**THE WAR WAS OVER,
YET THE BATTLE RAGED ON . . .**

KATHARINE LOUISE WESTON—A headstrong girl, she'd survived the ravages of the Civil War to become a woman obsessed, torn between the handsome Yankee she desired and the plantation that was her birthright.

BARON CAIN—War was his playing field; women his laurels of victory . . . until a fiery Southern beauty ensnared him with sweet kisses, daring him to tame her wild, willful heart.

BRANDON PARSELL—Drawn against his will to Kit's beauty, he wasn't sure he could manage her wild spirit . . . but he knew he could manage her plantation—if he could wrest it from his Yankee rival.

SOPHRONIA—She considered making a business of pleasure even as she longed for a deep and honorable love that seemed forever beyond her grasp.

MAGNUS—He loved Sophronia with a single-minded devotion, but could the power of his love mend her shattered dreams?

RISEN GLORY

RISEN GLORY

Susan Elizabeth Phillips

A DELL BOOK

Published by
Dell Publishing Co., Inc.
1 Dag Hammarskjold Plaza
New York, New York 10017

ISBN: 0-440-17285-3

Printed in the United States of America

First printing—December 1984

To my husband Bill,
with love and appreciation

ACKNOWLEDGMENTS

I am deeply indebted to the following:

National Cotton Council of America

American Textile Manufacturers Institution

My editor, Maggie Lichota, for her enthusiasm and insight

Charles Stone, who spent several patient hours teaching me to load and fire a Civil War revolver

My agent, Stephen Axelrod, who gave me the key to Kit

The men of the 17th Virginia Cavalry Battalion and Company H 119th New York Voluntary Infantry (Civil War Reenactment Units)

The staff of the Hillsborough Public Library, especially Sandra Jones and Rosemary Dotsko, for whom no question is too difficult

My parents, John and Louesa Titus, for their support and encouragement

Lydia Titus Kihm, Rosanne Kohake, Claire Kiehl Lefkowitz—sisters of blood and spirit, who gave me valuable suggestions

My wonderful sons, Ty and Zachary Phillips, who help me in so many ways

My readers, who have taken the time to write to me and tell me what is in their hearts

Susan Elizabeth Phillips
P.O. Box 486
Belle Mead, New Jersey 08502

Part One

A STABLE BOY

"When duty whispers low, *Thou must*,
The youth replies, *I can*."
Ralph Waldo Emerson, *Voluntaries III*

Chapter One

The old street vendor noticed him at once, for the boy was terribly out of place in the crowd of well-dressed stockbrokers and bankers who thronged the midday streets of Lower Manhattan. Cropped black hair that might have held a hint of curl had it been clean stuck out in spikes from underneath the brim of a battered felt hat. A patched shirt unbuttoned at the neck, perhaps in deference to the heat of early July, covered narrow, fragile shoulders. A pair of greasy, oversized breeches was gathered in at the waist with a strap of leather that might, at one time, have been part of a harness. The boy wore black boots that seemed too large for one so diminutive, and he held an oblong bundle in the crook of his arm.

The old street vendor leaned against the edge of his pushcart and watched curiously as the boy shoved his way through the crowd, looking neither to the right nor the left, but straight ahead, his eyes belligerent and wary. It puzzled the vendor that one so young should move so aggressively, as if the pavement itself were an enemy to be conquered.

The old man, whose name was Giuseppe Rospopa, was regarded by the other street vendors as something of a poet, although, as far as anyone knew, Giuseppe could not even write his own name. Still, he saw things others missed, and six days of the week he dispensed wisdom and his own kind of beauty along with the cakes and sugared buns that rested on trays in his wooden cart. Now the boy had caught his poet's imagination.

"You there, *ragazzo.* I got a pastry for you. Light as the kiss of an angel. *Vieni qui.*"

He watched as the lad jerked his head up and looked over at the cart piled so seductively with the gaily colored confections his wife, Rosa, still made fresh each day. He sensed the boy's hesitation as well as his hunger and could almost hear him counting the pennies that were doubtlessly concealed in the bundle he clutched so protectively.

"Come, *ragazzo.* It is my gift to you." He held up a fat cinnamon bun. "The gift of an old man to a new arrival in this, the most important city in the world."

Cautiously the boy approached the cart, one thumb stuck defiantly into the waistband of his trousers. "Jes' what makes you reckon I'm a new arrival?" His accent was as thick as the smell of Carolina jasmine blowing across a cotton field.

The old man concealed a smile. "Perhaps it is only a silly fancy, eh? But as soon as I see you, I say to myself—Giuseppe Rospopa, that one is a stranger to our proud city."

The boy shrugged and kicked at some litter in the gutter. "I ain't sayin' I am, and I ain't sayin' I ain't." He punched a grimy finger in the direction of the cinnamon bun nestled in the old man's hand. "How much you want for that?"

The old man's face crumpled in disappointment. "Did I not say it was a gift? Would you shame me?"

The boy seemed to consider this. Then he gave a short nod and held out his hand. "Thank you kindly."

As he took the bun, two businessmen in frock coats and tall beaver hats came up to the cart. The boy's gaze swept contemptuously over their gold watch fobs, rolled umbrellas, and polished black shoes. "Damn fool Yankees," he muttered under his breath.

The men were engaged in conversation and did not hear him, but the old man did, and as soon as his customers had left with their purchases, he looked over at the boy. "I think this city of mine is not a good place for you, eh? It has only been three months since the war is over. Our President is dead. Tempers are still high."

The boy took a bite of the bun and then settled down on the edge of the curb not far from the wheels of the pushcart. He laid his bundle carefully beside him and placed his battered hat on top.

"I didn't hold much with Mr. Lincoln," he said. "I thought he was puerile."

The old vendor's eyebrows shot up. "Puerile? *Madre di Dio!* What does this word mean?"

"Foolish like a child."

Giuseppe Rospopa was astonished. "And where does a boy like you learn such a word?"

For a moment the boy said nothing, and then, shading his

eyes from the noonday sun with the back of his hand, he squinted up at the old man. "Readin' books is my avocation. I learned that particular word from Mr. Ralph Waldo Emerson. I'm an admirer of Mr. Emerson." He took down his hand and began nibbling delicately around the edge of his bun, savoring each bite. "Course I didn't know he was a Yankee when I started to read his essays. I was mad as skunk piss when I found out. But by then it was too late. I was already a disciple."

"This Mr. Emerson. What does he say that is so special?"

A fleck of white icing clung to the tip of the boy's grimy index finger, and he flicked at it with a small, pink tongue. "Lots of things. He talks about nature and experience, about character and self-reliance. I reckon self-reliance is the most important attribute a person can have, don't you?"

The old man shook his head. "Faith in God. That is the most important."

"I don't hold much with God anymore, or even Jesus. I used to, but I reckon I seen too much these last few years. Watched the Yankees slaughter our livestock and burn our barns. Watched them shoot my dog Fergis. Saw Mrs. Lewis Godfrey Forsythe lose her husband and her only son on the same day. I've seen too much."

The street vendor looked more closely at the astonishing boy that providence had sent that day to his own city, to his very street. A small, heart-shaped face, a nose that tilted up ever so slightly on the end. It seemed somehow a sin that, before long, manhood would coarsen those delicate features. How old was he? Twelve? Perhaps thirteen? Certainly there was no trace of beard beneath the grime on his cheeks.

"How old are you, *ragazzo?*"

Wariness crept back into the boy's young eyes, eyes that were a surprising shade of deep violet. "Old enough, I guess."

"What about your parents?"

"They're both dead. My mother died when I was born. My daddy died at Shiloh three years ago."

"And you, *ragazzo?* Why have you come here to my city of New York?" The old man regretted the question as soon as he had uttered it, for he saw that he had gone too far.

The boy popped the last bit of bun into his mouth and stood up, wiping the tips of his fingers on his breeches. "Got to protect what's mine," he said shortly. Then he picked up the bundle, tucked it back under his arm, and settled the felt hat down over his head. "Thank you kindly for the cinnamon bun. It's been a pleasure makin' your acquaintance."

The old man nodded his head gravely. "The pleasure has been mine."

The lad began to walk away, and then he hesitated. Slowly he turned back to the old street vendor. "By the way," he said, "my name's Kit. And I'm not a boy."

The lunchtime crowd on Lower Broadway had thinned, and Kit could now walk more easily. As she made her way uptown toward Washington Square according to the directions she had received from an old woman on the ferry, she regretted the impulsiveness that had allowed her to reveal so much to the street vendor. After all, a person bent on murder shouldn't go around advertising herself. Except it wasn't murder. It was justice. Still, sure as the sun came up in the morning, the Yankee courts wouldn't see it that way, so she had better make certain they never found out that Katharine Louise Weston of Risen Glory plantation near what was left of Rutherford, South Carolina, had ever been within spitting distance of their godforsaken city.

She clutched the bundle more tightly under her arm. Inside was her daddy's six-shot Pettingill's self-cocking army percussion revolver, a train ticket back to Charleston, Emerson's *Essays, First Series,* a change of clothing, and four dollars and twenty-eight cents. A bed at a boardinghouse cost fifty cents a day. She would need food. Four dollars and twenty-eight cents wouldn't last long, but if she was careful, it might last a week. That should about do it.

She wished she could get it over with right away, but she had to allow herself time to watch him and get to know his ways. Killing him was only half the job. Not getting caught was the other half.

For the first time since she had stepped off the ferry, she studied her surroundings. It wasn't exactly that she had been afraid, but up until now, Charleston was the largest city she had ever seen, and New York certainly wasn't anything like Charleston.

The broad, tree-lined street was jammed with traffic. Carriages and omnibuses jockeyed for position with drays and wagons carrying everything from ice to pigs. Buildings five, six, even seven stories high towered over the noisy confusion. Well-dressed shoppers mingled with peddlers hawking their wares in strange languages. Next to the doorway of an oyster saloon was an organ grinder with a monkey on a chain.

She sidestepped quickly, barely avoiding a pile of garbage on the pavement—kitchen slops mixed with manure and cinders. Kit wrinkled her nose, which, up until that moment, had never shown any sign of being the least bit fastidious. Only Yankees would put their garbage out where people could step on it!

Still, as she walked on, she had to admit there were some fine sights. Beautiful churches, elegant hotels, emporiums with great marble doorways.

As she gazed at the prosperity around her, she was suddenly filled with bitterness. The city seemed to be untouched by the war that had torn apart the South. Richmond destroyed by Grant. An ugly scar cut through Georgia. Atlanta and Columbia reduced to smoldering rubble. If there was a God, she hoped He would see to it that William T. Sherman's soul roasted in hell for all eternity.

A man carrying a pick and shovel on his shoulder bumped into her, sending her sprawling up against a lamppost. "Hey, boy! Watch where you're going!" he exclaimed.

"Watch yourself," she snarled, shaking a small fist at his back. "And I'm not a boy!" But the man had already disappeared around the corner.

Kit sagged down and rested her back against the post while she rubbed her aching shoulder. Was everybody blind? Ever since she'd left Charleston nearly a week ago, people had been mistaking her for a boy. She sighed. It was probably for the best. A boy wandering alone was not nearly as conspicuous as a girl, and the trip had been a difficult one. Since the Yankees had torn up whole stretches of railroad track, passengers coming north had been forced to travel by an unsatisfactory combination of rail and wagon.

As she looked down at her breeches and scuffed black boots, she realized she shouldn't be so surprised. It was just that she wasn't used to it. Folks back home never made that mistake. Of course, they'd all known her since she was born, and they knew she didn't have any patience with dresses and perfumes and girlish gewgaws.

For years they'd clucked their tongues at her, telling her she'd be sorry—things would be different when she was older. Well, now that she was older, she still wasn't sorry.

Of course, she had to admit they'd been partially right. Things were different. The changes in her body, for example. Both of her undershirts were too tight for her. She tried to console herself with the knowledge that they at least flattened out her chest so she didn't have to look down at the small breasts she had grown. And her monthly flow—that had been even more unwelcome than her breasts.

Despite her developing body, on that July day when Kit Weston first arrived in New York City, she was more child than woman. Giuseppe Rospopa had been mistaken when he had guessed her to be twelve or thirteen. Even if he had known she was a girl, he would not have believed she was older than fourteen. But the truth was, only five months before, Kit had marked her sixteenth birthday.

Her age was something she didn't like to think about, for it left her feeling vaguely uneasy. The birthday had seemed to be an accident of the calendar, just as the changes in her body seemed to be accidents. At sixteen, everyone knew that a girl stood on the threshold of womanhood, but for Kit, the prospect was unappealing and somehow frightening. She was like a horse confronted with too high a fence. She was balking.

At the sight of a policeman moving in her direction, Kit quickly jumped to her feet and inserted herself into the midst of a group of shoppers. Her tired legs rebelled at the sudden movement, but she ignored her exhaustion. Time enough for sleep later.

A well-dressed woman with pale blond hair brushed past her, and she was abruptly reminded of her stepmother. She scowled at the thought of Rosemary Weston. From the moment Garrett Weston had met her, he had been moonstruck, even though Rosemary was several years older than he and her blond beauty was beginning to grow hard. She made no secret of her dislike for children and coldly informed him that she would have nothing to do with his eight-year-old daughter. Still, he married her.

Within a month Kit had been moved to a separate cabin near the slave quarters. With the exception of the kitchen where she took her meals, the rest of the house was denied her. She quickly learned to stay out of Rosemary's sight. A stinging slap on the cheek or a boxed ear was the least of her punishments if she forgot.

Never the most doting of fathers, Garrett Weston seemed barely to notice that his only child was receiving less care than the children of his slaves. He was too obsessed with his beautiful, sensual wife.

The neighbors were scandalized. That child was running wild! Bad enough if she'd been a boy, but for a girl, such neglect would lead to disaster.

When Rosemary, who had little interest in local society, ignored their pointed hints that the child must, at the very least, wear acceptable clothing, they sought out Kit themselves and pressed their daughters' cast-off dresses on her. Kit traded the dresses for britches and boys' shirts. She had learned very quickly that her new life had its advantages.

Maybe sometimes at night she did cry and have bad dreams, but all in all, she thought, she had it better than most children. The men, both black and white, of the plantation and neighboring sawmill taught her how to ride and fish. She could climb the peach trees in the orchard any time she wanted, swing from ropes in the barn, read without fear of censorship whatever books she stole on her early-morning forages into the library. And if she scraped her knee or caught a splinter in her bare foot, she could always run to Sophronia, the cook. By the time she was ten, she could shoot, cuss, ride a horse bareback, and had even smoked a cigar.

The war, of course, changed it all. She'd been twelve when the first shots were fired at Fort Sumter. Not long after that, Garrett Weston had joined the Confederate Army. He turned over the management of the plantation to Rosemary, but as Kit's stepmother never rose before eleven in the morning and did not care for the outdoors, Risen Glory began to fall into disrepair. Kit tried desperately to take her father's place, but the war had put an end to the market for Southern cotton, and she was too young to hold it all together.

The slaves ran off. Garrett Weston was killed at Shiloh. Bitterly Kit received the news that he had left the plantation to his wife. There was a trust fund for his daughter, but Rosemary was to administer it.

Two months before Kit's sixteenth birthday, the Yankees rode up the long drive to the handsome two-story house. From the veiled look exchanged between Rosemary Weston and the red-haired captain from Ohio who led the detachment, Kit suspected he would spend the night in her bed. The next day the captain ordered the barns burned and the livestock slaughtered. Rosemary's generosity had at least spared the house, and for the first time in eight years, Kit was grateful to her stepmother.

Still, when Rosemary died in an influenza epidemic shortly after Lee's surrender at Appomattox, Kit hadn't been able to shed a single tear. She could finally get on with her life. The war was over, Risen Glory would now be hers, and somehow she would restore its original grandeur.

Abruptly recalled to the present by the clanging bell on a passing fire engine, Kit dipped her hand into her pocket and closed her fingers around a crumpled scrap of paper. She didn't need to look at it. The address was stamped on her memory. And before she found a place to stay for the night, she was determined to see the house for herself, maybe catch a glimpse of the man she'd come so far to kill. Even if her motives weren't patriotic, she was going to do what no man in the entire army of the Confederate States of America had been able to do. Major Baron Nathaniel Cain didn't know it, but his days on God's good earth were about to come to an abrupt end.

Chapter Two

Cain was bored. Flora Van Ness was a delectable little piece—no one could argue about that—and in another few minutes when she was in his bed, he wouldn't be sorry he had asked her to dine with him this evening. But at the moment he was regretting the impulse that had brought her here to the dining room of the fashionable town house he had won in an all-night poker game not long after he'd arrived in New York.

He saw by her eyes that she was ready for him, but he didn't hurry with the brandy he had just poured for himself. He took women on his own terms, not theirs. Besides, brandy this old shouldn't be rushed. The former owner had kept an excellent wine cellar, the contents of which, along with the furnishings of the house, Cain owed to iron nerves and a pair of kings.

Reaching for a silver box that had been placed near his chair, he lifted the lid and pulled out a thin cigar. "Do you mind?" he asked, not really caring whether she did or not. She shook her head. He clipped the end of the cigar, rolled it once between his lips, and lit it.

He was a dangerously handsome man, with pewter-gray eyes, a lean, chiseled nose, and a strong chin. He had a thick moustache that was a shade darker than his tawny hair and gave his face the reckless look of a man who was living his life on the cutting edge.

As he leaned back in his chair, he saw the way Flora's eyes caught on the ugly puckered scar that disfigured the back of his right hand from the knuckles to the wrist. It was one of several that he had accumulated on various parts of his tall, muscular frame, and all of them seemed to excite her. She lowered her gaze to her dinner plate, but not before he saw the tip of her tongue flick briefly over her lips. It amused him.

She laughed nervously. "I don't think you've heard a word I've said all evening, Baron."

"Of course I have. You were telling me how angry your father would be if he knew you were dining alone with me tonight."

She tossed her fair curls. "You can't really blame him, can you? Considering your reputation with women. What father wants to have to marry off a daughter who's suspected of being damaged goods?"

"Flora, sweet, your goods were damaged long before I ever met you." She gave him a hurt, reproachful look, and he suppressed a sigh. What a silly little fool she was. But then, most of them were. Pampered society women attracted by his military exploits and his face.

Cain knew that women considered him handsome, but he took little interest in his looks and certainly no pride. The way he saw it, his face had nothing to do with him. It was an inheritance from a weak-willed father and a bitch of a mother who had spread her legs for any man who caught her eye.

He had been fifteen when he had begun to notice women watching him. At first he was surprised and then amused to hear them rave about his tawny hair and gray eyes. But now, at twenty-eight, there had been too many women, and their adulation merely annoyed him.

Flora shifted nervously in her seat, her silk gown rustling against the brocade upholstery. "Baron?" she began tentatively. "There's something I've been meaning to talk to you about. I—I hope you don't think I'm being too forward, but I believe it's only fair to tell you that my father has some very definite plans for me that could involve you."

"Oh?"

"As you know, the Van Ness Emporium is one of the largest dry goods stores in New York. My father has no other children, so any man that I marry can expect someday to take his place. My father has made it clear to me that he would not be totally averse to having you in the family. Of course, he would have liked it better if you hadn't resigned from the army. And you would have to be more discreet about your—hobby."

"Your father doesn't approve of gamblers, Flora?"

"Really, Baron, I'd hardly call you a gambler. After all, you only play at the tables of the wealthiest and most famous men in New York. It's more of a social activity."

His gray eyes regarded her levelly. "There's nothing social about it. It's the way I earn my living. And, Flora, I've never misled you. I made it clear from the beginning that I have no intention of marrying, now or ever."

"Yes, I know that, but . . ."

"Would you like me to take you home now?" he asked softly as he rose from his chair.

"No!"

Without even being aware of it, Flora found herself standing. He was the most exciting man she had ever met. Half the women in New York would give anything to be where she was right now. She didn't care that he wouldn't marry her. She didn't care that he wasn't entirely respectable. All she cared about was having him touch her, feeling the weight of his muscular body pressing down on hers, tracing those magnificent scars with her fingers. A small shiver traveled down her spine as he approached her.

"No," she repeated, this time more clearly. "I'm not ready to go home yet."

With the tips of his fingers, he led her from the dining room. They walked up the carpeted stairs silently and into the dimly lit bedroom. She looked up at him, her lips moist and willing. Lifting his hands, he cupped her bare shoulders, then slid his palms slowly downward over her upper arms, taking the small, capped sleeves of her dress with him. He extended his thumbs, letting them travel over the tops of her breasts, pushing the tight, constricting fabric down, out of the way.

With a small cry she lifted her arms and encircled his neck. Her breasts tumbled free like two pale melons served up to him. They were full and ripe, and he did not know why they didn't feel better in his hands.

He kneaded them more roughly than he intended, and she gave a small exclamation of pain. He let her go abruptly.

"Don't," she muttered quickly. "Don't stop." She pulled his hands back to her breasts and squeezed hard against his fingers. "Hurt me, Baron," she whispered. "Hurt me just a little. Please."

In the dark she could not see his mouth curl in a cynical twist. "Always a lady, aren't you, Flora?" he drawled.

And then he did what the lady asked.

Later, as she slept, Cain leaned back against the mahogany headboard, one arm crossed over his naked chest. He stared straight ahead, not really seeing the comfortable room.

He was ten when his mother had run off, leaving him alone with his debt-ridden father in a bleak Philadelphia mansion that was falling into disrepair. Three years later his father died, and a committee of women came to take him to an orphan asylum. He ran away that night. He had no destination in mind, only a direction.

He spent the next ten years on the back of a horse and grew to manhood drifting from one Texas border town to another, herding cattle, laying railroad tracks, and getting drunk. The West was a new land that needed educated men, but he would not even admit that he knew how to read.

Women fell in love with the handsome boy with the sculptured features and the cold gray eyes. There were olive-skinned Mexican beauties, wealthy ranchers' daughters, and accommodating farmers' wives. Whores and virgins, he set them on fire, and they knew they could not be satisfied until they had all of him.

But there was something hard and cold inside him that none of them could penetrate. Tenderness and affection, gentle feelings that take root and flourish in a child who has known love, were absent in him. Whether they were dead forever or merely frozen, even Cain did not know.

For a while he farmed. Then he drifted to California to pan for gold, but he soon discovered that he could find more gold over a poker table than in the creeks. He became a gambler. When the war broke out, he crossed back over the Mississippi River for the first time in twelve years and enlisted, not to help preserve the Union but because he was a man who valued his own freedom above everything else, and he could not stomach the idea of slavery.

He joined Ulysses S. Grant's hard-bitten troops, catching the general's eye in Tennessee when they captured Fort Henry. By the time they reached Shiloh, he was a member of Grant's staff. He was nearly killed twice, once at Vicksburg when they broke the South's spine, then four months later at Chattanooga, charging Missionary Ridge in the battle that opened the way for Sherman's march to the sea.

The newspapers began to write of Baron Cain, dubbing him the "Hero of Missionary Ridge." They praised him for his courage and patriotism. Later, when he made a series of raids through enemy lines, his celebrity was assured. Ulysses S. Grant was quoted as saying "I would rather lose my right arm than lose Baron Cain."

What neither Grant nor the newspapers knew was that Cain was a man who lived to take risks. Danger, like sex, excited him.

Maybe that was why he played poker for a living. He could risk everything on the turn of a card. Except now, for some reason he couldn't explain, the excitement had begun to pale. The cards, the city, the women, all of it.

Flora stirred beside him. Abruptly he reached over and smacked her plump rump. "Come on, buttercup. Wake up. Time to go home to Daddy."

Chapter Three

Kit jerked awake to the sound of an unfamiliar male voice. Clean straw pressed against her cheek, and for an instant she felt as if she were home again in the barn at Risen Glory.

". . . see about it. Why don't you turn in, Magnus? You've had a long day." The voice was coming from the other side of the wall near her head. It was deep and crisp with none of the elongated vowels and whispered consonants of her homeland.

Memory washed over her. Sweet Jesus! She had fallen asleep in Baron Cain's stable!

Cautiously she pushed herself up on one elbow, trying to peer through the darkness. She'd watched the front of Cain's house for several hours that afternoon without seeing anyone enter or leave. Finally she had gone around to the back only to discover that the yard behind the house was too open to provide her with a safe observation point.

The whicker of a horse had drawn her attention to the stable. She had noticed a small window that looked out on the yard, and when she was certain there was no one around, she had dashed across the open space and slipped inside. Unfortunately, as the afternoon shadows had lengthened, the warm, comfortable scent of horses and fresh straw had proven too much for her, and she had fallen asleep in the back of an empty stall.

"You plannin' to take Saratoga out tomorrow?" This was a different voice, the familiar, liquid tones reminding her of home, although his speech was less heavily accented than the Negroes there and showed evidence of a formal education.

"I might. Why?"

"Don't like the way that fetlock's healin'. Better give her a few more days."

"Fine. I'll take a look at her tomorrow. Good night, Magnus."

"Night, Major."

Major! The man with the deep voice was Baron Cain! Quickly Kit slipped out of the stall and crept to the window. She peered over the sill just in time to see a man disappear inside the lighted house. Cursing softly, she sagged down against the wooden wall. A whole day wasted! She'd missed her chance to get a glimpse of Baron Cain's face.

One of the horses stirred in the next stall, and Kit sighed deeply. If she'd tried, she couldn't have made a bigger mess of things. Someone had to have been in the stable to feed the horses while she was asleep. It was nothing short of a miracle that she hadn't been discovered and run through with a pitch-fork. It must be nearly midnight, she was in a strange Yankee city, and she'd nearly got herself found out the first day.

For a moment she felt a traitorous tightening in her throat. Resolutely she settled her battered hat more firmly over her head and stood up. No good crying over milk that was already spilled. Tomorrow would take care of itself. For now, only one thing was certain. She had to get out of this stable and find a safe place to spend the night.

After she had fetched her bundle, she crept to the doors and listened. She had seen Cain go into the house, but where was the man called Magnus? Cautiously she pushed the door open and peered outside. Light from the curtained windows lay like a still yellow pond on the open ground between the stable and the carriage house.

She slipped outside and pressed her back against the side of the building while she listened. The yard was silent and deserted. As quietly as possible, she pushed the stable door closed, wincing when one of the hinges squeaked. She waited a few minutes, but there was no movement near the house.

Peering through the shadows, she studied the high brick wall that separated the yard from the alley running behind it. From her experience that afternoon, she knew that the iron gate in the center was kept locked and that she would have to climb over the wall, but the prospect did not bother her. The bricks were covered with stout vines of Virginia creeper, and there were plenty of toeholds. No, it was the dash she must make across the yard that left her uneasy. Once more she glanced toward the house. Then she took a deep breath and ran.

As soon as she was free of the stable, she knew something

was wrong. The night air, no longer masked by the smell of horses, carried the faint, unmistakable odor of cigar smoke.

Tensing her muscles, she sprang across the yard and snatched at a vine on the wall. It came away in her hand. Her bundle fell forgotten to the ground as she clutched another vine. This one held. She sensed rather than saw something move behind her as she frantically pulled herself up the wall. Just as she reached the top, something jerked hard on the seat of her trousers. For an instant she flailed at the empty air, and then she slammed, belly first, to the ground.

"Well, well, what do we have here?" a deep voice drawled lazily as the sole of a boot settled firmly into the small of her back.

The fall had knocked the wind out of her and sent waves of pain through her side, but still she recognized the voice of the man she had come so far to kill. The man who was holding her down with his foot was her sworn enemy, Major Baron Nathaniel Cain!

Rage overcame her pain. She dug the heels of her hands into the dirt and tried to push herself up, but his boot held her firmly.

"Git your damn foot off me, you dirty sonvabitch!" she gasped.

"I don't think I'm quite ready to do that," he said calmly.

It was more than she could bear. "Let me up!" she stormed. "You let me up right now!"

"You're awfully feisty for a thief."

"Thief!" She banged her fist into the dirt. "I never stole anything in my life. You show me a man who says I have, and I'll show you a liar!"

"Then what were you doing in my stable?"

Her mind went blank. What excuse could she give that he would believe? The pressure on her back showed no sign of easing.

"Sleepin'!" she gasped in desperation. "I was sleepin'."

His foot did not move.

"It's true!" she exclaimed, improvising rapidly. "I came here lookin' for a job workin' in your stable. Nobody was around, so I went inside to get out of the heat while I waited for somebody to show up. Musta fallen asleep. When I woke up, it was dark.

Then I heard voices, and I got scared somebody would see me and think I was tryin' to harm the horses."

"It seems to me that somebody looking for work should have had enough sense to go knock on the back door," he said dryly.

It seemed that way to Kit, too, but she wasn't about to back down now. "I'm shy."

Slowly the weight lifted from her back. "I'm going to let you up now. You'll regret it if you try to run, boy."

"I'm not a—" She caught herself just in time before she had revealed her true sex. "I'm not about to run," she amended. "Haven't done anything wrong."

"That remains to be seen."

As she rose to her feet, the moon came out from behind a cloud and the yard was washed in silver, clearly illuminating the man who stood before her. Dressed in a white shirt, fawn trousers, and calf-hugging leather boots, he was standing easily, a hand lightly balanced on his hip, his cigar still clenched between his teeth.

Carefully she looked him over. He was not at all what she had expected. He was much bigger, for one thing. Broad-shouldered and muscular, he exuded an unmistakable aura of power and danger. And she couldn't help but notice that he was incredibly handsome.

"If you've finished your inspection, how about telling me what you have in there," he said, jerking his head toward the base of the wall where her bundle lay.

Kit was not averse to telling a lie if she could get away with it, but now she realized the truth would serve her better. She pulled the bundle from the weeds and opened it. "A change of clothes, a copy of Mr. Emerson's *Essays,* and my daddy's six-shot Pettingill's revolver." She did not mention the train ticket back to Charleston tucked inside the book. No matter what happened, he must never find out where she was from. "Nothin' of yours in here."

"What's a boy like you doing with Emerson's *Essays?*"

"I'm a disciple of his."

There was a slight twitching at the outer corner of Cain's thick moustache as he absorbed this unusual piece of information. "You have any money?"

She bent over to rewrap her bundle. "Course I got money. In

the pocket of my spare shirt. You think I'd be so puerile as to come to a strange city without any money?"

"How much?"

"Four dollars and twenty-eight cents."

"You can't live for long in New York City with only four dollars and twenty-eight cents," he said mildly.

"I told you I was lookin' for a job."

"So you did. You know, don't you, that I should turn you over to the police. Trespassing is against the law."

Kit had taken his measure and knew that she mustn't back down. Baron Cain was a man who respected strength. She picked up her bundle and thrust her chin forward defiantly. "Hit don't make no never mind to me what you do. I ain't done nothin' wrong."

He crossed his arms over his chest. "Where are you from, boy?"

Kit looked him square in the eye. "Michigan."

At first she did not understand his burst of laughter, and then she realized her mistake. Quickly she tried to recover. "That's a lie. I'm not from Michigan. I'm from Alabama. But with the war just over, I'm not anxious to advertise that fact."

Cain was still chuckling. "Then you'd better plan on keeping your mouth shut." He gestured toward the bundle. "Aren't you a little young to be carrying a gun like that?"

"Don't see why. I know how to use it."

"I'll just bet you do," he muttered. "Why did you leave home?"

"No jobs anymore."

"What about your parents?"

Kit repeated the story she'd told the street vendor. When she was done, she anxiously studied his face for some reaction, but she could decipher nothing from his expression, and so, when he finally spoke, his words were a surprise to her.

"How would you like to work for me as my stable boy?" he said gruffly. "The boy I had quit last week."

"Your stable boy?" Kit murmured weakly.

"That's right. You'd take your orders from my head man, Magnus Owen. He's a Negro, so if that's going to offend your Southern pride, you'd better tell me now." When she did not reply, he continued, somewhat more gently. "You can sleep over the stable and eat in the kitchen. Salary is three dollars a week."

She kicked nonchalantly at the dirt with the toe of her scuffed boot, but in reality her mind was racing. If she'd learned anything today, she'd learned that Baron Cain wasn't going to be easy to kill, especially now that he had seen her face. Working in his stable, she realized, would give her access to him that she couldn't otherwise have. It would also make her job twice as dangerous.

She tucked her thumbs into the waist of her trousers and looked up at him. "Two bits more, Yankee, and you got yourself a stable boy."

She fell asleep that night too exhausted to take note of her surroundings, and so she was pleasantly surprised the next morning when she inspected her room above the stable. Not only did it smell agreeably of horses and leather and dust, but it was comfortably furnished with a soft bed, an oak rocker, and a faded rag rug. Most important, it possessed a window that looked out over the back of the house. The small room also boasted a once handsome washstand, but that she ignored.

After she had used the whitewashed privy behind the stable, she fetched water from the pump in the yard and filled the horses' buckets, talking softly to the animals as she got acquainted. The stable held four horses, a matched pair for the carriage and two hunters. Kit's immediate favorite was a large bay with a long, elegant neck.

As he nuzzled her shoulder with his muzzle, she felt some of the tension inside her ease. Everything was going to be all right. For the next few days she'd do her job and keep her eyes open, waiting until the time was right. And she wasn't going to get caught either. From what she'd seen of him last night, she realized Baron Cain was a dangerous man. But she had an advantage he didn't have. She knew her enemy.

"His name is Apollo."

"What?" She spun around to see a handsome young Negro with rich chocolate skin and large, expressive eyes standing on the other side of the half door that separated the stalls from the center aisle of the stable. He was in his early to mid twenties and tall, with slim shoulders and a slight, supple build. A black-and-white mongrel waited patiently near his heels.

"That bay," he amplified. "His name is Apollo. He's the major's favorite mount."

"You don't say." Giving the bay a final pat on his neck, Kit opened the door and stepped out of the stall.

The mongrel sniffed at her while the young man looked her over critically. "I'm Magnus Owen. Major said he hired you last night after he caught you sneakin' out of the stable."

"I wasn't sneakin'. Well, not exactly, anyway. That major of yours just has a naturally suspicious nature, is all." She looked down at the mongrel. "That your dog?"

"Yep. I call him Merlin."

"Looks like a no-account dog to me."

Magnus's smooth, high forehead puckered indignantly. "Now why you go and say somethin' like that, boy? You don't even know my dog!"

Kit reached over and absentmindedly scratched behind Merlin's ears. "Stands to reason. I spent yesterday afternoon asleep in that stall over there. If Merlin was any kinda dog, he'd of been mighty indignant about that."

"Merlin wasn't even here yesterday afternoon," Magnus said. "He was with me."

"Oh. Well, I guess I'm just inherently prejudiced. The skunk-pissin' Yankees killed my dog Fergis. Never saw a better dog than Fergis. I mourn him to this day."

Magnus's expression softened a little. "What's your name, boy?"

She paused a moment before answering. It would be easier for her to use her own name, but she had to make certain she didn't link herself to Risen Glory.

Behind Magnus's head she spotted a can of Finney's Harness Oil and Leather Preserver. "Name's Kit," she said. "Kit Finney."

Magnus looked at her suspiciously. "Kit's a mighty funny name for a boy."

She thought quickly. "My folks were admirers of Kit Carson, the Injun fighter."

Magnus seemed to accept her explanation and was soon taking her through the stable and outlining her duties. Afterward, they went into the kitchen for breakfast, and he introduced her to the housekeeper.

Edith Simmons was a stout, gossipy woman with thinning salt-and-pepper hair and strong opinions. She had been cook and housekeeper for the former owner and had only agreed to stay on when she had discovered that Baron Cain was unmarried and there would be no wife to tell her how to do her job. Edith believed in thrift, good food, and, above all, personal cleanliness. It was obvious from the beginning that she and Kit were natural born enemies.

"That boy is too dirty to eat with civilized people!" Mrs. Simmons's lips were compressed into a tight, disapproving line.

Kit was furious at the housekeeper's snobbery, especially when Magnus agreed. She was too hungry, however, to argue for very long, and so she stomped into the pantry and splashed some water on her face and hands. She refused to touch the soap.

As she ate the sumptuous breakfast, she ignored the housekeeper and studied Magnus Owen. He interested her. From the way Mrs. Simmons deferred to him, it was obvious that he was an important figure in the household, unusual for a black man under any circumstances, but especially for one who was so young.

As Kit watched him, something tugged at her memory, but it was not until he finished eating and stood to leave that she realized what it was. Magnus Owen reminded her of Sophronia, the cook at Risen Glory and the only person in the world who understood her. Both of them had a funny way of acting as if they thought they were white.

It was not until afternoon that she had another chance to talk to him. She had finished her work and was sitting in the shade near the front door of the stable, her arm draped across Merlin, who had fallen asleep with his nose resting on her thigh. The dog did not stir as Magnus approached.

"Will you just look at this no 'count dog," she said softly. "If you were an ax murderer, I'd be dead by now."

Magnus chuckled and lowered himself down beside her. "I got to admit, Merlin isn't much of a watch dog. But maybe he'll get better as he gets older. Knew a dog like him when I was a boy back in Georgia. Turned into a fine bird dog. You got to remember that Merlin's young still. He was only a pup when the major found him rootin' around in the alley behind the house."

At the mention of Baron Cain, Kit's face darkened. She had seen him once already that day when he'd appeared at the door of the stable and curtly ordered her to saddle Apollo. Everything about him had irritated her—from the tight way his riding breeches clung to his thighs to the play of summer sun in his hair. He was so vital and alive, so handsome and arrogant.

She'd read that the Yankee newspapers called him the Hero of Missionary Ridge and that he'd fought at Vicksburg and Shiloh. Maybe he was even the man who'd killed her daddy. It didn't seem right, somehow, that he was alive when so many brave Confederate soldiers were dead. It seemed even more unjust that every breath he drew threatened the only thing she had left in the world.

"How long you known the major?" she asked cautiously.

Magnus plucked a blade of grass and began to chew on it. "Since Chattanooga. He almost lost his life savin' mine. We been together ever since."

An awful suspicion began to grow inside Kit. "You weren't fightin' for the Yankees, were you, Magnus?"

"Course I was fightin' for the Yankees!" he cried indignantly.

She didn't know why she should have been so disappointed, but she was. She liked Magnus. "But you said you were from Georgia. Why didn't you fight for your home state?"

Carefully Magnus removed the blade of grass from his mouth and turned to her. "You got a lot of nerve, boy," he said softly. "You sit here with a black man and, cool as a cucumber, ask him why he didn't fight for the people who was keepin' him in chains. Let me tell you somethin'. I was twelve years old when I got the papers freein' me. I came North. I got a job and went to school. But I wasn't really free, do you understand me? There wasn't a single Negro in this country could really be free as long as his brothers and sisters was slaves."

She was annoyed by his vehemence and his radical rhetoric. "It wasn't primarily a question of slavery, Magnus," she explained patiently. "It was a question of whether a state has the right to govern itself without interference. Slavery was just incidental to the main issue, doncha see?"

He looked at her with disgust. "Mighta been incidental to you, white boy, but it sure wasn't incidental to me." Without another word, he got up and walked away.

Black folks sure were touchy, Kit mused, as she watched his retreating back. But later, while she put out the second feed for the horses, she found she was still thinking about what he had said. It reminded her of several uncomfortable conversations she'd had with Sophronia.

Magnus did not appear for lunch, and Kit learned from Mrs. Simmons that he had gone to the feed store. She took advantage of his absence to question her about the running of the household and discovered that Mrs. Simmons and Magnus were the only servants who slept in the house. The two maids lived at home with their families.

Despite her condescending air, Mrs. Simmons obviously enjoyed having a fresh set of ears to fill with gossip, and before Kit had finished her second helping of creamed potatoes, she had learned about the private lives of the neighbors, the maids, the ice man, and even the delivery boy. Only when it came to her employer was Mrs. Simmons silent. Although disapproving of Cain's professional and amorous activities, the housekeeper had decided to look the other way.

Kit, however, learned something much more interesting than the details of Cain's personal life. She discovered that both Mrs. Simmons and Magnus had Saturdays off and spent the night elsewhere—Mrs. Simmons with her sister and Magnus in what the housekeeper described as a drunken and debauched manner best left undiscussed before young ears. Cain was alone in the house on Saturday night.

Kit could barely conceal her excitement. Today was Monday. Five more days. Now she knew not only how she was going to kill Baron Cain but when she was going to do it.

Chapter Four

Cain vaulted down off Apollo's back with a gracefulness unusual for a man of his size. "Take your time cooling him out, boy. I don't want a sick horse." He tossed Kit the bridle and began to stride toward the house.

She bristled with indignation. "I know my job," she called out. "Don't need no Yankee to tell me how to take care of a hot, sweaty horse."

The words were no sooner out of her mouth than she wished she could snatch them back. Today was only her second day. It was four more days until Saturday. This was no time to get herself fired.

Cain had stopped walking. He turned back to her, his gray eyes cool. "If you think you'd be happier working for somebody else, I can always find another stable boy."

"Didn't say I wanted to work for nobody else," she muttered sullenly.

"Then maybe you'd better try a little harder to hold that tongue of yours."

She kicked into the dirt with the dusty toe of her boot. "Yessir."

"And, Kit?"

"Yeah?"

"Take a bath. People around here are starting to complain about the way you smell."

"A bath!" Kit's outrage nearly choked her, and it was only with the greatest effort that she was able to control her temper.

Cain seemed amused by her struggle. "Was there anything else you wanted to say to me?"

"No, sir," she mumbled, her teeth tightly clenched.

"Then I'll need the carriage at the front door in about an hour and a half." With a curt nod, he left her.

As she walked Apollo around the yard, she released a steady stream of profanity. Killing that Yankee was going to give her more pleasure than anything she'd ever done in all her sixteen years. She'd blow his head off! What business was it of his whether she took a bath or not? She didn't hold with baths. Everybody knew they made you susceptible to influenza.

By the time Apollo was groomed and back in his stall, the edge had burned off her anger, but Cain's comment still pricked at her. Maybe she didn't bathe too often, but taking her clothes off made her feel uncomfortable, especially these last few years. It gave her a funny feeling to look down at her naked body, as if everything in her life was somehow slipping away from her control. For so long she'd fought anyone who wanted to make her look and act like a female. But now her own body was betraying her. And worst of all, there were even moments when she found a frightening kind of pleasure in what was happening to her.

At night when she lay in bed, she would sometimes reach under her shirt and cup a strange, bare breast. She would find the palm of her hand brushing over the tiny, growing bud at the tip, stroking it until her body was filled with a tingling that left her restless and discontent. Those were the nights when Kit knew that something she didn't entirely understand was happening to her.

She was still feeling grouchy and out of sorts an hour and a half later as she stood between the heads of the matched gray carriage horses and waited for Cain to come out the front door of his house. She had splashed some water on her face and hands and changed into her spare set of clothes, but the patched breeches and faded blue shirt were neither cleaner nor tidier than the clothes she had abandoned, and there was little improvement.

Cain, however, did not seem to notice. As he stepped into the open carriage, he was too preoccupied with the dreary prospect of the afternoon that lay ahead of him to be aware of his stable boy's appearance. The week before he had let Flora Van Ness persuade him into taking her on a drive through Central Park. Now he regretted it. His relationship with her was clearly over, but he suspected that she would take advantage of the privacy of their outing today to press him.

He had just resigned himself to the tiresome scene that would inevitably result when he became aware of Kit standing with his horses. Impulsively he called out, "Climb in the back, boy. It's about time you saw something of New York City."

Kit jerked her head up so quickly she nearly dislodged her hat. "Me?"

"I don't see anybody else around." He smiled. "Climb up. I'm going to need somebody to hold the horses." He did not add that he also hoped the boy's presence would forestall any more foolish declarations of undying love from Flora Van Ness.

Kit reluctantly did as she was told, knowing even as she settled down on the leather-upholstered rear seat that the situation could be dangerous for her. Baron Cain was no fool. The less time she spent in his presence, the better. Still, as he expertly maneuvered the carriage through the streets, her pleasure in the new sights began to overcome her uneasiness.

Cain called her attention to points of interest as they moved northward on Fifth Avenue, the most fashionable street in the city. They passed Delmonico's famous restaurant and Wallach's Theatre where Charlotte Cushman was appearing in *Oliver Twist.* Kit glimpsed the fashionable shops and hotels that surrounded the lush greenery of Madison Square. Farther north, she studied the glittering mansions of the wealthy and famous.

Cain drew the carriage up in front of an imposing brownstone and alighted in a single clean stride. "Watch the horses, boy. I won't be long."

At first Kit did not mind the wait as she surveyed the houses around her and watched the sparkling carriages with their well-dressed occupants flash by. But then the familiar bitterness rose inside her. The war had not affected this city at all.

"Baron, darling, you're an absolute wretch to have kept me waiting. Do you realize you're almost half an hour late?"

Kit looked up to see an elegant young woman with shining blond curls and a pretty pouting mouth come down the steps on Cain's arm. She was dressed in ruffled strawberry silk and held a lacy white parasol to protect her pale skin from the afternoon sun. A tiny froth of a bonnet perched on top of her head. Kit detested her on sight.

Cain helped her into the carriage and politely assisted her with her skirts. Kit's opinion of him sank even lower. If this was the kind of woman he fancied, he wasn't as smart as she'd figured.

She put her scuffed boot up on the iron step and swung herself into the rear seat. Flora's head jerked around in astonishment. "Baron, who is this filthy creature?"

Outraged, Kit sprang up from the seat, her hands already balled into small fists.

"Sit down, Kit," Cain said sharply.

For a moment she hesitated, and then, glaring venomously at the back of the pert strawberry and white bonnet, she reluctantly did as he said.

Cain eased the carriage out into the traffic. "Kit is my stable boy. I brought him along to stay with the horses in case you wanted to walk in the park."

The ribbons on Flora's bonnet fluttered indignantly. "Why on earth would I want to do that? It's much too warm to walk."

Cain shrugged but offered no explanation. Flora was furious. She had planned to take advantage of their outing today to pursue the subject of their future, but how was she to do it with a scruffy little stable boy breathing over her shoulder? She adjusted her parasol and settled into a silence that was loud with her displeasure. To her chagrin, Cain did not seem to notice. He was too busy pointing out landmarks to the little wretch.

Unlike Flora Van Ness, Kit was not given to sulking, and the pleasure of the bright summer afternoon and the new sights all around her soon overcame her earlier bitterness and her antipathy toward Flora. She did not even let the fact that Baron Cain was her tour guide destroy her mood. This was undoubtedly the only chance she would ever have to see New York City, and she was going to enjoy it.

When they reached the entrance to the park, Kit decided that the place was misnamed, for as far as she could see, it lay at the northern edge of the city. "Why do they call it Central Park?" she asked. "Doesn't look to me like it's central to anything."

"New York is growing fast," Cain explained. "Right now there's mainly open land around the park. A few shantytowns, some farms. But it won't be long before the city takes over."

She was about to voice her skepticism when Flora whirled around in her seat and fixed her with a withering glare. The message was unmistakably clear, and Kit resented it. She was not to open her mouth again.

Fixing a pretty smile on her face, Flora turned back to Cain and patted his forearm with a hand encased in strawberry lace.

"Baron, I have a most amusing story to tell you about Sugar Plum, my darling little pug."

Kit made a face and leaned back in the seat. She watched the play of light and shadow on her breeches as the carriage slipped along the tree-lined promenade that ran through the park, and then she found herself studying Flora's silly little bonnet.

Two women riding in a black landau passed them going the other direction. Kit noticed how eagerly their eyes sought out Cain. Women sure did seem to make fools of themselves over him, she mused.

One thing was certain. He knew how to handle horses. Still, that didn't count much with a lot of women. They were more interested in how a man looked.

She tried to study him objectively, to see what they saw in him. He was a handsome devil, no doubt about that. The color of his hair reminded her of wheat right before harvest time. He wore it longer than most men, so that it curled slightly over the back of his collar. As he turned his head to make a comment to Flora, his profile was etched clearly against the sky. There was something almost pagan about the smooth, high brow, the thin nose, and the arrogant line of his jaw. She remembered a book that had been a particular favorite of hers when she was younger. It described the ancient warriors and had one section that had been illustrated with engravings of Vikings. There was something about Cain's face that conjured up those engravings in her memory. She could almost see him standing in the bow of a long ship.

". . . and then Sugar Plum pushed the raspberry bonbon away with her nose and picked a lemon one instead. Isn't that the sweetest thing you've ever heard?"

Flora's twittering intruded on Kit's musings. That woman was a damn fool! Pugs and raspberry bonbons! She sighed. It was a long, painful release. It was also very loud.

Cain glanced back over his shoulder, glad for any interruption that would put an end to Flora's tiresome monologue. "Is something wrong, Kit?"

She tried to be polite. "I don't hold much with pugs."

There was a slight trembling at the corner of Cain's moustache. "Oh? Why is that?"

"You want my honest opinion?"

"By all means."

Kit darted a disgusted glare at Flora's back. "Pugs are sissy dogs."

Cain chuckled, much to Flora's irritation. "Really, Baron, I don't know what is so amusing. That boy is impertinent."

Cain ignored her. "You prefer mutts, Kit? I've noticed you spending an awful lot of time with Merlin lately."

"Merlin spends time with me," Kit declared, "not the other way around. I don't care what Magnus says. That dog's 'bout as worthless as a corset in a whorehouse."

"Baron!"

Cain made a queer, croaking sound before he recovered his composure. "Maybe you'd better remember there's a lady present, Kit."

"Yessir," she muttered, although she didn't really see what there was to get so riled up about.

But Cain's rebuke was much too mild for Flora's satisfaction. "That boy doesn't know his place," she snapped. "I would fire any servant who behaved so outrageously."

They were nearing the lake, and Cain pulled the carriage to a stop. "Perhaps it's a good thing that I'm his employer, then, instead of you."

He had not raised his voice at all, but the rebuke was clear, and Flora flushed. Nothing was going the way she had planned it, and it was all the fault of that vile child!

"Besides," Cain continued, his tone somewhat lighter, "my stable boy isn't an ordinary servant. He's a disciple of Ralph Waldo Emerson."

Kit quickly looked away from the family of swans she was watching glide between the canoes on the lake to see if he was making fun of her, but she could read nothing out of the ordinary in his expression.

Cain, thoroughly bored by now with Flora's posturings, laid his arm over the back of the leather seat and turned toward Kit. "Tell me, boy, is Mr. Emerson the only writer you read, or are there others?"

Flora's obvious indignation with Cain's question made Kit garrulous. "Oh, I read 'bout everything I can lay my hands on. Ben Franklin, of course, but I 'spect most everybody reads him. Thoreau, Jonathan Swift. Edgar Allan Poe when I'm in the mood. I don't hold much with poetry, but otherwise I have a generally voracious appetite."

"So I see," Cain said. "Maybe you just haven't read the right poets. Walt Whitman, for example."

"Never heard of him."

"He's a New Yorker. Worked as a nurse during the war."

Kit shook her head. "I don't reckon I could stomach a Yankee poet."

Cain lifted an amused brow. "Really, Kit, I'm disappointed. Surely an intellectual like yourself wouldn't let prejudice interfere with an appreciation for great literature."

She could feel her hackles rising. He was laughing at her!

"You know somethin', Major," she said with a smile every bit as artificial as Flora's. "It surprises me you even know the name of a poet, 'cause you don't look much like a reader to me. But I guess that's the way it is with most big men. All the muscle goes to their bodies, not sparin' much for the brain."

Cain nearly choked. He ignored the I-told-you-so look that Flora shot at him and studied Kit more closely. The boy couldn't be any older than twelve, at least a year younger than Cain had been when he'd run away. But Cain had nearly reached his adult height at that time, while Kit was small, probably not more than three or four inches over five feet.

For the first time Cain noticed how delicate the boy's grimy features were: the heart-shaped face, the small nose with its decided upward tilt, and the thickly lashed violet eyes. They were the kind of eyes women prized, although few possessed, but they looked foolish on a boy and would look even more outlandish when he was a man.

Kit refused to flinch under his scrutiny, and Cain felt a reluctant spark of admiration. The boy had spirit and courage, no one could deny that. The daintiness of his features probably had something to do with his pluck. Any boy who looked so delicate had obviously been forced to do a lot of fighting in his time.

Still, the child was too young to be on his own. He should be turned over to the authorities so he could be housed in an orphan asylum until he was older. But even as Cain considered the idea, he knew he wouldn't do it. There was something about that boy that reminded him of himself at that age—feisty and stubborn, walking through life with his chin thrust out, just daring somebody to take a swing at him. It would be like clipping the wings of a wild bird to put that boy in an orphanage. Besides, he was good with the horses.

Flora's need to be alone with Cain finally overcame her aversion to exercise, and she asked him to walk with her to the lake. There, the scene that he had hoped to avoid was played out with tiresome predictability, and Cain cursed himself for not having broken off the relationship sooner. It was his own fault. He had let Flora's expertise in the bedroom overcome his good judgment. Still, she was no great loss. Just last night he had been the bedpartner of a beautiful young widow who, in addition to being passionate, was blessed with a lively sense of humor. No, he was not going to miss Flora at all.

That evening after dinner Kit was sprawled down in her favorite spot outside the stable door, her arm propped comfortably on Merlin's warm back. She waved lazily to Magnus as he disappeared into the house, glad that the rift in their relationship had healed. She liked Magnus's soft voice and easy ways, and had promised herself not to engage him in any more political discussions.

But Magnus Owen wasn't the primary object of her thoughts that evening. Since she had returned from the carriage ride, she had been unable to think of anything except Flora Van Ness's pink-and-white bonnet. It was ridiculous! The bonnet was a silly-looking thing. Nothing more than a few pieces of satin and lace and a trail of ribbons. Yet she couldn't get it off her mind. She kept thinking of what she'd look like wearing it.

Sweet Jesus! What was wrong with her? She pulled off her own battered hat and slammed it down on the ground so suddenly that Merlin looked up in surprise.

"Don't pay me no never mind, Merlin," she muttered apologetically. "All these Yankees are makin' me queer in the head. As if I don't have enough on my mind without thinkin' 'bout bonnets!"

Merlin stared at her with soulful brown eyes. She didn't like admitting it even to herself, but she was going to miss him when she went home. Still, there was nothing she wanted so much as to be back at Risen Glory. She loved that plantation more than she loved anything in the world. It was the only thing in her life that had ever remained constant.

Apparently having decided that the mysterious human crisis was over, Merlin put his head down on her thigh. Idly Kit fingered one of his long, silky ears. She hated this city. She was sick of Yankees and the sound of traffic even at night, and, most of all, she was sick of people calling her "boy."

It was ironic, that's what it was. All her life she'd hated everything that had to do with being female, but now that everybody thought she was a boy, she hated that even worse. Maybe she was just some kind of mutation, a person who didn't have any sex at all. She tugged absentmindedly at a spike of dirty black hair that stuck out behind her ear. All she knew was that every time Baron Cain had called her "boy" today, she'd gotten a sick, queasy feeling.

The thought of Cain depressed her even further. The more she was with him, the more she hated him. He was so arrogant, so sure of himself. She had seen Flora's red-rimmed eyes after they had come back from their walk to the lake, and although she thought the woman was a silly fool, for a few seconds she'd felt a kinship with her. In different ways they were both suffering because of him.

She trailed her fingers down over Merlin's back and reviewed her plan. It wasn't foolproof, but it was the best she was going to be able to do, and all in all, she was satisfied. One thing was certain. When Saturday night came, she'd better not mess up, because, sure as the sun came up in the morning, she wasn't going to get another chance.

Chapter Five

Hamilton Woodward stood as Cain walked through the mahogany doors of his private law office. So this was the Hero of Missionary Ridge, the man who was emptying the pockets of New York's wealthiest financiers and being pursued by the city's most beautiful women. Not a flashy dresser, that much was in his favor. His pinstriped waistcoat and dark-maroon cravat of Damascus silk were expensive but conservative, and his pearl-gray frock coat had obviously been fashioned by a superior tailor. Still, there was something not quite respectable about the man. It was more than his reputation, although that was certainly damning enough. Perhaps it was the way he walked, as if he owned the room he entered.

The attorney walked around to the other side of his highly polished desk and extended his hand. "How do you do, Mr. Cain. I'm Hamilton Woodward."

"Mr. Woodward." As Cain shook hands, he made an assessment of his own. The man was middle-aged and portly. Probably competent. Definitely a lousy poker player.

Woodward indicated a leather armchair drawn up in front of his desk. "Please sit down, Mr. Cain. I apologize for asking you to see me on a Saturday, but this matter has already been delayed long enough. Through no fault of my own, I might add. I only learned of it yesterday."

He waved his plump hand toward a sheaf of documents that lay on his desk. "Gross inefficiency. I assure you, no one associated with my firm would deal with something like this in such a cavalier manner. Especially when it concerns a man to whom we all owe so great a debt. Your courage during—"

"Perhaps you could get to the point. Your letter said only that you wanted to speak with me on a matter of great importance." Cain made no attempt to hide his impatience. It irritated him when people praised his wartime exploits as if what he'd done were something to be unfurled like a flag and hung out for public display.

Hamilton Woodward was offended by Cain's brusqueness. It wasn't the way gentlemen did business. Still, from what he understood, the man didn't pretend to be a gentleman, so he couldn't be faulted for hypocrisy.

He picked up a pair of spectacles and settled the wire stems over his ears. "You are the son of Rosemary Simpson Cain—later Rosemary Weston?"

A shuttered expression came over Cain's handsome features. "I wasn't aware she'd remarried, but yes, that's my mother's name."

"*Was* her name, don't you mean?" Woodward said absently as he glanced down at a paper in front of him.

"She's dead, then?" It was said without expression. He might have been inquiring about the weather or the price of a handkerchief.

The attorney was mortified. His plump jowls jiggled in distress. "Mr. Cain, I do apologize. I assumed you knew. She passed on nearly four months ago. Forgive me for having broken the news so abruptly. Oh, dear, I had no idea . . ."

"Don't trouble yourself with apologies. I haven't seen my mother since I was ten years old. Her death means nothing to me."

After a moment's stunned silence, Woodward lowered his head and began nervously shuffling the papers before him. How could any man react so coldly to the death of his own mother? Finally, when he felt he had regained his composure, he picked up the top paper and cleared his throat.

"I have a letter sent to me by a man named W. C. Ritter, a Charleston attorney who represents your mother's estate. He has asked me to contact you and advise you of the terms of her will. To be brief, eight years ago your mother married a man named Garrett Weston. Weston was the owner of Risen Glory, a cotton plantation not far from Charleston, near the small town of Rutherford. When he was killed at Shiloh, he left the plantation to your mother. Four months ago she died of influenza, and she, in turn, has left the plantation to you."

Cain did not betray any of the surprise he felt. "I haven't seen my mother in seventeen years. Why would she bequeath a plantation to me?"

"Why, I have no idea, but Mr. Ritter did include a letter that she apparently wrote to you shortly before her death. Let me see. I have it here somewhere. Ah, here it is. Perhaps it will explain her motives." He passed a sealed letter across the desk.

Cain put it in the pocket of his coat without even glancing at it. "Tell me what you know about this plantation."

"It was apparently quite prosperous before the war, although I understand it has not been maintained, and like so many other Southern plantations, it's probably lost much of its value. With work, it might be reclaimed; however, I must advise you there's no money attached to this bequest. Weston lost almost everything during the war. There is, however, a substantial trust fund for his daughter, Katharine Louise."

This time Cain's surprise was evident. "Are you telling me I have a half sister?"

"No, no. She's a stepsister. You aren't related by blood. According to Mr. Ritter, the girl is Weston's child from his previous marriage. She does, however, concern you. It seems as though her grandmother left her quite a lot of money—fifteen thousand dollars, to be exact—to be held in trust for her until her twenty-third birthday or until she marries, whichever event occurs first. You have been appointed administrator of her trust and, of course, her guardian."

"Guardian!" Cain seemed to erupt from the deep seat of the leather chair.

Woodward was alarmed. "But of course, Mr. Cain. What else was your mother to do? The child is only sixteen. There is a substantial sum of money involved here, and apparently no other relatives."

Cain placed the tips of his fingers on the desk top and leaned forward over the gleaming mahogany surface. "I'm not going to take responsibility for a sixteen-year-old girl or a run-down cotton plantation."

"Well, that's up to you, of course, although I do agree that giving a man as—as worldly as yourself guardianship over an innocent young girl is somewhat irregular. Still, the decision is yours. It would seem necessary for you to go to Charleston and see the plantation first. You could speak with Mr. Ritter personally and advise him of your decision."

"There is no decision," Cain said flatly. "I didn't ask for this inheritance, and I don't want it. Write your Mr. Ritter and tell him to find another patsy."

Cain was in a black mood by the time he arrived home, a mood that was not improved when his stable boy failed to appear in the yard to take the carriage from him.

"Kit? Where the hell are you?" He called twice before Kit came racing out. "Damn it, boy! If you're working for me, I expect you to be here when I need you. As I remember, Monday is your day off, not Saturday. Don't keep me waiting again!"

He leaped down from the carriage and strode across the open yard to the house. The glare Kit threw at his back was dark with fury.

Once inside, Cain went straight to the library, a comfortable room with saffron draperies and deep-green upholstery. The sight of his stable boy had depressed him even further. Without being aware of it, he had somehow begun to feel responsible for Kit. It was a disagreeable discovery, especially coupled with today's interview. Since he had been thirteen years old, there had been no ties in his life, and that was the way he wanted to keep it.

Cain was a man with few possessions and none he'd ever let himself get attached to. During the war there had been no well-thumbed Bible tucked deep in his saddlebags. He kept no photographs, no mementos. He liked to read, especially American writers like James Fenimore Cooper and Walt Whitman, but when he finished a book, it didn't occur to him to keep it. He passed it on to the first person who showed an interest. He'd never permitted himself to get attached to anything or anyone, not even his horse, and he seldom kept an animal longer than a year. All in all, it was better that way. Possessions tied a man down.

He splashed some whiskey in a glass. Only after he had drained it did he pull the letter Woodward had given him from his coat and break the red wax seal. Inside was a single sheet of paper covered with small, nearly indecipherable handwriting.

April 17, 1865

Dear Baron,

I can imagine your surprise at receiving a letter from me after so many years, even if it is a letter from the grave. A morbid thought. I am not resigned to dying. Still, my fever will not break and I fear the worst. I do not know how much longer I will have the strength, so today I have decided to dispose of those few responsibilities I have left.

If you expect apologies from me, you will receive none. Life with your father was exceptionally tedious. I am also not a maternal woman, and you were a most unruly child, prone to running about and putting your dirty hands on my gowns. It was all very tiresome. Still, I must admit to having followed the newspaper stories of your exploits during the war with some interest. It pleased me to learn you are considered a handsome man.

None of this, however, concerns my purpose in writing. I was very attached to my second husband, Garrett Weston. He overlooked my indiscretions and made life very pleasant for me. It is for him that I write this letter. Although I have never been able to abide his daughter, Katharine, I realize she must have someone to watch out for her until she comes of age. Therefore, I have left Risen Glory to you with the hope that you will act as her guardian. Perhaps you will decline. Although the plantation was once the finest in the area, the war has done it no good.

Whatever your decision, I have discharged my duty.

Your mother,
Rosemary Weston

After eighteen years, that was all. Cain balled the letter in his fist. For an instant something that, in another man, might have been mistaken for pain flickered across his even features. And then, as quickly as it had appeared, it was gone. He pitched the crumpled ball of paper into the empty fireplace and stalked out of the room.

Kit kneeled in front of her open window and stared toward the dark house. She heard the clock on the Methodist church in the next block chime two. It was early Sunday morning, and Baron Cain was not going to live to see the dawn.

He had been home for over an hour now, and her worst fear, that he would bring a woman with him, hadn't been realized. Mrs. Simmons and the maids were gone, Magnus had left after lunch, Cain was in the house alone and the way was clear for her. She decided to give herself fifteen more minutes to make certain he was asleep.

The pre-dawn air that blew in the open window was heavy and faintly metallic, warning of a storm. She shivered even though her room was still warm from the afternoon's heat. Thunderstorms had always frightened her.

She tried to convince herself that this particular storm would make her work easier, hiding any noise she might make when she slipped into the house through the small pantry window she had unlocked so many hours earlier as she had washed her hands for dinner. But the thought brought her little comfort. Her imagination was too willing to provide an unpleasant picture of herself as she would be in less than an hour, running through the night streets with a thunderstorm crashing around her. If only the storm would blow over.

As if nature were laughing at her, there was a distant flash of lightning and a low, ominous rumbling. To distract herself Kit mentally reviewed her plan. Last night after she had cleaned and oiled her daddy's revolver, she had reread Mr. Emerson's essay "Self-Reliance" to bolster her courage. Then she had bundled up her few possessions and hidden them in the back of the carriage house.

After she killed Cain, she would grab them and make her way on foot to the ferry docks on Courtland Street in Lower Manhattan. It would be faster if she could take one of the horse cars that ran at night, but she was not certain exactly how to do it and had decided walking was safer. Even so, she should be at the dock in time to catch the first ferry for Jersey City and the train station that would mark the beginning of her journey back to Charleston.

The long nightmare would be over. With Cain's death Rosemary's will would be meaningless and Risen Glory would pass on to her. All she had to do was find his bedroom, aim her gun, and pull the trigger.

She realized she had to use the privy again and picked up the loaded revolver from the floor next to her. It was nearly time to leave anyway; he had to be asleep by now. Holding the wooden grip loosely in her hand, she crept down the stairs and out of the stable, being careful not to disturb Merlin on the way.

By the time she had finished in the privy, the thunder was louder. She tried to ignore it as she stealthily made her way around the corner of the house. The pantry window was set well above the ground, and she had hidden an empty nail keg behind the shrubbery so she would have something to climb on. Tucking the revolver into the waistband of her breeches, she reached into the bushes and pulled it out. Then she climbed on top and pushed up on the window frame.

It didn't budge.

She pushed again, harder this time, hooking the heels of her hands under the strips of wood that divided the window into panes. Nothing happened. She told herself it was the weather. The moisture in the air had swollen the wooden frame. If she just tried harder, it would give.

She shoved at the window until her undershirt was wet with perspiration, but it was no use. The window was locked.

Kit felt as if she had been punched in the stomach. She had known her plan wasn't foolproof, but it had never occurred to her that she wouldn't even be able to get into the house! Mrs. Simmons must have discovered the unfastened latch and secured it before she left.

Kit slumped down on the keg in despair just as the first drops of rain began to fall. Heavy and stinging, they hit her shoulders like a handful of pebbles flung through the air by a careless fist. She jumped up from the keg, forcing herself to action. There had to be a way to get inside!

She circled the house twice before she spotted an open second-story window in the back of the house. A maple tree, its branches thrashing wildly in the wind, grew nearby. It was impossible to tell in the dark how close the swaying tree limbs actually came to the house, but Kit knew she had no other choice. The window was her only hope.

Without giving herself time to think, she grabbed the lowest branch and pulled herself up. She had climbed halfway to the top when a bolt of lightning split open the skies. There was a thunderclap so close she could feel the tree quiver. She squeezed her eyes shut and clung desperately to the branch, terrified by the force of the storm and the realization that, in leaving the ground, she had become part of it.

She forced herself to go higher, edging out onto the limb that seemed to grow closest to the window. There was another thunderclap, which left the stink of brimstone hanging behind it in the air. She began to make soft, whimpering sounds as she moved her weight bit by bit out toward the end of the pitching tree limb, hoping against hope that it would reach far enough.

When she felt the branch sagging ominously beneath her

weight, she knew she could go no farther and peered through the rain trying to determine how close she had come. The skies lit, and to her despair she saw that at least five feet separated her from the side of the house.

She clung to the limb for what seemed like hours staring at the open window. Five feet or five miles, it made little difference. There was no way she could breach the distance.

The storm's fury had not abated by the time she slid to the ground, bedraggled and trembling. Her clothing was soaked through to her skin, and the brim of her hat had collapsed like a sodden pancake around her small head. She pressed her spine against the tree trunk, unshed tears hot behind her lids. Was this the way it was all going to end? Risen Glory taken from her because she couldn't get into a house?

She felt something brush against her legs and looked down to see Merlin staring up at her, his head cocked inquisitively to the side. She sank to her knees and buried her face in his wet, musty fur. "Oh, Merlin," she sobbed. "What in the name of Lord Jesus am I gonna do now?"

The mongrel scraped her cheek with his rough tongue, and then there was another blast of lightning and a crack of thunder. Merlin howled, and Kit jumped to her feet. Like a match to a powder keg, her fear ignited her determination. She wasn't going to let it happen! Risen Glory was hers! If she couldn't get into the house on her own, he would just have to let her in!

She dashed out from under the tree, fighting against the wind with each step she took. When she reached the back door, she threw herself against it, pounding the surface with her clenched fists, kicking at it with her boots, screaming for him to let her in. The wind ripped the words from her mouth and tossed them away, a splinter of wood speared her hand, but she barely noticed. With the storm raging at her back and tears of fear and frustration streaming down her face, she beat hysterically on the wooden surface.

The door flew open just as a jagged bolt of lightning shot down from the sky and struck the maple that had so recently sheltered her, splitting the trunk neatly in two. Kit screamed and threw herself inside, propelling her small wet form directly into the arms of Baron Cain.

"What the . . ." Carrying her with him, he took a fast step

backward to regain his balance. Although she weighed only a little more than a hundred pounds, she had come at him with the speed of a charging bull, plastering her cold, wet front against his naked, sleep-warmed chest.

"Kit, what's wrong? Has something happened?"

She jerked back from him, stumbling over Merlin in her haste to get away and sending herself sprawling down on the hard kitchen floor.

Torn between annoyance and amusement, Cain looked down at the bedraggled stable boy and wet mongrel lying in a tangled heap at his feet. He assessed the situation, and amusement won out.

"This thunderstorm a little too much for the two of you?"

Stepping over them, he went to the back door and pushed it firmly shut. Just as he turned back, Merlin stood and shook himself, showering Cain and the kitchen with water.

"Damn!" Cain jerked a towel from a hook near the sink and rubbed it over his chest. As if he realized his position was precarious, Merlin dashed out the side door into the hallway that led to Magnus's room, where he slithered under the bed and promptly fell asleep.

Kit had landed on top of the revolver that was tucked into her britches, and she bit her lip against the sharp pain that seared her hip. Quickly, while Cain was occupied drying himself, she shoved the weapon behind a basket of apples that sat next to the back door near where she had fallen. She couldn't let him see her gun until she was ready to use it, and she needed a few minutes to collect herself. She would have only one chance to kill him, and her hand had to be steady.

"I don't know which is worse," Cain growled as he passed the towel down his arm, "a scared boy or a scared dog."

"I'm certainly not scared of a little thunderstorm," Kit glowered.

Just then there was another crash from outside, and she leaped to her feet, her face turning pale.

"My mistake." Cain grinned.

Kit barely heard him, for at that moment she forgot the thunderstorm. Totally mesmerized, she stared at him as if she were seeing him for the first time.

He was nearly naked, wearing only a pair of dun-colored

trousers, slung low on his hips, the top two buttons left unfastened in his haste to get to the door. She had been around many scantily clad men working in the fields or at the sawmill, but now it was as if she'd never really seen any of them.

His chest was broad and muscular, lightly furred. A raised scar slashed across one powerful shoulder. Another jutted up over his bare abdomen from the open waistband of his trousers. His hips were narrow and his stomach flat, bisected by a thin line of tawny hair. Her eyes inched lower to the point at which the legs of his tight-fitting trousers met. There was an obvious bulge, forbidding and, at the same time, infinitely fascinating.

"Better dry yourself off."

She jerked her head up to see him staring at her, a towel extended in his hand, his expression faintly puzzled. Quickly she took the towel and reached under the collapsed brim of her hat to dab at her cheeks.

"It might be better if you took your hat off to do that," he offered.

"I don't want to take it off," she snapped, shaken by her reaction to his half-clad body. "I like my hat."

With a growl of exasperation, he headed out the side door of the kitchen into the hallway that led to Magnus's room. In less than a minute, he reappeared with a blanket.

"Take off those wet clothes before you get sick. You can wrap this around yourself."

She stared at the blanket and then at him. "I'm not takin' off my clothes."

"Don't be ridiculous." Cain frowned. "You're cold."

"I'm not cold!" It was a lie. The storm was chilling the air, and her teeth were beginning to chatter.

"Damn it, boy! It's three o'clock in the morning, I lost two hundred dollars at poker tonight, and I'm tired as hell! Now get out of those damned clothes so we can both get some sleep. You can use Magnus's room tonight, and I'd better not hear another sound out of you until noon!"

"Are you deaf, Yankee?" she cried, desperately fighting against the exhaustion and frustration that was threatening to overcome her. "I said I wasn't takin' off any clothes!"

Cain was not used to being thwarted by a stable boy, especially one who hadn't grown even a trace of fuzz on his cheeks. Without taking his eyes from her, he put the blanket down.

Kit saw by the grim set of his jaw that her time had run out and realized, too late, that hiding her gun had been a mistake. She should have killed him as soon as she got in the kitchen. Whirling around, she dashed toward the basket of apples.

Cain saw only that she was heading toward the back door and believed she was trying to escape him by running outside. Angry that a slip of a boy was defying him, he sprang across the kitchen floor. Kit sensed him behind her and jerked to the side to avoid him, but Cain was too quick for her. He shot out his hand and caught her by the upper arm.

"Let me go, you sonvabitch!" she screamed, trying to punch at him with her fists.

"Not a chance, boy," Cain growled, holding her easily at arm's length. "I told you to take off those wet clothes, and by damn, you're going to do what I say!"

"You can rot in hell, Yankee!" She swung at him again and again, but the only part of him she could reach was the arm that was holding her, and her blows bounced off the iron-muscled flesh as harmlessly as thistledown.

"Stop it, boy, before you get hurt!" He shook her once as a warning.

"Go fuck yourself!"

Her hat flew off her head as she felt herself being lifted off the floor. There was a clap of thunder. Cain threw himself down on a kitchen chair and tossed her across his outstretched knee.

"I've had all I'm going to take of that foul mouth of yours." His open palm slammed down hard on her buttocks, and a cry, composed as much of surprise as it was of indignation, escaped her. "If your father didn't have enough sense to beat some manners into you, then I do." Once again his hand came down, but this time her exclamation was edged with pain as she felt the first faint burning in her tender flesh.

"Let me go, you rotten bastard!"

She regretted the profanity as soon as it was out of her mouth, for now Cain showed her no mercy. He slammed his open palm again and again against her buttocks until they were on fire, burning with pain so keen it was all she could do to keep herself from begging him for mercy.

When he finally stopped, he jerked her to her feet, careful to keep a firm grasp on her arm. For a moment she stood quietly, and then she made a quick slash at her nose with the top of her sleeve.

Cain felt some of his anger slip away when he saw the tears that had clouded his feisty stable boy's violet eyes. Then Kit's small white teeth began to chatter, and he was abruptly reminded of the cause of their dispute. Using his free hand, he reached for the top button of her wet shirt.

It was as if he had taken a knife to her. With a growl low in her throat, she bared her teeth and jerked back from him. The movement was so unexpected that Cain nearly lost his grip on her. As he reached out to grasp her more firmly, his forearm brushed across the front of her chest.

Kit caught her breath when she heard his muffled exclamation. Before she could react, his arm had grabbed her wrists and whipped them behind her back. Eyes the color of frozen pewter stared down at her, wordlessly raking her dainty features. Without warning, he reached up with his fist and grasped the front of her shirt and the old, worn material of her undershirt. She felt a sharp, downward jerk. There was the sound of rending fabric, the faint patter of buttons skittering across the wooden floor. And then the cool air touched her flesh, and her small, coral-tipped breasts were exposed to his gaze.

The humiliation that gripped her was suffocating. To have any man see her naked breasts was degrading enough, but that the man should be Baron Cain was more than she thought she could bear. He released her slowly, and she fumbled for the torn edges of her shirt.

"What kind of game are you playing?" he asked grimly.

She clutched the shirt together with her fist and glared up at him, trying desperately to conceal her humiliation behind an expression of belligerence. Still, she couldn't quite meet his eyes. "I needed a job," she managed.

"And you got one by passing yourself off as a boy."

"You're the one who assumed I was a boy. I never said any such thing."

"You never said any different either." He picked up the blanket and tossed it to her; then he walked toward the hallway door. "You've got exactly two minutes to get out of those clothes. When I come back, I'll expect some answers. And don't get any ideas about running away. That'd be your biggest mistake yet."

She clutched the blanket in front of her. "Don't you worry, Yankee!" she spat out. "I don't have the slightest intention of runnin' away."

But the door had already closed, and she had no way of knowing if he'd heard her.

With Cain out of the room, she flung down the blanket and raced toward the basket of apples to retrieve the revolver. Only after she had twirled the cylinder to make certain all six chambers were ready was she satisfied. Then she set about trying to repair some of the damage to her shirt. There was one button several inches below her breasts that was still intact. She fastened it and then gathered the tattered shirttails together and tied them into a knot at her waist.

The result was unsatisfactory, and she looked down at herself with dismay. Without the protection of her undershirt, the shape of her small breasts was clearly evident. There was also a deep V of exposed flesh extending down to the single button. That the flesh was none too clean despite the drenching it had received from the storm totally escaped her notice.

Outside in the narrow back hallway, Cain was cursing himself for having been so easily fooled. How could he have believed for one moment that she was a boy, especially when he had studied her features and seen how delicate they were? Plowing his fingers impatiently back through his already disheveled hair, he tried to decide how old she was. Thirteen? Fourteen? Christ. He knew a lot about women, but not ones that young. When did they start growing breasts?

Still, it didn't really matter how old she was. She was too young to be on her own. It was one thing to have left her alone when he thought she was a boy, but that was all over now. She was going to have to have somebody to look out for her, and it sure as hell wasn't going to be him! Damn! How could he have been so stupid?

Without bothering to knock, he stalked back into the kitchen. She was sitting at the wooden table, her hands folded out of sight in her lap. His eyes flickered down over the wet shirt that now revealed all too clearly her true sex. For the moment he decided to ignore the fact that she had disobeyed his orders to take off her clothes and concentrate on the more important issue.

Resting one hand lightly on his hip, he walked over to the foot of the table. "Where's your family?"

"I told you," she said quietly. "They're dead."

"You don't have any relatives at all?"

"None I ever heard about."

Her composure annoyed him. "Look, a child your age can't run around New York City alone. It isn't safe."

"Only person's given me trouble since I got here's been you."

She had a point, but he chose to ignore it. "Regardless," he said stiffly, "tomorrow I'm going to take you to some people who'll be responsible for you until you're older. They'll find a place for you to live."

"You talkin' 'bout an orphanage, Major?" She seemed almost amused.

"Yes, I'm talking about an orphanage!" he exploded. "You're sure as hell not going to stay here! Damn it, you have to have someplace to live until you're old enough to look after yourself."

"Doesn't seem to me I've had too much trouble up till now. Besides, I'm not exactly a child. I don't think orphanages take in sixteen-year-olds."

"Sixteen!"

"And five months," she added unnecessarily.

Cain was incredulous. Once again she had managed to take him by surprise. He stared down the length of the table at her—ragged boy's clothing, a grimy face and neck, short black hair, stiff with dirt. In his experience, sixteen-year-olds were nearly women. They wore dresses and took baths. But then, it should have been obvious to him by now that there was nothing about her that bore the slightest resemblance to a normal sixteen-year-old girl.

"Sorry to spoil all your nice plans for orphanages and such, Major." She smirked.

He was suddenly glad he'd spanked her. "Now you listen to me, Kit—or is your name phony, too?"

She shifted her weight ever so slightly in her chair. "Nope. It's my real name all right. Leastways it's what most everybody calls me. Except it's not Finney. It's Weston. Katharine Louise Weston."

It was her last surprise. Before Cain could react, she was on her feet and he was looking down into the barrel of an army revolver.

"Son of a bitch," he muttered through lips that barely moved.

Without taking her eyes from him, she came around the edge of the table, the gun that was pointed at his heart held steady in her small hand. "Doesn't seem to me you're so particular about cussin' when you're the one doin' it."

He took a step toward her and was immediately sorry. A bullet whizzed by his head, just missing his temple.

"You don't move unless I tell you, Yankee," Kit snarled. "Next time it'll be your ear." Despite the boldness of her words, she felt a faint trembling in her knees.

"Maybe you'd better tell me what this is all about."

"It's self-evident, isn't it?"

"Humor me."

The faint air of mockery in his voice made her furious. "It's about Risen Glory, you black-hearted sonvabitch. It's mine! You got no right to it."

His eyes narrowed into thin slits. "That's not what the law says."

"I don't care about no law. I don't care about wills or courts or any of that. What's right is right. Risen Glory is mine, and no Yankee's takin' it from me."

"Don't you think if your father had wanted you to have it, he'd have left it to you instead of Rosemary when he died?"

"Where that woman was concerned, my daddy didn't have the sense he was born with!" Kit exclaimed. "She made him blind and deaf as well as a fool."

"It's a habit women associated with your father seem to have," he said dryly.

Kit was suddenly determined to wipe the mockery from his voice, to hurt him as she'd been hurt. "I suppose I should be grateful to Rosemary," she sneered. "Hadn't of been for her easy ways with men, the Yankees would of burned the house as well as the fields. Your mother was well known for sharin' her favors with anybody who asked."

Cain's face was expressionless. "She was a slut."

"That's God's truth, Yankee. And I'm not gonna let her get the best of me, even from the grave."

"So now you're going to kill me." He sounded slightly bored.

She could feel her palms beginning to sweat. "That's right," she retorted defiantly. "Without you standin' in my way, Risen Glory will be mine, just what should of happened in the first place."

He nodded his head slowly, his face empty of expression. "I see your point. All right, I'm ready. How do you want to go about it?"

"What?"

"Killing me," he said. "How are you going to do it? Do you want me to turn around so you won't have to look me in the face when you pull the trigger?"

Kit was outraged. "What kind of fool jackass thing is that to say? You think I could ever respect myself again if I shot a man in the back?"

"Sorry, it was just a suggestion. I was trying to make it easier for you, that's all."

"Don't you worry 'bout me, Yankee. You worry 'bout your own immortal soul."

Slowly she lifted her arm and sighted down the barrel of her revolver. It felt as heavy as a cannon in her hand.

"You ever killed a man, Kit?"

"Shut up!" she shouted. The trembling in her knees had spread upward, and she could feel her arm begin to shake. Cain, on the other hand, looked as relaxed as if he'd just finished a Sunday nap.

"Hit me right between the eyes," he said softly. "It'll be fast and sure that way. Standing so close, the back of my head will blow off. That'll be messy, but you can take it, can't you, Kit?"

Now the gun was visibly shaking. "Shut up!" she screamed. "Shut up!"

"Come on, Kit. Get it over with."

"Shut up!"

The gun exploded. Once, twice, three times. Four. Five. And then the click of an empty chamber. On the wall behind where Cain had been standing were five holes forming the outline of a man's head.

With the first shot Cain had hit the floor. As the kitchen once again fell silent, he looked up to see Kit standing with her shoulders slumped, her arms at her sides. The revolver dangled uselessly from her hand.

He eased himself up and walked over to the wall that had received the lead balls originally intended for him. As he studied the perfect arc, he slowly shook his head with admiration.

"I've got to say this for you, kid. You're one hell of a shot."

For Kit the world had come to an end. She had lost Risen Glory, and she had no one to blame but herself.

"Coward," she whispered, dry-eyed and trembling. "I'm a damn, lily-livered coward."

Chapter Six

Kit spent the next day huddled miserably in the stable with a book called *The Sybaritic Life of Louis XV,* which she'd randomly pulled off a shelf in the library. She wasn't permitted to work with the horses anymore, or to sleep in her pleasant leather-and-dust-scented room above the horses' stalls. Cain's orders had been precise. Until he had decided what to do with her, she would sleep in the house, in the small, second-story bedroom he had half led, half dragged her to shortly before dawn. She was to do no work in the stable, and above all, she was not to consider running away. Not only would he have her arrested for attempted murder, but he would make certain she never again set foot on Risen Glory.

She was convinced that he was bluffing about the arrest—the Hero of Missionary Ridge was hardly going to publicize the fact that he had been held at gunpoint by a girl—but she took his warning about Risen Glory more seriously. Until she knew what his plans were, she had no choice but to remain where she was.

For a while she read *The Sybaritic Life of Louis XV,* and then she dozed, dreaming disjointedly of thunderstorms, guns, and the King of France romping with his mistress, Madame de Pompadour, across the green fields of Risen Glory. When she awoke, she felt groggy and heavy-limbed. As she slumped dejectedly outside Apollo's stall, her elbows resting on the greasy knees of her breeches, she knew she was never going to be able to hold her head up again. When it had come time to prove herself, she had failed abysmally. It was just that, in all her planning, it hadn't occurred to her that she was going to have to kill an unarmed man while she was looking him square in the eye!

If only he had tried to wrestle the gun away from her, she could have killed him easily. That would have been self-defense. But he'd just stood there, talking to her in that low, quiet voice about how the back of his head was going to blow off.

The stable door creaked open, letting in a few feeble rays of light from the overcast afternoon. Merlin scampered across the floor and flung himself at Kit, nearly knocking her hat off in his exuberance. Magnus followed at a more leisurely pace, his boots stopping near her own.

"I'm not in the mood for conversation right now, Magnus," she murmured, refusing to lift her eyes.

"Can't say I'm surprised," he snapped. "This morning the major told Mrs. Simmons and me what happened last night. That was some trick you pulled, *Miss* Kit." It was the form of address she was accustomed to hearing at home, but he made it sound like an insult.

She jumped to her feet, wincing slightly as the sudden movement reminded her of the pain in her tender buttocks. "Don't you get snooty with me, Magnus Owen! What happened last night was between me and the major. It's none of your business."

"Far as I'm concerned, there's nothin' about you that's any of my business anymore." With that, he picked up an empty bucket and left the stable.

Infuriated by his rebuke, she put down her book, picked up a brush, and headed into the stall that housed Saratoga, a spirited russet mare Cain sometimes rode. She didn't care what Cain's orders were! If she didn't busy herself, she would go crazy!

She was running her hands down Saratoga's hind legs when she heard a noise behind her. Jumping up, she whirled around to see Cain standing in the center aisle of the stable regarding her with granite-hard eyes.

"My orders were clear, Kit. No work in the stable. Why have you disobeyed me?"

"The Good Lord gave me two strong arms," she snapped. "I'm no good at sittin' idle."

His voice was edged with mockery. "Grooming horses is hardly considered an appropriate activity for a young lady."

Kit planted one small hand on her hip. "I don't care what other people consider appropriate or not appropriate. If there's work to be done, I believe in doin' it. A sybaritic life doesn't appeal to me. Besides, whoever groomed Saratoga last did a sorry job. I found dirt in his fetlock. You gonna end up with a horse sufferin' from mud fever."

"I'll speak to Magnus about it," he said tightly. "In the meantime you stay away from the stable."

She opened her mouth to protest, but he was too quick for her. "No arguments, Kit. I went to see Hamilton Woodward today, the attorney who told me the conditions of Rosemary's will. I want you cleaned up and in the library in half an hour so I can talk to you." He turned on his heel and strode out the stable door, his powerful, long-legged gait strangely graceful for a man of his size.

Kit reached the library first. In token obedience to Cain's orders, the center of her face was a well-scrubbed oval, although neither the perimeter nor the rest of her seemed to have benefited from the washing. She began pacing the maroon and gold border of the Kashan carpet in boots that still bore traces of the stable, finally stopping in front of an open window to gaze out over the quiet street.

The lamp in front of the house had been lit, and she could see a moth futilely flinging its fragile wings against the amber globe. It struck her that she and the moth had much in common. Abruptly she turned away and began gnawing an already ragged fingernail. No matter what happened, she had to keep her wits about her.

The door opened and Cain came into the room. He was dressed in his customary at-home uniform of fawn trousers and white shirt, open at the throat. His eyes flicked over her. "I thought I told you to get cleaned up before you came in here."

"I washed my face, didn't I?"

"It's going to take a hell of a lot more than a face-washing to clean you up." He frowned. "How can you stand to be so dirty all the time?"

"I don't hold much with baths."

"Seems to me there are a lot of things you don't 'hold much' with. But I'll tell you this—you're going to get clean before you spend another night here even if I have to scrub you myself. Edith Simmons is threatening to quit, and I'll be damned if I lose a housekeeper because of you. Besides, you stink up the place."

Kit's violet eyes flashed in outrage. "I do not!"

"Hell you don't." He settled into an upholstered armchair on the opposite side of the room from where she was standing. "Even if it's only temporary, I *am* your guardian, and right now you're taking orders from me."

For a moment Kit didn't move, and then she shook her head once as if she were trying to clear it. When she spoke, her voice was little more than a whisper. "What you talkin' about, Yankee? What do you mean, 'guardian'?"

"You didn't know?" He seemed amused. "I'm disappointed. I didn't think there was anything that got past you." He briefly outlined the details of the guardianship and her trust fund.

She had known about the money for years. Her grandmother, a woman she barely remembered, had left it to her when she died. It had been a constant source of resentment to Rosemary, fueling her dislike of her stepdaughter. At his wife's urging, Garrett had consulted one lawyer after another, but he had not been able to break the trust. Although Kit understood that fifteen thousand dollars was a great deal of money, as far as she was concerned, it was useless. She needed it now, not seven years from now!

"The guardianship is Rosemary's joke from the grave," Cain concluded. "She's made me responsible for you until you're twenty-three."

"You're lying! I don't believe you! That damn lawyer didn't say anything to me 'bout a guardian!"

By now Cain was well acquainted with Kit's temper. "Did you give him a chance?"

Her mind flew back to her short interview with Willard Ritter, Rosemary's attorney. With a sinking heart she remembered how she had angrily ordered him out of the house after he'd told her about Cain's inheritance. She hadn't given him an opportunity to say anything more.

A remark Cain had made earlier came back to her, and she clung to it like a drowning man to a lifeline. "What did you mean about it bein' a temporary state?"

"You sure as hell don't think I'm going to let myself be saddled with you for the next seven years, do you?" The Hero of Missionary Ridge actually shuddered. "Early tomorrow morning, I'm leaving for South Carolina to get this mess straightened out. Even that's more than I'd intended to do. Mrs. Simmons will watch over you until I get back. It shouldn't be much more than three or four weeks."

Her hands were beginning to shake, and she clasped them behind her back before he could see. "How you plannin' on straightenin' things out?"

"I'm going to find you another guardian, that's for damned sure."

She dug her fingernails into her palms, terrified of the next question, yet knowing she must ask it. The words came out in a queer, breathless rush. "What's gonna happen to Risen Glory?"

He studied the toe of his boot. Was he ashamed to meet her eyes, or was he merely indifferent? "I'm going to sell it," he said flatly.

Something like a growl erupted from Kit's throat. "No!"

Now Cain met her eyes unflinchingly. "I'm going to sell Risen Glory, Kit. And that's final."

It was impossible! How could something this awful be happening to her? She did not even hear him call for Mrs. Simmons.

"Yes, sir?"

"Get her out of here, Edith," he growled, thrusting Kit toward the housekeeper. "And give her a bath."

"Certainly, sir." Mrs. Simmons took Kit from him, her ample chest visibly puffing up at the challenge.

"And burn those rags she's wearing. You can buy her some clothes tomorrow. *Dresses!*"

"Of course, sir."

As Edith Simmons led a curiously unprotesting Kit from the room, Cain sighed and poured himself a stiff measure of brandy. He had planned to dress and then go to the Astor House for a high-stakes game in one of the hotel's luxurious private dining rooms. Later there was an invitation from a famous opera singer who had assured him that he was always welcome to call, no matter how late the hour. Now it all seemed like too much trouble. What the hell was wrong with him anyway?

He had nearly finished his brandy when he heard a scream followed by a crash coming from above his head. Swearing loudly, he jumped up from his chair and dashed out into the hall.

Upstairs, the bathroom was a shambles. Shattered glass lay near the copper tub. A container of talc rested on its side atop the marble basin, its contents dusted over the fine silver faucets and handsome black walnut wainscoting. Clothing was scattered across the floor. Only the warm, perfume-scented water in the enameled tub was undisturbed, its surface smooth and pale gold in the glowing light of the gas jets.

Kit was holding Mrs. Simmons at bay with a mirror, the tortoiseshell handle clenched in her fist like the hilt of a saber. With the other hand, she gripped a towel in front of her nakedness.

Totally absorbed by her misery, she had barely noticed when Mrs. Simmons had led her from the library to the elegant bathroom, had hardly felt the clothing being removed from her body. It was not until the housekeeper had propelled her toward the tub that she had once again become aware of what was happening to her. That was when the struggle had begun.

Now she advanced on Mrs. Simmons, just missing the broken glass as she backed the unfortunate housekeeper to the door. "Nobody's givin' me a bath!" she shouted, the tendons in her small neck stretched taut. "You get out of here!"

"What the hell's going on?" Cain's voice sounded like thunder rolling down a mountain.

As he appeared in the doorway, Mrs. Simmons forgot herself so much as to grab his sleeve. "Mr. Cain! She tried to . . . to murder me! She threw a bottle of witch hazel at me. And then your china shaving mug. It missed my head by inches." Fanning her face with her hand, she moaned, "Oh, my neuralgia! I can feel an attack coming on. She should be locked up. Away from decent people. Never have I witnessed such behavior."

As Cain's flint-hard eyes found Kit, she realized, too late, that she had made a terrible mistake. "Go lie down, Edith," he said quietly. "I'll take over."

Even if the housekeeper had been inclined to protest the impropriety of her employer being left alone with his ward, who was, at that moment, clad only in a towel, his tone of voice left no room for argument. Without so much as a glance in Kit's direction, she stumbled down the hallway muttering darkly of neuralgia and asylums.

Cain's eyes drilled into Kit's, and then with deliberate slowness, he unfastened the cuffs of his white shirt and began rolling up the sleeves, exposing his tanned muscular forearms.

At the first sound of his voice, Kit had let the tortoiseshell mirror fall to her side. Now she raised it again. "Don't you come any closer, Yankee! When I threw the witch hazel bottle at Mrs. Simmons, I intended to miss. This time I won't!"

For all her bravado, she was badly frightened. Fully clothed, there was no man on earth she was afraid of, not even Baron Cain. But now with only a towel covering her body, she felt more vulnerable than she could ever remember. If only he hadn't taken her gun and locked it away. If she had it in her hand now, she could pull the trigger without a second thought.

"I mean it, Yankee! Not a step farther!"

"Don't you think it's about time you grew up?" His tone was iced with contempt. "You're sixteen—old enough to be thinking like a woman instead of a child—but you act like you're twelve. It was one thing to go after me, but tonight you threatened a woman who never did you any harm."

"She took my clothes and was gettin' ready to push me in that tub."

He crossed his arms and leaned against the door frame. "And now I'm the one who's going to put you in that tub," he said with determination.

Giving a cry that was half sob, half scream, she flung the mirror at him. But his relaxed posture had been deceptive. With lightning-quick reflexes he ducked, and the mirror crashed harmlessly against the wall.

His handsome features contorted with fury. "You little brat! You've finally pushed me too far!"

He sprang across the floor, glass crunching under the soles of his boots, and snatched her up in his arms. As she slammed against his chest, she felt something queer happening inside her, as if she'd jumped off a moving wagon or spun around too quickly. It was strange and unsettling.

She began to struggle more fiercely, but she might as well have saved the effort. For an instant he held her over the tub, and then he dropped her in, towel and all.

She sputtered with rage. "You filthy, stinkin'—"

That was as far as she got. A broad hand clamped itself to the top of her head and pushed her under the water.

When he did not immediately release her, she started to flail, splashing water everywhere. Still, he did not let her go. Her struggle grew more frantic. She began to panic as her lungs seemed to catch fire. Reaching up, she clawed at his forearm, pushing at it with rapidly diminishing strength. Finally, just at the moment when she felt her lungs would burst, he hauled her head to the surface by the hair.

She gulped in great, enraged lungfuls of air, finally managed to choke out, "You dirty—"

Before she could go any further, she was once again underwater. She fought him with what was left of her strength, but the struggle was shorter this time.

"Had enough yet?" he drawled after he had dragged her, sputtering and choking, to the surface.

He was resting on one knee at the side of the tub. The thin material of his shirt was plastered to his broad chest, and beads of water glistened on his face and even in his hair. She glared malevolently at him, her lips framing yet another curse.

It was then she realized that she had lost her towel in the struggle and that she was naked to his insolent eyes. Flooded with shame, she drew her legs up and crouched her shoulders over her bent knees, shielding her breasts and her lower parts from his gaze.

"Well? Do you want another dunking, or are you ready to cooperate?"

Although it nearly killed her, she nodded her head, her eyes fixed firmly downward.

"A wise decision," he said mockingly as he reached for the soap and began working it into her scalp. This time when he dunked her underwater, it was only to rinse out the suds. He lathered her hair a second time, rubbing her scalp so roughly she had to bite her lip to keep from crying out.

He went on to her face, not seeming to care that he was getting soap in her eyes and her mouth, merely shoving her heartlessly under the water when she began to sputter. He excavated first one ear and then the other, scrubbed her neck until she thought the skin would come off. Then he began to rake the sponge over the delicate curve of her back.

She clutched her thighs more tightly. He washed her shoulders, first the back surfaces and then reaching around to the front. Humiliation choked her. In seconds he would push her knees down so he could reach the rest. She could not bear to have him looking at the most intimate parts of her . . . to have him touching her.

Although she did not realize it, Cain was having his own misgivings about going further. Her efforts to shield herself had been sadly belated, for she had lost her towel as soon as he had dropped her in the tub, giving him ample opportunity to survey her naked flesh while he was holding her head so relentlessly under the water.

She was thin as a young filly, all bony arms and long, skinny legs. Even the hint of dark fleece below her belly seemed somehow innocent. What he saw was little more than a child's body, containing a child's mind, especially viewed by a man who favored ripe, experienced women.

And then one small, coral-tipped breast had risen above the surface of the water, and Cain had experienced a flicker of desire that was as unexpected as it was unwelcome. What the hell was the matter with him? She was just a child! When he finally began scrubbing her, he made a rougher job of it than he had intended.

Now as she huddled miserably over her knees, he felt some of his anger evaporating. "Do you want me to go on, or can you handle the rest?"

"I'll do it," she said hastily, not daring to lift her eyes.

He did not get up immediately. Instead he studied her for a moment as if he were making up his mind. Finally he set the sponge on top of her knees and stood up.

"I'll go get one of my shirts for you to put on. But I'm warning you, Kit, if I find a speck of dirt left on you when you're finished, we'll start all over again. And if that happens, I swear I'll wash every inch of you myself!" He strode from the bathroom leaving the door wide open.

Kit had always been a hard worker, but never had she applied herself more diligently. As she scrubbed, she glanced nervously toward the door, torn between her desire to finish quickly and her determination to spare herself any further humiliation. She washed herself twice, dislodging grime that had been comfortably residing in the nooks and crannies of her body for quite some time. When she was finally satisfied, she stood, ready to step out of the tub and fetch a dry towel from a neat stack on the shelf across the room. It was then she saw that broken glass surrounded the tub like a moat around a medieval castle. If she tried to step out, the soles of her feet would be cut into bloody ribbons.

She heard a small sound and looked up to see Cain standing in the doorway. She could feel herself growing cold and then hot as his eyes drifted down over her naked body. She wanted to cover herself with her hands, like Eve after the serpent had done his work, but she couldn't seem to move. She stood there, arms at her sides, frozen into immobility by feelings she did not understand.

Cain picked up a towel and extended it toward her, his eyes looking searchingly into hers. She snatched the towel from him and wrapped it tightly around her body. He looked down at the broken glass that surrounded her and quoted mockingly, "*'Every faculty which is a receiver of pleasure has an equal penalty for its abuse.'* Ralph Waldo Emerson."

With the towel wrapped protectively around her, Kit felt safe in responding. "Mr. Emerson also wrote, *'Every hero becomes a bore at last.'* If I didn't know better, I'd 'spect you inspired those very words."

Cain barely repressed a chuckle. So she still had some fight left in her. For some reason that pleased him. "I put one of my shirts in your bedroom. You'll have to wear it tonight. Tomorrow Mrs. Simmons will take you shopping for some decent clothes."

"I'm not wearin' any dress, Yankee, so you might as well get that idea out of your head before it takes hold."

Without a word he lifted her from the tub and carried her

over the broken glass into the hallway, where he set her down unceremoniously on the carpet. His brief moment of good humor had vanished.

"While I'm gone, you'll do exactly as Mrs. Simmons tells you. If you give her any trouble, I've left orders with Magnus to lock you in your room and throw away the key. I mean it, Kit. When I get back I want to hear that you behaved yourself. I intend to turn you over to your new guardian clean and respectably dressed."

Water from the dripping ends of her hair splashed down like tears onto her clean, thin shoulders. "You really gonna do it?" she asked in a voice so low he barely heard her.

"Find another guardian for you? Of course." He was surprised at her question. On this, at least, he had assumed they were in agreement.

"That's not what I mean." The knuckles of her fist were white where she clutched the towel. "You really gonna sell Risen Glory?"

Cain hardened himself against the undisguised suffering in her small face. He knew there was no way he could make her understand how impossible it was for him to be burdened with a run-down cotton plantation. He also knew that she wouldn't thank him for his decision to put the money from the sale into her trust fund.

"I don't have any choice," he finally said. "You'll see things differently when you're older."

Kit met his eyes unflinchingly. "The biggest mistake I ever made in my life was not killin' you." Turning on her heel, she disappeared down the hallway to her bedroom, her small, towel-draped form strangely dignified.

She stayed in her bedroom all the next day pleading a headache. Magnus and Mrs. Simmons were only too happy to leave her to her solitude, for they were each secretly unsure of their ability to control her, especially since their employer had left for South Carolina that morning. Mrs. Simmons had made a remarkable recovery from the events of the night before, a recovery that she attributed to the miraculous restorative powers of Dr. Worden's Female Pills for Weak Women. She spent the afternoon in Lord and Taylor's five-story white marble palace at Broadway and Grand, purchasing the clothing she considered suitable for her employer's ward.

Kit was staring out the window of her bedroom when Polly began bringing in the elegant Lord and Taylor boxes. She wore Cain's shirt, the tails of which came nearly to her knees, and nothing else, for all her clothing, including her boots, had disappeared.

"You want me to put these away for you, miss?" Polly asked after all the boxes were finally piled on the bed.

Kit shook her head. "No. Go away." She did not want to be with anyone until her mind was clear and she was absolutely certain about what she was going to do.

The idea had not burst full grown into her head like her ill-fated plan to kill Baron Cain. Instead it had come to her slowly throughout the day and then only after she had rejected everything else.

By the time the supper tray arrived in her room, she had made up her mind. She devoured the dinner of boiled cod, scalloped tomatoes, rice with green peas, blueberry muffins, and lemon cheesecake, glad that no one had insisted she come downstairs to eat.

After she was done, she began going through the boxes on the bed. She paid no attention at all to the unattractive dresses and serviceable petticoats Mrs. Simmons had purchased, setting aside only a pair of ugly black ankle boots, lisle stockings, drawers, and a chemise. She added *The Sybaritic Life of Louis XV* to the pile. She would use the time on the train to reread the book, just to make sure.

An hour before dawn the next day, Kit was dressed in the four garments and Cain's shirt. As she stared into the mirror, she realized it was no good. The chemise didn't hold her in at all. If her breasts still showed under a garment as oversized as his shirt, they would be even more noticeable under her own.

She bound herself with a strip torn from a new petticoat and was finally satisfied. When she had come north less than two weeks ago she had given no thought to disguising her sex, but now she was wiser. Besides, she would not have a gun with her this time. If she only knew where Cain had put it.

She slipped noiselessly down the stairs and out through the kitchen door. After she had retrieved her battered felt hat from the top of the trash bin, she made her way to the carriage house, where she found the bundle she had hidden away four days earlier. Shrugging off Cain's shirt, she donned her own along with her dirty patched britches, securing them around her waist with a length of twine. Then she placed the four dollars and twenty-eight cents she had arrived in New York with deep in her pocket. Tucking Ralph Waldo Emerson and Louis XV in the crook of her arm, she let herself out of the carriage house.

The key to the iron gate was kept inside the stable door, but Kit made no attempt to retrieve it. Instead she grabbed one of the stout vines and began to scale the high brick wall. She would leave the same way she had arrived.

Chapter Seven

Charleston was the proud matriarch of the South, an elegant city of walled gardens, rose-colored brick, and pastel frame houses. Lush with tropical growth, it smelled of jasmine and gardenia and wisteria. Everything about the city was exotic, even the names of the islands in its harbor, names like Yonges and Wadmallow, Folly and Kiawah.

The first families of Charleston were rice planters whose plantations graced the banks of the rivers of the Low Country. Cotton families were tolerated, but not truly accepted by the inner circle, and those who made their living in trade were not recognized at all. During the malaria season, from May to October, the rice planters left their plantations to live in Charleston behind filigreed iron gates in gracefully narrow three-story houses. They worshiped at St. Michael's Church, presented their daughters each January at the St. Cecelia Ball, and, all in all, behaved much like the European aristocracy.

Indeed, the true Charlestonians considered themselves aristocrats. Of course no one was so ill bred as to actually use the word, but it was understood nonetheless. They sent their sons to Oxford and their wives to Baden-Baden. Italian sculptors chiseled marble statues for their gardens. European actors performed at the Dock Street Theater. It was the most civilized city in America. It had history, tradition, and, even in defeat, dignity.

The eighteen-month siege of Charleston had taken its toll, and now, three months after Appomattox, the proud old city was badly damaged. Wharves were rotted, warehouses destroyed. Former slaves loitered outside the Freedmen's Bureau waiting for emancipation to live up to its golden promise. Once-elegant pastel houses were charred skeletons, and the buildings that were still standing bore scars from shrapnel and mortar shells.

The finest homes had been confiscated by the Union Army and their inhabitants forced to move to less comfortable residences. Fortunes as well as lives had been lost. Still, despite their empty, aching stomachs and threadbare clothing, the residents held their heads high, sweeping past soldiers in blue-and-gold uniforms as if they were invisible. After all, this was still Charleston, and there were traditions to be upheld.

Kit arrived in the city nearly a week after she had left New York. The train trip had been agonizingly slow, with frequent delays where the tracks had ended. She didn't have enough money for a berth in one of the new Pullmans, so she had slept sitting up in her seat. No one had spoken to her, and she had spoken to no one.

After a quick bite to eat from a vendor, she began to make her way toward the city's market. Risen Glory was another day's journey to the west, and she planned to hitch a ride part of the way on one of the farm wagons that were once again beginning to trickle into the city each morning with fresh produce, produce whose price was so badly inflated that only the Yankees and the wartime profiteers could afford to buy it.

Surprisingly, as Kit threaded her way through the crowded streets, her mind was not on the market or any of the sights around her. Instead, she was thinking about the interesting discovery she had made concerning herself in the days since she had left New York. She had discovered that she liked being clean.

Putting her dirty clothes on over her clean body had forced her to admit that Cain had been right about one thing. She did stink. It was funny she'd never noticed it before. Maybe taking baths wasn't such a bad idea after all.

Once she got to Risen Glory, she would wash and put on clean clothes. Not only was she tired of being dirty, but there was no sense in antagonizing the major any more than she had to. Her unexpected arrival was going to put him in a bad enough mood as it was.

Cain was fighting a losing battle with his temper. "Do you mean to tell me, sir, that there isn't any respectable person in this community who'd be willing to take over the guardianship of Miss Weston even if I were to offer compensation for time as well as expenses?"

The Reverend Rawlins Ames Cogdell nodded his stately white head. "You must understand, Mr. Cain. We've all known Katharine Louise a good deal longer than you have."

Rawlins Cogdell prayed that God would forgive him for the satisfaction he was taking in putting a spoke in this arrogant Yankee's wheel. Although neither of them had made any reference to the war, he knew very well who his guest was. The Hero of Missionary Ridge, indeed! How galling it was to be forced to entertain such a man. But what else was he to do? These days blue-uniformed occupation troops were everywhere, and even a man of God had to be careful not to offend them.

His wife, Mary, appeared in the doorway with a plate holding four tiny finger sandwiches, each one spread with a thin glaze of strawberry preserves.

"Come in, my dear. Come in. Mr. Cain, you do have a treat in store for you. My wife is famous for her strawberry preserves."

Although his visitor could not know it, the preserves were from the bottom of the very last jar Mary Cogdell had put up two springs ago when there was still sugar. And the bread was sliced from a loaf that had to last the Cogdells' another two days, for flour was nearly as scarce as sugar. Still, the minister was pleased she was offering it. He would sooner starve than let this man know how desperately poor they all were. If only there was some lemonade or some tea.

"None for me, my dear. I'll save my appetite for dinner. Please, Mr. Cain, take two."

Cain was not nearly as obtuse as Cogdell believed. He knew very well what a sacrifice the offering on the chipped blue willow plate was. Although he could not think of anything he wanted less, he took a sandwich and made the required compliments to Mrs. Cogdell.

Damn all Southerners! he fumed silently. Six hundred thousand lives had been lost because of their stiff-necked pride. He had seen it in Charleston when he had visited Rosemary's attorney, and now he was seeing it again in Rutherford, the small town near Risen Glory.

Their arrogance was all part of the disease of the slave system. The planters had lived like omnipotent kings on isolated plantations where they held absolute authority over hundreds of slaves. It gave them a conceit like no other group of men, a conceit that had spread across class barriers. Southerners had truly believed they were omnipotent. And defeat had only changed them superficially. A Southern family might be starving, but tea sandwiches would still be offered to a guest, even a despised one.

The Reverend Cogdell turned to his wife. "Please sit down, my dear. Perhaps you can help us. Mr. Cain finds himself on the horns of a dilemma, so to speak."

Mary reluctantly seated herself in her favorite rosewood chair and listened attentively as her husband outlined Cain's connection with Rosemary Weston and the fact that he wanted to transfer his guardianship of Kit. Mary had lived in Rutherford all her life and despite her quiet ways was not known for mincing words. When her husband was finished, she spoke her mind.

"I'm afraid what you want to do is impossible, Mr. Cain. Several years ago when Katharine Louise was still in her formative years, I can think of a number of families who would have been only too happy to take her in. But I'm afraid it's too late for that. My goodness, she must be sixteen by now."

"Hardly a Methuselah," Cain said dryly.

"Standards of behavior are different in South Carolina than they are in the North, Mr. Cain." The rebuke was softly spoken, but it was a rebuke nonetheless. "Girls of good family are raised from birth in the gracious traditions of Southern womanhood. Not only has Katharine Louise never shown any inclination to conform to these traditions, but she has frequently seemed to mock them. The families of our community would have to think first of their own children. They would not want them influenced by Katharine's unseemly ways."

Cain felt a spark of pity for Kit. What must it have been like for her to be raised by a stepmother who hated her, a father who ignored her, and a community that disapproved of her? As he asked these questions, it did not occur to him to relate them to his own early life.

Despite Mary Cogdell's disapproving air, she was, by Southern standards anyway, being straightforward with him, and so he was blunt in return. "Isn't there anyone in this town who feels affection toward Kit?"

Mary's small hands fluttered in her lap. "Good gracious, Mr. Cain! You misunderstand. There are many of us who are deeply fond of her. Katharine Louise is a generous and warm-hearted person. It's nearly impossible to dislike her. However, that does not alter the fact that she conducts herself outside even the most liberally defined boundaries of what is considered acceptable behavior."

Although the expression on Cain's face did not alter, he had played too much poker not to know when he was beaten. Willard Ritter had given him letters of introduction to four families in Rutherford: the president of the bank, the owner of a neighboring cotton plantation, a widow who ran the town school, and Rawlins Cogdell. He had received the same answer from all of them. Like it or not, he seemed to be stuck with Katharine Louise Weston.

As he rode back to Risen Glory on the bony mare he had hired at the livery stable, he found himself remembering his first glimpse of the house two days earlier. It rested at the end of a twisting overgrown drive—a handsome two-story structure made of brick covered with stucco. Since its construction in 1816 by Garrett Weston's father, the stucco had weathered to a warm shade of cream with the shape of the bricks and mortar beneath clearly visible.

Live oaks hung with Spanish moss shaded each end of the house and draped gray-green veils over the corners of the tiled roof. Once-manicured flower beds were overgrown with azalea and smilax and holly. Magnolia trees scattered their waxy leaves across the knee-high grass of the front yard. Still, despite the general air of neglect, peeling paint, and broken shutters, the house was sturdy.

The center of the house curved out from the front in a graceful bow. On that first day Cain had dismounted and begun to climb the steps only to be met at the top with a shotgun held by an old black man whom he later learned was Eli, the majordomo of Risen Glory for the past thirty years.

"Thas far enough. Miz Kit says I is to shoot anybody try to git pas' me."

Cain rested one dusty boot on the bottom step. "Miss Kit needs to have her breeches tanned." He did not add that he'd already done the job.

"You sure nuff right 'bout that, mistuh. But I still has to shoot you if you comes any closer."

It took Cain nearly a quarter of an hour to convince Eli to put down his gun. Of course he could have disarmed the old man without difficulty, but he knew he was going to need his cooperation, so he took his time explaining his relationship to Kit and Rosemary Weston. When Eli finally realized that the visitor was family and not one of the fancy scalawags that had been preying on the countryside, he put down his shotgun and welcomed Baron Cain to Risen Glory.

The interior of the house was gracefully proportioned, with high ceilings and low, paned windows. The first floor had been designed with a wide center hallway to carry the breeze. Arranged on each side of the hallway were several sitting rooms, a music room, and the library. The dining room was conspicuously empty, for Sherman's troops had carted the handsome teak table outside and used its surface to butcher the plantation's remaining livestock.

On the second floor were bedrooms of various sizes, as well as a storage room that at one time had served as a schoolroom, first for Garrett Weston and then, until Rosemary's arrival, for Kit. A master bedroom complete with its own sitting room stretched across one side of the house.

Only the library showed any signs of care, and they were recent. The rest of the house was shabby and dust-shrouded with scarred furniture and faded draperies. Rosemary had been an indifferent housekeeper with no interest in giving the servants the supervision they needed, and the deterioration had begun even before the war had started.

Cain, however, paid little attention to the neglect, for the house held no interest to him. Instead that first day as he had stood at a window in the master bedroom and gazed speculatively out over the abandoned fields, he had found himself thinking about New York City and how it had begun to suffocate him like an overly possessive woman.

He spent the rest of the afternoon on his horse inspecting the ruins of the outbuildings, crawling over broken machinery, picking up rusted tools, and occasionally stopping as he paced across an empty field to bend down on one knee and pick up a handful of rich soil. It trickled like warm silk through his fingers.

Now, two days later, as he stepped into the wide center hallway, he was more preoccupied with thoughts of Kit than with the fertile soil of Risen Glory. Despite his lack of success with the others he had spoken to, he had somehow hoped he could persuade Cogdell and his wife to take responsibility for her. The money he was offering under the guise of compensating them for their time would make the difference between penury and comfort in their household. Still, they had refused him. Damned Southern arrogance!

He was just ready to call for Eli when he noticed mouthwatering cooking odors coming from the kichen at the back of the house. Despite the fact that he was hungry, he frowned, for he had already discovered that Eli couldn't cook, and as far as he knew, there was no one else in the house. The rest of the former slaves had gone off after the Union Army, enticed by the promise of forty acres and a mule, and he had resigned himself to a slice of stale bread and a slab of cold ham for dinner.

As he took his first step toward the kitchen, a small, familiar figure appeared at the end of the hallway and stood silhouetted against the window.

"Evenin', Major."

At first there was an ominous, electric silence in the quiet hallway, and then Cain released a stream of oaths that made even Kit look at him with new respect. It also made her very nervous.

She took a deep breath. "I sure hope you're hungry," she

chattered brightly, hoping to postpone, if only for a moment, what she knew was to come. "I got some fried chicken and hot buttermilk biscuits just beggin' to have somebody with a big appetite get close to them. Looks to me like you might be the man. Eli and I moved a table into the dining room so we could eat there. Course it's kinda scratched up, but it's a genu-wine Sheraton. You ever heard of Sheraton, Major? He was a Englishman and a Baptist to boot. Doesn't that seem strange to you? Seems like only Southerners should be Baptists. I—"

"That's enough!" His anger transformed his handsome features into a brutal mask. He took a step toward her, and she instinctively caught her breath, certain he was going to kill her. Sweet Jesus, she had known he would be mad at her, but never had she expected anything like this!

"You just made one mistake too many." There was a cold, flat quality to his voice that knotted her stomach. "From the very beginning you've refused to do as you were told. This time you've gone too far."

He grabbed her arm and, with a jerk that made her stagger, began dragging her down the hallway toward the stairs.

Kit's mind whirled frantically. What was he going to do with her? Lock her up? Beat her? Maybe even kill her? She was suddenly furious. She'd endured so much this past week: the awful train trip, the bone-jarring wagon ride, a hike today of nearly fifteen miles that had left her feet covered with blisters. She'd used the last of her money to buy food for tonight's dinner, taken a bath in the kitchen, and changed into a clean shirt and clean britches so she didn't smell, and now he wasn't even going to give her a chance.

"You hypocrite!" she spat out through clenched teeth. "You damn hypocrite. You would of done the same thing!"

Cain was so startled by her ridiculous statement that he paused for a moment in his purposeful march toward the stairs. "What are you talking about?"

Kit stomped her foot on the worn hallway carpeting, bringing up a small puff of dust. "Do you think you'd of stayed up there in New York City while somebody was takin' away the only thing in all your life you ever cared about? Would you of sat in that fancy bedroom readin' books while it all slipped away? You're a hypocrite, Baron Cain! If you'd been in my shoes, you'd of done the same thing I did! You'd of got yourself back to South Carolina as fast as you could, and then done anything you had to so you could keep what was yours."

"And I can just imagine what you decided you had to do."

Before she knew what was happening, he had released her only to begin raking his hands systematically over her body. She gasped with indignation as he roughly pressed her breasts and her waist, then moved his palms down over her belly, her hips, and finally her legs. He found what he wanted strapped to her calf.

"Were you planning to use this on me when I was awake or when I was asleep?" he sneered, dangling the bone-handled knife in front of her eyes.

"If I didn't have the guts to kill you with a gun, I'd hardly do it with a knife," Kit said bitterly.

He pocketed the weapon, making no attempt to hide his skepticism. "I suppose you were carrying this to clean your teeth?"

"Don't be a jackass! You took my gun. I could hardly come all this way by myself without some kind of protection. I found that in your carriage house."

"If you're not planning to kill me"—his voice was a mockery of politeness—"just what do you have in mind?"

Nothing was going the way Kit had hoped. They stood at the bottom of the stairs barely a foot apart, Cain towering threateningly over her diminutive frame. She hadn't wanted to antagonize him so badly. Now everything was ruined. All her dreams. All her plans.

And then she felt a dim flicker of hope as she realized he was no longer grasping her arm. Temporarily, at least, he seemed to have forgotten that he was in the process of dragging her up the stairs. After a moment's hesitation, she decided to press her luck.

"Why don't we eat dinner first, and then I'll tell you. Food's hard to come by. No sense in lettin' it go to waste." She held her breath.

Cain hesitated. Now that the first hot flame of his temper had cooled, he recognized that there was some truth in her observation. In coming to South Carolina, it was true that she was only doing what he would have done had the circumstances been reversed. Still, there was a difference. He was a man. She was only a small slip of a girl.

"All right," he snapped. "We'll eat. But afterward you and I are going to have a serious talk."

She flashed a bright, happy smile at him before she turned to scamper back toward the kitchen. "Supper'll be on the table in fifteen minutes," she called over her shoulder.

Fifteen minutes later Cain entered the dining room. Kit was already there, setting a platter of fried chicken down on the scratched Sheraton table that she and Eli had placed in the center of the nearly empty room.

He finally noticed what had escaped him earlier. Everything about her was clean, from her cropped hair to the plaid shirt with a button missing at the neck and the pair of dark-brown britches that hung so loosely on her small hips. He suppressed a smile. Until now he hadn't imagined that anything short of force could convince her to bathe voluntarily. She was obviously prepared to go to drastic lengths this evening to please him.

"Sit down and eat, Major," she said as she dropped somewhat nervously into the chair across from him. "I sure hope you're hungry."

Cain stared down at the platter piled high with crisply fried golden brown chicken, at the plate of steaming buttermilk biscuits, and the bowl of dandelion greens. Abruptly he seated himself, the rumbling in his stomach reminding him of how long it had been since he'd eaten decent food. His questions could wait.

It was the best meal he'd had since he left New York. Although the food was simple, it was well prepared, and he gave it his full attention, failing to notice as he ate that Kit was doing little more than toying with her food.

When he had finally eaten his fill, he said, "I thought everybody around here had left except Eli."

Kit set down the chicken wing she had been nibbling on. "They have. Course I expect Sophronia to come back any time, soon as she finds out I'm home. Sophronia won't go off as long as I'm at Risen Glory."

Cain pushed himself slightly back from the table. "Sophronia?"

"She's our cook. She sort of looks after me."

He frowned. "She doesn't do a very good job of it."

A stinging retort sprang to Kit's lips, but she held it back and contented herself with a small shrug.

Cain was no longer able to contain his curiosity. He leaned back so his chair was resting on its rear legs. "Kit?"

"Uhm?"

"Who cooked this meal?"

Her eyes flew open in surprise. "Why, I did, Major. Who'd you think?"

"You!" The front legs of his chair banged to the floor. "I don't believe it. This food is delicious."

"Course it's delicious. I'm a superior cook. Sophronia taught me how years ago." Kit pursed her lips in exasperation. "You know, Major. I don't understand you at all. You wouldn't let me keep workin' in the stable once you found out I was a girl. But now, even though you know I'm a girl, you're surprised that I can cook."

She was about to go on when she remembered her vow to do her best not to irritate him. Quickly she got up and walked over to the sideboard where she picked up a dusty bottle.

"I dug out one of the bottles Rosemary hid away before the Yankees came. Thought you might like to have a glass of brandy. Celebrate your arrival at Risen Glory."

Cain took the bottle from her. Trust his mother to take better care of the liquor than she did of her stepdaughter. "Tell me how Risen Glory got its name," he said as he pried out the cork. "It's unusual."

Kit leaned one elbow on the sideboard. "It happened not too long after my granddaddy built the house. A Baptist preacherman came to the door askin' for a meal, and even though my grandma was strict Methodist, she fed him. Well, they got to talkin', and when he heard the plantation didn't have a name yet, he said they should call it Risen Glory on account of it was almost Easter Sunday. It's been Risen Glory ever since."

A shadow of a smile flickered across Cain's face and then disappeared. He poured a small measure of brandy into the bottom of a cut-glass water goblet, fishing out a piece of cork with his finger before he took a sip.

"I think it's time you tell me what you're doing here, Kit."

Her stomach gave an unexpected lurch. To steady herself, she wandered over to the open doors that led from the dining room to the overgrown garden and stepped outside. It was dark and quiet, and she could smell the sweet odor of honeysuckle on the night breeze. How she loved it all. The trees and brooks, the gently rolling fields. She remembered the last time she had seen them white with cotton. They were going to be that way again, no matter what she had to do.

Slowly she turned and stepped back into the lighted room. "I came to make a proposal to you, Major."

"I resigned my commission some time ago, Kit. Why don't you just call me Baron?"

She shook her head. "If it's all the same to you, I'll just go on callin' you Major for now."

"Suit yourself." He shrugged. "At least it's better than some of the other things you've called me. Now suppose you tell me about this proposal of yours."

Kit took a deep breath. "Well, as you might of guessed, your part of the bargain would be to agree not to sell Risen Glory until I can buy it from you."

"I kind of figured that," he said dryly.

"You wouldn't be stuck with it forever," she hastened to add. "Just until I can get my hands on the money in my trust fund. I'll take it off your hands as soon as I can."

She paused, waiting for him to make some response, but he merely sipped his brandy and watched her noncommittally. She caught her bottom lip between her teeth. This was going to be the hardest part.

"Now I realize you'd expect somethin' in return." Although she had made a statement, her rising inflection gave it the sound of a question.

"Of course," Cain said solemnly.

"Well, what I'm preparin' to offer is a little bit unorthodox, but if you think about it, I know you'll see that it's fair." Again she paused.

"Go on."

The words came out in a great rush. "I'm offerin' myself to you as your mistress."

"My mistress!" Only with the greatest effort was Cain able to choke back his laughter. He took a long, steadying sip of brandy and then busied himself studying the peeling plasterwork on the ceiling just above his head. "What makes you think I'd be interested?" he finally managed.

Kit looked at him as if he were dull-witted. "Well, it stands to reason, don't it? Even you got to admit I'm a lot better company than those sorry excuses for females in New York City. At least if Miss Flora is any example. I don't giggle or simper, and I certainly don't talk about pugs. With me, you wouldn't have to worry about goin' to all those balls and dinner parties. We like the same things—bein' outdoors, huntin', fishin', ridin' horses. We could have a good time."

It was too much for Cain. The laughter he had tried so hard to suppress refused to be contained any longer.

Kit glared at him. "You mind tellin' me what you think is so damn humorous?"

Gradually Cain brought himself under control. Setting his glass down on the table, he got up and walked over to the open doorway where Kit stood.

"Do you have any idea what mistresses do?"

"Of course," Kit snapped, still uneasy over his laughter. "I read *The Sybaritic Life of Louis XV.*"

Cain looked at her blankly. He knew there was a connection somewhere, but he was damned if he could figure out what it was.

"Madame de Pompadour," Kit explained, realizing he didn't understand. "I got the idea from readin' 'bout her. She was Louis XV's mistress."

What Kit did not add was that Madame de Pompadour had also been the most powerful woman in France, controlling her ruler and her country just by using her wits. The possibilities had fascinated her even as she read the book, and slowly the idea of offering herself to Cain had taken root. As his mistress she could surely manage to exert some control over the fate of Risen Glory. Besides, she didn't have anything but herself to bargain with.

Cain began to speak, thought better of it, and then began again. "Kit, being a man's mistress involves more than hunting and fishing," he said gently. "Do you know what I'm talking about?"

Kit felt a flush creeping slowly upward from her neck. This

was the part she hadn't let herself dwell on too much, the part the book hadn't covered at all.

"I know what you're talkin' about," she muttered, even though, for all her worldliness, it wasn't entirely true. Having been raised on a plantation had exposed her to some of the more rudimentary facts of animal reproduction at an early age. It had also allowed her to draw certain conclusions about human reproduction, some of which were accurate and a great number of which were not. Still, although she was astute enough to realize she didn't have all the details quite right, she did know the whole process was disgusting. She also knew it had to be part of her bargain. For some reason it was important to men, and women were expected to put up with it.

Cain looked down at her. She was so worldly and yet so incredibly naive. Her proposal no longer seemed quite so funny. Damn it! This was just another example of how ill-equipped she was to look after herself. And he was responsible for her! For a man who didn't believe in keeping either books or horses, the thought was a bitter one. He pulled a cheroot from his pocket, lit it, and wandered out through the doors to the garden.

Kit's sense of uneasiness grew. Why didn't he say something? Finally, when she could no longer bear it, she followed him outside. He was standing by a rusted iron bench, gazing out toward the orchard.

"Well, what do you think?" she asked.

The glowing ember at the end of his cheroot cast flickering orange shadows across his face. "I think it's the most ridiculous thing I've ever heard," he said flatly.

She could feel panic beginning to well up inside her like some great suffocating force. This was her last chance to keep Risen Glory. She had to make it work.

"Why is it so ridiculous?" she demanded.

"Because it just is."

"You tell me why?" She knew she was shouting, but she couldn't seem to help herself.

"For God's sake!" Cain exclaimed, spinning around to face her. "I'm your stepbrother and, I might add, your guardian. I couldn't find a single person who was willing to take you off my hands. Judging by your recent behavior, I can understand why."

"Bein' my stepbrother doesn't mean anything and you know it," she cried. "It's purely a legal relationship. That's no reason. No reason at all!"

"All right, I'll tell you why," Cain said, the panic in her enormous child's eyes making him brutal. "Men aren't looking for a hunting companion when they're selecting a mistress. They want a woman who looks and acts and dresses like a woman. One who knows how to smile and talk softly and make love. Now that pretty much leaves you out, doesn't it?"

Kit swallowed hard, hating him for making her set aside her pride. "I could learn."

"Oh, for God's sake!" He stalked to the other side of the overgrown gravel path and put one hand on his hip. "I've already made up my mind. I decided yesterday that I'm not selling Risen Glory right away."

"Not sellin' . . ." For a moment Kit couldn't seem to find her breath, and then a great wave of happiness washed over her. "Oh, that's wonderful!" She wrapped her arms around her chest and hugged herself, then she spun out in a great circle. "Not sellin' Risen Glory! Whooee!"

"Hold on."

At the note of command, Kit felt a sharp prickle of warning. She stopped abruptly and looked at him.

"There's a condition, Kit." He stepped forward into the amber pool of light spilling out from the dining room, nothing in his manner or expression betraying the fact that he had just that moment thought of the condition and realized it was the answer to his most pressing problem.

"What condition?" she asked suspiciously.

"You have to return to New York and go to school."

"School!" Kit was incredulous. He couldn't be serious! "What do I need some stupid school for? I'm self-educated. Besides, I probably already know more than half the teachers."

"Not that kind of school," Cain said. "I'm talking about a finishing school. A place that teaches deportment and etiquette and all the other female accomplishments you don't know a damn thing about."

"Finishing school!" She was horrified. "Now that's the stupidest, most puerile—" She saw the storm clouds gathering in his expression, and she quickly changed tack. "Let me stay here. Please. I won't be any trouble, I promise. I can sleep out back. You won't even know I'm around. And I can make myself useful all kinds of ways. I know this plantation better than anyone. Please let me stay. You won't regret it. I promise. Swear to Jesus."

"That's enough, Kit." He cut her off coldly and decisively. "I'll hear no arguments about this. You'll do as I say, or I'll sell Risen Glory so fast you won't know what happened, and you won't have even a prayer of getting your hands on it again."

He hoped she wouldn't call his bluff, because now that he had seen the plantation, he had no intention of selling it.

The moonlight washed Kit's pale, stricken features with silver. "How long do I have to go to this school?"

"Until you can behave like a lady," Cain snapped. "So I guess that's up to you."

"That's not good enough. You could keep me there forever."

"All right. Let's say three years."

"And then what happens? Will I be able to buy Risen Glory back from you with the money in my trust fund?"

"We'll discuss that when the time comes," he said. "And, Kit, just so I don't have to lie awake tonight waiting for you to try to stick a knife between my ribs or shoot me in the head with a gun, it won't do you any good to kill me. If I die, Risen Glory will be sold automatically. If they don't hang you, you'll probably receive the money, but you won't have the plantation."

Slowly she walked back into the lighted dining room. She would be exiled from all she loved, not just for a few weeks but perhaps for years. How could she bear it? Yet even as she thought of the impossibility of leaving, she knew she had no choice. Baron Cain had seen to that.

Hatred rose like bile in her throat, bitter and choking. She thought of how she had just humiliated herself, offering to be his mistress when he'd already made up his mind not to sell. He would pay for everything, she vowed. Her humiliation. Taking what was hers. Someday when her exile was over and Risen Glory was safe, she would see to it that he paid.

"What's it going to be, Kit?" He had entered the room behind her.

She could barely force out the words. "You don't give me much choice, do you, Yankee?"

A woman's voice, throaty and seductive, rippled from the hallway into the room. "Well, well, well. Will you jes' look at what that chile brought back with her from Noo York City."

"Sophronia!" Kit pitched herself across the dining room and into the arms of the figure who stood in the doorway.

Cain stared at the newcomer with surprise. So this was Kit's Sophronia. She was hardly what he had envisioned.

Without question, she was one of the most exotically beautiful women he had ever seen. Probably not more than nineteen, she was slim and unusually tall for a woman, towering over Kit. She had high, chiseled cheekbones, pale caramel skin, and slanted golden eyes that slowly lifted as he studied her. Their gazes met and held over the top of Kit's head, and then Sophronia disentangled herself and walked toward him, moving with the languid sensuality that made her simple blue cotton dress seem like a gown of the finest silk. When she was directly in front of him, she stopped and held out her slim hand.

"Welcome to Risen Glory, Boss Man."

Part Two

A TEMPLETON GIRL

"Manners are the happy way of doing things."
Ralph Waldo Emerson, *Culture*

Chapter Eight

Just like Jonah into the belly of the whale, Kit thought, as she began mounting the steps that led to the Fifth Avenue entrance of the Templeton Academy for Young Ladies. There was even something about the forbidding building that reminded her of a whale, perhaps the fact that the great gray stones were sleek and wet in the drizzle of the early September afternoon. How was she going to survive three years in such an awful place?

She swore as she tripped on the hem of her dress, and a strong arm reached out to steady her. She jerked away from his touch as if she had been burned. Ahead of her the glass panes of the narrow windows that flanked the imposing front door caught her reflection, and she flinched. She looked like a child dressed up in her spinster aunt's clothes.

The hat on Kit's head was as far removed from Flora's frothy pink-and-white chapeau as galoshes are from dancing slippers. Made of dun-colored felt, it sat like a squashed gravy boat on top of her short, ragged hair. The material of her ocher jacket was of good quality, but cut so amply that the shoulder seams nearly reached the middle of her upper arms. The brown serge dress beneath was even worse. Devoid of any ornament, it was much too large for her thin frame, and so long that the hem dragged on the wet pavement.

A few days after they had arrived in New York, Sophronia had warned Kit that the garments were too big and she should try them on so they could be altered, but Kit had refused to abandon her boy's clothing until the last minute. Finally, just before she was to leave for the Templeton Academy, she had permitted Sophronia to help her dress. When the last garment had been settled in place, she had stared at her reflection in the mirror.

"I look like a jackass!"

Exasperated, Sophronia had thrust her hands on her hips, the long, elegant fingers splayed. "What you expect? I told you those clothes was too big for you, but you wouldn't pay me no never mind. You ask me, this is what you get for thinkin' you know so much more than everybody else!"

Kit stiffened with anger. Sophronia had been acting hateful ever since the long train trip north when she'd been all "yes, sir," and "no, sir," to Cain, always taking his side to Kit's disadvantage. And it hadn't gotten any better after they'd arrived in New York. Since Magnus had laid eyes on Sophronia, he was walking around in a daze. Even Mrs. Simmons couldn't stop talking about Sophronia being a jewel.

Kit rounded on her, giving vent to the pent-up frustrations of the past weeks and an aching feeling that Sophronia was betraying her. "Don't you sass me," she stormed. "You been puttin' on airs ever since you stepped on that train in Charleston, and I don't like it. Just 'cause you're in New York City now don't mean you got cause to start actin' uppity!"

Sophronia's elegant nostrils quivered. When she finally spoke, her voice was thick with emotion. "You think you can say anything you want to me just 'cause my skin's a shade darker than yours. Well, I'm not your nigger slave no more, Kit Weston. You understand me? You understand what I'm sayin', girl? I don't belong to you! I don't belong to nobody 'cept Jesus!"

Kit's eyes darkened with anger and hurt. "Sometimes I hate you, Sophronia," she said crossly. "You don't show any gratitude. I did everything for you. I taught you how to read, even though it was against the law. I taught you your sums. I hid you from Jesse Overturf that night he wanted to lie with you. Now you've turned on me, takin' that Yankee's side against mine every chance you get!"

"Don't you talk to me 'bout gratitude," Sophronia snapped. "I spent the last five years of my life, since I was fourteen years old, keepin' you out of Miz Weston's sight. And every time she caught you and locked you in that closet, it was me who let you out. I took a whippin' for you! So I don't want to hear nothin' 'bout no gratitude! You're a noose around my neck, you know that? Suffocatin' me. Cuttin' off my life's breath. If it wasn't for you—"

Abruptly Sophronia broke off as she heard footsteps approaching outside the door. Polly appeared and announced that Cain was waiting for Kit in the hallway below.

Without quite knowing how it happened, the two combatants

found themselves in each other's arms. Finally Kit pulled away and started to walk out the door.

For a moment Sophronia was quiet, and then she said softly, "You mind yourself at that fancy school, hear?"

Kit was abruptly recalled to the present as Cain's arm swept in front of her to open the heavy oak door, and the scene with Sophronia faded from her mind. She instinctively pulled back, wary of even the slightest brush with him. If Cain noticed, he gave no sign.

The quiet elegance of the foyer at the Templeton Academy for Young Ladies made it clear to all who entered that it was an institution patronized only by the privileged. The floor was paved with alternating squares of black and white marble. In the corner standing next to a richly upholstered Grecian couch was a plaster column topped by a bust of Socrates, bearing the interesting inscription "Sons are the anchors of a mother's life."

A uniformed maid appeared and led them into a small reception room furnished entirely in the style of the Second Empire, with a rolled-arm couch, lyre-backed chairs, and matching tables supported by thin curved legs capped with brass lion's paw feet. Kit sat down clumsily in one of the chairs, the ocher of her jacket clashing disastrously with the purple upholstery.

Cain scowled at her. She looked hideous, worse than when she wore her breeches. Whatever could have possessed Edith Simmons to buy such ugly garments?

If only he hadn't been so busy these past few weeks, he might have thought to ask to see them, but there had been so much to attend to—overseeing the sale of his town house, buying supplies to take back to South Carolina, and most important, spending a few profitable evenings at the city's poker tables. There had also been his conference with Hamilton Woodward. It was Woodward who had recommended the Templeton Academy, where his own daughter was currently enrolled. In exchange for a healthy fee, he had also agreed to stay in contact with Kit and send Cain periodic reports on her progress.

It was money well spent as far as Cain was concerned. Woodward would look after Kit while he concentrated on the business of growing cotton. The less contact he had with Kit Weston, the better for both of them. After today, she would be out of his life—for three years anyway. And by then she'd be nineteen. He would marry her off to some impoverished Southern gentleman who was willing to overlook her faults in exchange for her trust fund.

There was a rustle of black bombazine, and Elvira Templeton, the widow of the school's founder, entered the room. She as a large woman with iron-gray hair and strong, severe features. Extending her hand, she advanced toward Cain.

"I'm sorry to have kept you waiting, Mr. Cain. I was conferring with the rector about Sunday's sermon. I am Elvira Templeton."

Cain acknowledged her greeting. They exchanged pleasantries and then Mrs. Templeton turned to Kit. "This, I assume, is your ward. You will rise, Katharine, when a person older than yourself enters a room. To remain seated is boorish and ill-mannered. I will not remind you of this again."

Kit glared up into the tiny, marble-hard eyes and remained stubbornly seated. Across the room Cain cleared his throat in warning. She sullenly rose to her feet.

Mrs. Templeton sucked in her withered cheeks and then abruptly inflated them. "Very good, Katharine. Now you may sit."

She turned back to Cain, failing to notice that Kit was remaining stubbornly upright. "As I'm certain Mr. Woodward told you when he recommended our school," she went on, "the Templeton Academy has the highest standards. Our curriculum includes French, music, dancing, embroidery, watercolors, the recitation of poetry, the rudiments of horticulture, and a class which I teach myself entitled Modern Management of Home and Husband. Our students embody all that is meant when one speaks of gracious behavior in a young woman."

"I'm sure Katharine will fit right in," Cain said solemnly.

There was a noise in the hallway. He took advantage of Mrs. Templeton's temporary distraction to push hard on Kit's shoulder and send her sprawling back down into her chair.

Mrs. Templeton returned her attention to them, not appearing to notice anything amiss. "I have put Katharine in a room with Mr. Woodward's daughter Elspeth. Although she is a year younger, they will be in the same class. It seemed a sensible arrangement. As I informed him, we don't usually keep girls past their eighteenth birthday, but considering what he told me of Katharine's unfortunate past, I have agreed to make an exception. As I tell my girls, charity begins at home. Now, Katharine, you may say your good-byes to Mr. Cain while I call one of the older girls to show you to your room."

Mrs. Templeton's black skirts had barely cleared the doorway before Kit shot out of her chair, fists clenched. "Charity!" she exclaimed. "Ain't nobody gonna mention Kit Weston and charity in the same breath! That old she-devil! I'll roast in hell before I stay here!" Catching her cumbersome skirts up much higher than was proper, she stalked toward the door.

"It's your choice, Kit. But if you walk out, you've lost your last chance at Risen Glory."

Cain's words stopped her as effectively as an iron bar. She turned slowly back to him, the force of her hatred somehow frightening on a face so young. "I'll never forgive you for what you've done to me, Baron Cain," she hissed. "And I swear on my mama's grave that someday you're gonna pay for it. If it takes my whole life, I swear to Jesus I'm gonna make you suffer the way I've suffered."

Cain's face was expressionless. "Good-bye, Kit." He turned on his heel and left the room.

The upper floors of the Templeton Academy were as sparse and utilitarian as the first floor was elegant. The younger girls slept in dormitories, eight to a room, while the older girls shared tiny, spartan quarters furnished with a pair of identical beds and bureaus, two small shelves for books, and a set of wire hooks. Although every corner of the school was kept spotlessly clean, there was nothing in the way of luxury on the upper floors. The girls were discouraged from adding personal touches to their quarters—tacking fashion plates from *Godey's Lady's Book* on the walls or tying back the plain muslin curtains with pretty ribbons. Rules were strict, and any infractions were dealt with severely. Still, it was a privilege to be accepted at the academy, and they were proud to be Templeton girls.

Kit stood hesitantly on the threshold of the third-floor room that she would share. A group of five girls, all identically dressed in the Templeton uniform of navy-blue dresses with white collars and cuffs, and, for inside wear, white aprons, were jammed together at the room's single window overlooking the street.

"Oh, Margaret, isn't he the handsomest man you ever saw?"

"His profile is even better than Lord Byron's in the portrait hanging in Mrs. Templeton's office."

"And he's so tall. I just love tall men, don't you, Elspeth?"

The girl identified as Elspeth gave a long sigh. She had crisp brown curls and a pretty, fresh face. At fifteen, her bosom was already well developed, a fact that both pleased and embarrassed her. "Imagine, he was right here in the academy and none of us were allowed to go downstairs," she grumbled. "It's so unfair!" And then, with a giggle: "My father says he's not really a gentleman."

More giggles.

"I heard that Madame Riccardi, the opera singer, has gone into a decline since she learned he was moving to South Carolina."

A tall, slim girl who had so far contented herself with staring out the window now elected to join the conversation. She was the most striking of the four and had an air of worldliness that the others lacked. "I'm sure I would go into a decline, too, if he were my lover."

"Lilith Samuels!" The girls were deliciously horrified.

"Oh, you're all such innocents." Lilith regarded them disdainfully. "A man as sophisticated as Baron Cain has a dozen mistresses. Everybody knows it. I'm sure they are all suffering terribly now that he is leaving the city."

Elspeth shook her head woefully. "I just can't believe it. In another two days, he'll be gone forever. I didn't think I would ever stop crying after my father told me."

"You don't even know what true sorrow is, Elspeth Woodward." Lilith sniffed. "I love him far more than any of you. Just remember, I'm the only one of you who has actually met him."

Unoffended by Lilith's rebuke, Elspeth grabbed her friend's arm. "Tell us about it again, Lilith. I just love the part where he saw you coming down the stairs and winked. I'm sure I would have fainted if it had been me."

Lilith sighed with self-importance. "Oh, all right. It was last spring at my parents' ball to celebrate the end of the war—"

She broke off as she turned away from the window and saw Kit standing in the doorway.

Lilith knew at once who she was. For weeks she had been dreading this moment. But now as she surveyed Kit's comic appearance, she could barely conceal her delight. This girl was no threat to her at all.

Since last spring when Lilith had actually spoken with Baron Cain at her parents' ball, she had been the most important student at the academy and the authority on all matters related to the Hero of Missionary Ridge. It was not a role she intended to give up easily, and as she studied the ridiculous-looking girl in front of her, she decided she would not have to.

The Templeton Academy was a relentlessly female establishment. At the time in their lives when the girls were most interested in the opposite sex, they had been denied all contact with it. As a result the more romantic of them wove elaborate fantasies around famous and unattainable men, the most popular being the Hero of Missionary Ridge.

On the night of their annual Christmas outing to the Lyceum Theater Cain had been in the audience seated in a box directly across from the girls. They all had recognized him at once. The month before some of them had even cut out a sketch of him that had appeared in the *Tribune.* But not even his picture had prepared them for their first sight of him, resplendent in his navy-and-gold uniform. As a group, they had fallen in love, and ever since that night he had been the subject of tireless speculation.

When Elspeth Woodward had told her friends that his ward was coming to the academy, the girls had exhausted themselves in discussion. They knew they should snub her because she was a Southerner and an enemy. On the other hand, she would be their closest link with *him.* She could tell them everything they wanted to know: what he liked to eat for breakfast, what color hair he found most attractive on a woman, whether he really made his living playing cards.

Now, one by one, the girls turned to see why Lilith had stopped speaking. There were a few muffled giggles as they took in the newcomer's appearance, and then the room fell silent. They looked at each other uncertainly. Elspeth Woodward nibbled on the inside of her bottom lip, a habit she had fallen into when she was nervous. Each of the girls waited for one of the others to make the first move. Lilith Samuels saw their indecision and took advantage of it. Tilting her head high, she swept past Kit without a word. After a moment's hesitation, the other girls followed, leaving only Elspeth behind.

Elspeth did not know what to do. Her father had asked her to be kind to the newcomer, but she looked so strange. Why was she wearing those silly clothes? They were much too large for her. And what had happened to her hair?

Elspeth was not a leader by nature. She loved being part of a group, especially one that included Lilith Samuels and Margaret Stockton, the most popular girls at the academy. It wasn't fair for her father to ask her to jeopardize her friendships for a stranger.

"You must be Katharine," she said reluctantly, her innate good manners winning out. She stepped forward and offered a none too steady hand. "I'm Elspeth Woodward. We'll be sharing this room."

When Kit did not move, Elspeth slowly lowered her hand and continued bravely. "The maids will be bringing up your trunk soon. I'll help you unpack if you like."

Kit's lips narrowed into a thin, fierce line. "You put one finger on anything belongs to me, and I'll slap you silly! And that goes for all those other whey-faced bitches, too. I catch them in this room again, I'll kick their skinny asses straight to hell!"

Elspeth's jaw went slack with horror. Never in her life had anyone spoken to her so harshly. With a tiny, terrified sob, she dashed past Kit out of the room.

As soon as she was gone, Kit slammed the door shut. She kicked hard at the leg of the bureau and then threw herself down on the bed and cried.

At first when the dinner gong sounded, Kit did not move. Then she sat up and slowly swung her feet over the side of the bed. Even if it killed her, she had to face them, and the longer she put it off, the harder it would be. She dipped her fingers in the pitcher on top of her bureau and patted her eyes with the cool water. After drying them on her sleeve, she stepped out into the hallway and joined the stream of chattering girls in their crisp, white-aproned uniforms as they moved toward the stairs.

The dining room was long and narrow, somewhat gloomy despite palms growing from squat bronze urns placed in the corners. A wrought-iron chandelier hung from the ceiling, its gas jets glowing inside frosted glass globes. Sturdy trestle tables lined with identical black wooden chairs ran the length of the room.

Even if her hair had not been so short and ragged, Kit's brown dress alone would have made her conspicuous in a sea of navy-and-white uniforms. That and her connection with Baron Cain. She could feel the stares of the older girls as she took a seat at the end of one of the tables. She realized too late that everyone else was still standing.

The sound of a spoon tapping the side of a glass preceded the voice of Elvira Templeton. "Everyone will rise for grace."

Forty pairs of eyes turned in Kit's direction. She slithered to her feet, hot with embarrassment.

The prayer was short but ardent. This time Kit waited until the others were taking their seats before she sat down herself. No sooner was she settled than Mrs. Templeton once again tapped her glass.

"Girls, before we begin our meal, I would like to introduce a new student to all of you. Katharine Weston, will you please stand up." Kit reluctantly rose to her feet, her mouth set in a grim line and her eyes fixed firmly in front of her.

"In keeping with the Templeton tradition of hospitality," the headmistress continued, "I would like all of you to make Katharine feel welcome. As we move through the week, let us keep in mind the Thirteenth Chapter of Hebrews, verse number two. 'Be not forgetful to entertain strangers, for thereby some have entertained angels unaware.' You may begin eating."

Lilith Samuels tittered. Elspeth had told her of the encounter with Kit after Lilith had found her, white-faced and shaken, sitting in an empty classroom, and Lilith had wasted no time spreading the story among the older girls. An angel unaware, indeed! Now they all joined Lilith, their giggles hidden from the ears of Elvira Templeton by the sounds of serving dishes being passed down the tables.

Kit, however, could hear them clearly, and it was not difficult for her to guess the reason for their amusement. Elspeth Woodward had certainly wasted no time spreading her story! As she sat down, she glared across the table at the younger girl.

Elspeth was taking a biscuit from a basket when she felt Kit's eyes on her. She looked up and flushed, dropping the biscuit in her confusion. Kit felt a stab of satisfaction. The girl might have a pretty face and long curly brown hair, but she was going to find out that she had better steer clear of Kit Weston. All of them were going to find that out!

For the rest of the meal, she made no effort to be polite. Several of the girls, beginning to feel guilty about their display of bad manners, tried to make amends, but Kit either ignored their attempts at conversation or glared at them so contemptuously that they retreated. By the time the bread pudding was passed around, she was firmly established as an outcast.

After dinner she was summoned to the first-floor reception room, where Hamilton Woodward was waiting for her. After a curt nod he began to outline the legalities of the guardianship that bound her and his own role in her affairs. "Your schooling is being paid for with the interest from your trust," he said. "Also, your clothing and a small weekly allowance. As Mr. Cain has no doubt told you, the principal can't be touched until your twenty-third birthday or until you marry, whichever comes first."

"Beg pardon?" Kit sat up straighter in her chair. "Would you mind explainin' that last part again?"

He seemed annoyed with the interruption. "There's nothing to explain. The money is being held in trust for you until you marry or until you turn twenty-three. It goes without saying, of course, that you can only marry with the permission of your guardian."

He went on to detail the specifics of the arrangements he had made with Cain, but Kit was barely listening. She hadn't known that the trust would end if she married. For a moment she turned the idea over in her mind, but then she discarded it. Cain hadn't even wanted her as his mistress; she could hardly expect anyone to want her as a wife. Besides, she had no intention of ever marrying. She wasn't that desperate.

That night Elspeth did not appear in their room until minutes before bedtime. Kit, wearing a voluminous white flannel nightgown, was already lying down, arms crossed behind her head, staring at the ceiling as she reviewed the conversation with Hamilton Woodward for the hundredth time, trying to find some way out.

Elspeth gave a tiny, nervous gasp as she tripped over the leg of a chair that Kit had moved out of place. Kit regarded her scornfully. She looked like a scared rabbit. Probably afraid Kit was going to murder her in her sleep. With a snort of contempt, she turned her back on the younger girl.

But sleep did not come easily to her. She found herself reliving the humiliating night she had offered herself to Cain as his mistress. What a fool she had made of herself! The sound of his laughter still pounded in her ears. Under the bed sheet, her ragged fingernails cut tiny half moons into the palms of her hands. Someday she was going to make him pay.

Chapter Nine

The Templeton Academy used a system of demerits to maintain order. For every ten demerits a girl acquired, she lost privileges for a week. By the end of the following day, Kit had accumulated eighty-three. (Taking the Lord's name in vain was automatically ten.)

Mrs. Templeton called her into her office and threatened her with expulsion if she did not immediately begin to follow the rules of the academy. Cursing would not be tolerated. She was to participate in all her classes. Her room and her clothing must be kept neat. She had been provided with two uniforms, and she must begin wearing them. Above all, she must make every effort to correct her grammar. Ladies did not say "ain't" or "I reckon." A lady referred to objects as "unimportant." Never! Absolutely never was anything to be referred to as being "useless as toad spit"!

Kit remained stoic during the interview, but afterward she found herself trembling. If she was expelled, she would have broken her agreement with Cain and lost her last hold on Risen Glory. No matter what, she couldn't let that happen.

The next morning she appeared on time at her first class,

neatly dressed in her new navy-blue and white uniform, minus only the required corset. Taking a seat in the farthest corner, she sat quietly, speaking only when she was addressed directly. She had already concluded that the safest course for her was to talk as little as possible.

Within several days the teachers began to suspect that she was slow-witted. The girls were certain of it. Only Elspeth remained unconvinced. Too often she had returned to her room to find Kit with her head buried in a collection of essays by Ralph Waldo Emerson.

By the end of September, Kit was nearly desperate. With the exception of French, which she was picking up easily, the rest of her classes were agonizingly difficult for her. Music was torture. The girls were expected to sing prettily and play the piano. Not only couldn't Kit carry a tune, but the only instrument she knew anything about was the jew's harp, and she had quickly discovered that a jew's harp was not considered an appropriate instrument for a young lady.

Dancing class was even worse. Her natural gracefulness as she rode a horse or raced barefoot across a field deserted her the moment she heard the music. The girls in the class partnered each other, and as none of them ever chose her, she was forced to dance with the teacher, a brisk, middle-aged woman who announced at the end of one particularly trying session that Katharine Weston was the clumsiest young woman it had ever been her misfortune to teach.

She performed a little better at embroidery, simply by pretending she was mending a piece of harness, but the weekly sessions in deportment were an unmitigated disaster. She had no idea at all how to carry on a polite conversation, and every time she opened her mouth to speak, either her grammar or her ignorance of social customs betrayed her.

When Kit was not in class or confined to her room to work off the demerits she had earned in her first weeks, she was in the library poring over the newspapers for news of her homeland. She read everything she could lay her hands on about Andrew Johnson, the new President. A Tennessee Democrat and former slaveholder, he had been the most prominent Southern advocate of the Union cause, regarded as a hero to the North and a traitor to the South. Now Southerners were beginning to look upon him differently, for he was one of a dwindling group of politicians who was advocating a moderate reconstruction policy toward the defeated Confederacy. She read with trepidation about men named Stevens and Sumner and Chandler who wanted to impose military rule on the South and upset the delicate racial balance by registering black males to vote. Surely the more moderate policies of the President would prevail. She ached with homesickness.

Lilith Samuels took pleasure in each one of Kit's failures. She tried to make the girls forget that any connection existed between Kit and their idol, Baron Cain. They snickered at her mistakes, at first behind her back and then openly. As far back as Kit could remember, she had gone through life with her fists swinging. Now her whole future depended on keeping her temper. If she fought them as she wanted to, she knew she would be expelled, and so she gritted her teeth and walked away.

To keep some measure of her self-respect, she stored away every insult. Each time the girls mimicked her accent or her grammar, each time they giggled at her cropped hair or laughed when she caught her unaccustomed skirts on a chair, she made a mental note of it. She collected the insults and stored them away like pieces of dry tinder to fuel her determination for revenge. Baron Cain was going to pay for every slur.

Only Elspeth did not join in Kit's persecution, although she was not completely certain why. Goodness knew, Katharine Weston deserved what she got. From the very beginning she'd been hateful, looking down her nose at everybody, cursing Elspeth, making her feel like an interloper in her own room. She was always leaving her things scattered around so that Elspeth was forced either to pick them up or earn a demerit herself for living untidily. And Mrs. Templeton refused to let her change rooms! It was all so unfair.

Still, despite the fact that Lilith Samuels had begun to notice, Elspeth held herself apart from the group when they tied Kit's nightgown into knots or tore up a Confederate flag and put the pieces under her covers. Vindictiveness was as foreign to her nature as compromise was to Kit's.

One evening after she had earned Lilith's displeasure by dissuading the girls from gluing the pages of Kit's French book together, she returned to her room to find Kit sitting on the bed reading a letter. Several of her books were scattered on the floor, her discarded nightgown and yesterday's underwear were lying in a heap on the chair, she had spilled water, and three of her bureau drawers were standing open.

Elspeth's normal sweet temper deserted her. "I'm not picking up after you anymore, Katharine Weston," she declared. "You get all of this cleaned up before we have room inspection!" Despite her anger, she was surprised at her own boldness. Although she didn't like acknowledging it even to herself, she was more than a little afraid of her roommate.

Unfortunately, Elspeth had picked the wrong time to take her stand. Kit had just received a letter from Sophronia filled with praise for Risen Glory's new owner. Glad to have a target on which to vent her anger, Kit jerked up her head and glared at Elspeth.

"Since when you think you can give me orders? I'll clean up when I've a mind to and not before."

Elspeth held her ground, even though her hands were trembling. "There's going to be a room inspection tonight, and I'm not getting a demerit because of you!"

"I don't give a damn 'bout no room inspection!" Kit snarled, crumpling the letter in her fist and throwing it down on the floor. "I got so many demerits already, a few more won't make a difference. If you're so all-fired anxious to have this room clean, you clean it yourself!"

"You're hateful!" Elspeth declared, tears clouding her pretty brown eyes. "You're the most hateful person I've ever met in my whole life."

Kit saw the tears and hardened her heart against a momentary pang of guilt. The girl was a silly fool, crying like a baby because she couldn't have her own way. No more spirit than a mouse. She crossed her arms belligerently over her chest. "Then why don't you just go find yourself another room to live in?"

"Don't think I haven't tried!" Elspeth cried, crumpling the edges of her spotless apron in agitation. "I hate sharing a room with you. I'd give anything to get away. You're mean and stupid and vulgar and you live like a pig!" She regretted her outburst the instant it was over. Never had she spoken so unkindly to another human being.

But Kit was already on her feet. "And you're a damn jackass!" she exclaimed, angrily dashing across the room to Elspeth's bureau. A small alarm sounded in her brain, warning her of the consequences of losing her temper, but she deliberately ignored it. Jerking open Elspeth's top drawer, she snatched up the neatly folded piles of underwear and tossed them on the floor.

"I'll show you what it's really like to live with a pig! I'll show all of you!" She went on to the next drawer. "You're all bitches! Smirkin' at me! Laughin' in my face!" A stack of nightgowns and black lisle stockings joined the petticoats. "I hate this school! I hate all of you! You're all silly, pampered little bitches!" Only after the contents of the bottom drawer had joined the rest did she pause to catch her breath.

Elspeth's quiet sobs punctuated the sudden silence. The room was a shambles. Clothing and underwear were everywhere—littering the floor, scattered across the beds. A glove from Elspeth's second best pair had even landed in the water pitcher.

"What is the meaning of this outrage?"

The girls' eyes flew to the doorway as Elvira Templeton's deep voice thundered through the room. Too late, Kit realized what she had done.

The headmistress stormed into the room like a great, ironclad battleship with black bombazine sails. "I don't have to ask who is responsible for this shocking display! I have tried from the beginning to be patient with you, Katharine, but I shall try no longer. You will be out of this school tomorrow morning. Mr. Woodward will be notified immediately."

Kit could feel the eggshell walls of her fragile world collapsing around her. It couldn't be happening, not after she'd tried so hard—swallowing snubs, walking away from insults. "You mean I'm expelled?" she stammered.

Mrs. Templeton was not unmoved by the small, stricken face, but she knew she must think of the greater good. "That's exactly what I mean, Katharine. I can no longer keep you here as a student. You are not a good influence."

Kit slowly lowered her head. She would die before she'd let them see her cry.

"I'm the one who was responsible," a small voice interjected softly. "You mustn't expel her. I emptied the drawers. I made the mess."

Kit's head shot up in astonishment. Elspeth stood with her hands clasped tightly in front of her apron, her bottom lip trembling ever so slightly.

"You, Elspeth?" Mrs. Templeton exclaimed. "I don't believe it!"

"I did it," Elspeth said stubbornly. "It's not fair to punish Katharine for what I did."

Mrs. Templeton looked at her uncertainly. "But why, Elspeth? Why would you do such a thing?"

"I lost my temper. Katharine and I had an argument, and I lost my temper."

"That's not true!" Kit exclaimed, finally coming to her senses.

But Elspeth cut her off. "She's just trying to take the blame for me. She knows how angry my father will be."

It wasn't often that Elvira Templeton was at a loss. She looked at both girls closely. She was almost certain that Elspeth, who had been a model student at the academy since she was eight years old, was lying to protect her roommate. On the other hand, she wasn't certain.

Taking a deep breath, she made her decision. "Very well," she said severely. "Katharine, you will not be expelled *this time.* However, several serious infractions of the rules have taken place. Since I do not want to punish either of you unjustly, I will punish you both equally. Today is Friday. Beginning at this moment, you are both confined to your room until Monday morning. You will leave only to use the necessary and to attend church. On my desk Monday morning I expect to see a one-thousand-word essay from each of you on the subject of an individual's responsibility to the institution that serves her. Any more incidents such as this will not be dealt with so leniently. Do I make myself understood?"

"Yes, Mrs. Templeton."

"Yes, ma'am."

With an imperious nod of the head, she swept from the room. As soon as the door had closed behind her, Kit whirled on Elspeth. "You silly fool! Why'd you go and do such a thing? You could of got yourself thrown right out of this school!"

Elspeth sank miserably down on the edge of her bed, finally overcome by the reality of what she had done. She wondered if

Mrs. Templeton would notify her parents. How would she ever explain to them? She couldn't even explain it to herself.

Kit advanced on her, not taking the time to try to understand why she was so angry. "Don't you expect any gratitude from me!" she shouted. "I didn't ask you to take the blame. Just remember that!"

"Please leave me alone," Elspeth murmured with quiet dignity. "I don't want your gratitude. I don't want anything except for you to leave me alone."

If Elspeth had screamed at her, Kit could have borne it better. As it was she felt horribly ashamed, like a bully who had tied a firecracker to a kitten's tail. She walked away from Elspeth, stepping across the small, littered room to the window. Below her, fashionable carriages with glowing brass lamps mounted on their sides swept along Fifth Avenue toward the theaters and restaurants that were the nighttime oases of wealthy New Yorkers.

Slowly she turned her attention back to the room. Elspeth was still sitting motionlessly on the bed looking down at her hands clasped in her lap. Kit reached over and picked up one of her white cambric nightgowns, then began to fold it. It was not a very good job, and she tried again with little more success.

"If you don't want me to make an entire mess of it, Elspeth," she said quietly, "maybe you better show me how you fold these things."

Elspeth looked up in surprise. For a moment neither girl spoke, and then Elspeth slowly rose from the bed and walked over to Kit. "If you fold it lengthwise, it's easier," she said, taking the nightgown from her and demonstrating.

Kit plucked a garment from the floor and copied Elspeth's motions. "Your way sure is better than mine," she conceded as she surveyed the finished product. She set it down on the bed and picked up another. For a while the girls worked quietly. Finally Kit spoke.

"I reckon I owe you a apology. I been actin' mean and spiteful ever since I got here. That first day you showed me courtesy and I spit in your face. I'm not proud of that. It's just that I'm not used to bein' around females. I'm not makin' excuses, you understand. I just want you to know that I'm not naturally acrimonious."

"I guess I never thought you were," Elspeth said hesitantly. "Despite the way you were acting. Besides, I didn't like the way the rest of the girls were treating you."

"They're mean-minded bitches, every one of them," Kit declared emphatically. "I reckon you're the only decent person in this school."

"That's not true," Elspeth said, her brow wrinkled earnestly. "Oh, maybe some of the girls are insensitive, but most of them are awfully nice if you just give them a chance. I think you scare them a little. You're so ferocious."

"Me?" Kit was genuinely astonished. "How could I scare them? I'm a failure at everything I've done here." There was no self-pity in her observation, she was merely stating a fact. "You know as well as I do, Elspeth—it's been a disaster from the very beginning." She slumped down despondently on the bed. "I don't know how I'm gonna last three years."

"Why three years?" Elspeth asked. "You'll be nineteen by then. That's awfully old to be going to school."

Kit dropped her hand and began to fidget with the gray wool coverlet. Ordinarily she didn't believe in sharing her private business with other people, but she realized she wanted to confide in Elspeth. There was something comforting about the girl's gentle curiosity, and Kit sensed that, despite what had happened between them the first day, Elspeth was not one to spread tales.

"Do you really want to know?" she finally asked, part of her hoping Elspeth would say no.

"If you want to tell me."

Kit thought about it. "I guess I better. I've been carryin' so much around inside me for so long, it must be what's makin' me act so mean." For the first time since their conversation had begun, she looked Elspeth full in the face. "Did you ever love somethin' real hard, Elspeth? So hard you'd do just about anything in the world to protect it?"

Elspeth immediately nodded her head and lowered herself next to Kit, the old bed springs protesting against the additional weight. "My little sister Agnes. I love her that way. She's not like other children. Even though she's almost ten, she can't read or write. But she's so sweet, and I love her dearly. I'd never let anybody hurt her."

Kit considered what Elspeth had told her and then nodded her head. "That's the way I feel about Risen Glory. . . ."

She talked for nearly an hour. Only when she reached the more recent parts of her story did she hold back. Elspeth would never understand about her masquerade as a stable boy and her attempt to kill Cain. Still, she couldn't completely hide the depth of her hatred for him, even though she could see it shocked the younger girl.

"Don't you understand, Elspeth?" she concluded. "I'm impotent. If I get expelled, he'll sell Risen Glory—which just goes to show you how little he really cares about that plantation. And if I do manage to last three years, it's not gonna do me one bit of good. I still won't have control of my trust fund, so I can't buy Risen Glory back from him even if he agrees to sell it to me."

Elspeth's small forehead puckered. "I don't understand. If he's your guardian, he controls your trust. Couldn't he just take the money and give you Risen Glory?"

Kit shook her head. "No. It has to do with principal and interest. The interest is what's payin' for my schoolin'. But even he can't touch the principal. Your daddy said that was supposed to protect me, but it's like I've been hogtied. The only way the bank'll release the money before I'm twenty-three is if I get married." There was a pause. "Which I ain't."

Now Elspeth was her father's daughter. "If you did marry, the money would pass into the control of your husband. It's the way the law works. You couldn't spend it without his permission."

Kit shrugged. "It's all academic, far as I'm concerned. There's no man in the world I'd shackle myself to." Unbidden, the memory of Cain's humiliating words came back to her. "Besides," she added bitterly, "I was raised all wrong to be a wife. Only thing I can do right is cook."

Elspeth was immensely sympathetic, but she was also eminently practical. "But that's why we're all here! To learn how to be proper wives. The girls from the Templeton Academy are renowned for the successful marriages they make. That's part of what's so special about being a Templeton girl. Men come from as far away as Baltimore to attend the graduation ball."

"It doesn't make any difference to me if they come from far away as Paris, France. You'll never see me at any ball."

But Elspeth was paying no attention to Kit's grumbling, for she had been struck with a sudden inspiration. "I've got the answer!" she exclaimed as she leapt up from the bed, sending a pile of neatly folded petticoats tumbling back to the floor. "All you have to do is find the right husband as soon as you graduate. Somebody who's sweet and kind and wants to make you happy. Then everything will be perfect. You wouldn't be Mr. Cain's ward any longer, and you'd have your money."

"You're a real nice girl, Elspeth, and I'm ashamed of how I misjudged you at first, but I still got to tell you that's the most ridiculous idea I ever heard in my entire life. Besides, gettin' married wouldn't do me any good. All it'd mean is that another man'd have my money."

"If you picked the right man," Elspeth explained patiently, "it'd be the same thing as having it yourself. Before you get married, you could ask him to buy you Risen Glory for a wedding present." She clapped her hands merrily, caught up in her vision. "Oh, wouldn't that be romantic! Maybe you could even go there for your honeymoon!"

Husbands and honeymoons and wedding presents. . . . It was as if Elspeth were speaking a foreign language. "That's plain foolishness," Kit declared. "What man's gonna want to marry me?" Neither of them seemed to notice that Kit had not actually rejected Elspeth's romantic plan, but was merely questioning its feasibility.

Elspeth thought seriously about Kit's question. What man, indeed, would marry such a girl? "Stand up!" she finally ordered, her voice containing the same no-nonsense note of command as Elvira Templeton's. Kit rose reluctantly to her feet, telling herself she was only doing so to humor her new friend.

Elspeth began to study her, tapping her finger thoughtfully on her cheek. "You're awfully thin, and your hair is horrible. Of course it will grow," she added politely. "And it is a beautiful color. Even now it would probably look quite nice if it were cut a little straighter. Your eyes are too big for your face, but I think that's all part of being so thin." Taking Kit's arm, she pulled her out into the center of the room and then slowly circled her, being careful not to step on the clothing strewn in her path. By the time she had completed her circuit, she was well satisfied. "You're going to be awfully pretty someday, so I don't think we'll have to worry about that."

"Just what *will* we have to worry about?" Kit asked, a dangerous glint in her eyes.

But Elspeth was no longer intimidated by Kit, for she had glimpsed the softness of her heart. "Everything else," she said firmly. "You have to learn to talk and to walk. What to say and, even more important, what not to say. You'll have to learn absolutely everything the academy teaches."

"And just how am I gonna do that?" Kit snapped. "I haven't exactly made a success of it so far."

"No, you haven't, have you?" Elspeth said, her smile impish. "But then, you haven't had me helping you, either."

Chapter Ten

"Never, Miss Weston, have I seen eyes so beautiful. Like two spring violets floating in a pitcher of cream. I have not slept in weeks thinking of those magnificent eyes. I vow I shall not rest until you agree to become my wife."

Kit batted away the hand that was attempting to clutch hers. "Then you're going to be one sleepy man, mister, 'cause I'd never marry anyone as fat and ugly as you. Even if I am half desperate."

"Katharine Louise Weston!" Elspeth jumped up from her position on bended knee at her roommate's feet. "Now you say what I taught you!"

Kit grinned. Elspeth looked like a ferocious kitten. Even though only a year separated them, she somehow seemed much younger than Kit. Perhaps it was the light sprinkle of childish freckles across the bridge of her nose, or maybe it was her simple goodness. Regardless of the reason, Kit loved her dearly. Elspeth, who had always been a follower, had now become the leader.

It was mid-March, barely three weeks after Kit's seventeenth birthday. For the past six months, Elspeth had successfully steered Kit through the dangerous shoals of the Templeton Academy. Never far from her side, she had drilled her at every spare moment, nagged her, corrected her, and yet somehow always known when Kit could be pushed no further and had given her the time she needed to adjust to a world that was as strange to her as a foreign land. She refused to take personally Kit's frequent, if short-lived, bursts of ill temper, and had nearly managed to stop blushing at her roommate's lapses into profanity, a feat that was made considerably easier by the fact that she didn't actually understand most of the words.

Kit jumped up from the chair they had placed in the middle of the room for their rehearsal and hugged her friend. "Sorry, Elspeth, but I couldn't resist teasing you. Besides, it don't—doesn't seem natural to say what you taught me—'Thank you, kind sir, for the honor you have bestowed upon me.' No Southern lady would say it that way." Kit's patriotism was a constant source of contention between them, and Elspeth opened her mouth to protest, but Kit cut her off, waving a finger in admonition. "I am Southern, Elspeth, no matter how much you want to forget it."

"All right." Elspeth sighed, knowing when she was defeated. "How would a Southern lady say it?"

Kit called up memories of the women of Rutherford. "Well," she said thoughtfully, "I guess a Southern lady would clasp her hands in front of her bosom like this"—she proceeded to demonstrate—"tilt her head ever so slightly to the side, and say, 'I declare, sir, I don't know when I've been so flattered, 'deed I don't.' "

Elspeth nodded her head approvingly. "Very nice. All right, when you get a proposal, you can do it your way. Now before we go to bed, remember you promised to help me with my algebra."

The months that had elapsed since the weekend of Elspeth and Kit's confinement to their room had been surprisingly gratifying ones for Kit. Although she had never officially agreed to Elspeth's romantic scheme to save Risen Glory, neither had she rejected it. Just knowing there was a plan, no matter how distasteful, gave her some measure of peace.

One thing was certain. She would not allow Baron Cain to run her life until her twenty-third birthday. By that time she would have lost Risen Glory for good. She only hoped she would be able to think of something less drastic than getting married to end Cain's guardianship and regain her home. If not, she knew she would just have to do as Elspeth said and find the right husband. It no longer seemed quite so impossible as it had before.

Although Kit made light of it to Elspeth, she was secretly delighted with the changes in her own appearance. She kept her hair immaculately clean, and Elspeth had tidied its ragged edges with her silver embroidery scissors until it formed a glossy cap of shiny black curls around her face. Even though her hair was too short to be fashionable, barely reaching the starched white collar of her uniform in the back, she had noticed some of the other girls beginning to regard it enviously. With part of her allowance, she had purchased a collection of narrow satin ribbons. Elspeth had taught her how to thread them through her short curls to keep them from tumbling forward into her face. The academy food, which was as ample as it was filling, had begun to round out some of the sharp angles of her body. Her eyes no longer seemed quite so ready to leap from her face. She was also moving more gracefully as she gradually became accustomed to the long skirts of her uniform and the heavy petticoats beneath.

Other changes that were happening inside Kit were not as apparent, even to herself, but as she freed the long-denied feminine side of her personality, she began to feel less restless. Still, she desperately missed the freedom of her old life. The sedate daily strolls in two neat rows, six girls to a row, up and down the same small section of Fifth Avenue pavement were more torture than exercise and left her with a nearly uncontrollable longing to throw herself on the back of a horse and ride until she caught the wind.

Even so, she was almost happy. With Elspeth as her partner, she gained confidence in dancing class, she could pick out "Home Sweet Home" on the piano (her request to learn "Dixie" had been flatly denied), and just after the new year, she was given permission to begin taking classes in algebra, ancient history, and English literature that had recently been added to the curriculum. Only Elvira Templeton was not surprised by Kit's progress. She had realized the day she had read Kit's essay entitled "The Responsibilities of a Woman to the Institution Serving Her" that the academy's most difficult student had a keenly incisive mind.

Correcting her speech was proving to be one of the most difficult of Kit's tasks as she discovered that the habits of a lifetime are not easily broken. The only job more difficult was trying to establish an easy relationship with the other students.

Elspeth insisted that Kit overcome her prejudices against the members of her own sex and learn how to enjoy being with other women. At first Kit flatly refused, but Elspeth proved to be remarkably stubborn about the issue, drawing Kit into conversations at the dinner table and dragging her along to visit the girls in their rooms. At first the girls felt uneasy in her presence, but as she said little, they gradually became accustomed to her and began to behave as if she were not there.

Late in the evenings if it was quiet and the group small enough, the talk would turn to Eve's Shame. Each spring Elvira Templeton delivered a lecture on the subject to all the senior girls. Over the years the lecture had become legendary, passed down from one group of girls to another. All of them knew it by heart long before they had actually heard it.

Behind carefully closed doors, in sepulchrally hushed tones, Mrs. Templeton spoke to them of the dark side of men and marriage, what she referred to as "Eve's Shame." She spoke of pain and duty, of obligation and endurance. She advised them to keep their minds pure and let their husbands have their way, no matter how shocking and horrible it all might seem. She suggested they recite verses from the Bible or try to recall from memory the recipe of a cake they had particularly enjoyed. But never once did she tell them exactly what Eve's Shame involved. It was left to their fertile imaginations.

Elvira Templeton regarded her lecture as informative and progressive in an age where such matters were never discussed. The girls were terrified, emerging from the room pale and shaken, even though they had known in advance what they would hear.

Eve's Shame was the subject of endless speculation among them. They pooled their ignorance. One girl reported that her mother had an aunt who had gone insane on her wedding night. Another had heard there was blood. But of them all, Kit and Fanny Jennings, whose father owned a Thoroughbred farm not far from Saratoga, were the most terrified, for only they had watched horses mate, only they had seen the shuddering of a reluctant mare as she was covered by a trumpeting stallion. They did not speak of it to the other girls, but they recognized the fear in each other's eyes.

Slowly Kit came to realize that the girls at the academy were as different as the blossoms in a fruit orchard. Some of them were silly—prattling on for hours about a young man that they fancied had smiled at them in church or, even worse, Baron Cain himself. Lilith Samuels was openly malicious. She sensed there was something wrong between Kit and Cain, and she never missed an opportunity for a barbed remark. But there were others she came to admire: Fanny Jennings, who was counting the days until summer vacation when she could ride to her heart's content; Louisa Coate, who painted beautiful watercolors of ships and the sea that were so real you could almost taste the salt spray; Jessica Kessler, who seemed to love books as much as Kit did and who, although she hotly denied it, was rumored to have secured a copy of Charles Darwin's forbidden book, *The Origin of the Species,* and actually read it. The only girls who continued to openly snub her were those who had lost brothers or fathers in the war. Elspeth protested they were being unfair, but Kit understood the girls' hostility. For her, too, the war was far from over.

As Kit's grammar improved, she began to gain confidence and speak more freely to her classmates, although never about politics. Much to Lilith's chagrin, some of the girls started turning to her for help with their compositions or their algebra. But friendship had its price. They also began questioning her about Baron Cain.

"Tell us what he's really like, Kit. Please!"

How she yearned to tell them! But she bit back the words, knowing that if she spoke the truth—that he was wicked and hateful and a bully to boot—she would once again find herself an outcast.

They continued to press her. She finally thought of something to tell them.

"He's tall."

"We know that, silly! Tell us something we don't know."

She began to gnaw at the inside of her bottom lip, a habit she had picked up from Elspeth. Eventually she made a begrudging concession. "He keeps a good stable."

This piece of information was greeted with protracted groans. Only Fanny Jennings was interested.

As summer drew nearer Kit realized she would have to remain at the Templeton Academy, which stayed open for those students whose parents were traveling or otherwise too busy to be bothered with their offspring. Elspeth was to join her parents at their summer home in fashionable Long Branch, New Jersey.

Elspeth begged her father to let Kit join them. At first he would not hear of it. Although he had instructed his daughter to be pleasant to his client's ward, he did not want her to grow too close to a young lady with such an unfortunate past. Elspeth spent the weekend pleading with him and finally, with her mother's support, managed to melt through his resolve. He wrote Cain for permission.

The two girls were nearly giddy with excitement. Kit dreamed of being able to ride a horse again, of having some small measure of freedom after the suffocatingly structured existence of the academy. Elspeth laughed at how much livelier Long Branch would be with Kit in attendance. She described the stretch of beach where they would be permitted to wade and the clam bake that was always the highlight of the summer. What a glorious vacation it would be!

Cain's reply was terse. Under no circumstances would he give his permission for Kit to leave the Templeton Academy.

Dry-eyed and furious, Kit stalked the narrow perimeters of the room until long after midnight, refusing to talk of what had happened. It was left to Elspeth to shed tears over the ashes of their wonderful plans. She felt doubly betrayed. Even in the face of Kit's criticism, she had maintained her devotion to Baron Cain. How could the man she had desperately loved for so many months have acted so cruelly?

On the first day of June, Kit stood at the window and watched as Elspeth waved sadly up at her before she disappeared into her father's carriage. Kit tried to tell herself it was only for three months, that Elspeth would be back in September. But it didn't help. All she could think about was that she had suffered another loss. Mother . . . father . . . home . . .

friend. . . . Was that all her life was to be? A series of losses, little deaths, each one of which left her more alone than before.

She let go of the muslin curtains she had pushed back and, overcome with self-pity, turned to face her empty room. Once again Baron Cain had taken something away from her, and she could do nothing about it because as long as he was her guardian, he was in total control of her life. If he wanted her to remain at the academy, she must remain. If he dictated that she was to leave, she must leave. He could lock her in an attic for the next six years and the law would support him. She was a victim of his merest whim. It was a hopeless situation.

Without bothering to consider the consequences, she dashed from her room, down the back stairs, which smelled of steam and boiled chicken from the kitchen, and out through the rear door. She dashed around the corner of the gray stone building and stepped out onto Forty-fifth Street. Leaving the academy unattended was strictly forbidden, but she had to have some time alone with the decision she now saw she had to make.

She walked rapidly down the street, not seeing the neat brownstone row houses or the black wrought-iron fence that separated the houses from the pavement. Elspeth had been right all along. The only way a woman could have power was through a man. No matter how horrible the prospect, she was going to have to find herself a husband.

She would approach the problem logically. Unlike other girls, she was not blinded by romantic visions of orange blossoms and ivory lace. She trusted her judgment. She had to find a man with an easy disposition, someone who was not too smart and could be easily steered in the proper direction. It wouldn't be simple, but surely if she didn't let herself get sidetracked by unimportant issues like age or attractiveness, she could find exactly the man she needed. Getting Cain's permission to marry would undoubtedly be easier than getting his permission to go on vacation with Elspeth. He would be permanently rid of her, a fact that would make him nearly as happy as it made her.

She was seventeen now. If she had been placed at the academy according to her age, September would be the beginning of her final year instead of her next-to-last year. She had heard all about that final year from Elspeth.

In the early spring the senior girls began to attend teas and small, well-chaperoned gatherings with carefully selected young men. All of these activities led up to the climax of their years as Templeton girls—the May graduation ball. This event officially announced to the world that now they were women ready for marriage.

Reaching Park Avenue, she slowed her steps and resolutely turned around. She would use the next year and a half wisely, preparing for that special springtime as carefully as any man had ever prepared for a career. And when the time came, she would find a husband. Then Baron Cain would have lost his hold on her. Through her husband she would take control of the money in her trust fund and, if the Fates smiled on her—please, Jesus, let them smile—she would be able to buy Risen Glory and finally have it for her very own!

Chapter Eleven

Fresh spring flowers filled the ballroom of the Templeton Academy for Young Ladies. Pyramids of multicolor tulips in white ceramic pots screened the empty fireplaces, while cut-glass vases stuffed with lilacs lined the mantels. Even the mirrors had been draped with swags of white azaleas.

Along the ballroom's perimeter, clusters of fashionably dressed guests looked toward the charming rose-bedecked gazebo that had been erected at the end of the ballroom and through which the most recent graduates of the Templeton Academy were soon to pass. Despite the differences in age, physical appearance, and sex, the guests possessed a curious similitude. It was not just their fashionable garb, the expensive jewels that rested upon the withered chests of the older women, or the luxurious moustaches and side whiskers of the men. Instead, the guests shared a smugness, self-righteousness, and complacency that is only possible when one does not have to worry about how one is going to pay the butcher for the next day's mutton.

Generously sprinkled in among the parents and more important relatives of the graduating students were members of New York City's most fashionable families—Schermerhorns, of course, and Livingstons; several Jays, and at least one Van Rensselaer. No one who was anyone in New York would think of missing the Templeton Academy's Graduation Ball, and certainly no socially prominent woman would consider letting any one of her marriageable sons miss the occasion. It was the best place in New York to find a suitable daughter-in-law. Naturally one could dream of a bride from among the British nobility, but since that was generally not practical, a Templeton girl was the next best thing.

In small clusters around the room, the bachelors had gathered, their ranks thinned by the war, but still numerous enough to please the mothers of the debutantes. The younger men were carelessly confident in their immaculate white linen and black broadcloth, despite the fact that the sleeves of several tail coats hung empty and more than one who had not yet seen his twenty-fifth birthday walked with a cane. The older bachelors, their coffers overflowing from the profits of the booming post-war economy, signaled their success with diamond shirt studs and heavy gold watch chains draped across thickening bellies.

For the gentlemen from Boston, Philadelphia, and Baltimore, tonight was the first time they would view the newest crop of New York's most desirable debutantes, and so they turned to the New York gentlemen who, for the past six weeks, had been attending the teas and sedate Sunday afternoon receptions that led up to this evening's ball.

The local bachelors had already staked out the winners in this year's sweepstakes. There was the beautiful Lilith Samuels, who'd grace any man's table. And her father was to settle ten thousand on her when she married.

Margaret Stockton. Not a good mouth. Her teeth were crooked and unattractively bucked, but she would bring nearly eight thousand to her marriage bed, and she sang quite well, a pretty quality in a wife.

Elspeth Woodward. Not as much money there. Five thousand at the outside. But sweet-natured and pleasant to look at. A dutiful wife who wouldn't give a man a moment's trouble. Definitely a favorite.

Unfortunately Fanny Jennings was out of the running. The youngest Vandervelt boy had already spoken with her father. Quite a pity, since she was worth a good eighteen thousand.

As the recital of the favorites came to an end, one of the men, a Bostonian, looked puzzled. "But isn't there another I've heard talk about?" he inquired. "Southerner, I seem to remember."

The men of New York kept their faces carefully expressionless. One of them cleared his throat. "Ah, yes," he said. "That would be Miss Weston."

Just then the orchestra began to play a selection from the newly popular "Tales from the Vienna Woods" and one by one the members of the graduating class were announced. Dressed in white ball gowns, they came out through the gazebo, pausing for just a moment at the top of the rose-petal-strewn stairs before they stepped down onto the ballroom floor and took the arm of a father or brother or favorite uncle.

Inside, they were nearly sick with excitement, but they were women now, and so they refused to permit such a childish emotion access to their smooth young faces. Lilith was cool and as poised as a goddess. Elspeth smiled so prettily that her oldest cousin, who had, up until that moment, thought of her as little more than a nuisance, began to think again. Fanny Jennings tripped ever so slightly on the hem of her skirt as she came forward, and although she wanted to die, she refused to let her mortification show. Margaret Stockton, even with her bad mouth, looked fetching enough in her white gown to make her mother's eyes cloud with tears and her father decide he had been much too pessimistic about his daughter's prospects.

"Katharine Louise Weston."

There was an almost imperceptible movement among the gentlemen of New York City, a slight tilting of heads, a vague shifting of position. The gentlemen of Boston and Philadelphia and Baltimore sensed that something special was about to happen and fixed their attention more closely on the front of the ballroom. She came toward them, her form dim at first in the back shadows of the gazebo and then gradually becoming clearer as she walked forward and finally stopped at the top of the petal-strewn steps.

They saw at once that she wasn't like the others. This one was no tame tabby cat to curl up at a man's hearth and keep his slippers warm. This was a woman to make a man's blood surge, a wildcat with lustrous black hair pulled back neatly from her face with silver combs only to fall in a riotous tangle of thick dark curls down over the back of her head and the slim column of her neck; an exotic cat whose eyebrows were thick and dark instead of thin, fine arches, whose widely spaced violet eyes were so heavily fringed it seemed impossible that the very weight of the lashes was not holding them closed; a jungle cat with a mouth that was much too full for fashion but so ripe and moist that a man could think of nothing else but drinking from it.

Her gown was fashioned of eggshell satin with a billowing chiffon overskirt caught up by lavender bows. The neckline was heart-shaped, softly outlining the contours of her breasts. The bell-shaped sleeves were finished in a tight, wide cuff of Alençon lace. The gown was beautiful and expensive, but she wore it almost carelessly, as if it were of little importance to her. One of the lavender bows had come undone at the side and, as she stepped down the stairs and out into the ballroom, revealing pretty, eggshell satin slippers with small, spool-shaped heels, several sets of observant eyes couldn't help but notice that her stride was a shade too long for the skirts to sway prettily.

Hamilton Woodward's youngest son stepped forward as her escort for the promenade. As he offered his arm, he whispered something to her. She threw back her head and laughed, showing small, white teeth. Each man who watched wanted that laugh to be his alone, even as he told himself that a more delicate young lady would perhaps not have laughed quite so boldly.

The gentlemen from Boston and Philadelphia and Baltimore watched as the graduates were led by their escorts through the first dance. "Who was this Miss Weston?" they asked under cover of the music. "Where did she come from?"

At first the gentlemen from New York were vague. She was connected with Hamilton Woodward somehow. No one knew much about her. Some talk that Elvira Templeton shouldn't have let a Southerner into the academy so soon after the war, especially when her family was unknown.

Gradually their comments became more personal. Quite something to look at, of course. Hard to keep your eyes off her, as a matter of fact. But a dangerous sort of wife, don't you think? Seemed a bit wild. Wager she wouldn't take the bit well at all. Difficult for a man to keep his mind on business with a woman like that waiting for him at home. If she waited. . . .

Only as the evening progressed did the gentlemen from Boston and Philadelphia and Baltimore learn the rest of it. It was most curious. The incomparable Miss Weston was actually the ward of the Hero of Missionary Ridge, who was noticeably absent. In the past six weeks she had captured the interest of a dozen of New York's most eligible bachelors, only to turn cool. These were young, handsome men from the wealthiest families—men who would one day run the city, even the country. As for those she did seem to favor, that was what galled the most, for she picked the least likely men! Bertrand Mayhew, for example, who came from a good family, of course, but not much money and, God knows, he was completely lost now that his mother had died. Then there was Hobart Cheney. The man had neither money nor looks, and he stuttered so badly that it was nearly impossible to understand him. The delicious Miss Weston's preference was incomprehensible. She was passing over Van Rensselaers and Livingstons and Jays for Bertrand Mayhew and Hobart Cheney!

Not that the mothers weren't glad, of course. Most of them enjoyed Miss Weston, but they said she wasn't up to scratch as a daughter-in-law. She was forever tearing a flounce or losing a glove. Her hair was never neat, they complained; always a lock tumbling down behind her ear or curling at her temples. No, she would not make the right sort of wife at all.

The fathers felt differently. They also knew that she wouldn't make the right sort of wife for their important sons. But at least they understood. . . .

There was another man who thought he understood only too well. Across the ballroom Hamilton Woodward relinquished his daughter into the arms of his eldest nephew and then sat down on one of the small gilt chairs next to his wife. He scowled at the adoring expression on his son's face as he handed Kit Weston over to her next partner. If the boy had thoughts in that direction, he was going to find himself badly disappointed. No son of his was going to marry a woman who was damaged goods.

Never had he regretted anything so much as he regretted persuading Elvira Templeton to accept Kit Weston at the academy. It had been an enormous error of judgment on his part, but how could he have known what kind of girl she was? At least Elspeth did not seem to have been tainted by her. He would always be thankful for that.

He looked with satisfaction at his daughter as she circled the floor, her brown hair caught up in a charming chignon adorned with a wreath of pink rosebuds. Elspeth was a daughter to be proud of. She was just like her mother, sweet and well mannered, and so good to her poor sister Agnes. She'd never given him a moment's worry, at least not until three weeks ago when he had belatedly realized the danger of her friendship with Kit Weston.

Although Cain had steadfastly refused to give permission for Kit to spend summers with them in Long Branch, he had given Woodward authority to grant or withhold permission for outings and small trips. Woodward had seen no harm in asking Kit to join them in Long Branch for four days at the end of April.

On the second night of their holiday something had awakened him. It had been unseasonably warm for several days, and he had gone downstairs, ambling out onto the broad wooden veranda to smoke his pipe. The moon had been full that night, and almost immediately he had seen them walking rapidly up over the bluff that separated the house from the beach.

She was barefoot, her black hair hanging in a wild tangle about her face, her dress unbuttoned at the neck. Walking slightly behind her was his groom.

Woodward didn't remember now what he had yelled out at them as he ran down the porch steps. All he remembered was the sight of her swollen mouth, the shocking way her dress was unbuttoned, revealing the pale flesh of her bosom. He had roughly pushed her inside, wanting to get his groom out of the way before he dealt with her.

The boy had been mutinous and sullen, just as the Irish always were when they were confronted with authority. In the end after he'd been lectured and dismissed from his job, the little mick had turned nasty.

"She came beggin' for it," he had snarled as Woodward mounted the steps of the veranda to go back into the house. "I swived her good, mister, and don't you be doubtin' it. And I wasn't the first one either. That wee filly's been covered before."

Woodward had felt ill as he entered the parlor to confront Kit. It was unthinkable that something like this could have happened under his own roof. When he could finally speak, he kept his voice low so he would not awaken his family, for he was determined they should never learn of what had happened.

At first she had predictably tried to deny that anything had happened at all, but when she discovered that her partner had branded her a harlot, she had finally fallen silent, realizing that any more protestations of innocence were futile.

Woodward found himself in a quandary. It was clearly his duty to see that she was immediately expelled from the academy before she contaminated any of the other girls, but if her behavior became public knowledge, the scandal would almost certainly rub off on Elspeth. Everyone knew the two girls were inseparable.

So he had gone to the bookstand in the corner of the parlor and lifted off the heavy leather-bound Bible that lay open on top. Then he had made her swear a solemn oath that she would conduct herself with discretion during her last month at the academy and that she would not mention anything of what had happened to Elspeth.

After he'd sent her upstairs, he sat down to write a letter to Cain. He described everything that had happened, even recording the exact words the groom had spoken, although he had never performed a more repugnant task.

"We can only pray that there will be no permanent consequences of your ward's promiscuity," he had concluded, refraining from suggesting that Cain find her a husband as soon as she returned to South Carolina. Whatever Baron Cain might be, he was not stupid. Woodward felt sure that within two weeks of the little harlot's return to Risen Glory, he would have given her away to the first man who looked in her direction.

Perhaps it was just as well Hamilton Woodward did not know that the day before the graduation ball Kit had received a terse letter from Baron Cain, the first he'd ever written her. The letter informed her that, as a result of her recent conduct, she was to remain in New York City for at least another year, taking up residence at the St. Nicholas Hotel with Miss Dorthea Pinckney Calhoun, a Southern lady who was currently living in New York City and had been highly recommended as a respectable chaperone by the Reverend Rawlins Cogdell. Under no circumstances was she to return to Risen Glory.

Throughout the first few dances, Kit had been well aware of Woodward's disapproving eye upon her, but she had refused to let him spoil her evening, concentrating instead on entertaining her partners with her own breathless style of Southern conversation, which she had discovered seemed to amuse them. Now, however, her partner was poor Hobart Cheney, who was barely capable of maintaining a conversation under the best of circumstances, let alone when he was counting so vigorously under his breath and trying to remember the dance steps. To address him now would be very unkind, and a Templeton girl was never unkind. Still, she wished she could chat with him so she could take her mind off Hamilton Woodward's baleful glances.

Damn that man to everlasting hell! Even as she thought of the evening on the beach at Long Branch, she could feel her cheeks grow hot. Couldn't he have seen that she was trying to escape that horrid groom, not encourage him?

In all fairness, she knew she was partly to blame for what had happened. One of the many lessons she had learned at the Templeton Academy was that ladies never went off by themselves, even in the broadest daylight, and certainly not late at night. But the prospect of being alone on the deserted beach with nothing but the sound of the surf and her own breathing to keep her company had been too delicious to resist. Still, as soon as she had seen the young groom scampering down the bluff to the beach, she should have known he had more on his mind than talking about horses as they had done that afternoon. But she had certainly not expected him to attack her!

She shivered involuntarily as she remembered his wet lips grinding away at her mouth like a pestle working against a mortar, the rough hand that had grabbed at her breasts. How surprised he had been when her fist had caught him hard in the belly, the blow giving her just enough time to get away from him. She wished she'd had a bullwhip!

So many times in the past few weeks, she'd told herself that it was all for the best, even that awful moment when she had realized that Hamilton Woodward actually believed the groom's obscene accusation and that there was nothing she could say to convince him that she was innocent. It would be all that much easier for her, she knew, when she and the man she had chosen arrived at Risen Glory to obtain Cain's permission to marry. Woodward's letter would take care of any possible objections Cain might raise. And then with her inheritance safely in her hands, she could set about the business of getting Risen Glory away from Baron Cain. Money was power. That was something else she'd learned at the Templeton Academy. Still, she could not help but chafe at the injustice of Hamilton Woodward serving as judge and jury, passing sentence on her without once considering that she might be telling the truth.

Her partner stumbled, and she quickly led him back into the steps, giving him a bright smile so he would not notice that he was actually following her. Poor Mr. Cheney, he would never know how close he had come to being her chosen husband. If he had been a trifle less intelligent beneath his stutterings and stumblings, she might have picked him. As it was, Bertrand Mayhew presented the better choice.

She glimpsed him standing off by himself near the orchestra, waiting for the first of two dances that she had promised him. She felt the familiar heaviness that always settled over her when she looked at him or spoke with him or, indeed, thought of him at all. He was not much taller than her own five feet five inches, with a receding hairline and a belly that was not receding but protruding, instead, below the waistband of his trousers like a woman's.

Perhaps it wasn't so unusual that Bertrand Mayhew had some womanly characteristics. At forty, he had lived all his life in the shadow of his mother, obeying her every wish, quaking beneath her commands. Now that she was dead, he was lost and desperately needed another woman to take her place. Kit had decided she would be that woman.

Elspeth was furious with her, of course, pointing out, quite logically, that Kit could have any one of a dozen eligible men, both young and old, who were not only much richer than Bertrand Mayhew but a hundred times less distasteful. Elspeth couldn't understand, no matter how often Kit tried to explain, that she wanted power from a marriage, not riches. A husband who expected her to behave like a properly submissive wife was of no use to her at all.

Kit didn't doubt for a moment that, as a wife, she could

wheedle dresses and bonnets by the dozens, even jewels if she desired them, from the men who seemed more than ready to offer for her. But she was also clear-sighted enough to know that nothing in her entire arsenal of tricks could convince any one of them, with the possible exception of Hobart Cheney and the definite exception of Bertrand Mayhew, to step down from his business and live permanently at Risen Glory. Certainly she could have convinced several of them to buy the plantation for her as a wedding present. But what good would it be to own Risen Glory if she had to live in New York City?

There was nothing for her to do but firmly suppress the part of her that wished she could find a husband who was a shade less repugnant and tell Bertrand Mayhew that she would marry him. Tonight, after the midnight supper, she would take him to the front reception room to show him the newest collection of stereoscopic views of Niagara Falls and then she would lead him to the question. It wouldn't be difficult. When it came to dealing with men, she had discovered that there was very little that was difficult. Within a month they would be on their way to Risen Glory.

She wasted no thought at all on the letter she had received from Baron Cain the day before, instructing her to remain in New York City. Her life was about to become her own, and she would never let him stand in her way again.

The music ended with a flourish, and instantly Bertrand Mayhew appeared at her side. "Miss—Miss Weston?" He pulled a handkerchief from his pocket and mopped his damp, pink brow as if he were the one who had just finished dancing. "I was wondering—That is to say, did you remember—"

"Why, if it isn't Mr. Mayhew." Kit tilted her head to the side and looked up at him through the thick veil of her lashes, a gesture she had practiced for so long under Elspeth's tutelage that it had now become second nature to her. "My dear, dear Mr. Mayhew. I was afraid—terrified, in fact—that you had forgotten me and gone off with one of the other young ladies."

Bertrand Mayhew was horrified. "Oh, my, no! Oh, Miss Weston, how could you ever imagine I would do something so ungentlemanly. Oh, my stars, no! My dear mother would never have—"

"Quite so." She excused herself prettily from Hobart Cheney

and then linked her arm through Mr. Mayhew's, not caring that the gesture was an overly familiar one for an unmarried woman to make to a man who was not a relative. "Now, now. No long face, you hear? I was only teasing."

"Teasing?" For a moment he looked as baffled as if she had just announced she was going to ride naked down Fifth Avenue, and then his thick lips twitched into a smile. "Ah, yes. Teasing."

Kit repressed a sigh. Just then the orchestra began to play a lively galop. Setting the palm of her left hand lightly on his fleshy shoulder, she led him into the dance, trying to shake off the overwhelming sense of depression that was settling around her.

They had circled the ballroom twice when she saw a man coming through the doorway on the arm of a woman several years older than he. There was something vaguely familiar about him that caught her attention and made her pulses quicken uncontrollably. By the time the couple had made their way to Mrs. Templeton to pay their respects, she had recognized him.

"Mr. Mayhew," she said weakly, "would you mind very much if we don't finish this dance? I—I would appreciate it if you would escort me over to Mrs. Templeton. She is speaking with someone I know. Someone I have not seen since I was a child."

The gentlemen from New York, Boston, Philadelphia, and Baltimore noticed that Kit had stopped dancing and was walking toward the doorway. They looked with interest and no small amount of envy at the man who had just entered the ballroom. What was it about the pale, thin stranger that had brought such an attractive flush to the cheeks of the elusive Miss Weston?

Chapter Twelve

Brandon Parsell, former cavalry officer in South Carolina's famous "Hampton's Legion," had something of the look of an artist about his pale, sensitive features, even though he was a planter by birth and knew nothing about art beyond the fact that he liked that fellow who painted horses. His hair was brown and straight, combed from a side part over a fine, well-molded brow. He had a neatly trimmed moustache and conservative side whiskers that ended just below his ears. His face was not the kind that inspired easy camaraderie with members of his own sex. None of the men present, for example, would have considered nudging Brandon Parsell in the ribs and inviting him to accompany them to Ida Thompson's fashionable bordello on Twelfth Street for whiskey and a tickle. It was, instead, a face that women liked, as it brought to mind novels about chivalry and called up memories of sonnets and odes to nightingales and Grecian urns.

The woman at his side was Eleanora Baird, the plain, somewhat overdressed niece of his employer. He acknowledged her introduction to Mrs. Templeton with a courtly bow and a well-chosen compliment. Listening to his easy Southern drawl, no one would have guessed at the loathing he felt for all of them: the glittering guests, the imposing hostess, even the Northern spinster whom duty required he escort that evening.

And then, from nowhere it seemed, he felt a sharp pang of homesickness, a yearning for the quiet night air of Holly Grove, his family's former home, a longing for the walled gardens of Charleston on a Sunday afternoon. There seemed to be no cause for the feeling, no reason for the crush of emotion that tightened his chest, no reason beyond the faint, sweet scent of Carolina jasmine borne on a rustle of white satin.

"Ah, Katharine, my dear," Mrs. Templeton called out in that strident Northern accent that jangled Brandon's ears. "I have someone I would like you to meet. A countryman of yours."

Slowly he turned his head toward the evocative jasmine perfume and, as quickly as a missed heartbeat, lost himself in the beautiful, willful face that met his gaze.

"Mr. Parsell and I are already acquainted"—she smiled—"although I can see by his expression that he doesn't remember me. Shame, Mr. Parsell. You've forgotten one of your most faithful admirers."

Although Brandon Parsell did not recognize the face, he knew the voice. He knew those gently blurred vowels and soft consonants as well as he knew the sound of his own breathing.

It was the voice of his mother and his aunts and his sisters. The voice that, for four long years, had soothed the dying and defied the Yankees and sent the gentlemen out to fight again. It was the voice that had gladly offered up brothers and husbands and sons to the Glorious Cause. It was the voice of all the gently bred women of the South. The voice that had cheered them on at Bull Run and Fredricksburg, the voice that had steadied them in those long weeks on the bluffs at Vicksburg, the voice that had cried bitter tears into lavender-scented handkerchiefs and then whispered "never mind" when they lost Stonewall Jackson at Chancellorsville. It was the voice that had spurred on Pickett's men in their desperate charge at Gettysburg, the voice they had heard as they lay dying in the mud at Chickamauga, and the voice they would not let themselves hear on that Virginia Palm Sunday when they surrendered their dreams at Appomattox Court House.

Yet, despite the voice, there was a difference in the woman who stood before him from the women who waited at home. The white satin ballgown she wore rustled with newness. It bore no marks of having been made over, no brooch artfully placed to conceal a darn that was almost, but not quite, invisible, no signs that a skirt originally designed to accommodate a hoop had been taken apart and reassembled to give a smaller, more fashionable silhouette. There was another difference, too, in the woman who stood before him from the women who waited at home. Her violet eyes did not seem to contain any secret, unspoken reproach.

When he finally found his voice, it sounded strange, as if it were somehow detached from his body. "I'm afraid you have the advantage, ma'am. It's hard for me to believe I could have forgotten such an unforgettable face, but if you say it's so, I'm not disputin' you, just beggin' your forgiveness for my poor memory and hopin' you'll enlighten me."

Elvira Templeton, accustomed to the plainer speech of Yankee businessmen, blinked twice in rapid succession before she remembered her manners. "Mr. Parsell, may I present Miss Katharine Louise Weston."

There was an awkward pause. Every inch a gentleman, Brandon Parsell was too well disciplined to let his shock show on his face, but even so, he could not seem to find the words to frame a proper response. Mrs. Templeton noticed that, for some reason, Kit Weston seemed amused. She continued with the amenities, introducing Miss Baird and, of course, Mr. Mayhew. As she finished, the orchestra began to play the first strains of the "Blue Danube" waltz.

Mr. Parsell turned to Mr. Mayhew. "Would you mind seeing that Miss Baird has a cup of punch, sir? She was just remarking that she was thirsty. Miss Weston, I believe this waltz is mine." It was an unforgivable breach of etiquette, but, for the first time in his life, he couldn't bring himself to care.

"Of course, Mr. Parsell." Kit smiled, presenting him with her gloved hand and wasting no thought at all on the young stockbroker to whom she had, only the day before, promised the first waltz.

They moved out onto the polished floor and into the steps of the dance without speaking. It was Brandon who finally broke the silence. "You've changed, Kit Weston. I don't believe your own mammy would recognize you."

"I never had a mammy, Brandon Parsell, as you very well know!"

He laughed aloud at her feistiness, not realizing until that moment how much he had missed talking to a woman whose spirit had not been broken, and then he pulled her closer into the circle of his arms. "Wait until I tell my mother and my sisters about you. We heard Major Cain had shipped you off to a school up North so he could have Risen Glory all to himself, but nobody knew what had happened to you after that. We don't talk to Major Cain, of course, and none of the hands workin' for him seems to know anything. Even Sophronia isn't sayin' much."

Kit did not want to talk about Cain or about Sophronia. "How are your mother and sisters?"

There was a nearly imperceptible clouding of Brandon's pleasant features. "As well as can be expected. We're livin' in Rutherford now. It's been hard on them, losin' Holly Grove. Watchin' the house set afire by the Yankees and then losin' the plantation because there was no money for taxes. I'm workin' at the bank now." His laugh was thin and self-deprecating. "A Parsell workin' in a bank. Times do change, don't they, Miss Kit Weston?"

Kit had been studying his face, taking in the clean, sensitive lines, observing the way his neatly trimmed moustache just brushed the strong upper curve of his lip, breathing in the faint smell of tobacco and bay rum that clung so pleasantly to him, but now she looked quickly down, not wanting him to see the pity she could feel welling up inside her.

Brandon Parsell and his sisters had been at the center of a carefree group of young people some six or seven years older than she, made up of the sons and daughters of the county's most influential families. As a child she had stood at the side of the road in her dusty britches and patched shirt and watched them ride by on horseback and in carriages to barbeques and balls and church socials, the young men carefree and handsome in their high-crowned hats and polished boots, the women beautiful in crinolined skirts, their pale complexions carefully shielded with beribboned parasols. And then, when the war had started, she had stood at the side of the road and watched the young men in their immaculate gray uniforms ride by on their way to Charleston.

The most splendid of them all had been Brandon Parsell, sitting on a horse as if he had been born in a saddle, wearing the gray uniform and plumed hat so proudly that her throat had congealed with fierce tears. To her, he had symbolized the spirit of the Confederate soldier, and she had yearned for nothing more than to follow him into battle and fight for the South at his side. Now Holly Grove lay in ruins and Brandon Parsell was working in a bank.

"What are you doing in New York, Mr. Parsell?" she asked, steering the conversation to a less painful topic and, at the same time, trying to steady herself against the faint giddiness that seemed to be attacking her knees.

"My employer sent me here to attend to the affairs of his widowed sister and her daughter, the young lady you just met. I'm returnin' home tomorrow."

"Your employer must think highly of you if he's willing to trust you with family affairs," Kit observed in a voice that was almost steady.

Again the self-deprecating sound that was nearly, but not quite, a laugh. "If you listen to my mother, she'll tell you that I am practically runnin' the Planters' and Citizens' Bank, but the truth is, anyone who can read could do my job. I hate to disillusion you, Miss Weston, but I'm little more than an errand boy."

"Oh, surely that's not so!"

"But it is," he insisted. "The South has been raised on self-delusion. Self-delusion is like mother's milk to us, the belief in our own superiority, our invincibility. Well, I, for one, have given up self-delusion. The South is not invincible, and neither am I."

The bitterness in his voice cut through her like the slicing edge of a knife, and she turned her head away, not wanting to hear any more from this man who outwardly appeared to be untouched by the war but who was so obviously scarred inside.

"You haven't been to Rutherford for at least three years, Kit," he continued more evenly. "Everything's different now. Carpetbaggers and scalawags are runnin' the state. Even though South Carolina's about to be readmitted to the Union, nothin's changed. Yankee soldiers still patrol the streets and look the other way when respectable citizens are accosted by riffraff. The state legislature's a joke, controlled by Northerners, illiterate Negras, and Southern Republicans." He spat out the last word as if it were snake venom, for the scalawags—white Southerners who had turned their backs on their own and joined the Republican party—were regarded with even more contempt than the Northerners who had flocked South after the war, carpetbags in hand.

"Livin' here in New York City, you can't have any idea what it's like," he concluded.

Although there was no trace of censure in his words, she felt unaccountably guilty, as if she were somehow shirking her duty. For three years she had devoured the newspapers, following every detail of the formation and implementation of the hateful Reconstruction Acts, keeping abreast of the bitter battle between Congress and the President, the battle that had culminated in the impeachment trial, ending just the day before with Congress failing by one vote to oust Andrew Johnson from office. But reading about what was happening was not the same as being there to live it, and she had never quite been able to shake the feeling that she was somehow betraying her homeland by deserting it to go to school in New York.

When the music ended, her guilt was replaced by a queer

mixture of regret and something very close to panic. She was not ready for the dance to be over. Not yet. Not before she'd had a chance to sort through the strange jumble of feelings Brandon Parsell's presence had provoked.

The couples around them were walking off the ballroom floor, but he made no move to release her. "I imagine you already have a partner for the supper dance."

She did. Bertrand Mayhew. "As a matter of fact, I do, Mr. Parsell. But as you're a neighbor and leaving New York tomorrow, I'm certain my partner will not object to stepping aside."

Without taking his eyes from hers, he lifted her hand and brushed the back of it with his lips. "Then he's a fool," he said softly.

It was not long after Brandon left her side to return to Miss Baird that Elspeth swooped down on her and dragged her to the upstairs sitting room that had been set aside for the ladies to tidy themselves.

"Who is he, Kit? All the girls are talking about him. Margaret said she overheard Mrs. Templeton say he's a neighbor of yours. Why haven't you told me about him? He's so handsome. He looks like a poet."

Kit hesitated, reluctant to talk about Brandon Parsell, even to Elspeth. Fortunately, at that moment Elspeth was distracted from her interrogation.

"Oh, look at your dress, Kit! Your bows are coming untied and you already have a spot on your skirt. Why can't you be tidier? Yesterday when you put out your hand to Fanny's mother, you had a hole in your best pair of gloves. And look at your hair. It's tumbling about as if it's never seen a brush." She pushed Kit down in front of a large mahogany-framed mirror and, snatching out the filigreed silver combs that she'd given Kit on her nineteenth birthday, she began to tidy the thick, dark curls. "I don't know why you wouldn't let me put your hair up in a chignon for tonight," she grumbled. "It looks so wild. Like you just stepped out of bed."

"For the same reason I wouldn't let you lace me into a corset," Kit retorted. "It makes me feel as if I'm suffocating. I want to be able to breathe. And when I dance, I like to feel my hair swinging against my neck and the tops of my shoulders."

Elspeth sighed as she replaced one of the silver combs. "I don't know why I bother to scold you. You should have been giving *me* lessons these past few years. You hardly do anything the way a young lady is supposed to, yet you have half the men in New York at your feet. Even Lilith doesn't have your following. I've just about made up my mind to be jealous and stop speaking to you."

For once Kit did not respond to her friend's bantering. Without knowing it, Elspeth had struck a sensitive nerve. She caught Elspeth's eyes in the mirror's reflection. "Everything isn't always what it seems," she said. "There's something not quite nice about the way some of them look at me, as if I'm not wearing any clothes. They don't look at you that way, or even Lilith, and she's such a flirt. I think there's a failing inside me."

Elspeth immediately wound her arms around her friend's shoulders, hugging her from behind. "Kit, don't talk that way, ever. There's nothing wrong with you. It's just that you're so beautiful, I don't think they can help it."

Kit squeezed Elspeth's hand and then jumped up from her chair and walked toward the door. "His name is Brandon Parsell, and he's taking me into supper."

"Supper?" Elspeth called out. "I thought Mr. Mayhew. . . ." But it was too late. Kit had already left.

Mrs. Templeton's staff had outdone themselves. The damask-covered buffet tables groaned beneath trays of ham and turkey and veal. A half-dozen white china platters banded in gold bore the most fashionable dish that could be served in New York that spring, canvasback duck. Oysters by the dozens quivered on sparkling beds of shaved ice. There were salads and cheeses, jellies and sorbets, and, amid the cakes and pastries, colorful Nesselrode puddings made with the finest cream.

On straight-backed chairs in the corner of the dining room, Kit and Brandon were laughing over a story he had just finished telling her. Throughout the midnight meal, Brandon had kept her entertained with lighthearted gossip and amusing tales of the people she had known since birth. She realized that there was a great deal he was not telling her, but she didn't press him. That could come later. For tonight, she wanted to laugh and dance and be happy.

She was already thinking about seeing him again, even

though she knew he was leaving for Rutherford the next day, even though she knew that she should be with Bertrand Mayhew at this very moment, showing him stereoscopic views of Niagara Falls and leading him to a proposal of marriage. But she couldn't seem to summon the will to excuse herself from the man who sat beside her, his hazel eyes filled with admiration as he gazed at her. He was so different from the Northern men she had met, soft-spoken and gallant, able to voice a compliment without stumbling over the words, yet thoroughly and unmistakably masculine, even as he balanced a white china punch cup on his knee.

A waiter came by for the second time with a tray of petits-fours and stopped in front of them. She started to reach for one and then caught herself just in time. Not only had she already had two, but she had also devoured every bite of the enormous quantity of food she had piled on her plate. If Elspeth had noticed—as most assuredly she had—Kit would be receiving another one of her friend's famous lectures in the morning.

"Ladies are supposed to eat sparingly. A morsel of this. A tiny sip of that. You eat like every bite of food is going to be your last, Kit Weston!"

Brandon took the accusingly empty plate from her and handed it, along with his own, to a second waiter. "I confess to enjoyin' a pipe after eatin'. Would you be agreeable to showin' me the garden? That is, of course, if you don't mind the smell of tobacco."

"I'd be happy to, Mr. Parsell." Kit smiled, rising from her chair and taking his arm as he led her toward the doors that had been left open at the end of the dining room and out into a small brick-walled garden. "And no, I don't mind tobacco at all," she continued. "When I was younger, I even smoked it myself." No sooner had the impulsive words left her mouth than she wished she could snatch them back.

Brandon frowned slightly. "As I recall, your childhood was an unfortunate one, best forgotten." And then the frown disappeared and admiration took its place. "It's truly amazin' how well you've managed to overcome the adversity of your upbringin'. But then, you're a plucky little woman, aren't you? Otherwise you wouldn't have been able to live for so long with these Yankees."

"They're not all bad, Brandon," she responded, thinking of Elspeth and Fanny and even Mrs. Templeton.

He led her toward the brick path that skirted the edge of the garden, its ruddy surface just visible in the flickering multicolored light of the gay paper lanterns that had been strung in a haphazard zig-zag over their heads. "Have you made a lot of friends while you've been here?"

There was something about his question that did not sound like a casual inquiry. "No," she replied. "I wouldn't say I've made a lot. Too many of the girls lost relatives in the war. But I do have a few."

"And what about the Yankee gentlemen? Are any of them your friends?"

She hesitated. "I have acquaintances."

"No proposals of marriage?" he asked.

"Let's just say that I haven't let it go that far."

They walked in silence for a moment before Brandon spoke. "I'm glad."

Without quite knowing how it happened, they were standing still. Gently he clasped her shoulders and turned her toward him. She felt the whisper of a breeze ruffling her hair. The paper lanterns fluttered, casting first green and then blue shadows across his cheek. He was going to kiss her. She knew it would happen, just as she knew she would let him.

She gazed up at him openly, surveying the mouth that, any second now, was going to claim hers, sliding her eyes across the full upper lip and the shorter lower one. They were moist and slightly parted, revealing the bottom edge of two front teeth that, from such a close vantage point, she could see were endearingly crooked.

Slowly his head began to dip. Her eyelids fluttered closed, anticipating the intimacy that, up until that moment, she had only thought of with revulsion. She felt the warmth of skin drawing nearer to skin and then heard the sound of a muffled exclamation as, abruptly, his hands released her.

"Forgive me." His words were queerly strangled.

Her eyes flew open. "What's wrong?"

"I apologize. I—I nearly forgot myself."

"You were going to kiss me," Kit stated frankly.

Abruptly he turned away from her. "I'm ashamed to admit

it's all I've been able to think about since I first set eyes on you. A man who presses his attentions on a lady is no gentleman."

Kit was thoughtful. "Doesn't it make a difference whether the lady is willing or not?"

He turned back to her, something strangely tender in his expression. "Oh, Kit, you're so innocent and trustin'. You don't know much of the ways of men, do you?"

"I think I do. Except for Sophronia, I was practically raised by men. The ones at the sawmill and on the plantation, at least. They taught me how to shoot, how to ride, how to do most everything that's useful."

"It's hardly the same thing." Brandon frowned. "Listen to me, Kit. You mustn't let any man, even myself, take advantage of you."

"Is a kiss 'taking advantage'?"

"Kisses lead to greater liberties, I'm afraid."

She could feel herself flush as memories of Eve's Shame and the terrifying lecture she had heard only a few weeks before welled up inside her. As if sensing her dismay, Brandon reached inside his pocket for a pipe and a worn leather tobacco pouch. He refilled the wooden bowl, tamping it down with his thumb, then he walked over to the brick wall and leaned gracefully back against it, the pipe cupped in his hand.

"I don't know how you've been able to stand livin' in this city," he said. "Even this garden doesn't really smell like a garden. The fumes from the factories and the garbage from the streets overpower everything. It's not much like Risen Glory, is it?"

"I hardly notice it anymore," Kit admitted, sitting down on a narrow iron bench not far from where he was standing. "But it took me a long time to get used to it. Sometimes I thought I'd die of homesickness."

"Poor Kit. You've had a rough time of it, haven't you?"

Surprisingly she could feel her eyes misting at the gentleness in his tone, and she fought against her weakness. "I haven't had it as bad as some. Not as bad as you, Brandon. At least Risen Glory is still standing."

"Risen Glory," Brandon said. "It's a fine plantation. Always has been. I'll say this for your daddy—he might not have had much sense where womenfolk were concerned, but he sure knew how to run a plantation." There was a hollow, hissing sound as he drew on his pipe only to discover that it had gone out. He relit it and then, after a moment's pause, walked over to her. "I'm going to tell you something I've never told another livin' soul."

"What's that?" She pulled her skirts aside and he sat down next to her.

"I used to have a secret hankerin' after Risen Glory," he confessed. "Risen Glory's a better plantation than Holly Grove ever was. The land's always been better. It's a cruel twist of fate that the best plantation in the county is in the hands of a Yankee."

"I'm going to get it back, Brandon," she said quietly, absent-mindedly running her finger along the cold underside edge of the bench.

His voice was suddenly weary and old. "Kit, don't make the same mistake all the others are makin'. Remember what I said about self-delusion."

"It's not self-delusion," she responded sharply. "I've learned about money since I've been in the North, Brandon. Money is the equalizer. It gives people power. Money is spoken about openly here; it's not like in the South. I have money, Brandon. At least I will have whenever I decide to marry. And I'm going to buy Risen Glory back from Baron Cain."

For a moment he said nothing. Another couple entered the garden and began to stroll down the opposite border. He watched them thoughtfully. "It's going to take a lot of money," he said. "Baron Cain has some crazy idea about spinnin' his own cotton right there at Risen Glory. He's begun buildin' a mill on the northeast corner of the plantation, right alongside the county road. Steam engine came just last month from Cincinnatuh."

This was news she hadn't heard, but she couldn't think about it now. "I'll have fifteen thousand dollars, Brandon."

"Fifteen thousand!" In a land that had been stripped of everything, it was a fortune. And then, abruptly, he was on his feet. "You shouldn't have told me that," he said, almost harshly.

"Why not?"

Instead of answering, he put out his hand and drew her somewhat abruptly to her feet. "I'll take you back inside now."

"Now?" She pulled back sharply. "Tell me what you mean."

He tapped the bowl of his pipe on the bottom of his shoe, stalling for time. "All right," he said finally. "I admire you, Kit. I was hopin' that after you returned to Risen Glory, I could call on you and we could get to know each other better. But what you've told me casts a shadow over my motivations, don't you see?"

Kit, whose own motivations were so very much more shadowy than his, nearly laughed. "Don't be a goose, Brandon. You're far more a gentleman than I am a lady. I could never doubt your motivations. And, yes, you may call on me at Risen Glory. I intend to return just as soon as I can make the arrangements."

As quickly as that, she had made her decision. She couldn't marry Bertrand Mayhew, not just yet anyway. And she didn't care what Cain had written in his letter. She was going back to Risen Glory as soon as possible.

That night, just before she fell asleep, she told herself that she wasn't taking all that great a risk. If things didn't work out, she could always write Bertrand and ask him to come for her. But first she had to give herself a little time. After three years, what did another few weeks matter? The dream of having both Risen Glory and Brandon Parsell was suddenly too wonderful for her to set aside lightly.

Part Three

A SOUTHERN LADY

"We boil at different degrees."
Ralph Waldo Emerson, *Eloquence*

Chapter Thirteen

Sophronia sat at the small mahogany desk inlaid with holly that stood in the corner of the sun-drenched rear sitting room at Risen Glory. She studied the list she had just completed, checking it against menus for the next three weeks that she had laboriously written out in her uneven scrawl. She was going to need sugar and more salt, and they were nearly out of flour. She didn't usually let supplies run so low, but then she'd had a lot on her mind lately.

She had dreamed about Kit again last night. It was nearly three years since they'd last seen each other. Kit hadn't even bothered to write her for over a year now. Sophronia toyed with the silver inkwell in front of her. Somehow they managed to quarrel, even in letters. You'd think she would be happy to hear how well Risen Glory was doing under Baron Cain's management.

Falling victim to the restlessness that had been plaguing her for weeks, she got up from the desk and began wandering around the comfortable rear sitting room, taking in the new rose damask upholstery on the settee and the blue-and-white Delft tiles that bordered the fireplace, their illustrations of Adam and Eve in the Garden of Eden finally freed of the accumulated grime of Rosemary Weston's indifferent housekeeping. Idly she straightened one panel of the white lace curtains that hung at the windows.

The sitting room shone with beeswax, fresh paint, and care, as did each room of the house. Her touch was everywhere, from the dining room, where she had pushed the other servants aside and cleaned the hand-painted Chinese wallpaper herself with bread crusts, to the master bedroom with its cool green walls and richly striped silk bed hangings, taken down only the month before and replaced with gossamer-thin mosquito netting for the summer. Risen Glory had never looked better, and it was all because of her.

Sometimes she hated herself for working so hard to make this house beautiful again. Working her fingers to the bone for a white man, just as if there'd never been a war and she was still a slave. And then she'd go into Rutherford and hear all the white ladies talking about how lazy the niggers were now that they were free. She didn't know what it was to be lazy! She'd been working for as long as she could remember, picking cotton in the fields when she couldn't have been more than four years old and then working here in the big house since she'd been six or seven.

Now she was the housekeeper, having taken over the job three years ago at Baron Cain's request. She had discovered almost immediately that he expected the house to be clean and comfortable but would not be bothered with the details of how it was done. For this, he paid her a generous twenty-five dollars a month, far more than any other housekeeper she knew of. But despite the money, and despite the pride she could not seem to help but take in doing a good job, Sophronia was far from satisfied.

Deliberately she turned toward her reflection in the gilt pier glass that hung between the room's two windows. She knew she had never looked better. She wore her waist-length black hair pulled severely away from her face and smoothly coiled high on the back of her head, allowing not even a single silky tendril to escape and curl around the sharply chiseled bones of her face. The severe hairstyle added to her already considerable height of nearly six feet, and that pleased her. With her exotically slanted golden eyes and her pale caramel skin, she looked like one of the young Amazons pictured in a book she kept in her bedroom.

Only her dress irritated her. She had made it herself, and it was pretty enough with its pale-peach gingham fabric and moss-green ribbons at the throat and sleeves, but it wasn't what she wanted for herself. She didn't want to wear homemade gingham dresses, no matter how skillfully constructed. She wanted to be able to visit the best dressmaker in Charleston and have gowns especially designed to complement her exotic beauty. She wanted perfumes and silks, champagne and crystal. But most of all, she didn't want to run white folks' houses anymore. She wanted to run her own, one of those small pastel houses in Charleston with a maid to tend her and a butler to answer the door. She would have had it by now, too, if it hadn't been for Magnus Owen.

As always, at the thought of Risen Glory's overseer, Sophronia's beautiful features hardened. He had spoiled it all for her. If it hadn't been for him, she would be Baron Cain's mistress by now instead of his housekeeper, and she would have her pastel residence in Charleston.

She walked over to the desk, picked up the list she had just made, and then closed the lid with a satisfactory bang. Damn his soul! Following her everywhere with those dark eyes of his. Sometimes looking at her like he felt sorry for her. Sweet, blessed Jesus! If that wasn't enough to make her laugh! Magnus Owen, who had wanted her so badly from the first moment he laid eyes on her that he might as well have been wearing a sign around his neck, having the gall to feel sorry for her!

It was laughable, really, for him to even imagine she would let him touch her. Magnus Owen, or any other black man for that matter. She had worked too hard for that, grooming herself, studying those around her, modifying her speech until she could make herself sound almost like the white ladies in Rutherford. Soon now she was going to have everything she wanted —the house, the rich gowns, the maid—and she was going to earn it in the only way she could, satisfying a white man's lust.

At the thought, an involuntary shudder swept through her body and an image of pale white limbs wrapping themselves around her flailing golden brown ones assaulted her. Just then the door of the sitting room swung open and Magnus Owen stepped into the room.

The three years he had spent as Risen Glory's overseer had wrought subtle changes in Magnus. The muscles beneath his soft butternut shirt and dark-brown trousers were sleek and hard. Although his build was as slim as ever, there was a taut wiriness about it now that had been lacking before. His face was still smooth and handsome, looking younger than its twenty-seven years, but now, as happened whenever he was in Sophronia's presence, there were subtle lines of tension etching his features.

"I heard you wanted to see me," he said. "Is somethin' wrong?"

"No, nothin's wrong, Magnus," Sophronia replied, a deliberate note of condescension in her voice. "I understand you're goin' into town later this afternoon, and I wanted you to pick up some supplies for me." She walked over to him, her skirts swaying gracefully as she moved, and extended the list.

Magnus snatched it from her, making no effort to hide his irritation. "You mean to tell me you called me in from the fields just so I could be your errand boy? Why didn't you send Jacob for this or wait until this afternoon when I came in?"

"I didn't think about it," she said innocently, perversely glad that she had been able to ruffle Magnus's even temper. "Besides, Jacob is busy cleanin' vegetables for dinner."

Magnus's jaw tightened. "And I suppose cleanin' vegetables is more important than takin' care of the cotton that's supportin' this plantation?"

Sophronia arched one finely shaped brow. "My, my. You do have a high opinion of yourself, don't you, Magnus Owen? You think this plantation's goin' fall apart, just 'cause the overseer had to come in from the fields for a few minutes?"

A tiny vein began to throb at the side of Magnus's forehead, more in response to her patronizing manner than to her deliberate breach of the unwritten rules of plantation hierarchy. He lifted one work-roughened hand and splayed it on his hip. "You got some airs about you, woman, that are gettin' mighty unpleasant. Somebody needs to take you down a peg or two before you get yourself in real trouble."

"Well, that somebody sure 'nuff won't be you." Sophronia smirked, lifting her chin in the air and sweeping past him into the hallway.

Magnus's hand whipped out and caught her arm. Sophronia gave a small gasp of alarm as he pulled her back into the parlor and slammed the door shut. "Thas right," he drawled softly, in the sweet, liquid tones of his plantation childhood. "I keeps fo'gettin' Miz Sophronia too good for the res' of us po' black folk."

Her golden eyes sparked with anger at his mockery of her, an emotion that slowly changed to apprehension as Magnus pressed her body up against the back of the door with his own.

"Let me go!" she cried, shoving her hands against his chest. But even though they were the same height, he was much stronger and she might as well have been trying to move an oak tree with a puff of thistledown. He pushed his narrow hips against her dress until the heat of him seemed to burn through her skirt and petticoats into her very flesh.

"Magnus, let me go!" There was an edge of panic to her plea.

But he had been goaded by her once too often, and even patient men can be pushed to impatience. He pinned her shoulders to the door behind her with the palms of his hands, not holding her hard enough to hurt her, just firmly enough to keep her still so he could have his say.

"Miz Sophronia thinks jes' cause she act like she white, dat she gwine wake up some mornin' an' find out she *is* white," he taunted. "Den she don' eber half to talk to none of us black folk again, 'ceptin' maybe to gib us orders."

With a sob she turned her head away from him and pressed her eyes closed, trying to shut out his scorn. But Magnus was not finished with her. He continued, his voice softer but his words no less wounding. "If Miz Sophronia only white, den she don' eber half to worry none 'bout no black man wan' to take her in his arms and make her his woman and hab chillun by her. She don' half to worry none 'bout no black man wantin' to sit by her an' hold her when she feel lonesome, an' grow old lyin' in a big ole feather bed right next to her. No, Miz Sophronia don' half to worry 'bout none of dat. She too fine for all dat. She too *white* for all dat!"

"Stop it!" Sophronia screamed, lifting her hands and pressing them over her ears to shut out his cruel words.

Magnus eased his own hands from her shoulders, suddenly ashamed of the pain he was causing her. He stepped back, freeing her body, but she did not move. She stood frozen in position, her spine rigid, her hands pressed to her ears. Only the tears coursing down her cheeks gave evidence that she was a woman made of flesh and blood and not some incredibly lifelike statue.

With a muffled groan, Magnus took the stiff body in his arms and began stroking her back, crooning softly into her ear. "There now, girl. S'all right. I'm sorry I made you cry. Last thing I want in this world is to hurt you. There now, everything's goin' be all right."

Gradually the tension ebbed from her body, and for a moment she sagged against him. And then her pride returned and, with it, an anger directed as much at her own weakness as it was at him. She jerked away, proud and haughty despite the tears that still coursed down her cheeks.

"You got no right to talk to me like that. You don't know me, Magnus Owen. You just think you do."

But Magnus had his own pride. "I know you got nothin' but smiles for any rich white man looks your way, but you won't even spare a glance for a black man looks in your direction."

"What can a black man give me?" she snarled, standing in the center of the room, her hands balled into tight fists at her side. "Black man got no power, Magnus! My mother, my grandmother, her mother before her—they all loved black men, and their men loved them right back. But when the white man came skulkin' through the door of their cabins at midnight, weren't one of those black men could stop him from havin' her, weren't one of those black men could keep his children from bein' sold away, weren't one of those black men could do more than stand by and watch when the woman he loved was tied naked to a post and whipped until her back ran red with blood. Don't you talk none to me 'bout black men!"

Magnus took a step toward her, his arms reaching out with a will of their own only to return to his sides as she jerked away from his touch, walked to the window, and turned her back to him. "Times are different now, Sophronia," he said gently. "The war's over. You're not a slave any longer. We're all free. Things have changed. We can vote."

"You're a fool, Magnus! You think just 'cause the white man says you can vote, things goin' be any different? It don't mean nothin'."

"Yes, it does! You're an American citizen now. You're protected by the laws of this country."

"Protected!" Sophronia's voice dripped with scorn, and her spine stiffened with contempt. "There's no protection for a black woman 'cept what she makes for herself!"

"By sellin' her body to any rich white man who comes along? Is that how?" he growled.

She whirled around, lashing out at him with her sharp, punishing tongue. "You tell me what else a black woman has to barter with? Men been usin' our bodies for centuries and givin' us nothin' in return for it 'cept a passel of children we couldn't protect. Well, I want more than that, and I'm goin' have it, too.

I'm goin' have me a house and clothes and fine food. And I'm goin' be *safe!*"

Her words were like knife wounds, leaving him feeling helpless and emasculated. "Sellin' yourself into another kind of slavery," he accused. "Is that how you're goin' get your safety?"

Sophronia's eyes did not waver as they bore into his. "It's not slavery when I choose the master and set the terms. And you know as well as I do that I'd have it all by now if it wasn't for you."

Magnus shook his head. "The major wasn't goin' give you what you wanted, Sophronia."

"You're wrong," she declared haughtily. "He would of give me anything I asked for if you hadn't spoiled it all."

Magnus began to wander aimlessly about the light-splashed sitting room trying to frame his thoughts. He finally stopped and rested his hand on the carved back of the rose damask settee.

"There's no man in the world I respect more than Baron Cain," he said. "He saved my life, and I guess I'd do about anything he asked me. He's fair and honest, and every man who works for him knows it. He never asks anybody to do anything he hasn't done himself. The men admire him for that, and so do I. But he's a hard man with women, Sophronia. I never saw one yet could bring him to heel."

"He wanted me, Magnus," Sophronia insisted. "If you hadn't bust in on us that night, he would of give me whatever I asked for."

Slowly Magnus walked toward her. When he reached her, he put out his hand and, with his index finger, lightly traced a path across the top of her shoulder and down the curve of her arm. Instinctively she recoiled, although the feeling of it was strangely pleasant.

"And if he had," Magnus asked, "would you been able to hide that shiver that comes over you every time a man so much as touches your arm? Even though he's rich and good-lookin' and white, would you been able to forget that he's also a man?"

Magnus had struck too close to the nightmare shadows that lurked in the dark corners of her soul and haunted her dreams. She turned away from him and blindly made her way toward the desk, where she took a deep breath, struggling for control.

When she was finally sure she could speak without her voice betraying her, she turned back to him and said coldly, "If there's nothin' else, I got work to do. If you won't get the supplies for me, I'll send Jacob to town."

For a moment Magnus considered trying once again to pierce through the shell she had so swiftly rebuilt around herself, his beautiful, sad Sophronia. But then he knew he couldn't bear hurting her again.

"I'll get your supplies for you," he said brusquely, and turning on his heel, he left the room.

Sophronia stared at the vacant doorway. For a brief instant, she was filled with an overpowering longing to fling herself after him, and then, just as quickly, the impulse was gone. Magnus Owen was her enemy. She could never let herself lose sight of that fact. It was he who had kept her from becoming Baron Cain's mistress. She wandered over to the window and absentmindedly outlined the center pane with an almond-shaped fingernail as the memory of that winter night swept over her.

From the very beginning there had been an awareness between herself and the master of the house, a charged tension that both pleased and frightened her. She let her hips sway seductively whenever she walked by him, forced her breasts to brush against his upper arm as she set food before him, watched him with moist lips and inviting eyes, practiced every one of the tricks she had made herself learn. And through it all, she had managed to ignore Magnus Owen standing off to one side whenever he saw them together, watching her with eyes that seemed to pierce into the farthest reaches of her soul.

Cain had been at Risen Glory for nearly six months when it happened. It was mid-February, a rainy wintry night with howling gusts of wind sweeping down the chimneys and rattling the shutters. After dinner she had gone to the library, first stopping outside the door and making herself unfasten the top buttons of her dress so that the creamy swells of her breasts were exposed before she entered the room.

Cain looked up from the desk where he was busy with the plantation's calf-bound ledgers. She could still remember the way he had watched her as she had walked toward him, her body moving with languid sensuality, a silver tray bearing a bottle of brandy and a single glass on her upraised palm. She remembered the sight of his rugged, long-limbed frame slowly uncoiling from the leather chair behind the desk, the way he had walked toward her like a great, golden lion.

She had deliberately led him to that moment, but as he took the tray from her and set it down on the edge of the desk, she began to feel the familiar stirrings of panic. There was something even more frightening about this man than other men, something hard and dangerous. The scarred hand with its long, tapered fingers reached out and closed around her shoulder. The unmarred hand, bronzed by the Carolina sun and ironically darker than her own pale-caramel flesh, cupped her chin. His head dipped slowly toward her, but in the instant before his lips could lay claim, they both heard a small intrusive sound behind them. They turned their heads together to see that the library door was open.

As long as she lived, she would never forget the sight of Magnus's smooth features transformed by rage into an ugly stone mask as he saw her standing ready to submit to Cain's embrace. Even now she could hear the rumble deep in his throat as he charged into the room and threw himself at the man he had always regarded as a friend, the man who had once saved his life.

The suddenness of the attack took Cain by surprise, and Magnus caught him hard in the jaw with his fist. Cain staggered backward, barely managing to keep his balance. With finely honed reflexes, he recovered, splaying his legs and bracing himself for Magnus's assault.

She watched in horrified fascination as Magnus came at him, swinging his fists with deadly purpose. But Cain refused to fight him. He sidestepped and lifted his arms to block the blows. Magnus swung again and again, but Cain made no attempt to return the punishment, concentrating instead on using his forearms to deflect Magnus's fury.

Gradually Magnus's blows lost their force as some semblance of sanity returned to him. Finally his arms sagged to his sides, and he stood before Cain, his forehead beaded with sweat, his chest heaving with exertion.

Cain lowered his own arm and looked deep into Magnus's tortured eyes. Then he gazed across the room at Sophronia. Slowly he bent over to right a chair that had been upended in the struggle. "You'd better get some sleep, Magnus," he said gruffly. "We have a big day ahead of us tomorrow. You can go, Sophronia. I won't be needing you anymore." The careful way he spoke those final words left no doubt about his meaning.

That had been the end of it. She could not believe that he didn't turn Magnus over to the law for hitting a white man or, at the very least, fire him, but the next day as she rode into town in the buggy, she saw them silently working side by side, clearing brush from one of the fields. As far as she knew, they never spoke of the incident at all, but even so, some uniquely masculine kind of understanding seemed to have passed between them.

In the following weeks, she had tried to hint to Cain that Magnus had no hold on her, but it was as if he did not hear her words, and since that time he had distanced her by treating her with formal courtesy.

All of it had happened more than two years ago, and yet she was still at Risen Glory, still wearing gingham dresses and working as a housekeeper. She could not go on like this much longer. Somewhere there had to be a white man other than Baron Cain whose touch did not make her skin crawl. She was twenty-two years old. It was time she began living her life.

She thought of James Spence, the ruddy-faced Northerner who was mining phosphate to the south of town. He had made it clear to her that he was not averse to using some of his profits to make her happy. He was clean and rich and he could give her what she wanted. She was going to have to make up her mind soon.

She released the edge of the curtain she had been holding between her fingers and stepped back from the window. After Kit came home, then she would decide.

She smiled wryly to herself at the thought of seeing Kit again, and felt some of the chill lift from her for the first time in weeks. The major might think that just because he'd written a letter saying Kit was to stay in New York for another year, she'd stay, but Sophronia knew her too well. That girl would be back to Risen Glory before the month was over. And as far as she was concerned, it was about time, too.

Chapter Fourteen

The elegantly dressed young woman seemed out of place in the shabby hired carriage with its water-stained upholstery and stale smell of old tobacco and Macassar oil. She was dressed in a dove-gray gown with soft rose piping at the waist and hem and a row of rose pearl buttons down the sleeves. A waterfall of pale-gray lace threaded with rose ribbon cascaded from the base of her slim throat, emphasizing the firm, round swelling of her breasts.

Her dark hair was dressed simply, almost severely, in the Spanish style—parted at the center and pulled back into an elegant coil at the nape of her neck. Wispy tendrils curled at her temples and over the front of her ears, brushing the tiny drops of jet that hung from her shell-like lobes.

On her head perched a small hat in the same soft rose shade as the piping on her gown. A fluffy gray plume curled down from the brim, its tip ending level with the left edge of her brow. Of the face beneath the hat, only a moist red mouth was visible, for the rest of the woman's features were covered by a black veil as light as a spider's web with tiny, sparkling dew drops of jet clinging to its honeycombed surface.

Although the features beneath the veil were obscured, it was still possible to see that the face was a beautiful one, possessing a high, smooth brow, a small, straight nose, and a pair of luminous violet eyes. What was not so evident was her impatience with this last leg of the long journey she had begun several days before and her longing to have some respite from the incessant chatter of her traveling companion.

"I declare, Katharine Louise, my throat is so parched, I can't seem to think of anything but a cool glass of lemonade. My Darcy used to make the best lemonade. Just that little hint of tartness that makes it refreshin'. Are you parched, too, darlin'?"

Kit repressed a sigh and reached down to smooth out her skirt. This was one day of her life when she was determined not to appear disheveled. "It won't be much longer, Miss Dolly," she reassured the older woman. "Risen Glory is only a few miles from here, and I'll have someone make you a nice glass of lemonade as soon as we arrive."

"Not too much sugar, you hear? I don't like it with too much sugar."

"Yes, Miss Dolly." Kit shifted her weight slightly so that her back was turned toward her companion, shutting off further conversation. She fixed her gaze firmly out the window on the familiar landscape passing by. Traveling with Dorthea Pinckney Calhoun had proved to be more than a little trying.

As soon as Kit had made her decision to return to South Carolina, she had realized that she must bring a suitable chaperone with her. Staying at Risen Glory while Baron Cain was in residence, with no one but the servants to provide respectability, would cause gossip, and she was not going to give him any excuse to send her away from her own home. And so she had gone to the St. Nicholas Hotel and called on Dorthea Calhoun, the companion whose name and address had been so conveniently provided by Cain's letter. It had not been difficult to convince Miss Calhoun that there had been a change of plans and that the two of them were to return to South Carolina. The older woman was more than delighted. She was a Southerner, born and bred, and her stay in the North as companion to a distant cousin had left her both unhappy and frightened.

Never had a woman been more appropriately named than Dolly Calhoun. With her tiny stature and her faded blond corkscrew curls, she resembled nothing so much as an aged china doll, an impression that her mode of dress further emphasized. Although she had celebrated several birthdays since her fiftieth, she favored frilly white gowns with pastel sashes and wide skirts beneath which she never wore any fewer than eight whispering petticoats. She was a natural coquette, looking out at the world through teacup-blue eyes and batting the lashes of her wrinkled eyelids at any man she judged to be a gentleman. She always seemed to be in motion. Her hands in their lacy fingerless mitts fluttered, her faded curls bobbed like tiny springs, her ribbons and sashes and fringes were never still, and when something upset her, her tiny cupid's-bow mouth quivered like a baby's. Her bonnets were as frivolous as her dresses and, like her dresses, showed signs of having been made over more than once.

But Dolly Calhoun bore her poverty with gentility. She smelled of sweet lavender talcum powder and the peppermint drops she loved to suck. She talked of cotillions and cough remedies and a set of porcelain temple dogs that had disappeared along with her girlhood. She was sweet and harmless, more than a little annoying, and, as Kit quickly discovered, slightly mad. Unable to accept the defeat of her glorious Confederacy, she had permitted herself the small luxury of slipping ever so slightly back in time so that she could forever live in those first days of the war when hopes were high and thoughts of defeat unthinkable.

In the beginning her habit of referring to events that had happened seven years before as if they were occurring that very day had been unnerving to Kit, but gradually she was coming to accept Miss Dolly's genteel madness as her way of coping with a life over which she had lost control. Kit thought of Brandon Parsell and his assertion that the South had been raised on self-delusion. It was true of Miss Dolly, perhaps even of Brandon himself, but it was certainly not true of her. She knew exactly what she wanted from life, and she was going to get it, too.

It was because of this very determination to control her own life that her attraction to Brandon worried her. She must never let her emotions cloud her judgment, as she had seen happen to so many of the girls at the academy the moment they were attracted to a young man. Still, she could not honestly say she regretted her decision to come South without Bertrand Mayhew's marriage proposal. The possibility of being able to substitute Brandon Parsell for the unfortunate Mr. Mayhew had been irresistible. She wouldn't let herself act foolishly, however. If Brandon showed the smallest sign of posing a threat to her wishes to buy Risen Glory, she would cut him out of her life as cleanly as a diseased limb from a tree. She would let nothing get in her way. As much as she was attracted to him, she had to remember that he was merely a means to an end for her.

The carriage tilted sideways as it swung into the long, winding drive that led to Risen Glory, and Kit could feel her whole body grow tense with anticipation. After three years, she was finally home again. She noticed at once that the two deep grooves that had rutted the drive for as long as she could remember had been leveled and the surface spread with fresh gravel. The weeds and undergrowth had also been cut back, making the road wider than she recalled. Only the trees seemed to have resisted change, remaining just as she remembered them —an undisciplined assortment of buckthorn and oak, blackgum and sycamore, here and there a persimmon, bearing only a promise of the heavy russet fruit it would drop after the first frost. In a moment they would round the final curve, and she would be able to see the house set against the great, moss-draped live oaks with the low, spreading branches that she had spent her childhood climbing and swinging from and, occasionally, using as a hiding place from her stepmother's wrath.

But when the carriage finally cleared the trees and rounded the bend, Kit did not even glance at the house, for something far more important had caught her attention. Beyond the gentle slope of the lawn at the front of the house, beyond the orchard and the outbuildings, beyond the house itself, stretching as far as her eyes could view, were the fields of Risen Glory, fields looking as she had not seen them since the days before the war. The plowed ground was covered with long, seemingly endless rows of young cotton plants, stretching across the rich, dark soil like narrow green ribbons.

She abruptly banged her fist on the roof of the carriage, startling Dolly Calhoun so that the older woman let go of the peppermint drop she had been about to slip into her mouth and lost it in the frilly white folds of her dress. The driver brought the horses to a halt. Without waiting for him to climb down and open the door for her, Kit jumped out and waved him on to the house.

As the carriage pulled off, she slowly walked away from the drive and climbed the gentle rise of a grassy hillock. Then she lifted the veil that covered her face, pushing it up on the small brim of her hat so she could have an unrestricted view of the fields and the new life they contained.

She judged the plants to be about six weeks old. The seedlings had probably been thinned several weeks earlier, at least if he knew his business they had. Although she was not close enough to see for certain, the plants should already be covered with tight buds, buds that in another few weeks would open into creamy four-petaled flowers that looked like small hollyhocks, the flowers that would give birth to the cotton bolls.

She lifted her gloved hand, shading her eyes from the late-afternoon sun, and slowly turned her head, taking it all in. Even under her father's efficient management, she could not remember Risen Glory having looked like this. The outbuildings that had been destroyed by the Yankees had all been rebuilt, as had the building where the plantation's cotton was ginned. There was a new whitewashed fence around the paddock. Off to the northeast she could see a freshly plowed field in an area that had once held scrub. Everything about the plantation looked well tended and prosperous.

Her gaze finally came to rest on the house from which she had been exiled at so young an age. It was both the same and different. The front of the house still bowed out in the same graceful arch. The color had not changed; it was the exact shade of warm cream that she remembered, slightly tinted now by rose colored light as the sun settled lower in the sky.

But there were differences. Even from the distance, she could see that the house had an air of being cared for that it had formerly lacked. The red tile roof seemed to have been repaired near the twin chimneys where the tiles had come off, the shutters and front door had received a fresh coat of shiny black paint, the glass in the windows sparkled clean, like sunlight on a still summer pond.

How different it all was from what she had seen on her long journey south. From the dirty window of the train, she had gazed out on a land stripped of its wealth, on houses that were only shells, on broken wagons and rusted plows, on bony horses with drooping heads and cows whose udders hung empty. Fields that in the early days of June should have been green and bursting with new growth lay uncultivated. Amid such devastation, Risen Glory stretched in front of her, an oasis of beauty and prosperity.

The changes should have gratified her, offering as they did indisputable proof that Risen Glory had been tenderly cared for in her absence. But the emotion that surged through her bore no resemblance at all to gratitude. If at that moment she had been called upon to put a label to the sickness that gnawed at her insides as she stood staring out at her home from the grassy hillock, she would have identified it as anger. However, it wasn't really anger that coursed through her proud young body. Instead, it was a deep and bitter jealousy, the jealousy of one who has been absent from a child or business or home for some period of time, only to return, expecting disaster, and find that all had flourished during the absence with more health and vigor and speed than would have been possible had the owner been present. It was a bitter pill, but by refusing to give it a name, Kit escaped swallowing it.

She settled the delicately beaded veil back over her face and walked determinedly toward the house with her characteristic long stride, moving too quickly to be considered truly ladylike, but still undeniably graceful. The door of the carriage was open, and Dolly Calhoun was waiting inside, her cupid's-bow mouth beginning to quiver at being so precipitously deserted just as they had arrived at their destination. Kit gestured to the driver, who had finished depositing the last of the trunks on the piazza, to help her companion out of the carriage, then she paid the man and, with a reassuring smile at Miss Dolly, climbed the front stairs and lifted the brass knocker.

Kit did not recognize the young maid who answered the door, and this lack of recognition in a place where she had once known every face deepened her resentment. She would have given anything at that moment to have seen Eli's dear, familiar face, but the old man had died the previous winter. The maid glanced curiously at them and then at the array of trunks and bandboxes piled on the piazza.

"I would like to see Sophronia," Kit said.

"Miz Sophronia not here," the maid replied.

"When do you expect her?"

"The Conjure Woman done took sick this mawnin' and Miz Sophronia go off to take her some med'cine. Don' know when she be back."

"Is Major Cain here?"

"He be comin' in from the fields any minute now, but he ain't here yet."

Kit smiled to herself. With any luck, they would be firmly settled in before he arrived home. She clasped Miss Dolly gently by the arm and steered her through the doorway, past the astonished maid.

"See that our trunks are taken upstairs at once," Kit ordered. "This is Miss Calhoun. Show her to her room and have someone bring her a glass of lemonade and something to eat. I'll wait for Major Cain in the front sitting room."

Nothing in the girl's limited experience as a maid had prepared her for a situation like this. Still, there was something about this elegantly dressed and fashionably veiled woman that didn't encourage argument. Besides, Miz Sophronia would give her the sharp edge of her tongue if she left company standing in the hallway.

"Y-yes, ma'am," she stammered. "I take you to the sittin' room."

"Never mind. I can find it myself. You just see to Miss Calhoun."

Kit turned to Miss Dolly, anxious to see her safely tucked away before Cain's return. She was more than a little worried about how her nervous companion was going to react to sleeping under the same roof with a former officer in the Union army. She had tried once to talk to her about Baron Cain, but she had not seemed to be listening, and Kit had soon given up the effort.

"Why don't you lie down until supper, Miss Dolly. You've had a long day."

"I think I will, darlin'," Miss Dolly murmured, patting Kit's arm distractedly. "I want to look my best this evenin'. I only hope the gentlemen won't talk about politics all through dinner. With General Beauregard in command at Charleston, I'm sure none of us have any need to worry about those murderous Yankees."

"I'm sure you're right." Kit gave Miss Dolly a gentle prod toward the maid, who was regarding the elderly woman with open-mouthed bewilderment. "Now you go along and I'll look in on you before dinner."

Only after they had disappeared up the stairs did Kit take time to study her surroundings. As she took in the polished wooden floor and the fresh white paint and the colorful arrangement of spring flowers sitting in a pink glass bowl on the hall table, a sprinkle of saffron pollen dusting the highly polished surface, she suspected that Sophronia was more than a little responsible for the transformation of the house. She remembered how particular Sophronia had always been about the condition of the kitchen and knew how Rosemary's slovenliness had always galled her.

She crossed the hall and stepped into the front sitting room. It, too, bore evidence of Sophronia's care. By New York City standards the room was hopelessly old-fashioned. There were no India shawls draping the tables and the mantelpiece. The chairs were not covered in heavy red upholstery. The settees did not have high wooden backs, elaborately carved with fruits and flowers and vining grape leaves. Nor were the surfaces of the room cluttered with china figurines or candy dishes or stuffed birds under glass domes. Instead, the room was spare and cool with ivory walls, apple-green moldings, and yellow silk taffeta curtains rippling in the breeze from the open windows.

The furniture was not new. It was the same comfortable hodgepodge Kit remembered of cherry and mahogany tables and chairs made in the styles of the early nineteenth century by the fine cabinetmakers of Charleston and Philadelphia. But now the chairs and settees were newly covered in shades of green and gold and ivory, and the entire room smelled of lemon oil and beeswax instead of mildew. Not a speck of tarnish marred the shining silver candlesticks that rested on top of a small lacquered chest, and the grandfather's clock with its round brass dial engraved with the faces of the sun and the moon was working for the first time in Kit's memory.

Kit listened to the mellow, rhythmic ticking echoing in the quiet room, and her features tightened with resentment at all the changes of which she had had no part. It was as if she were a stranger in her own home.

Baron Cain watched as Vandal, his new chestnut stallion, was led into the stable. He was a good horse—deep girth, powerful legs with plenty of bone, strong, sloping shoulders. Cain had won him in a poker game in Charleston the month before from an old riverboat gambler who should have known better than to pull to an inside straight. It was hard to find good horseflesh in the South, and he was glad he'd decided to play that night, something he'd had neither the time nor the inclination for since he'd left New York. Of course, Magnus had been mad as hell, but he was always mad when Cain brought home a new horse because he knew they'd soon be getting rid of one of the old ones. In Cain's opinion, Magnus let himself get too attached to the animals. But then, there was a softness about Magnus that disturbed Cain. Look at the way he was behaving about Sophronia.

Cain shook his head in disgust. He hated to see Magnus make such a fool of himself over a woman. Where was his pride, letting Sophronia treat him like he was dirt under her feet? Cain would have gotten rid of her long ago—certainly after that incident in the library—if he hadn't been fairly certain Magnus would go right after her. If there was anything he couldn't abide, it was a woman making a fool of a man and a man letting her get away with it.

As he strode from the stable toward the house, he wondered why Magnus didn't just take her and be done with it. Once he'd had his fill of that lush body of hers, he'd come to his senses. There wasn't anything one woman had that couldn't be found on another, and there was no woman in the world worth losing a night's sleep over.

Dismissing thoughts of Magnus and Sophronia, he gazed around at all he'd accomplished in three years. Not once had he regretted his decision to leave New York and come to Risen Glory. For the time being he was satisfied with his life here, despite his isolation from his neighbors and the annoyances connected with living in a conquered land. He'd had some experience growing cotton in Texas before the war, and Magnus had been raised on a cotton plantation. With the help of a healthy supply of agricultural pamphlets, the two of them had managed to produce a paying crop last year. Although Cain did not feel any more deep affinity for the land he owned than he did for his horses, he was enjoying the challenge of restoring the plantation more than anything he'd done in years. Recently, however, he had given Magnus responsibility for the cotton crop so he could concentrate his own energies on building the new mill.

Cain stuck his hands deep in his pockets and grinned as he thought about the mill. Compared to the great textile mills of the northeast, his factory was small indeed—two and a half stories high and not much bigger than a large house. He wouldn't even have a power loom for weaving cloth when he began operation; it was to be a spinning mill only, taking the ginned cotton, cleaning it, carding it to straighten the fibers, and then pulling and twisting them into yarn.

The South had always shipped the bulk of its cotton to England, where it was spun into thread and then woven into cloth. In the years since the war, a small handful of men with money had begun to build a few scattered mills that took cotton from the gins and spun it into thread. As a result of these spinning mills, compact cotton spools could be shipped to England instead of the bulky cotton bales, yielding a thousand times the value for the same tonnage.

Cain had seen the opportunity and decided to take it. He had invested some of his money before he'd left New York, and last year's profits had repaid him for what he'd put into Risen Glory. He could have reinvested everything, but the idea didn't appeal to him. Instead he'd decided to gamble it all on the spinning mill. Now he was as close to being broke as he'd ever been. He doubted he could lay his hands on two hundred dollars ready cash if he had to, with all his money tied up in the plantation and the mill. But he'd always liked taking risks, and at that moment, he was as contented as he'd ever been in his life.

He had approached the back door and was running the muddy soles of his boots over the black wrought-iron boot scraper that was driven into the ground when Lucy, the young maid who had let Kit into the house, raced down the steps to meet him. In the time since Lucy had settled Miss Dolly into her room, she had grown increasingly worried about what she had done. As far as she knew, no guests were expected, and the woman with the veil had not even given her name. Now she was hoping that if she explained how it wasn't really her fault that she'd let two strange women in the house, he wouldn't blame her if she'd done the wrong thing. Unfortunately, the master of the house had always terrified her, and her words began tumbling all over themselves as she tried to tell him what had happened.

". . . Miz Sophronia didn't say nothin' 'bout nobody comin' today. She gib me de debbil fo' sure. I works hard from mawnin' to night. And den dis woman takes herself off into the sittin' room and say she gwine wait for you, and I—"

He finally cut her off. "Is she there now?"

"Yes, Major." Lucy nodded her head in agitation. "And dat's not all. She brung—"

"Damn!" It was a mechanical curse, and not even very loud, but it terrified Lucy, who mistakenly believed it was meant for her. With a howl, she threw her apron up over her head and scrambled back up the steps and into the house.

Cain shook his head in exasperation. He had received a letter the week before announcing that a member of the Society to Protect Widows and Orphans of the Confederacy would be calling upon him for his contribution. The buggy was gone, so Sophronia wasn't home, and he would have to see to it himself.

The visitor irritated him, although he should have become used to it by now. From the beginning the respectable citizens of the neighborhood would have nothing to do with him. They gave him their coldest nod when they passed him on the road and refused the pleas of their marriageable daughters to receive him. If that had been the end of it, he would have been relieved instead of annoyed, for he wanted as little to do with all of them as possible. Unfortunately, he was one of the few people in the neighborhood with any cash at all, and there was apparently an unwritten rule among the women that it was acceptable for them to call upon him whenever the coffers of their favorite charity dipped too low. For the past year it seemed as if he were being continually plagued with visits from matronly women who watched him with pursed lips and nervous eyes, and he suspected that the charities were merely a face-saving excuse to get a glimpse inside the lair of the infamous Hero of Missionary Ridge.

Even in hostile South Carolina, he had not lacked for female companionship. From a word dropped here and there by some of the servants, he had discovered, to his amusement, that his exploits with women had become the subject of much speculation among the residents of the neighborhood, despite the fact that he generally restricted himself to the pleasures so abundantly available in Charleston and turned aside offers closer to home. He regarded the interludes as pleasant—certainly necessary—but easily forgettable.

His neighbors were not so worldly. The men were openly disapproving and secretly envious, while the reactions of the women varied in direct proportion to their age and marital status. What all of them recognized, but none of them would openly admit, was the undeniable fact that Baron Cain was, by far, the most interesting person to come into their lives since the war.

Chapter Fifteen

Cain was not in the best of humor as he stalked down the hallway toward the sitting room, dressed in the same clothes he had worn all day in the fields, a pair of close-fitting tobacco-brown trousers and a white shirt still damp with sweat. Damned if he was going to extend the courtesy of changing his clothes for a guest he didn't invite. He was tired of being plagued by these tiresome women.

What he saw when he entered the door of the sitting room was hardly what he had expected. She was standing looking out the window, her back toward him, the skirt of her dove-gray dress rippling ever so gently in the breeze. At the sound of the door opening behind her, she slowly turned to face him. Her slim young body and mysteriously veiled face immediately intrigued him.

He knew at once that he had never seen her in the neighborhood and concluded that she was one of the respectable daughters who was so carefully tucked away from the slightest contact with the infamous Yankee who had settled in their midst. She stood quietly under his open appraisal, making none of the nervous movements of hands and fingers that women tend to make when they are uneasy. Idly he wondered what household calamity had resulted in so enticing a morsel being sent to take her mother's place. As his eyes touched the moist red mouth that peeked out from beneath the bottom edge of the veil and then raked down over the demure cascade of gray lace that fell from her throat, accenting the supple curves of her breasts, he thought with some amusement that her parents would have done better to have kept this one safely locked away at home, out of his reach.

While Cain was studying her so intently, Kit was conducting her own uneasy perusal of him from behind the honeycombed cells of her veil. Three years had passed since she had last seen him, and now she found herself looking at him through different, more mature eyes. At thirty-one, he was more ruggedly handsome than she remembered. The sun had bronzed the chiseled planes of his face and streaked the top of his crisp, tawny hair a lighter color. The darker hair at the temples and in his thick moustache gave his face the rugged, totally masculine look of a man who belonged outdoors.

She saw that he was still dressed for the fields and found herself strangely unsettled by the sight of the muscular body that his informal dress revealed all too clearly. The white shirt that stretched across his broad chest was rolled up at the sleeves, revealing tanned, hard-tendoned forearms. His tobacco-brown trousers clung to his narrow hips and hugged the powerful muscles of his thighs.

Everything about him was overpowering and terrifyingly masculine. She had the uneasy impression that the spacious room in which they were standing had shrunk in size since he had entered it. Even standing still, he radiated an aura of power and thinly leashed danger. How could she have forgotten? What curious, self-protective mechanism had made her reduce him in her mind over the years, unconsciously bringing him down to the level of other men? It had been a mistake, one she must never make again. Baron Cain was not like other men. To forget that was to invite disaster.

Cain was aware of her scrutiny. The silence stretched between them. He observed with interest and a small degree of admiration that she seemed to have no intention of being the first to speak. Her composure marked a degree of self-confidence not often found in a woman so young. Curious to test its limits, he broke the silence with deliberate brusqueness.

"You wanted to see me?"

Kit felt a stab of satisfaction. So he did not know who she was. She had worn the veiled hat deliberately, hoping this would happen, hoping to give herself that small edge of advantage before he recognized her. Although she knew the masquerade could not last for long, she needed as much time as she could muster to size up her opponent with wiser eyes than those of a sixteen-year-old child.

"This room is quite beautiful," she said simply, determined to appear cool and dispassionate under his calculating eyes.

Cain noticed that her voice was low and husky and distinctly Southern, although its accent was, perhaps, not quite so pronounced as the accent of the local women. There was also something vaguely familiar about it.

"My housekeeper is responsible," he said.

"You're fortunate to have so talented a housekeeper."

"Yes, I am." He walked farther into the room, moving with the easy rolling gait of a man who spends much of his time on horseback. "She usually takes care of calls like yours, but she's gone out on some kind of errand."

"She's gone to see the Conjure Woman," Kit said, wondering who he thought she was and what he meant by "calls like yours."

"The Conjure Woman?" He quirked an inquiring brow.

"She makes spells and tells futures." Kit could not quite hide her scorn at his ignorance. After all, he had been at Risen Glory for three years. "She lives about five miles from here. She's sick, and Sophronia's gone to see her."

"You know Sophronia?" he asked.

"Yes, I know her," she replied with deliberate nonchalance.

"So you are from around here?"

She nodded but made no effort to elaborate. He indicated a chair. "You didn't give Lucy your name."

"Lucy? Do you mean your maid?"

He nodded his head.

"No. No, I didn't, did I?"

She walked toward the chair he had offered and then past it, to the fireplace to study a small English tea chest that rested at one side of the mantel. He noticed that she walked with a bolder step than other women of his acquaintance. She also seemed indifferent to the fashionable clothes she wore, making no effort to position herself to best advantage. It was as if her clothing meant little to her, something to toss on in the morning and, once she had done up the fastenings, to forget.

He decided to press her. "Your name?"

"Is it important?"

"Maybe."

"Why, I wonder?" she responded. "Does knowing a name make the person who possesses it any different?"

Cain was intrigued as much by the provocative way she avoided answering his question as he was by the faint fragrance of jasmine that drifted from her skirts and tugged at his senses. He made his way over toward the chair she had ignored and sat down on it, stretching out his long legs and crossing them casually at the ankle. Her back was toward him, and he found himself wishing she would turn around so he could get a closer look at the captivating features of the face he had glimpsed through the veil.

"A lady of mystery," he mocked softly, "coming into the enemy's lair without a zealous mother to serve as chaperone. Not very wise."

Her shoulders lifted in a small shrug. "I don't always behave wisely."

There was a short pause before Cain spoke. "Neither do I."

Kit felt a tremor of uneasiness and knew that somehow the encounter was slipping from her control. To cover her loss of composure, she moved away from the fireplace and over to the grandfather's clock, absorbing herself in the intricately engraved scrollwork of the gleaming brass dial.

Cain's gaze slipped down from the wisp of rose-colored hat to the thick, dark coil of hair resting on the nape of her neck. He wondered what it would look like unfastened, tumbling down naked white shoulders.

"Should I expect a jealous husband to come banging on my door looking for his wayward wife?" he inquired lazily.

"I have no husband."

"No?" He uncoiled from the chair and slowly approached her from the back, choosing his next words deliberately. "Is that why you're here? Has the supply of eligible men in the county dipped so low that well-bred young ladies are forced to scout in the enemy camp?"

He finally had her attention. As she whirled around, he could just make out flashing eyes and a small nose with delicately flaring nostrils.

"I assure you, Major Cain," she said icily, "I have not come to see you to scout for a husband. You have an elevated opinion of yourself."

"Do I?" He moved a step closer until his legs were only inches away from her skirt.

Kit told herself that the queer, queasy feeling that had come over her was merely a result of her certainty that he was going to recognize her. She wanted to step back, away from his overpowering nearness, but she forced herself to hold her ground. He was a predator, and like all predators, he fed off the weakness of others. To a man like Baron Cain, even the smallest retreat would be construed as a victory, and she refused to show him any sign of vulnerability, no matter how unsettling this encounter might become.

"Tell me, mystery lady," he said, his voice deep and teasing, "what else would a respectable young lady be doing visiting a man by herself? Or is it possible that the respectable young lady isn't as respectable as she seems to be?"

"I—I don't know what you mean." Her words came out breathless and uncertain. To cover her weakness, she drew up her chin and unflinchingly met his gaze with her own. If he recognized her, so be it.

If she had but known it, the unspoken challenge in the veiled eyes—were they blue or a darker, more exotic color?—stirred him far more than anything else she could have done. There was something different about this woman. She was no simpering coquette, of that he was certain. No hothouse orchid, either. Rather she reminded him of a wild rose, growing tangled and unruly in the deepest part of the woods, a wild rose with prickly thorns ready to pierce the flesh and draw blood from any man who touched her.

The untamed part of him responded to the same quality he sensed in her. What would it be like to work his way past those thorns and pluck this wild rose of the deep wood?

Even before he moved, Kit understood that something was about to happen. She wanted to break away—knew she must break away—but her legs would not respond to her will. As she gazed up into the chiseled face that hovered over hers, she tried to remember that this man was her deadly enemy, that he held possession to everything that was dear to her—her home, her future, her very freedom. But she was young and ripe, a creature of instinct, and the blood was beginning to roar so loudly in her head that it was blotting out her reason.

Slowly Cain lifted his scarred hand and gently cupped it around the side of her slim neck. The delicate pulse that lay just beneath her skin jumped under the touch of his work-roughened palm, a touch that was surprisingly gentle and maddeningly exciting. She knew she had to pull back out of his reach, but her legs, along with her will, refused to obey.

He lifted his thumb and slid it upward along the curve of her jaw and under the edge of the honeycombed veil, dipping it into the soft valley behind the lobe of her ear. With the tip of his thumb, he intimately caressed the silky hollow, sending quivers of sensation coursing through her skin. Then he lifted his left hand and, finding the matching recess behind the other ear, began exploring it in a gentle, intimate invasion that stole her sense of will.

He moved his thumbs forward, brushing over the delicate shells of her ears and through the silky tendrils of curl that feathered at her earlobes, his soft breathing rippling the bottom edge of her veil. Then he tipped her head back and lowered his lips to the soft, moist wild-rose mouth that had beckoned him from the first moment he had seen it.

The ugly encounter on the beach at Long Branch had not prepared Kit for Cain's experienced kiss, a kiss that drove out thought and reason, replacing all that was rational with all that was not.

His lips covered hers, gently at first, softly persuading. She was dimly aware of the pleasant brush of his moustache against her skin, the strong masculine scent of him. Her hands lifted of their own accord and clasped his sides. The feel of warm-muscled flesh and hard-ridged ribs through the thin material of his shirt became part of and at one with the kiss. And then even that awareness disappeared as she lost herself in a swelling sea of sensation.

Slowly his lips opened and began to move over her closed ones. One of the hands that held her head prisoner slid down along the delicate line of her spine to the small of her back, pressing her body closer to his until the narrow space that had been between them disappeared altogether. His chest pressed against her breasts, his hips against the flatness of her stomach.

And then the moist tip of his tongue began its soft sorcery, gently inserting itself between her closed lips and sliding leisurely along them. The intimacy inflamed her already reeling senses, sending a wild rush of hot sensation pouring through every part of her body.

They lost their identities. There was no past and no future. They had become man and woman. For Kit, Cain no longer had a name. He was the quintessential man, fierce and demanding. And for Cain, the mysterious veiled creature, hot and demanding in his arms, was all that a woman should be but never was.

He grew impatient. His tongue began to probe more deeply, determined to slip past the barrier of her teeth and gain full access to the sweet interior of her mouth. The unaccustomed feeling brought a faint flicker of sanity to Kit's fevered mind. Something was wrong. . . .

In a cold, condemning rush, reality returned to her. With a cry she snatched her lips away and jerked her body back until it was free of the dangerous heat of his.

Cain, more shaken by her response than he cared to admit, dropped his hands and looked down at her. He had found the thorns much too soon. . . .

She stood before him, breasts heaving, her hands balled into fists at her sides. With a pessimistic certainty that the rest of her face could never live up to the promise of the mouth, he reached out and hooked his index finger under the edge of her veil. With a flick, he pushed the soft webbing up onto the brim of her hat.

Recognition did not come immediately, perhaps because he took in the separate features of her face instead of the whole. He saw the smooth, intelligent forehead, the thick, dark slashes of eyebrows, the heavily lashed violet eyes and determined chin. All of it, together with the wild-rose mouth from which he had drunk so deeply, spoke of a vivid, unconventional beauty and made a mockery of his pessimism.

Then there was an uneasiness, a nagging feeling of familiarity, a sense of something unpleasant lurking just on the other side of his memory. He saw the nostrils of her small, straight nose quiver like the wings of a hummingbird. He watched as she set her jaw and lifted her chin. In that instant, he knew her.

The pale-gray irises of his eyes rimmed themselves in black.

Kit saw it happen and dimly understood its significance, but she was too stricken by what had passed between them to take it in. What insanity had possessed her? What madness had led her to such wild abandon in the arms of this man who was her mortal enemy? She felt sick and angry and more confused than she had ever been in her life.

She was suddenly aware of a disturbance coming from the hallway, a series of rapid clicks, as if a sack of parched corn were being spilled on the bare wooden floor. The noise grew louder, and then a streak of black fur darted into the room, skidding to a stop on white-mittened paws. It was Merlin. He turned his attention to the strange new person who occupied the room and cocked his head to the side to study her. It did not take him nearly as long as it had taken Cain to guess her identity. With three barks of welcoming recognition, he raced over to greet his old friend.

"Merlin!" Kit fell down on her knees as the dog hurled himself at her. Oblivious to the damage his dusty paws were inflicting on her dove-gray traveling dress, she hugged his warm short-haired body to her and let his wet, rough tongue lap at her face. Her hat fell to the carpet, loosening her carefully arranged hair, but she didn't notice.

Cain's voice, like a polar wind rushing down the sides of a glacier, shattered the reunion. "You're still the same little headstrong brat you were three years ago, aren't you?"

Kit looked up at the handsome features, strangely distorted by the force of his anger, and said the first thing that came into her mind. "You're just mad because the dog was smarter than you were."

Chapter Sixteen

Not long after Cain had stalked out of the sitting room, having first informed her that she was to meet him in the library immediately after dinner for a long and undoubtedly difficult interview, Kit heard a familiar voice.

"Lucy! I've told you a dozen times not to let that dog in the house."

"I know, Miz Sophronia, but he jes' keep slippin' right pass me."

There was the sound of brisk, efficient footsteps, and then Sophronia swept into the sitting room. Lucy had not managed to work up enough courage to explain about the strange women who had appeared at the door, so Sophronia was not expecting to find the room occupied by anyone other than Merlin. To her surprise, she saw a woman kneeling on the floor with the mongrel.

Sophronia's features automatically arranged themselves in the cool, impersonal expression she used to receive visitors. "Good afternoon. May I—" Recognition sprang into her eyes at the mischievous grin on the stranger's face. "Kit! Oh, my! Is it really you?"

"It's me all right, Sophronia." The two women ran into each other's arms. Merlin, enjoying the excitement, began circling them and barking at their skirts.

"Oh, hush, Merlin!" Kit cried. "Sophronia, it's so good to see you. You're even more beautiful than I remember."

"Me!" Sophronia exclaimed. "Just look at you. What did they do to you, child? You look like you just stepped out of the pages of *Godey's Lady's Book.*"

Kit made a modest disclaimer, but she was pleased nonetheless by Sophronia's compliment. The two women sank down on the settee and, in a rush of disconnected thoughts and jumbled sentences, tried to catch up on three years of separation in the space of ten minutes, with Kit doing most of the talking. Now her earlier annoyance at Sophronia's skillful redecorating of the house seemed petty, and in between fragmentary stories of Elspeth, Miss Dolly, and life at the academy, she lavishly praised all Sophronia had done.

As Kit talked, Sophronia felt the familiar combination of love and resentment that always seemed to plague her where Kit was concerned. But now there was a new dimension. Before, Kit had been a child and an outcast with no one to take care of her. Now she was a woman with stories of friendships of which Sophronia had no part. She was beautiful and poised and obviously at home in a world to which Sophronia could never belong. The old hurts began to throb again. With a promise to visit later that evening and a firm grasp on Merlin's old leather collar, Sophronia excused herself to oversee dinner.

During the interlude with Sophronia, Kit had managed to push her shattering encounter with Baron Cain to the back of her mind, but as she climbed the great walnut staircase to the bedroom Sophronia had suggested she occupy, it all came back in a rush. How could such a thing have happened to her? If it had been Brandon Parsell, she could have understood it better. He was a man she admired. But how could she have forgotten herself so entirely in the arms of Baron Cain?

Even as she thought about it, she felt a hot flush of shame creeping over her and, with it, the memory of Mrs. Templeton's lecture to the senior girls. A frightening thought wormed its way into her mind. Perhaps there was something very, very wrong with her.

The sight of the bedroom helped to lift her sagging spirits, despite the fact that it was second best to the master bedroom that Baron Cain occupied. The room Sophronia had assigned to her was decorated entirely in pale pink and soft green. Pink and green striped silk hung in gathers above the mosquito netting that draped the bed and was repeated in the swagged valances over the windows. The room reminded her of the inside of a ripe watermelon, close to the bottom where the pink meat joins the pale iridescence of the rind. It was cool and pretty, and she was glad it would be hers.

She dismissed a faint prickle of uneasiness at the sight of the room's second door. It led to a common sitting room that lay between her room and the master bedroom, where there was a similar connecting door. The thought of the adjoining room was somehow disquieting.

She stripped off her dress and, standing in her chemise and one petticoat, freshened herself at the washstand, smiling a little as she remembered those years not so very long ago when the idea of putting soap and water on her skin would have horrified her. Thoughts of her disdain for cleanliness led to a far more unpleasant memory—the night Baron Cain had scrubbed her naked body in his bathtub.

She cursed softly under her breath, a habit of which Elspeth had never entirely been able to break her. It seemed that no matter what she did, her thoughts ran full circle, always coming back to the one person she didn't want to think about, at least not until she had to go downstairs and confront him at dinner.

Lucy came into the room to unpack her trunks. For a moment Kit considered throwing on one of her oldest dresses and dashing outside to reacquaint herself with her home. But then she dismissed the impulse. In less than an hour she had to be downstairs, ready to do battle again. She did not want to hurry the reunion to which she had looked forward for so long. Morning would be soon enough.

She stretched out on the bed and tried to distract herself by reading a strange book she had found on a dusty back shelf in a bookstore not far from the academy. It had been written by a man named Herman Melville. According to the owner of the bookstore, Melville's tales of adventure in the South Seas had made him a popular writer during the 1840s. This book, however, had lost him his following. Instead of presenting his readers with an exciting adventure story, this one about whaling, Melville had told a darker, more complicated tale that had left his faithful readers bewildered. The book had not been a success.

Kit, however, had found the story engrossing, especially the inner workings of the main character's mind. She felt a strange sympathy for Captain Ahab, perhaps because she understood what it was like to be obsessed with a dream. For him, it was a great white whale; for her, this piece of land on which she had been born.

At the moment, however, even Captain Ahab's struggles couldn't hold her attention, and when Lucy had finished putting away her clothes, she tossed the book down on the pink-and-green striped counterpane and wandered over to the wardrobe to choose a dress for dinner. As she surveyed her new clothes, she felt a sharp stab of homesickness for Elspeth Woodward.

Thanks to Elspeth, Kit had a wardrobe that any woman would envy. It was Elspeth who had seen to it that her father provide Kit with a generous clothing allowance from her trust. She had quickly discovered, however, that Kit's taste in clothing was unpredictable. Sometimes she would buy a lovely dress that set her features off to perfection; other times, she would purchase a gaudy fringed and tasseled monstrosity that wasn't at all the kind of garment a well-brought-up young woman would wear.

Elspeth had never quite been able to discover whether Kit's buying habits were the result of an erratic sense of good taste or whether she had merely been bored with shopping that day and settled for whatever had been set before her. She suspected it was a little bit of both. As a result, she forbid Kit to go on any more shopping trips by herself. It was Elspeth who had either selected or approved each item in her friend's wardrobe.

Kit pulled out a pretty cotton frock with sprigs of gay blue forget-me-nots scattered over a white background. In the current fashion, the skirt was drawn up in soft folds to reveal an underskirt of a solid color, in this case the same blue as the forget-me-nots. It was a dress she had loved on sight. Its scooped neckline was cool and left the back of her shoulders bare.

Impatiently she pulled the hairpins from her hair. It had been confined long enough. She brushed it out until it crackled and then caught it back from her face with the silver filigree combs Elspeth had given her for her birthday so that it tumbled, free and lush, in a riot of curls that spilled down over her shoulders. With a quick dab of jasmine scent at her wrists, she was ready.

She knocked on the door of Miss Dolly's room with some trepidation. How was her fragile companion going to manage sitting at the dinner table with a Yankee war hero? Belatedly it occurred to her that she should have considered more carefully before bringing someone like Miss Dolly into such a difficult situation. She knocked a second time. When there was no response, she pushed the door open and found her worst fears realized.

Miss Dolly sat huddled in a rocking chair in the corner of the darkened room, her tiny features crumpled, tears streaking her wrinkled cheeks. Her hands, encased as always in their lace mitts, held the tattered fragment of what had once been a baby-blue handkerchief.

Kit shut the door quickly and dashed to her side, kneeling next to the rocking chair. "Miss Dolly! What's wrong?"

At first the older woman didn't seem to have heard her, and then she slowly turned her head and gazed down into Kit's upturned face. "Hello, darlin'," she said vaguely. "I didn't hear you come in."

"You've been crying!" Kit exclaimed, grasping the woman's bird-frail hands in her own strong young ones. "Tell me what's wrong."

Miss Dolly managed to shape her cupid's-bow mouth into something resembling a smile. "Nothin', really. Silly memories. Makin' rag babies with my sisters when we were children. One of the penalties of old age."

"You're not old, Miss Dolly. Why, just look at you in your pretty white dress. You look as young and as fresh as a spring day."

"I do try to keep myself pretty," Miss Dolly acknowledged, straightening a little in her chair and making a dab at her wet cheeks. "It's just that sometimes, on days like today, I find myself thinkin' about things that happened a long time ago, and it makes me sad."

"What kind of things?"

Miss Dolly patted Kit's hand. "Now, now, darlin'. You don't want to hear my ramblin's."

"They're not ramblings," Kit declared with conviction, forgetting that only a few hours earlier that very habit had been driving her to distraction.

"You've got a good heart, Katharine Louise. I knew it the moment I set eyes on you. That was why I was so glad when you told me we were coming back to South Carolina." The smile faded. "I didn't like it in the North. Everybody had such loud voices. I don't like Yankees, Katharine. I don't like them at all. They frighten me."

"You're upset about meeting Major Cain, aren't you?" Impulsively Kit laid her head on the older woman's knee. "I should never have brought you to Risen Glory. It was selfish of me. I knew I couldn't stay here without a chaperone. I was just thinking of myself, not of how it would affect you."

"Now, now, Katharine Louise. Don't you be blamin' your sweet self for a silly old woman's foolishness." She picked up a silky black curl in her fingers and toyed with it.

Kit lifted her head. "I don't want you to stay here if it's going to make you unhappy."

As soon as the words had left her mouth, she wished she

could snatch them back, for Miss Dolly's teacup-blue eyes widened in alarm. "But I don't have anyplace to go!" she exclaimed, pushing herself up from the rocking chair with great agitation. "I'll be just fine, you'll see. Just fine." She was beginning to cry again. "Silly foolishness. That's all it is. You just wait for me outside while I freshen up, and then we'll go right downstairs for dinner. I won't be a minute. Not a minute."

Kit jumped to her feet and threw her arm around the frail, trembling shoulders. "Miss Dolly, you calm yourself. I'll never send you away, not as long as you want to stay with me. I promise, you hear me?"

She could feel the small body begin to quiet. "You won't send me away?"

"Never," Kit insisted, intent only on easing the older woman's unhappiness and giving no thought at all to the difficulties she might have keeping such a promise. She smoothed the puffy white sleeves of Miss Dolly's gown and then, with a quick peck on the soft, withered cheek, she crossed the room and opened the door. "Now you make yourself pretty for dinner."

Miss Dolly glanced nervously at the hallway that lay beyond the safe haven of her room. "All right, darlin'," she said weakly.

As Kit reached out for the knob to pull the door shut behind her, she gently teased her companion, trying to lighten the older woman's apprehension. "You just pretend to yourself that Baron Cain is General Lee in disguise." She smiled. "Then you won't be half so worried."

She closed the door an instant too soon to see Miss Dolly's head shoot up and all the pale-blue ribbons on her lace cap begin to quiver.

Ten minutes later, it was a confident Miss Dolly who descended the stairs next to Kit. "Hold still a minute, darlin'. Your pretty dress is all crooked. The overskirt isn't caught up properly on the right side." She clucked her tongue as she adjusted the garment. "I do wish you'd be a little more careful when you dress, Katharine Louise. I don't mean to be critical, but sometimes you don't look quite as neat as a young lady should."

"Yes, ma'am," Kit answered docilely, so relieved to see Miss Dolly was her old self again that she didn't mind being fussed over. If Baron Cain did anything tonight to frighten her, she'd kill him with her own bare hands!

Just at that moment Cain came out of the door of the library. He was dressed casually in a pair of black trousers and a white shirt, his hair still damp from his bath. The insult of his informal attire pricked at her. Didn't the man have the common courtesy to dress for dinner when he knew there would be ladies at the table?

He looked up and watched them coming toward him, Kit leading with Miss Dolly slightly behind her. For an instant, Kit thought she saw a strange emotion flicker in the depths of his eyes, but then it was gone, leaving his expression as inscrutable as ever. The memory of their hot, abandoned kiss washed over her. To her consternation, she could feel her heart beginning to pound, and she took a deep breath to steady herself. The evening that lay ahead was going to be a difficult one. She must force herself to forget their earlier encounter and concentrate instead on remaining poised and alert.

As she came to the last step, she suddenly realized she had forgotten about Miss Dolly. She quickly turned to her companion, ready to soothe the older woman, only to discover that Miss Dolly showed no signs at all of needing soothing. Instead, she was beaming her most coquettish smile at Baron Cain and holding out one lace-encased hand.

"My dear, dear general," she chirped, tripping down the last two steps and across the hallway as lightly and gracefully as a debutante. "I cannot tell you what an honor this is for me, sir. You will never know the hours and hours I have spent on my poor knees, prayin' for your safety in these tryin' times. But never, never, never in my wildest dreams did I ever imagine I would have the honor of meetin' you. I am Dorthea Pinckney Calhoun, of the Columbia Calhouns."

She thrust her tiny hand into Cain's large one, which was still hanging at his side, and dropped him her deepest curtsy. Cain stared down at the top of her frilly cap in bewilderment, but before he could respond, the cap bobbed back up, the head it contained barely coming to his middle shirt button.

"You must know, General," Miss Dolly twittered with much fluttering of her eyelashes, "if there is anything, anything at all I can do to make you comfortable during your stay here at Risen

Glory, you need only ask. From this moment, this very instant on, you must consider me your devoted servant."

Cain finally managed to tear his gaze away from Miss Dolly's wrinkled eyelids, which were batting at him with such alarming speed that he was afraid the poor woman would blind herself, and look at Kit for enlightenment. To his displeasure she was standing frozen on the bottom step, one hand clutching the banister, as she stared at Miss Dolly with a bewilderment that matched his own.

Cain cleared his throat. "I believe—I'm afraid, madam, that you've made a mistake. I'm not entitled to the rank of general. Indeed, I hold no military office at all now, although some still refer to me by my former rank of major."

This attempt at clarification was greeted by a trill of girlish laughter. "Oh, my, my! Silly me! You've caught me like a kitten in the cream." She lowered her voice to a conspiratorial whisper, which still could have been heard in the attic. "I forget that you are in disguise. And a very good one it is, I might add. No Yankee spies could possibly recognize you, although I think it's a shame you had to shave off your beard. I do admire beards."

Cain, his patience at an end, turned toward Kit. "What the hell's she talking about?" he barked.

"Now, now, no need to fret." Miss Dolly placed her fingers on Cain's arm. "I promise when we are in company, I shall be very discreet and only address you as major, dear general."

Cain's voice was full of warning and as dark as a thundercloud. "Kit. . . ."

Miss Dolly clucked her tongue. "There, there, General. I don't want you to worry your head for an instant about Katharine Louise. She's completely trustworthy, I assure you. And a more loyal daughter of the Confederacy does not exist anywhere on God's good earth. She would never betray your true identity to anyone. Isn't that so, darlin'?"

Kit tried to reply. She even opened her mouth. But nothing seemed to come out.

Miss Dolly was clearly annoyed with her charge's lack of response. She plucked up the chicken-skin fan that dangled from her bony wrist by a frayed purple cord and waved it in Kit's direction. "Tell the general that's so, darlin', this very instant. We mustn't have him worryin' unnecessarily about betrayal. The poor man has enough on his mind without your addin' to his burden. Go on, now. Tell him he can trust you. Tell him."

"You can trust me," Kit croaked.

Cain glared at her murderously.

Miss Dolly lifted her head and sniffed the air with great satisfaction. "If my nose isn't betrayin' me, I do believe I smell chicken fricasse. I'm more than a little partial to fricasse, 'deed I am, especially if it contains just a bitty dash of nutmeg."

She linked her arm through Cain's, propelling him in the direction of the dining room. "You know, General, there is a distinct possibility that we are distantly related. According to my great-aunt, Phoebe Littlefield Calhoun, her father's branch of the family is connected through marriage to the Virginia Lees."

Cain stopped dead in his tracks. "Are you trying to tell me, madam—Do you actually believe that I am General Robert E. Lee?"

Miss Dolly opened her cupid's-bow mouth to respond and then closed it with a giggle. "Oh, no, you shan't catch me that easily, General." She waggled her finger at him. "It's naughty of you to test me like this, especially after I distinctly informed you that you could rely on my discretion." Like a schoolgirl reciting a well-learned lesson, she intoned, "You are Major Baron Nathaniel Cain. Katharine told me that quite clearly."

And then she favored them both with a broad, conspiratorial wink.

Chapter Seventeen

Dinner was a disaster. Cain scowled throughout the meal. Kit picked at her food and silently blamed herself for planting the seed of Miss Dolly's latest madness, while the object of their ill humor chirped on and on about fricassees and distant relations and the medicinal qualities of camomile until both of them were ready to throttle her. As the meal drew to an end, she began making ominous references to an informal poetry recitation in the parlor. This brought Cain back to a state of full attention.

He set down his fork and looked directly at her. "I'm afraid that will be impossible, Miss Calhoun." His eyes traveled to Kit, and he gave her a venomous glare. "Katharine Louise has brought back some secret dispatches with her from New York City. I'm afraid I must meet with her privately"—one tawny brow slashed upward—"and *immediately!*"

Miss Dolly fairly beamed with pleasure. Here at last was something she could do. "Why, of course, General. You don't need to say another word." And as quickly as that, she hopped up from the table. With a departing waggle of her fingers, she left them alone in the dining room.

The silence was deafening. Kit suddenly found herself engrossed in the slice of Martha Washington cake that, up until that moment, had remained untouched on her dessert plate. She knew the confrontation had to come, but now that it was time, she wasn't ready for it.

There was the sound of a chair being pushed back from the table. "In the library, Kit," Cain commanded.

"I . . ."

"Now!" He swept around the corner of the table and pulled her up from the chair by her arm. With an indignant exclamation, Kit tried to jerk away, but she quickly realized her struggles would win her nothing more than a loss of dignity, for his grip was unyielding.

She glared at him scathingly. "I'm not accustomed to being manhandled."

"That's not what I hear," he drawled contemptuously.

Hamilton Woodward's letter! With all that had happened since her arrival, she had forgotten the obscene letter the lawyer had written about her behavior on the beach at Long Branch. And then comprehension hit her like a dash of cold water thrown in her face. Her insane surrender to Cain's kiss that afternoon would almost certainly have confirmed the letter's awful accusations about her in his mind! She could feel the hot color rushing into her cheeks as he propelled her out the door and toward the library.

And what if it had? she thought, furious at herself for caring about his opinion at all. Wasn't that what she wanted? If he thought she was free with her favors, he would be only that much more anxious to get rid of her. No matter how it stung her pride, she would follow her original plan and refuse to deny any accusations he might make. Let him think as he pleased. All the better for her!

The library at Risen Glory was much as Kit remembered it, with its old mahogany desk and comfortable leather-upholstered chairs, their seats sagging slightly in the middle. The carpet was the same, too, although the Oriental design had faded now from its original crimson and black to less dramatic hues. The room faced south and had been designed with a generous number of windows so that it remained light and cheerful despite the somber leather-bound books that lined the walls. It had been her favorite room at Risen Glory, and she resented the unfamiliar cigar-filled glass humidor on the desk top and the Colt army revolver that rested in a red-lined wooden box next to it. Most of all, she resented the portrait of Abraham Lincoln that hung above the mantelpiece in place of "The Beheading of John the Baptist," the painting that had been there for as long as she could remember.

Behind her back she heard him splash some liquor into a glass. Then she heard a soft creak. She turned to see that he had slouched down in the chair behind his desk and watched as he propped his heels up on the cluttered mahogany surface and crossed his ankles.

His posture infuriated her. No gentleman of her acquaintance would dream of sprawling so informally in the presence of a lady. And here she was, standing at the foot of his desk like a supplicant!

Deliberately she crossed to the far side of the room and studied the shelf of books in front of her with unseeing eyes. It did not take her long to understand what was happening. Earlier that afternoon when she had been veiled, he had treated her very much like a woman, and she sensed that he had been intrigued by her. But now that he knew her identity, it was as if the three years that had passed since they had last seen each other hadn't taken place, and she was once again a child—a child he seemed determined to treat like a stable boy! Well, she would show him that child did not exist any longer!

With a soft rustle of her skirts, she turned to him. He was quietly studying her over the rim of his brandy glass.

"That portrait of the former president is out of place at Risen Glory," she rebuked him quietly. "It insults my father's memory."

"From what I hear, your father insulted his own memory."

Kit refused to flinch. "Nevertheless, he was my father, and he died bravely."

Cain regarded the depths of his glass sourly. "There's nothing brave about death." Abruptly he looked back up at her, the planes of his face harsh and angular in the dim lamplight of the room. "I told you to stay in New York."

"Our agreement was for me to stay there for three years," she replied calmly. "I fulfilled my part of the bargain."

"Part of the agreement was for you to conduct yourself properly. The way I see it, you're the one who went back on your word." Without taking his feet from the desk top, he leaned to the side and opened the middle drawer, extracting a piece of folded stationery that he slapped down on the desk. "Don't forget that your reputation has preceded you. This letter makes for interesting reading, although I wouldn't want to show it to anybody who was easily shocked."

"Did you ever consider that Mr. Woodward might have exaggerated?" she asked, even though she had vowed not to try to exonerate herself.

"Did he?"

She couldn't help herself. "Yes. The letter's a lie."

Cain's eyes traveled with lazy insolence down over her breasts and waist and hips before slowly returning to her face. "Forgive me if I'm skeptical," he drawled, "but don't forget that I've already had a small sample of your idea of acceptable behavior." He took a slow sip from his glass. "If this letter's such a lie, how about explaining to me why you slipped into my arms so easily this afternoon."

She couldn't explain. She didn't understand it herself. Why had she tried to defend herself to him when she had known he wouldn't believe her? Well, she'd learned her lesson. Now she would show him!

She cocked her head to the side and regarded him with a small, deliberately sly smile. "I like men. Is that a crime?"

Cain slammed his feet to the floor and catapulted from his chair. "You little tramp," he ground out through gritted teeth.

His anger as he glared at her over the top of the desk frightened her, but she held her ground. "I'd forgotten what a hypocrite you are, Major," she sneered, "but it's all coming back to me with painful clarity. You have the morals of an alley cat yourself, but now you're suddenly full of righteous indignation because Kit Weston isn't lily-white. Well, you and your morality can go to hell!"

She turned to stalk from the room, but he was too fast for her. As quickly as a hawk swooping down on a rabbit, he charged around the side of the desk and across the room, catching her by the soft flesh of her exposed shoulder and spinning her around to face him.

"I said you were a tramp, and that's exactly what you are! But, by damn, you can do your whoring someplace else. I told you to stay in New York for another year, and this time you're going to do what I say."

She choked back her anger and forced herself to regard him calmly. "I thought you wanted to be rid of me."

"More than I've wanted anything in a long time."

"Well then, I suggest you let me stay at Risen Glory. It won't be for long, I promise you. Believe me, I want to be rid of you even more than you want to be rid of me."

"Why should I let you stay here?"

Despite his grasp on her shoulder, she decided she held the upper hand. "So we can put an end to this ridiculous guardianship, of course." She gave him a smile that was deliberately patronizing. "There are several men who would like to marry me. I just need a few weeks to make up my mind which one I'm going to choose."

Slowly he released her shoulder and dropped his hand to the side. "And are these men aware that their prospective bride is hardly the virgin a man expects to find in his wedding bed?"

Her scornful expression told him exactly what she thought of his hypocrisy. "That's really none of your business, is it?"

He shrugged. "No, I guess it isn't." Walking over to the fireplace, he leaned an elbow on the mantelpiece and crossed one calf indolently over the other. "I must admit, you surprise me. Somehow I can't see you as a devoted wife."

"I'm nineteen," Kit replied. "Hardly a child anymore." An image of Lilith Samuels sprang into her mind—Lilith sprawled across her bed, holding court with her opinions about men and marriage to the group of younger girls that idolized her. "Marriage is what every woman wants, isn't it?" she said with the same wide-eyed vacuousness she had seen so often on Lilith's face. "A husband to take care of her, pretty clothes, a piece of jewelry on her birthday. What more could a woman want from life?"

Cain scowled. "You know something? Three years ago when you were my stable boy, you were a thorn in my side, but I have to admit, I had a certain amount of respect for you. You were brave and ambitious, willing to fight for what you wanted. The Kit Weston I knew then wouldn't have been satisfied with clothes and jewelry. I don't think that little stable boy would like the person you've become very much."

Although his assessment was unfair, it still stung. "And who's responsible for the person I've become?" Kit retorted. "You were the one who wanted me to go to finishing school."

Cain suddenly seemed bored with the conversation. "It's all in the past now." He stepped away from the fireplace and placed one hand loosely on his hip. "All right, you can have one month, and then I want you out of here, husband or no husband." He jerked his head toward the hallway. "One other thing, Kit. That woman has to go. I want her out of this house tomorrow."

"No!" Kit exclaimed, remembering the promise she had made. "It's out of the question." And then, more calmly: "As I recall, you're the one who sent me to her, and I can't possibly stay here without a chaperone."

His mouth twisted sardonically. "Seems to me like it's a little late to be worrying about respectability. Kind of like closing the barn door after the cow has been stolen. Besides, I don't think she's going to be much of a chaperone as far as the neighbors are concerned. As soon as anyone talks to her, they're going to realize she's crazy as a loon."

Kit immediately rose in hot defense of her elderly companion. "She's not crazy!"

"You could have fooled me."

"She's just a little different."

"More than a little." Cain looked at her, his expression openly suspicious. "Just how did she get the idea that I was General Lee?"

Kit told him what had happened when she went to Miss Dolly's room. "She was so frightened of you," she concluded. "I was just trying to tease her into a better mood. I had no idea she would take me seriously."

He shook his head in annoyance. "And now you actually expect me to go along with this charade?"

"It won't be hard," Kit pointed out quite reasonably. "She does most of the talking."

There was no yielding in Cain's expression, and Kit knew she had not convinced him to change his mind about Miss Dolly's leaving. She could think of only one resource left at her disposal, a resource she was loath to use. But as she remembered Miss Dolly's frightened tear-streaked cheeks, she knew she had no other choice.

She slid the tip of her tongue over her dry lips, and then she slowly walked toward him. She stopped a bare foot in front of him and extended one small hand, placing it on his upper arm. "Please, Baron," she murmured softly, tilting her head to the side and looking up at him through a thick battery of black lashes. "I promised her she could stay. She doesn't have anyplace else to go." So unnerving did she find it to be in such close contact with him that she did not even notice she had finally used his first name.

He lifted her hand from his arm, but did not release it. "Don't toy with me, Kit," he said, his voice low and slightly husky. "As you reminded me so long ago, the relationship between us is purely a legal one. Believe me, I have no compunction at all about taking what you seem to be offering so freely."

Kit snatched her hand from his and tried to back away, only to bump up against a chair. "I'm not offering you anything," she cried.

Cain ambled over to her and reached out his hand. With his index finger, he traced a burning path down the side of her neck and over the bare skin of her throat. His finger traveled lower until he reached the edge of her bodice and the warm, gentle slopes that marked the beginning of her breasts.

"It's only a matter of time," he taunted softly, his finger lightly tracing the soft mounds of flesh.

"You bastard!"

But he snatched the curse from her lips with his mouth, swooping his head down to claim her with a brutality that sucked the breath from her body. It was a violent, marauding kiss, a mark of possession and conquest that held nothing of tenderness. His fingers dug into the flesh of her arms, slamming her body against his and tilting her head backward so he could have complete access to her. This time he did not permit her teeth to form a barrier to his entry, but plunged his tongue into her mouth, raping the virgin recess with a ruthlessness that brought Kit none of the pleasure she had known in his arms that afternoon, but only the deep, instinctive fear of a woman confronted for the first time with the dark side of a man's desire.

He drank until he was sated. When he finally pulled away, he stared down at the swollen, branded mouth, but instead of remorse, his cold gray eyes showed a primitive kind of satisfaction—the satisfaction of a man who has begun to avenge himself for some unnamed betrayal.

"The old lady can stay as long as you're willing to pay the price," he hissed softly. "I'll collect the next installment when I'm ready." He left the room without a backward glance. A few moments later she heard the front door close and knew he had gone out.

It was some time before Kit could move. She gingerly brushed the back of her hand over her injured mouth and stared at the empty doorway, stunned and frightened by what had happened. She had gotten what she wanted—both she and Miss Dolly could stay at Risen Glory—but the cost had been terrifyingly high.

Cain did not return to Risen Glory for several hours, but when he did, Kit was still awake, lying motionless in her bed as she listened to the distant sound of his footsteps on the stairs.

In his bedroom Cain stripped off his clothes in the dark and climbed naked into bed. He crooked one arm behind his head and stared at the ceiling. An image was printed there in the darkness of a wild rose mouth with bruised, petal-soft lips.

Without either of them knowing it, there had been a subtle shifting, a passage breached that could never be recrossed. The time of being man and child had passed forever.

Chapter Eighteen

Despite her restless night, Kit was up early the next morning. She searched through the clothes Lucy had unpacked for her until she found what she wanted, the one outfit in her wardrobe that Elspeth had never seen. She pulled the form-fitting khaki breeches on over her long, slender legs and then slipped her arms into the soft boy's shirt, drawing it closed over her lace-edged chemise. As she fastened up the row of buttons at the front, she regretted the shirt's long sleeves, but she knew they were necessary. Her arms would be brown as a butternut if she left them exposed to the sun. She consoled herself with the knowledge that the white material was as thin and fine as the fabric of her undergarments and would undoubtedly be cool.

She tucked her shirttails into her breeches and fastened the short row of buttons at the front snugly over her flat stomach; then she drew on her boots, enjoying the way the soft brown leather molded to her narrow feet and her calves. They were the first pair of good riding boots she had ever owned, and she could not wait to try them out.

Her hair hung in a single long braid at the back. Soft tendrils curled at her temples and in front of the tiny, silver ear studs that were fastened in her lobes. To shade her face, she had bought a boy's black felt hat with a flat brim and a thin leather cord that fastened beneath her chin to hold it on.

When she finished dressing, she studied her reflection in the cheval glass. For the first time since she had purchased her outfit, she had misgivings. Despite her masculine dress, no one could possibly mistake her for a boy. The clinging material of her shirt outlined her breasts with far more definition than she had anticipated, and the slim cut of the breeches made for a boy clung to her womanly hips like a second skin.

She shrugged off her misgivings about her scandalous attire. What did it matter? She only intended to wear her unorthodox outfit as she rode on Risen Glory land. When she was riding about the neighborhood, she would wear her new riding habit no matter how much she detested its confinement. She grimaced at herself in the mirror as she remembered that she would also have to ride sidesaddle, something she had only done a few times on occasional outings in Central Park. How she had hated it. Riding sidesaddle had robbed her of the feeling of power that she loved when she was on horseback and left her feeling awkward and unbalanced.

She let herself out of the house quietly, passing up a chance at breakfast because she did not want Sophronia to see her. Sophronia had come to her room last night not long after the awful interview with Baron Cain. Although Sophronia had listened politely to Kit's stories, she had volunteered little about her own life during the past three years. When Kit had pressed her for details, she had spoken of neighborhood gossip and the weather, impersonal topics that revealed nothing of herself. Only when Kit had asked her about Magnus Owen did she seem to be the Sophronia of old, haughty and snappish.

With the excitement of their first reunion over, Kit had noticed subtle changes in Sophronia. She had always been something of an anomaly, but now she seemed even more so. It wasn't just the outward changes in her produced by pretty clothes and a good diet. There was something more. Kit received the distinct impression that Sophronia resented her. Perhaps the feeling had always been there. Maybe it had just taken time and distance for Kit to be aware of it. What made it even more puzzling was that beneath that resentment, Kit thought she could still feel the old, familiar force of Sophronia's love.

Deliberately dismissing thoughts of Sophronia and what her reaction would be at seeing Kit's riding attire, she headed for the horses. As she walked with her characteristic long-legged stride across the open yard behind the house, she delicately sniffed the air. It smelled exactly as she remembered it, of good, rich earth and fresh manure. She even caught the distant scent of skunk, not altogether unpleasant when its source was far away. Merlin came out to greet her, and she stopped to scratch behind his ears and throw a stick for him to fetch.

The horses were not yet in the paddock, so she let herself into the stable, a new building erected on the foundation of the old one that had been burned. The heels of her boots clicked on the old stone floor, which was swept as cleanly as when Kit had attended to it. Tack hung in orderly rows on wooden pegs not yet darkened with age.

There were ten stalls in the stable, four of which were currently filled, two with carriage horses. The stalls that she suspected held the draft horses were empty as was another stall, somewhat larger than the others, which undoubtedly housed Cain's mount. Slowly she inspected the other two horses. She dismissed the first almost immediately. She was an old horse, a sorrel mare, obviously gentle but with no particular sparkle. She would be a good mount for a timid rider, but Kit had little interest in riding an animal whose primary concern would be returning to the stable for a good feed.

It was the other horse that caught her attention, a midnight-black gelding with a white blaze running down the center of his face. He was a large, powerful-looking animal, nearly eighteen hands, she judged, and his eyes were alert and lively.

She reached out a hand to stroke the long, elegant neck. "What's your name, boy?"

The animal whinnied softly and tossed his powerful head.

Kit laughed. "I think we're going to be good friends."

Just then the stable door opened behind her, and she turned to see a young boy, perhaps eleven or twelve, come in.

"You Miz Kit?" he asked curiously.

"Yes," she replied.

"I'm Samuel. Major done tole me if you comes to the stable today, I'm 'posed to tell you he want you to ride Lady."

Kit looked suspiciously toward the old sorrel mare. "Is that Lady?"

"Yez'm."

"Sorry, Samuel," she declared, stroking the gelding's silky mane, "but I have no intention of riding that horse. I want you to saddle this one."

"That's Temptation, ma'am. And the major was most particular 'bout that. He say you leave Temptation alone and ride Lady, and he say if I let you ride Temptation, he gwine hab my hide first and then he gwine hab yours!"

Kit bristled. How dare he talk about her that way! She looked over at the old sorrel and then at Temptation. Never had a horse been better named! Damn Cain! If last night had not happened, she would throw his threat back in his face and ride the horse she pleased, but the encounter in the library had made her cautious.

"Saddle Lady for me," she instructed him brusquely. "I'll talk to Major Cain about this personally."

As she had suspected, Lady was an unsatisfactory mount, more interested in nibbling the grass and the tops of bushes than in racing through the woods or along the edge of a field. Kit soon gave up trying to urge the mare beyond a sedate trot and turned her attention to the changes around her.

The old slave cabins had been painted and repaired. Each had its own garden, and she waved at several women who were tending them while their small children played in the shade of the nearby buckthorns.

When she came to the edge of the first planted field, she slid down off Lady's back and walked over to inspect it. As she had suspected when she had observed the fields from a distance the day before, the young cotton plants were covered with tight buds. A lizard slithered in the dirt near her boots, and she smiled. Lizards and toads as well as birds such as martins and mockingbirds preyed on the bollworms that could be so destructive to the cotton plants. It was too early to tell, of course, but it looked as if Baron Cain had the beginnings of a good crop. The thought was both pleasing and disturbing.

As she stood looking out across the land she knew so well, she could feel an unpleasant tightness building up inside her. It was all far more prosperous than she had imagined. For the first time it occurred to her that the money in her trust fund might not be enough to buy the plantation back from him, but she quickly pushed the thought aside. Somehow she was going to have to get access to the plantation's books. She did not let herself consider the awful possibility that he might not be willing to sell.

She strode over to Lady, who was nibbling away at a patch of new clover, and snatched up the bridle she had not bothered to secure. Leading the horse to a stump, Kit stepped up on it and gracefully climbed back into the saddle. Then she headed toward the small, secluded pond where she had spent so many pleasant summer hours swimming. It was just as she remembered it, with its clean spring-fed water and willow-lined bank. She promised herself a swim as soon as she was certain she would be undisturbed.

Leaving the pond, she rode on to the tiny cemetery where her mother and her grandparents were buried and paused outside the iron fence. Only her father's body was missing, buried in a mass grave in Hardin County, Tennessee, not far from Shiloh Church.

Her eyes wandered to the far corner by the fence where Rosemary Weston lay alone. Kit's features hardened as she considered how her stepmother, who had brought her so much misery when she was alive, was still bringing her misery three years after her death. How like his mother Baron Cain was. He had the same ruthless selfishness, the same cruelty about him that she had had.

Pulling the reins taut, she grimly set out toward the southeast corner of the property and the new spinning mill. Just before she rounded the last stand of trees, she saw a big, chestnut stallion tied off to the side and decided it must be Vandal, the horse Samuel had told her about while he was saddling Lady. She saw at once that the stallion was a fine animal, but she was disappointed that Cain had sold Apollo. And then she rounded the trees and caught her first sight of the spinning mill.

It was an oblong brick building, two and a half stories tall, with many windows. The building was much smaller than the pictures she had seen of the New England textile mills along the Merrimac River, probably not much bigger than the plantation house, but to Kit it was huge and threatening. It was going to make everything so much more complicated for her.

The mill was alive with noise. From inside, she could hear the sound of hammering and see workers passing by the windows. Outside, a half-dozen men were working on the roof, climbing ladders with stacks of shingles slung on their backs and nailing them on. Kit suspected that the shingles had been made from the cypress trees that grew in the nearby swamp and whose wood, when it cured, was waterproof and nearly as hard as granite.

The men working on the roof had all shed their shirts. One of them, who was nailing on shingles, straightened and a wave of muscles rippled beneath the sun-burnished skin of his back.

Even though he was turned away from her, she recognized him at once. Slowly she rode closer to the building and dismounted.

A burly man pushing a wheelbarrow saw the beautiful young woman in the boy's clothing and nudged the man next to him. Both of them stopped what they were doing to stare at her. Gradually the construction site fell silent as, one by one, the men stepped out of the building or peered through one of the open windows to see what had caught their co-workers' attention.

Cain became conscious of the sudden silence and looked down. From the roof he could see the top of a flat-brimmed hat, but not the face beneath it. Still, he did not need to see the face to recognize his visitor; one look at the slim, womanly body so clearly revealed by the white shirt and tight-fitting khaki breeches told him everything he needed to know.

He climbed across the roof and swung his foot onto the ladder, descending with the catlike grace of a much smaller man. At the bottom he turned toward her and began to survey her with every evidence of enjoyment. His eyes traveled once over her body and then returned to linger on the most intimate parts for a more leisurely inspection.

Kit could feel her cheeks flaming with embarrassment. At that moment she wanted nothing so much as to be wearing the modest riding habit she had formerly shunned. It was bad enough that these men were ogling her without Cain making it worse. He was her guardian! She had somehow expected him to reprimand her for her dress. Instead, he seemed to approve of it!

There was a crinkling at the corner of his moustache, and he murmured, just loudly enough for her to hear, "There ought to be a law against ever putting a body like yours in a dress." Before she could voice the sharp retort that was on its way to her lips, he took her arm and led her toward the doorway. "Come on. I'll show you around."

Although the construction of the building was nearly completed, there was actually little to see. Other than the steam engine that would power the machinery, none of the other equipment had been installed yet. Kit decided it was just as well, for she was having a difficult time concentrating. While Cain pointed up to the ceiling and talked about overhead belt drive and spindles, all she could think about was that she wished he had put on his shirt before he had decided to act as a tour guide.

She met a middle-aged man with ginger hair and whiskers whom Cain introduced as Jacob Childs, a New Englander he had hired away from a mill in Providence to operate the mill at Risen Glory. She learned for the first time that Cain had made several trips North during the past few years to visit the textile mills of New England. Somehow it galled her that he had never once stopped at the Templeton Academy to check on her.

As they stepped back outside, she refused to give him the satisfaction of knowing that his mill had interested her at all. "I want to talk to you about Temptation," she snapped.

"What about him?" Cain replied absentmindedly, his attention on the womanly curves the breeches revealed, curves that were much more apparent in the sunlight than they had been in the dim interior of the building.

Kit was uncomfortably aware of the onlookers hanging on to every syllable of their conversation. She moved closer to Cain and dropped her voice to a furious whisper. "I want to ride him! Surely you can't expect me to be satisfied with that poor excuse for a horse." She pointed an accusing finger at Lady, who was, at that moment, idly decapitating a patch of buttercups.

Cain finally forced his attention to her face. "Temptation's too much horse for a woman. I know Lady isn't much, but you'll have to make do."

"I've been riding horses like Temptation since I was eight years old," Kit hissed angrily. "Temptation might be too much horse for some women, but he's not too much for me!"

"Sorry, Kit, but that horse is a handful, even for me."

"And just what does that have to do with me?" Kit scoffed loudly, her anger making her forget the men who were enjoying every moment of the confrontation between their boss and the lady wearing pants. "I'll bet I'm ten times the rider you are."

"You think so?" Cain said slowly.

"What do you say we just see," she challenged. "You on Vandal and me on Temptation. We'll start at the gate next to the barn, race past the pond to the maple grove, and finish right here."

"You're not going to bait me into anything, Kit."

"Oh, I'm not baiting you, Baron Cain." Kit's mouth curved into a slow, sly smile. "I'm challenging you."

For a moment he studied her, and then he walked over to a sawhorse and grabbed his shirt. As he buttoned it, he issued a few brief orders to the men. Then he picked up a worn western hat, whose stained sweatband and sun-faded tan brim testified to many years of comfortable wear, settled it on his head, and walked over to Vandal.

"I'll meet you at the stable," he said brusquely as he climbed up into the saddle. Wheeling the stallion around, he rode from the clearing without waiting for her.

Eager for the oats that awaited her, Lady made the homeward journey somewhat faster than Kit had expected, but they still arrived well after Cain. When Kit rode into the yard, Temptation was already saddled and Cain was checking the cinch strap. Kit dismounted and handed Lady's bridle to Samuel. Then she walked over to Temptation and ran a hand down his muzzle.

"Ready?" Cain said shortly.

"I'm ready."

He gave her a leg up and she swung into the saddle. As soon as Temptation felt her weight, he began to prance and sidestep. For a moment she thought the gelding was going to try to throw her, and she concentrated all her skill on keeping him under control. When the horse had finally settled down, she looked around to see if Cain had been watching, but he was mounting Vandal and did not seem to be paying any attention to her.

As she rode from the yard, Kit was intoxicated by the sensation of leashed power contained in the animal beneath her, and she could barely restrain herself from giving him his head. She reluctantly reined in when she reached the gate near the barn.

Cain pulled up beside her, and Kit looked over at him. "First one who makes it back to the mill wins," she said. "Are you ready?"

Cain slowly tipped up the front of his hat with his thumb. "I'm not racing you, Kit."

"Not racing!" Kit was furious. She wanted to race him, desperately wanted to compete with him at something where his size and strength would not give him an advantage over her. On horseback the differences between man and woman would disappear, and she would have her chance to prove to him that Kit Weston was no simpering piece of fluff he could manhandle whenever he felt the urge.

"What's the matter?" she taunted. "Are you afraid you'll get beat by a girl in front of your men?"

Cain squinted slightly in the blaze of the late-morning sun. "I don't have to prove anything to you, and I don't have to prove anything to them, either."

His quiet self-assurance made her uncomfortable. "Then why did you come back here with me if you weren't going to race?"

"You were doing a lot of bragging back there. I wanted to see if any of it was true."

"It's true all right," she retorted defiantly.

"Talk's cheap, Kit. Let's see what you can do with a horse." Before she could respond, he had set off.

Kit watched him for a moment as he let Vandal break from an easy trot into a canter. He rode well for a large man; relaxed and easy, he seemed to be an extension of his horse. The memory of her earlier boastfulness now made her feel small. She sensed that he was as good a rider as she, yet he'd felt no need to brag about his abilities.

Shaking off her sudden mood of self-reproach, she leaned forward and patted Temptation's sleek black neck. "All right, boy. Let's show him!" Pulling the reins taut, she set off after him.

Temptation proved to be everything she had hoped. At first she kept him abreast of Vandal and held him to a canter, but then, as she sensed the horse straining to go faster, she let him have his head. Veering away from the planted fields, she turned the horse into an open meadow. They tore across it at a fierce gallop, and as she felt the raw power of the animal beneath her, all else disappeared. There was no longer a ruthless man with cold gray eyes watching her. There was no yesterday or tomorrow, nothing but the magnificent animal who seemed to have become part of her very body.

Ahead of her she glimpsed a low hedge. With the barest pressure of her knees, she turned the horse toward it. As they thundered closer, she crouched low in the saddle and leaned forward, holding her knees tight to his flanks. She felt the great surge of power as Temptation effortlessly cleared the barrier.

When they were well past it, she reluctantly slowed him down to a trot and turned him back. It was enough for now. If she pushed the horse harder, Cain might accuse her of being reckless, and she would give him no excuse to deny her the right to ride Temptation.

Cain was waiting for her at the entrance to the meadow. She reined in beside him and wiped the perspiration from her cheeks and the bridge of her nose with her sleeve.

Cain turned toward her, his saddle creaking slightly as he moved. "That was quite an exhibition."

She kept silent, determined not to repeat her earlier boastfulness.

"Did you ride at all when you were in New York?" he inquired politely.

"Not really."

With a slight tug on the reins, he turned Vandal toward the stable. "Then you're going to be sore as hell tomorrow."

Kit watched his retreating back with open-mouthed astonishment. Was that all he was going to say? Digging her heels into Temptation's flanks, she quickly caught up with him.

"Well?" she said belligerently.

"Well what?"

"Are you going to let me ride this horse or not?"

Cain grinned. "Don't see why not. As long as you don't put a sidesaddle on him, you can ride him."

Kit silently reveled in her victory all the way back to the stable. She reached the yard slightly ahead of Cain and dismounted while Samuel held the bridle.

"Take your time cooling this horse out," she instructed the youngster. "And put a blanket on him. I rode him hard."

Cain drew up in time to hear her orders. He dismounted, regarding her with amusement. "Leave him alone, Kit. Samuel's nearly as good a stable boy as you were."

She glared at him, but he merely chuckled and walked away from her toward the barn.

Chapter Nineteen

Kit's muscles ached as she descended the stairs the next morning. In contrast to the breeches she had worn the day before, she was dressed in a fetchingly demure dress of palest lilac voile with a delicate white lace shawl tossed around her slim shoulders. From her fingers dangled the lavender sashes of a floppy leghorn hat.

Miss Dolly stood by the front door waiting for her. "Now don't you look as pretty as a picture," she cooed with a tiny clap of her hands. "Just fasten up that button on your glove, darlin', and you'll look perfect."

Kit smiled as she fastened the offending button and then, centering herself in front of the long, narrow mirror that hung near the door, began putting on her hat. "You look awfully pretty yourself," she said.

"Why, thank you, darlin'. I do try to keep myself nice, but it's not as easy as it once was. I don't have youth entirely on my side any longer, you understand. Now just look at you. Not a single gentleman will be able to keep his mind on the Lord with you sittin' in the congregation lookin' like a piece of Easter candy waitin' to be devoured."

"Makes me hungry just watching her," drawled a lazy voice from behind them.

Kit spun around, dropping the sashes she had been carefully arranging into a bow. Cain was leaning against the doorjamb of the library. He was dressed in a pearl-gray morning coat with charcoal trousers and waistcoat and a thinly striped cravat of burgundy and white.

Her eyes narrowed suspiciously at his formal dress. "Just where do you think you're going?"

He lifted a brow as if he were mildly surprised at her question. "To church, of course."

"Church!" Kit exploded. "We didn't invite you to go to church with us!"

"Katharine Louise Weston!" Miss Dolly exclaimed, her hand going to her throat with a small, nervous flutter. "Whatever can you be thinkin' of, addressin' the general so rudely? I specifically requested that he escort us. You'll have to forgive her, General. She spent too long on horseback yesterday. She could barely walk when she got out of bed this morning, and it's made her cranky."

"I understand completely," Cain replied with a sympathetic concern in his voice that was completely at odds with the amusement dancing in his eyes.

Kit angrily plucked up the sashes of her hat and turned back to the mirror, but she couldn't seem to make them form a bow.

"Miss Calhoun, maybe you'd better tie that for her before she destroys it."

"Certainly, General." Miss Dolly walked over to Kit, clucking her tongue. "Here, darlin'. Tilt up your chin and let me."

Kit gave Cain a scalding glare and then submitted herself to Miss Dolly's ministrations. She felt like a child with Miss Dolly fussing over her while Cain looked on, making no effort to hide his enjoyment of her discomfiture. Finally the bow was arranged satisfactorily, and Kit followed her companion out the front door to the waiting carriage.

Cain helped the older woman in and then offered his hand to Kit. She batted it away and hissed at him angrily. "Why don't you stay home where you belong?"

Cain's lips curved into a mocking smile. "Not a chance. I wouldn't miss your reunion with the good people of Rutherford for anything in the world."

Our Father who art in heaven . . . Jewellike puddles of shimmering topaz and lapis lazuli and amethyst settled over the bowed heads of the congregation as sunlight streamed through the stained-glass windows. In Rutherford, they still talked of what a miracle it was that those windows had escaped destruction by that spawn of Satan, William Tecumseh Sherman.

Give us this day our daily bread, and forgive us our trespasses as we forgive those . . .

Kit was uncomfortable sitting in her lilac finery amid the faded dresses and pre-war bonnets of the women around her. She felt as if she had somehow committed a breach of etiquette by being fashionably dressed in the midst of such abject poverty, and vowed to wear a more subdued outfit the next time she attended church.

For thine is the kingdom and the power and the glory . . .

As the congregation recited the familiar words, her mind wandered back to her childhood and the ramshackle clapboard church, not far from Risen Glory, that served as the spiritual home for the slaves from nearby plantations. It was there that Sophronia had taken her every Sunday because Garrett and Rosemary refused to make the weekly trip to the white community's church in Rutherford, and Sophronia, even though she was a child herself, was determined that Kit should hear the Word.

Now Kit could not help but compare this sedate congregation as they lifted their heads and politely turned their attention to the words of the Reverend Rawlins Cogdell and the members of the shabby slave church, jubilantly crying out their praises to the glory of the Lord. She had lost too much of her faith when she had stopped attending that slave church, although she knew it was not the lack of a church that had made her lose faith, but the events of her own life. In her mind she could see the wooden building with its peeling paint and sagging steps as it probably was at that very moment, bursting at the seams with enthusiastic worshipers. Sophronia would be there, and Magnus.

Her forehead puckered into a small frown as she thought of Magnus. She had run out to meet him yesterday afternoon when she had spotted him heading toward the stables. But it had been a subdued reunion. Although Magnus had seemed happy to see her, the old informality between them was gone. She was now a white woman, fully grown, and he was a black man.

A fly buzzed a lazy figure eight in front of her. She stole a glance at Cain, glad that Miss Dolly was seated between them. His attention was turned politely toward the pulpit, his expression as inscrutable as ever. Farther over in the row in front of her sat another man whose attention was not as firmly fixed on the front of the church. Kit gave him a slow smile and then tilted her head ever so slightly so that the straw brim of her hat shielded her face from further view. Later on, when they stood to sing the final hymn, she would favor Brandon Parsell with another smile.

As she had hoped, he was attending church today. He had tried to get to her side before the service, but she had been surrounded by a group of women, all eager to confirm for themselves the startling news that Kit Weston had come back from New York City, a beautiful, well-mannered young lady. Before she returned to Risen Glory, Kit was going to have to make certain that Brandon found his chance to speak with her. She only had a month, and she couldn't waste a day of it.

The final hymn was sung, Brandon received a smile that made him feel better than he'd felt any time since he'd returned from New York City, and the congregation slowly filed down the center aisle. The people of Rutherford were faced with a dilemma, and they knew it. Regardless of her past, Kit Weston was one of their own. To snub her socially was unthinkable. Yet as long as she was living at Risen Glory under Major Cain's guardianship, they could hardly accept her and continue to reject him.

Slowly, first one person and then another nodded to him. A gray-haired gentleman asked him about his cotton crop. A plump woman with a marriageable daughter thanked him for his contribution to the Bible Society. The conversations were reserved, but the message was clear. The barriers against Baron Cain had to come down.

Later they would remark to each other that it was only for Kit Weston's sake, of course, that they had acknowledged him. Not for anything would they admit how pleased they were to finally have an excuse to draw the fascinating Yankee into their small, insular circle. It did not occur to any of them that the Yankee might not wish to come.

Standing off to the side of the church, an elegant woman with an air of sophistication that set her apart from the other members of the congregation watched what was happening with some amusement. So this was the notorious Baron Cain. Although she was a stranger to the community, having lived in the large brick house on the outskirts of Rutherford for only three months, she had heard all about the owner of Risen Glory. Nothing she had heard, however, had quite prepared her for her first sight of him. Her eyes made a sweeping path from his shoulders down to his narrow hips. He was magnificent.

Veronica Gamble was a Southerner by birth, if not by inclination. Born in Charleston, she had married the portrait painter, Francis Gamble, when she was barely eighteen. They had immediately left both her family and his and gone to Italy. For fourteen years, they had divided their time between Florence, Paris, and Vienna, where Francis had charged outrageous prices for outrageously flattering portraits of the wives and children of the aristocracy. On Sunday afternoons artists, politicians, and nobility attended their salon, which had become famous throughout Europe.

When her husband died the previous winter, she was left comfortably well off, if not wealthy. On a whim, she decided to return to South Carolina and the brick house that her husband had inherited from his parents. It would give her time to assess her life and decide what she wanted to do with her future.

At thirty-one, she was striking in appearance. Her auburn hair was pulled softly back from her face and fell in lustrous curls over the nape of her neck. Setting off its coppery hues were a pair of slanted eyes, almost as green as her fashionable Zouave jacket. On any other woman her full underlip would have been obtrusive, but on her it was frankly sensual. She was considered by everyone to be a great beauty, but in actuality her features were too angular, her thinly chiseled nose too long. No man, however, had ever seemed to notice. Instead, they saw a sophisticated woman of intelligence and wit who watched those around her with a slightly jaundiced eye and waited patiently to see what life had in store for her.

She eased her way toward the double doors at the back of the church where the Reverend Cogdell was greeting his flock as they filed out.

"Ah, Mrs. Gamble," he said as he caught sight of her. "How pleasant to have you with us this morning. I don't believe you've met Miss Calhoun. And this is Mr. Cain of Risen Glory. Where has Katharine Louise gone? I wanted you to meet her, too."

But Veronica Gamble had no interest at all in either Miss Calhoun or anyone named Katharine Louise. With wise eyes she smiled into the openly admiring face of the man who towered over her. "Mr. Cain," she acknowledged with a graceful inclination of her head. "I've heard a great deal about you. Somehow I had expected horns."

Rawlins Cogdell winced, but Cain tossed back his head and laughed. "I only wish I could have been as fortunate to have heard of you," he replied.

Veronica slipped her gloved hand into the crook of his arm. "The matter is easily remedied."

From the pavement outside the church, Kit had heard Cain's laughter, and it had momentarily distracted her from her conversation. She quickly turned her attention back to Brandon.

His pleasant, regular features were even more attractive than she had remembered. A stray lock of straight brown hair tumbled over his smooth forehead, and he brushed it away impatiently as he talked. She noticed how different his small, neatly trimmed moustache was from Cain's thick, piratical one. Everything about the two men was different. Brandon was polite and easy to be with, every inch a Southern gentleman. As she looked at the soft line of his mouth, she suddenly wondered what it would feel like to kiss it. It would be pleasant, she was certain. Far different from Cain's frightening assault. She determined to find out the first chance she got.

Brandon lowered his voice. "I've thought about you quite often since we met in New York."

"Oh?"

"Would you like to ride with me tomorrow afternoon? The bank closes at three. I could be at Risen Glory within the hour."

Kit nodded graciously. "I'd enjoy riding with you, Mr. Parsell." She saw he was ready to say more and decided their first meeting had lasted long enough. "Until tomorrow, then." With a smile, she turned away from him toward a group of young men who had been patiently waiting for a chance to speak with her.

As they vied for her attention, she noticed Cain deep in conversation with a strikingly attractive auburn-haired woman. Something about the attentive way the woman was gazing up at him grated on her, and she found herself hoping Cain would look over and see her so well surrounded by masculine company. She was disappointed, however, for as far as she could tell, he did not seem to notice her at all.

She was suddenly aware of Miss Dolly engaged in animated conversation with the Reverend Cogdell and his wife. The longer Miss Dolly talked, the more bewildered her pair of listeners looked.

Hastily disengaging herself from her disappointed admirers, she sped to Miss Dolly's side. "Are you ready to leave, Miss Dolly?" she asked, somewhat breathlessly.

"Why yes, darlin'. I was just chattin' with the Reverend Cogdell and his dear wife Mary. We haven't seen each other in years, don't you know, even though our families are related. We were just discussin' the recent events at Bull Run. Grown-up conversation, darlin'. Nothin' for you to worry your pretty little head about."

Perhaps Cain sensed disaster, for he suddenly materialized at Kit's side. "Miss Calhoun, the carriage is waiting for us."

"Why, thank you, General—" Miss Dolly gasped and pressed her fingers to her mouth. "I—I mean Major, of course. Of course I mean Major. Major Baron Cain. Silly me." With all the ribbons on her bonnet aflutter, she scampered toward the carriage.

The Reverend Cogdell and his wife stared after her in openmouthed astonishmemt.

"She thinks I'm General Lee living in disguise at Risen Glory," Cain explained politely.

Rawlins Cogdell began to wring his pale, thin hands in agitation. "Major Cain, Katharine, I do apologize. When I recommended Dolly Calhoun for the post of chaperone, I had no idea —Oh, dear, this will never do."

Mary Cogdell's small brown eyes were filled with remorse. "I'm afraid this is all my fault. I'm the one who brought Miss Dolly to my husband's attention. We had heard she was nearly destitute, but we had no idea she was feebleminded."

Kit opened her mouth to protest, but Cain cut her off. "You needn't worry about Miss Calhoun. Kit wants her to stay at Risen Glory. She's made all the necessary arrangements with me." Kit was the only one who noticed the brief, pointed pause before the word "arrangements."

"But Katharine can not possibly stay at Risen Glory with you," the minister protested. "Not without a proper chaperone in attendance, and Dolly Calhoun is hardly a proper chaperone. Why, she must have spoken to a dozen people today. By this afternoon everyone in the county will know about her. It isn't respectable. Surely you must understand, Mr. Cain. There will be gossip. You're far too young a man. . . ."

"Kit is my ward," he said dryly.

Rawlins Cogdell looked at him sharply. He was not a fanciful man, but he seemed to sense a strange tension between Kit Weston and Baron Cain, and he did not like it at all. This situation boded no good.

In the meantime, his wife was trying to convince Kit of the impossibility of the arrangement. ". . . an innocent young woman, so it would not, of course, occur to you how it might look to others."

"Mrs. Cogdell, I don't really care what other people think. I've been away from Risen Glory for three years. I don't intend to leave again so quickly."

Mary Cogdell looked at her husband helplessly. What both of them wanted to say, but neither of them could politely phrase, was their conviction that she was far too young and beautiful to be living so loosely chaperoned in the same house with the worldly Major Cain.

Cogdell had the unsettling sense that Cain was reading their minds and knew exactly what was troubling them. He imagined he saw a small smile flicker across the man's features before he inclined his head politely toward them.

"If you'll excuse us now, Reverend Cogdell, Mrs. Cogdell. We have to be going. Thank you for your concern, but please don't trouble yourselves any further." He took Kit lightly by the arm and led her toward the carriage.

Cogdell shook his stately white head. "There's going to be trouble there," he muttered. "I can feel it in my bones."

Magnus drove the buggy with Sophronia seated at his side and, in the back, Samuel, Lucy, and Rose, the cook. When they had first left the church, he had tried to make conversation with Sophronia, but she had answered him brusquely and he had soon given up. Kit's return had upset her, although Magnus didn't understand why. There was something strange about Sophronia's relationship with Kit.

Magnus looked over at her, sitting like a beautiful statue at his side. He was tired of all the mysteries surrounding her. Tired even of his love for her, which was bringing him far more misery than happiness. He thought of Deborah Watson, the daughter of one of the men working on the cotton mill. Deborah had made it clear that she wanted Magnus's attention. Damn it! He was ready to settle down. The war was behind him, he had a good job, and Risen Glory's small, neat overseer's house situated at the edge of the orchard pleased him. His days of hard drinking and easy women were over. He wanted a wife and children. Deborah Watson was pretty. Sweet-natured, too, unlike the vinegar-tongued Sophronia. She'd make a good wife for him. However, instead of cheering him up, the thought made him feel even more unhappy.

He was distracted from his bleak ruminations by the sight of a crimson-and-black buggy with a gold stripe running down its side coming toward them. Magnus didn't recognize the buggy, but he knew it was too new to belong to any of the locals. Probably a Northerner. Carpetbagger, most likely.

Magnus sensed Sophronia straighten beside him and look more closely at the approaching vehicle. It was not long before he recognized the driver as James Spence, the owner of the new phosphate mine. Magnus had had little contact with the man. From what he knew of him, he was a good businessman. He paid an honest day's wage for an honest day's work and didn't cheat his customers. Still, Magnus didn't like him, perhaps because Sophronia so obviously did.

As the buggy drew nearer, Magnus realized to his displeasure that Spence was not an unattractive man. He tipped a biscuit-colored beaver hat, revealing a thick head of black hair, parted neatly in the center, and a set of trim side whiskers. "Good morning, Sophronia," he called out. "Nice day, isn't it?" He did not so much as glance at any of the other occupants of the buggy.

"Mawnin', Mr. Spence," Sophronia replied with a sassy smile that set Magnus's teeth on edge and made him want to shake her until she begged for mercy.

Spence replaced his hat, the buggy passed, and Magnus recalled that this was not the first time he had seen Spence show an interest in Sophronia. He remembered observing the two of them in conversation several times when he had driven Sophronia into Rutherford to do some shopping. His hands tightened involuntarily on the reins. He was going to talk to Sophronia as soon as he could get her alone.

The opportunity came late that afternoon. He had changed from his Sunday best into a comfortable pair of dark-blue trousers and a faded blue shirt, and was sitting with Merlin on the front porch of his house, leaning idly against the wooden railing as he enjoyed his day of leisure.

A flash of amber in the orchard caught his attention. He looked more closely and saw Sophronia in the amber and brown dress she had worn to church that morning. She was walking among the cherry trees, gazing up into the branches, and he guessed she was trying to judge whether there was enough fruit left to justify another picking.

Getting up from his comfortable position, he took the two front steps in one long stride, and then, stuffing his hands deep into his pockets, ambled toward the orchard. "Looks like you might as well let the birds enjoy what's left," he said when he reached her.

Sophronia had not heard him come up behind her, and now she whirled around. "What do you mean, sneakin' up on me like that?"

"Wasn't sneakin'," Magnus replied with an easy grin. "I guess I'm just naturally light on my feet."

But Sophronia refused to respond to his bantering. "Go away, Magnus. I don't want to talk to you."

"Well, that's just too bad, 'cause I'm goin' talk to you anyway."

Without uttering a word, Sophronia turned her back to him and began to walk toward the house. In a few quick steps, Magnus had planted himself in front of her. "We can talk here in the orchard," he said pleasantly, "or you can take my arm and we'll walk over there to my house, and you can sit in that big old rocker on my front porch while I say what I have to say."

"Let me by, Magnus!"

"You want to talk here? That's fine with me." He took her by the arm and steered her up against the gnarled trunk of the apple tree behind her, using his muscular body to block any chance she had of slipping past him.

"You're makin' a fool of yourself, Magnus Owen!" Sophronia

hissed, her slanted eyes alive with small, golden fires. "Most men would of taken the hint by now. I don't like you! When you goin' get that through your thick skull? Don't you have any pride? Doesn't it bother you to be chasin' after a woman who doesn't care anything about you? Don't you know that half the time I'm laughin' at you behind your back?"

Magnus flinched, but he didn't move away. "You just go ahead and laugh at me all you want," he said. "My feelin's for you are honest ones, and I'm not ashamed of them. You're the one should be ashamed. You sat in that church this mornin' singin' hymns and cryin' out praises to Jesus Christ, and then you walk out the door and the first thing you do is start makin' eyes at James Spence."

"Don't you judge me, Magnus Owen!"

"You listen to me, Sophronia. That Northerner may be rich and good-lookin', but he's not your kind. When you goin' stop fightin' what you are?"

Magnus's words made her uneasy, but not for anything would she let him see that. Instead, she tilted her head provocatively to the side and rested it against the rough bark of a tree branch, thrusting her breasts ever so slightly forward as she did. A stab of triumph shot through her at his quick intake of breath. This time she would punish him for interfering, and she would punish him in the way that would hurt him most.

"You jealous, Magnus?" She lifted her hand and placed it on his arm, kneading the warm, hard flesh beneath his sleeve with seductive fingertips. She was too intent on taunting him to notice that the masculine contact did not produce that awful crawling inside her she was so used to feeling whenever a white man touched her. "You wishin' it was you instead of him I was smilin' at?" she asked softly. "Is that what's botherin' you, Mistuh Overseer?"

"What's botherin' me is watchin' all those wars goin' on inside you and not bein' able to do anything about it," he said huskily.

"There aren't no wars goin' on inside me, Magnus," she replied with a silky certainty that was as false as a paste diamond.

"You don't have to lie to me, Sophronia. Don't you understand? Lyin' to me is like lyin' to yourself."

His gentleness made a tiny crack in the chrysalis of her self-protection. He saw it happen just as he saw through the sham of her seduction to the vulnerability behind it. He saw it all and knew he must kiss her, damned himself as a fool for not having done it sooner.

Slowly, ever so slowly, he lowered his head, as determined not to frighten her as he was to have what he wanted. He could see the knowledge of what was to come flicker in her golden eyes, see the tremor of fear, the hint of defiance. Nearer he came, pausing just at the point of illusion where his lips first sensed the warmth of hers, not touching, feathering her skin with his warm breath. She waited patiently, whether in fear or resignation, he did not know.

Softly, with no clear moment of metamorphosis, the illusion became reality, and his lips brushed hers in a tender boy's kiss, infinitely exciting because it was given by a man. Gently he kissed her, yearning to heal with his mouth her hidden wounds, to dissolve devils and tame demons and teach her gentle worlds of love and softness where evil did not exist and tomorrow was laughter and hope that knew no color, and forever was two loving hearts wedded in joy as one.

Her lips trembled under his like the wings of a trapped bird, frightened yet somehow sensing that her captor would do her no harm. His healing magic slowly began to seep through the pores of her skin like warm summer sun. He gently lifted her away from the tree and enfolded her in his arms, pressing her close to him. The maleness that had frightened her for so long did not seem so terrifying now, but strangely pleasant. How soft his mouth was, she thought. Soft and clean.

Much too soon, he pulled back from her, leaving her deserted and exposed. Her mouth felt abandoned, her skin cold despite the heat of the late June afternoon. She met his eyes, even though she knew it was a mistake, and drew a deep, shaking breath at the love and tenderness she saw there.

With a jerk she yanked herself away from him. "Leave me alone," she cried, sobbing. And then she fled, tearing across the orchard as if she were running away from devils, refusing to recognize that all the devils were inside her and that she could never outrace them.

Chapter Twenty

Kit heard the hooves of Brandon's horse crunching the fresh gravel of the drive that curved in an ellipse in front of the house. She rushed to the cheval glass to check her reflection for the dozenth time since she had finished dressing. There would be no khaki riding breeches today. She had resigned herself to proper dress, a sidesaddle, and poor Lady as a mount.

The memory of that morning consoled her. She had been up before dawn and racing across the fields on Temptation's back when the sky was still the pale, soft pink of the underside of a seashell. It had been a wonderful ride, wild and exhilarating, far different from what she could expect this afternoon.

She studied her reflection critically. It was the first time she had worn her new riding habit, and she had to admit that it was a flattering garment, no matter how much she disliked the idea of wearing it. Made of crimson broadcloth trimmed in black braid, the jacket fit her snugly in the bodice, accenting her small breasts and narrow waist. The full crimson skirt fell in graceful folds to the hem, which was decorated with a deep border of black braid, its swirling pattern looking like a long chain of script *L*'s.

She checked to make certain there were no hanging threads or hooks that had escaped her notice. The four large black frogs that held together the front of the snug jacket were all fastened. Her black hat, a feminine version of a man's stovepipe, but with a lower, softer crown and a wisp of a crimson gauze veiling trailing from the back, was on straight. Her hair was fastened in a neat bun at the nape of her neck, with only a few recalcitrant wisps escaping to soften its severity. She had polished her boots herself, unwilling to trust the soft leather to anyone else's care, and knew they were spotless.

Satisfied that she was looking her best, she snatched up her riding crop and left the room, giving no thought at all to the pair of black kid riding gloves that lay in her glove box and that were an essential part of the outfitting of any fashionable female equestrienne.

When she reached the hallway, she heard voices coming from the piazza and stepped outside where she discovered, to her consternation, that Cain was standing in the drive talking to Brandon. Once again she was struck by the contrast between the two men. Cain was much bigger, of course, but it was more than a difference of size that set them apart.

Brandon was properly dressed for riding in hat, coat, and trousers, with a bottle-green four-in-hand showing above the top of his vest. The clothes were old, Kit noticed, and no longer of the most fashionable cut, but they were neatly pressed and he wore them well. In contrast, Cain was bareheaded with an open-collared shirt rolled up at the sleeves and a pair of muddy trousers. He stood in an easy slouch, one hand stuffed into his pocket, a dirty boot propped up on the bottom step. Everything about Brandon indicated culture and good breeding, while Cain looked like a barbarian.

She clutched her riding crop more tightly in her hand and walked forward. Lady had been brought around as she had instructed and waited patiently next to the mounting block, the old sidesaddle she had found in the attic on the horse's back. Kit gave Cain a cold nod and Brandon a smiling greeting, which he returned effusively. The admiration in his eyes told her that the efforts she had taken with her appearance had not been in vain. There was no admiration, however, in Cain's eyes, nothing but mockery as he studied her fashionable garb.

Brandon made a motion to help her mount, but Cain was quicker. "Allow me," he said as he stepped forward.

"Thank you," she said coldly.

Brandon turned away with obvious displeasure to mount his own horse, and Kit slipped her fingers into Cain's outstretched hand. She stepped onto the mounting block and put the toe of her polished boot into the stirrup, then she swung herself up into the saddle. When she was settled with her upper leg hooked in place and the cumbersome skirts arranged, she looked down to see Cain still watching her.

"Now who's the hypocrite?" he mocked softly.

Before she could make a response, he had turned on his heel and was striding across the drive, the gravel crunching under the soles of his boots.

Brandon suggested they ride over to Holly Grove, his former

home, and Kit agreed, unwilling to risk running into Cain again if they stayed near Risen Glory. As they trotted down the drive toward the road, Kit noticed Brandon covertly studying the planted fields that stretched out on both sides of them, and her lips curved into a smile. He was already making plans.

Holly Grove, along with most of the cotton plantations in the area, had been put to the torch by the same men who had spared Risen Glory. After the war Brandon had returned to find a crumbled ruin and blackened chimneys already overgrown with wild grape vines and blackberry brambles. He had not been able to pay the punishing taxes on the land, and everything had been confiscated. Now it was all standing idle.

They dismounted near what had once been the smokehouse. Brandon tied the horses and then took Kit's arm and led her to the house. They had been chatting pleasantly as they rode, but now he fell silent as he gazed at the devastation around him. Kit felt her heart swell with pity at the pain she saw on his face.

"It's all gone," he finally said. "Everything the South believed in. Everything we fought for."

She stared up at the twin chimneys and repressed a shudder. They were like great ghostly fingers towering over her, rebuking her somehow.

"The Yankees laugh at us, you know," he continued. "They laugh because we believe in chivalry and honor. But look what happens when there's no chivalry and when honor is turned into a joke." He made a great stabbing gesture around him. "They take away our land, tax us until we can't buy bread." Slowly he shook his head. "Radical Reconstruction is the Almighty's curse on us. What have we done to deserve so much evil?"

"Maybe it was the slaves," Kit said, as much to herself as to him. "Maybe we're being punished for having kept human beings in slavery."

"Poppycock!" Brandon snapped. "You lived with the Yankees too long. Slavery is God's plan. You know very well what the Bible says about slaves."

She did know. She had heard it often enough, preached from the pulpit of the slave church by white ministers sent periodically by the plantation owners to remind their people that God approved of their enslavement and had left clear instructions regarding a slave's obligations to his master. Kit remembered Sophronia sitting by her side during these sermons, stiff and pale, unable to reconcile what she was hearing with her vision of a loving, forgiving Jesus.

"And just look at what's happened to the Negras now that they're free," he went on. "They're like small children, lost and bewildered, with no one to take care of them."

Sophronia and Magnus hardly fit Brandon's description as far as Kit was concerned, but she recognized his sincerity and held her tongue. Besides, she knew there were thousands of homeless Negroes all over the South who were depending on rations from the Freedmen's Bureau to keep them alive.

"Let's go back to the horses," Brandon said abruptly. He took her arm and led her away from the house, and they walked back along the overgrown path as silently as they had come.

Their mounts were peacefully grazing in the clearing near the smokehouse. A wild plum, uprooted long ago in a winter storm, lay on its side. Kit walked over to it and sat on the trunk. She was not ready to go back. There was something she had to do first.

Brandon came up beside her. "It was a mistake bringing you here."

"Why?"

He stared off toward the blackened chimneys in the distance. "Don't you see? It makes the differences between us all that much more apparent."

"Does it?" Kit countered. "Neither of us has a home, Brandon. Remember that Risen Glory's not mine. Not yet, anyway."

Now she had his attention. He gave her a searching look. She pulled off her hat and set it on the ground beside her. It was so warm. Much too warm to be wearing riding habits with long-sleeved jackets and cumbersome skirts. She plucked absent-mindedly at a piece of loose tree bark, peeling it off in her fingers.

"I only have a month, Brandon, and then he's going to force me to go back to New York." There. It was done. She had taken the initiative and gently pushed forth the issue that he was too much a gentleman to broach.

Brandon did not need to ask who she was talking about. "I

can't tolerate the idea of your living in the same house with that man," he said venomously as he sat down beside her on the fallen tree trunk. "Everybody who came into the bank today was talkin' about it. They say Miss Calhoun's senile and not a fit chaperone. That man's not a gentleman, Kit. You watch yourself with him, you hear? I don't like him. Don't like him at all."

She was warmed by Brandon's concern. He was so serious, so kind. "Don't worry," she said. "I'll be careful."

And then she deliberately tilted her face up to him, slightly parting her lips in open invitation. She had vowed she would not let this excursion end without kissing him. It was something she knew she must do to erase Cain's searing brand upon her mouth. Even as she thought it, she realized it was more than that. Cain's kiss in the library had been terrifying, a brutal violation, and she had hated it. But there had been his earlier kiss that same afternoon, the kiss that had set hot fires in her blood and made her forget everything, the kiss that was, in its own way, even more frightening than the brutal one. She must prove to herself that Brandon Parsell could spark those same fires.

His eyes were partially shadowed by the brushed beaver brim of his gray hat, but she could see him looking at her mouth. "I want you to kiss me," she said.

Her forwardness shocked him. She saw it at once in the frown that puckered his brow, and his attitude irritated her even as it endeared him to her. She reached up and gently lifted off his hat, noticing as she set it beside her own that there was a small, red line across the upper part of his forehead from the band.

"Brandon," she said quietly, "I only have a month. There isn't time for me to be coy."

Even a gentleman could not ignore so open an invitation. He leaned forward and pressed his mouth to hers.

Kit noticed that his lips were softer than Cain's and fleshier. They were also much sweeter, she decided, remaining politely closed. It was a tender kiss compared to Cain's burning, all-encompassing invasion that had sucked the very life from her. Brandon's lips were dry. That was pleasant. But his moustache seemed a little rough. Was that because it was so much shorter and spikier than Cain's?

Her mind was wandering, and she quickly brought her attention back to what she was doing. Lifting her arms, she threw them enthusiastically around his neck. At first his shoulders seemed a little narrow to her, but then she decided it was all in her imagination. They were really very solid. He began trailing kisses across her cheek and the line of her jaw. His moustache scratched the sensitive skin, and she jumped.

He immediately pulled back from her. "I'm sorry. Have I frightened you?"

"No, of course not." She nearly snapped at him. The kiss hadn't proven anything. Why couldn't he set aside his scruples just once and do the job right? No sooner had she thought it than she was contrite. Brandon Parsell was a true gentleman, that was why!

He dropped his head. "Kit, you must know that I wouldn't hurt you for anything in the world. I should have known such lack of restraint would only frighten you. Women like you are to be cherished. You need to be shielded from the harsher aspects of life."

She could feel a surprising misting of tears pushing at the back of her eyelids. How dear he was. So concerned about protecting her. So different from . . . "Brandon, I'm not made out of glass."

"If only I were in a position to shield you," he said, lifting his head. "Kit, I want you to know that if anything more permanent were to happen between us, I would never physically debase you. I would bother you as little as I possibly could with my own needs."

This was something she understood. When Mrs. Templeton had spoken with them about Eve's Shame, she had told them that there were many husbands who were most considerate of their wives, and if they were fortunate, they would marry such a man.

She was suddenly glad Brandon's sweet kisses had not set the raging fire in her that Cain's had, a response, it now occurred to her, that had probably been nothing more than a physical reaction to the rigors of her journey and the strange emotions of being home again. She was more certain than ever that marriage to Brandon was what she wanted. Not only was he handsome, but he was kind and considerate, everything a woman wanted in a husband. Even more important, she was very sure she could manage him.

He made her put on her hat so she wouldn't get sunburned and gently chastised her for forgetting her gloves. As he fussed over her, she smiled and thought of Elspeth. How she would have approved of Brandon Parsell.

They talked for a while about the disgraceful state of politics in South Carolina, or rather Brandon talked while Kit listened. She reminded herself that he was accustomed to a different sort of woman—quiet and retiring like his mother and his sisters—and she tried to restrain her normally impulsive tongue. Still, she managed to shock him with her well-informed opinions about Negro suffrage and the Fifteenth Amendment. Two small furrows gradually etched themselves between his eyes.

"Brandon," she said quietly, determined that he should understand from the very beginning, "I'm a well-educated woman. I have opinions and ideas. I've also been on my own for a long time. Most of my life, in fact. It's made me independent. I can't be what I'm not."

His smile did not quite erase the furrows between his eyes. "Your independence is one of the things I most admire about you. It's just going to take me a little while to get used to it. You're not like the other women I know."

"And have you known a lot of women?" she teased.

Her question made him laugh. "Kit Weston, you're one of a kind."

Their conversation as they rode back to Risen Glory was a happy combination of gossip and reminiscences. She promised to go on a picnic with him and two other young couples on Saturday and to let him escort her to church on Sunday. As she stood on the porch and waved good-bye, she decided that, all in all, the day had gone well.

Unfortunately, the evening did not. Miss Dolly waylaid her before dinner and asked her to use her sweet young eyes to sort through the button box for a dome-shaped mother-of-pearl that Miss Dolly just knew was in there someplace. The sorting was accompanied by a great gust of chatter punctuated with twittering and nose twitching and a fluttering of fingers and ribbons

—what button had been sewn on what dress, where the garment had been worn and with whom, what the weather had been like on that particular day. And then when they went into dinner, she ordered that all the windows be closed, despite the fact that the evening was warm, because she had heard rumors of a diphtheria outbreak in Charleston.

Cain managed Miss Dolly well and the windows remained open, but he scowled at Kit throughout dinner, breaking his silence only over dessert with a scathing inquiry about her outing with Brandon.

"We had a wonderful time, Major," she responded with forced equanimity, and then, politely, "There are not many gentlemen who are as pleasant to be with as Mr. Parsell."

She could see Cain framing a caustic reply and then remembering Miss Dolly's presence just in time. "And what did you and Mr. Parsell do all afternoon?" he finally inquired.

"We rode over to Holly Grove, and we talked about politics."

Cain's expression was openly skeptical. "That's all you did?"

"Yes, it's all," she snapped. "Not all men's interests when they're with young women are as narrow as yours."

Miss Dolly's fork clattered to her plate. "Katharine Louise, you're dawdlin' over your dessert. If you're finished, let's go to the sittin' room and leave the general to his cigar."

Kit was in no mood for retreat. "I'm not quite finished yet, Miss Dolly. Why don't you go? I don't mind the smell of cigar smoke."

Miss Dolly glanced nervously at Cain, who nodded his permission. She rose from the table, her napkin still in her fingers. For a moment she stood at her chair as if she were trying to gather her courage, and then she turned to Kit. "You watch your manners, darlin'. I know you don't mean anything by it, but sometimes you seem to speak sharply to the general. You mustn't let your natural high spirits get in the way of givin' him his proper respect." Her duty done, she scampered from the room.

Cain looked after her with some amusement. "I must admit, Miss Dolly's beginning to grow on me."

"I'm so glad to hear it," Kit replied disdainfully. "I won't have to worry about making *payments* for her anymore."

"She hasn't grown on me that much." He grinned.

Kit wasn't amused. "You really are reprehensible, do you know that?"

"Reprehensible? I don't know as I'd go that far. Of course, I admit I'm no Brandon Parsell."

"You're certainly not. Brandon's a gentleman."

"Did he behave like a gentleman with you today, Kit?" He leaned back in his chair, but there was nothing relaxed about his posture. "More to the point, did you behave like a lady with him?"

"Why you—" She choked back the epithet she had been about to hurl at him. This time he was not going to make her lose her dignity. She forced herself to study the delicate pattern of parasols and bridges and small hand-painted Chinese figures that covered the wallpaper. "I'll have you know that Mr. Parsell and I spent most of the afternoon discussing the political situation in South Carolina and the indignities the federal government has been forcing on us," she said with forced composure.

Cain pushed back his plate. "I can just hear the two of you now," he said, shaking his head in disgust. "Both of you sighing over what the Yankees have done to your poor state, moaning over all the injustices of the occupation—none of them the South's fault, of course. You two make quite a pair."

Kit could not believe anyone could be so callous. "Don't you have any human feelings at all?" she demanded. "You can see the horrors of Reconstruction all around you. People have had their homes taken from them. They've lost all their savings. The South is like a piece of glass being ground to bits beneath a Yankee boot heel."

"Very poetic." He picked up the brandy decanter sitting on a silver tray at his elbow, but before he could pour from it, he shoved the stopper impatiently back in the neck and returned the bottle to the tray with a bang. "Let me remind you of a few painful facts you seem to have forgotten. It wasn't the Union that started this war. Southern guns fired on Fort Sumter." His eyes regarded her with ill-concealed scorn. "You lost the war, Kit. You lost it at the expense of six hundred thousand lives. And now you expect everything to be just like it was. You talk about the horrors of Reconstruction. The way I see it, the South should be thankful the federal government has been as merciful as it has."

"Merciful?" Kit exclaimed, leaping to her feet. "Do you call what has happened here merciful?"

"You've read history. You tell me," he said slowly, his anger building. "Name any other conquering people who've dealt so leniently with those they've conquered. If this had been any country but the United States, there would have been thousands of men executed for treason after Appomattox. Thousands more would be rotting in prisons. Instead, there was a general amnesty, and now the Southern states are being readmitted to the Union." He slammed the palm of his hand down hard on the table, making the dishes jump. "My God, Reconstruction is a slap on the wrist for what the South has done to this country!"

Her knuckles were white where they gripped the back of the chair. "It's too bad there wasn't enough bloodshed to satisfy you!" she hissed. "What kind of man are you to wish the South more misery than it's already had?"

He shook his head slowly. "I don't wish it any more misery. I agree with the leniency of the federal policies. But you'll have to forgive me if I can't seem to work up any righteous indignation over the fact that people in the South have lost their homes."

"How can you be so vindictive?"

He said simply, "Men have died in my arms, Kit. Not all of them wore blue uniforms."

Slowly she released her grip on the chair and swept out of the room. She managed to make it to her bedroom without encountering Miss Dolly. Once inside, she kicked off her shoes and sank down into the ladder-backed chair next to her bed. He was wrong, of course. But there had been something about his last statement that had not seemed insensitive, and it bothered her.

To distract herself from troubling thoughts, she picked up the copy of *Moby Dick* that was lying on the table next to her. She wished she could go to bed; her head was pounding and she was exhausted from the strain of the day. But there was a job she had to begin tonight after the house was quiet and everyone was asleep. She'd already put it off too long, and she wasn't going to let anything keep her away from it any longer. Opening her book, she settled down to wait.

Chapter Twenty-one

The next few weeks brought a steady stream of callers to Risen Glory's front door. In better times the women would have arrived in fine carriages and been dressed in their prettiest gowns. Now they came in wagons drawn by plow horses, sitting on the front seats of broken-down buggies, or, in a few cases, on foot. Their gowns were shabby and their bonnets rusty with age, but they carried themselves as proudly as if they wore the latest designs from Paris.

Self-conscious about the extravagance of her wardrobe amid so much poverty, Kit dressed as plainly as she could for her first callers. But she soon discovered that the women were disappointed by her simple gowns. They made pointed references to the pretty lilac frock she had worn to church, and had her hat been trimmed in taffeta or satin? They had heard the gossip about her clothes passed from maid to cook to the grizzled old woman who sold she-crab from a tub on the back of a pushcart. It was said that Kit Weston's wardrobe was filled with beautiful gowns of every color and description. The women were starved for beauty, and they wanted to see them all.

Once Kit understood, she didn't have the heart to disappoint them. She dutifully wore a different dress each day and with several of the younger women finally abandoned subterfuge altogether and invited them to her bedroom so they could see for themselves.

It saddened her to realize that the clothes meant so much more to her visitors than they did to her. She would have been happy with a wardrobe of breeches and a few soft shirts. The dresses were pretty, but they were such a bother with all their hooks and laces and overskirts that were always catching on furniture. She found herself wishing she could give some of them away. The green Indian muslin, for example, to the pretty young widow who had lost her husband at Gettysburg. But the women were as proud as they were poor, and she knew better than to offer.

Not all her callers were women. A dozen men of various ages

and sizes made their way to her door in as many days. They invited her on buggy rides and picnics, surrounded her after church, and nearly got into a fight over who was to accompany her to a Chautauqua lecture on phrenology. She managed to turn them all down without hurting their feelings and attended with Brandon, his two sisters, and Miss Dolly.

Brandon was increasingly attentive, even though she frequently shocked him, causing those twin furrows of disapproval to form at the bridge of his nose. Still, he remained stolidly at her side, and she was certain he intended to ask her to marry him just as soon as enough time had elapsed to satisfy his sense of propriety. He was as aware as she that half of her month was over, and she suspected he wouldn't wait much longer.

She had seen little of Cain, even at meals, since the night of their disquieting conversation about Reconstruction. The machinery for the mill had arrived, and he was storing it away under canvas tarps in the barn and several of the larger sheds until they were ready to install it. Whenever he was nearby, she was uncomfortably conscious of him. His eyes, unfriendly and faintly mocking, seemed to be watching her, especially as she talked with the male admirers who attached themselves to her like bees to honey.

Gossip traveled quickly, and it wasn't long before Kit learned that Cain was frequently being seen in the company of the beautiful Veronica Gamble. Veronica was a source of mystery and speculation to the local women. Even though she was Carolina born, her exotic life-style after her marriage set her apart from them and made them regard her as a foreigner. There was even a rumor that her husband had painted a picture of her lying stark naked on a couch and that it was hanging right on the wall of her bedroom, bold as brass.

One evening Kit came downstairs for supper and, to her surprise, found Cain in the sitting room reading a newspaper. It had been nearly a week since he had last appeared for a meal, so she was surprised to see him. She was even more surprised to find him dressed in formal black and white, since she had never once known him to wear anything but casual dress in the dining room.

"Are you going out?" she asked hopefully.

He looked up from his paper. "Sorry to disappoint you, but I'm eating in this evening. We have a guest for dinner."

"A guest!" Kit cried in dismay, looking down at her creased gown and ink-stained fingers in dismay. "Why didn't you tell me?"

"This is my home, Kit. I don't have to keep you informed of my activities."

She glared at him indignantly. Her whole day had been a disaster, and this was the crowning blow. She had been up last night long after everyone else in the house was asleep. As a result she had slept late that morning and been forced to cut her ride short. Then Mary Cogdell and her husband had come to call and recounted to her, in excruciating detail, all the gossip that her unchaperoned stay at Risen Glory was producing. To give them credit, she understood they were genuinely concerned for her, but she still resented their interference. To make matters worse, Miss Dolly had soon joined them and insisted they roll bandages for the Confederate wounded while they chatted.

Afterward, Kit had taken a long walk and then decided to write Elspeth a letter in response to the one she had just received that morning. The letter had taken longer than she had expected, and she was left with no time to change for dinner. Since she hadn't expected anyone but Miss Dolly at the table, she hadn't been too concerned about the condition of her plain muslin dress, even though it had a noticeable mud stain on the saffron-colored skirt from her walk when she had knelt down in the dirt to free a baby field sparrow that had somehow gotten caught in a tangle of brambles. Not changing would mean a scolding from Miss Dolly, but then Miss Dolly scolded her about her appearance even when she was dressed well!

Lucy appeared at the door to announce the arrival of Veronica Gamble. As Veronica swept into the room, Kit's self-consciousness over her soiled gown turned into acute embarrassment. Veronica was wearing a stylish jade-green evening gown caught up to reveal an underskirt of bronze and black striped satin. A border of overlapping bronze and black lace trimmed the low décolletage of the gown, setting off skin as pale and opalescent as only a natural redhead can possess. Her hair was swept up into a sophisticated arrangement of curls and braids caught at the side by a crescent of bronze silk laurel leaves.

Kit was suddenly conscious that Cain was watching her. Something in his expression made her suspect that he was well aware of her embarrassment and even pleased by it. The thought made her furious. Was it possible he had wanted her kept in the dark about his guest? She immediately dismissed the idea as being fanciful. What reason would he have for wishing her to appear at a disadvantage before Veronica Gamble?

Cain introduced Kit and then Miss Dolly, who had just come into the room. Despite the fact that Veronica acknowledged the introductions graciously, Kit was barely able to conceal her dislike for the woman. Her sophisticated elegance made Kit feel young and awkward and just as disheveled as she looked. Miss Dolly seemed to share her aversion, although for a different reason. When Veronica noticed the newspaper Cain had been reading and remarked that her husband had been a great supporter of Horace Greeley, the noted newspaper editor and abolitionist, Miss Dolly developed a sudden headache and excused herself from dinner to go to her room.

Kit was left alone with the couple. She felt like a third wheel and silently cursed Sophronia for not having told her that Mrs. Gamble was expected for dinner. If she had known, she would have taken a tray in her room. It was outrageous for him to expect her to dine with a woman who, if all accounts were true, was probably his mistress by now.

Veronica sat on the settee, Cain in a green and ivory upholstered chair next to her. He should have looked ridiculous in such a chair—it was much too small for him—but instead he seemed as comfortable as if he were on the back of Vandal or crawling across the roof of his cotton mill. Veronica was telling him a story about a balloon ascension she had seen that had been accompanied by a pyrotechnical display. At one point as she described the antics of several onlookers, he tossed back his head and laughed, showing even white teeth.

The two might have been alone in the room for all the notice they were taking of her. Kit jerked up from her own chair, unwilling to sit and watch them a moment longer. "I'll go see if dinner's ready," she muttered.

"Just a minute, Kit."

She stopped and turned. Cain uncoiled from his chair and walked toward her. His eyes roamed over her crumpled frock as if he were seeing it for the first time, although she knew very well he had noticed it before. He stopped in front of her and reached out his hand so abruptly she nearly flinched. And then she felt his fingers tugging at her hair behind one of her silver combs. When his hand came away, it was holding a clump of burrs attached to a dry twig.

"You might at least have combed your hair," he said, frowning. "What have you been doing? Climbing trees?"

He made her feel as if she were nine years old, and she hated him for deliberately embarrassing her in front of a stranger. She was to hate him even more for his next words.

"Go to your room and change your clothes at once. You aren't coming to my table dressed like a stable boy."

There was no longer any reason for politeness. "I'm not coming to your table at all!" she snarled through clenched teeth, and then she nodded curtly in Veronica's direction. "If you'll excuse me, Mrs. Gamble, I'm not feeling well."

She fled to her room. Once inside, she collapsed on the edge of her bed, her hands trembling in fury. How dare he humiliate her like that!

In the sitting room Veronica watched Cain's rigid back with great interest and a small measure of sadness. Somehow she had hoped that the two of them. . . . Ah, well. One could not change what was not meant to be. Besides, she should have known. He was much too magnificent a man not to be difficult.

She felt a flash of pity for his young ward. Silly girl. For all her extravagant beauty, she did not know her own mind, and she certainly did not know his. She was much too young and inexperienced, of course, to understand why he was behaving in such a beastly manner toward her. But Veronica understood. She understood only too well.

Baron Cain was attracted to the girl, and he didn't like it one bit. He had brought Veronica here tonight, wanting Kit to appear at a disadvantage next to the sophisticated older woman. Of course, the foolish girl had lost her temper and played right into his hands. Still, Kit Weston struck Veronica as a most interesting young woman—certainly nobody's fool—and Veronica had a feeling the game was not over yet.

She tapped one long fingernail thoughtfully on the upholstered arm of the settee. Should she permit Cain to use her as a pawn in the struggle he was waging with himself and with his ward? It was a foolish question, and it made her smile. Of course she would permit it. He probably wouldn't allow her any choice in the matter anyway. Besides, it was all so deliciously amusing, she didn't really mind. Life was dull here, and it wasn't in her nature to be jealous of another woman over something as natural as sex.

With a gruff apology, Cain poured a glass of sherry for her and then excused himself. She could hear him taking the steps two at a time, and the impending violence of it excited her beyond measure. If only she could see what was about to happen in the room upstairs. If only she was the one in the room. . . . She sipped at her sherry, prepared to wait them out.

Cain didn't bother to knock on the closed door. He threw it open and then kicked it shut behind him. Kit shot up from the edge of the bed, too enraged by this violation of her privacy to feel any of the fear that was to come later.

"Get out of here!" she shrieked, stabbing a shaking finger toward the closed door. "This is my room, and you have no right to come charging in here."

"When I leave, I leave with you," he snarled. "I told you to change your dress, and that's what you're going to do. And then you're going to walk downstairs and sit at that table like a lady, and you'll never embarrass me in front of a guest again!"

"Embarrass you!" His audacity nearly choked her! "Why, you bastard! You hypocritical bastard!"

"Watch it, Kit! I tanned that little rump of yours once for your nasty tongue, and I'll do it again!"

"Get out of here!" Without taking time to think of the consequences of her action, she snatched up a heavy china figurine from the table next to her and hurled it at his head. He saw it coming and jerked to the side, but it still glanced painfully off his shoulder before it smashed to the floor.

His lips thinned into a vicious snarl. "You little bitch!" In three long strides he had closed the distance between them and caught her by the shoulders, shaking her hard. "For weeks I've stood by and watched you playing your silly little-girl's games with every man you meet, making them all hop and jump to your tune. Well, I don't play those kinds of games, especially with a little tramp like you!"

His hand went to her throat, and he yanked at the top button of her yellow dress. It flew off and rolled across the carpet. The other buttons quickly followed suit, and within seconds the front of her dress gaped open to the waist.

She was as terrified as she was blind with anger. She grappled for the edges of the garment, trying to pull them closed with her free hand while she kicked at him with her thin kid slippers. He dragged her by the arm across the room to her wardrobe and flung open the door. Reaching inside, he jerked out the lilac voile.

"You can either put this on yourself, or I'll put it on for you!" he growled.

The dress hung from his fist, no longer just a garment but a symbol of the clash of wills between them. For Cain it represented too many sleepless nights since she had come back to Risen Glory; for Kit, a kiss that she couldn't quite seem to forget.

"You can go to hell!" she raged. Forgetting all modesty, she let go of the front of her dress and punched at his chest with her free arm in a desperate struggle to shake him off.

Cain dropped the lilac voile to the floor and jerked the muslin dress down off her shoulders and arms. It settled at her hips, leaving her breasts covered by nothing more than her chemise.

Kit went insane with rage, kicked her legs at him, trying to hurt him with her arms and fists. She heard him grunt as one of her blows found its mark and then, tripping over the petticoats and the dress that was entangling her legs, sprawled to the floor.

No sooner had she hit the carpet than he crouched over her, his hands at her hips, and ripped off the ruined garment. She scrambled back to her feet, her lungs burning and her chest heaving from the struggle.

Never taking his eyes from her, he walked to the wardrobe, leaned over, and snatched up the lilac voile from the floor. She tried to gather her strength, aware that the struggle was far from over, no longer remembering why it was so important that she win it, knowing only that on this matter, she must not bend to his will.

She saw that his gaze had dropped, and then she felt the currents of cool air on her flesh. She looked down to see that the narrow strap of her chemise had given in the struggle and the material had fallen away, exposing one coral-tipped breast. With a gasp, she grabbed the edge of the garment and pulled it up.

Cain's eyes narrowed, their color changing from slate to pale smoke. He walked toward her and stopped. The lilac dress fell from his hand to the floor.

"I liked it better the other way," he said huskily.

As quickly as that, the battle between them had shifted to new ground.

Kit snatched up the gown. Afraid to take her eyes from him and further hampered by having only one hand to use since the other was still holding up her chemise, she had some difficulty finding the opening of her dress. She finally struggled into it, however, and yanked it up over her petticoats while he watched. She shoved her arms into the sleeves and then, reaching around to the back, tried to fasten it.

Cain stepped behind her and brushed away her hands. He began to secure the tiny hooks, starting at her waist and working upward. As he neared the top, he gathered her tangled black curls into his hands and pushed them forward over one shoulder. He saw her tremble at the gesture.

"You're a coward, Kit," he breathed softly into her ear.

"I—I don't know what you're talking about."

He leaned down. She felt his breath warm against the skin he had just exposed, felt his hands clasp her waist. And then he gently bit into the soft flesh at the side of her neck. "Liar," he whispered.

She pressed her eyes shut, felt his chest pushing hard against her back, felt the cool, wet spot on her neck where his tongue had touched her flesh. His hands slid up over her ribs and then, incredibly, over her breasts before they moved higher, above the edge of the unfastened neckline and then dipped down again, pushing the material out of his way so he could claim the soft, tender mounds beneath.

Kit's skin was hot and cold at once. She shuddered at the feeling of his callused palms holding her breasts so gently, shuddered at her own insanity in submitting to so intimate a caress.

There was a knock at the door, abruptly ending Kit's paralysis. She jerked away, appalled at her lack of resistance, and clutched her hands over the bodice of her dress.

"Who is it?" Cain barked out impatiently.

At the sound of his voice, the door flew back on its hinges. Sophronia stood on the other side, two pale smudges of alarm over her taut cheekbones. "What are you doin' in her room?" she exclaimed.

Cain's eyebrow slashed upward. "You forget yourself, Sophronia."

His rebuke was cold and direct, the openly expressed disapproval of an employer for the presumption of a servant, but still Sophronia could feel the iron shackles of her slave past closing around her. She took in Kit's disheveled state and the torn yellow dress on the floor. Unable to look at Cain, she spoke to Kit instead, forcing herself to use the even, impersonal tones of a well-trained servant. "Mr. Parsell is downstairs. He says he has a book to lend you. I put him in the sittin' room with Mrs. Gamble."

Kit was suddenly aware that her fingers were stiff from the tight grip she was still maintaining on the bodice of her dress. Slowly she relaxed and nodded to Sophronia. Then she looked at Cain and, with as much composure as she could muster, asked, "Would you invite Mr. Parsell to join us for dinner, Major? Sophronia will help me finish dressing, and I'll be downstairs shortly."

For a moment their eyes locked, stormy violet clashing with a gray as cold as winter sleet. Who was the winner and who the loser in the battle that had just been fought between them? Neither of them knew. There had been no resolution, no healing catharsis. The antagonism that crackled between them was as tangible as their own flesh.

Cain left without a word, but with a look that informed her quite clearly it was not over. As soon as he was gone, Kit peeled the lilac dress off with trembling hands and, while she scrubbed at the inkstains on her fingers, directed Sophronia to fetch a dress that was covered in protective muslin and hanging at the back of her wardrobe.

The garment had been outrageously expensive, and Elspeth had protested her purchasing it, arguing that Kit could put her money to better use by buying two more modest gowns. But the truth of the matter was that Elspeth had been uncomfortable about more than the cost of the gown. It was so extravagantly beautiful, so conspicuous, that even on the most demure female —which Kit certainly was not—it was likely to attract more attention than, perhaps, a well-brought-up young lady should wish to draw to herself. But such subtleties of fashion were beyond Kit. She only knew that she loved it with a passion she had felt for no other female garment and that she had to have it.

A silent Sophronia lifted the gown over her head. It fell in a crystalline cloud of ice and snow, shimmering and cool in the hot summer night. The overskirt of the dress was a billowing cloud of silver organdy caught up over gleaming white satin shot with silver thread. The tight-fitting bodice was covered with crystal bugle beads, which sparkled on the cloth beneath like night snow under a starry winter sky. More crystal beads lightly spangled the skirt, sprinkling down to the hem. The neckline was low, falling well off her shoulders to reveal the gleaming swells of breasts still faintly rosy from Cain's hands. Around her neck she fastened the necklace that went with the gown, a choker of crystal bugle beads dripping onto her skin like ice chips from a silver band.

Perhaps it was Kit's own vivid beauty, perhaps the silver thread and glittering beads, but the very air around her seemed to crackle with life as she moved across the room in the shimmering gown. Wordlessly Sophronia brushed out her hair. When she began to draw it into a neat knot, Kit shook her head. She would wear it free tonight, with only the silver combs. Everything about her must be as different from Veronica Gamble as possible.

She slipped on satin slippers with small spool-shaped heels, the ones she had worn at the Templeton Ball. They were eggshell instead of stark white and didn't match her gown, but she was too preoccupied to notice.

Sophronia brought her a cluster of tiny crystal drops, and she fastened them in her lobes. Then she turned to her friend for approval. "Well?"

Sophronia was busy tidying the dressing table in front of her. "Well, what?"

"You know very well what I'm talking about," Kit said impatiently. "How do I look?"

Sophronia pushed a crystal perfume bottle to the back of the dressing table. "Mirror's the best judge of that, I guess."

Kit sighed with annoyance. Sophronia was obviously in one of her difficult moods. "Really, Sophronia, you're so prickly. I don't know what's gotten into you since I came back."

"Maybe you should ask that question of yourself."

"Just what do you mean by that?"

Sophronia slammed a silver-backed hairbrush down on the dressing table with unnecessary force. "I mean the Kit Weston I knew wouldn't have found herself locked in a bedroom with a man who's not her husband!"

"Do you really think there was anything I could do about it?" Kit responded hotly. "I didn't invite him in. He wanted me to sit at the dinner table with that Mrs. Gamble, and I refused."

Sophronia splayed her fingers on her hips. "If you refused to have dinner with them, do you mind tellin' me just what you're doin' in that gown?"

"It's different now that Brandon's here."

"Is that why you're gettin' all dressed up?" Sophronia scoffed. "For Mr. Parsell?"

"Of course it's for him," Kit retorted. "And also for Veronica Gamble. I don't like that woman, and I intend to show her I'm no country bumpkin."

Sophronia's stiff features softened almost imperceptibly. "You can lie to me, Kit Weston, but just don't lie to yourself. You'd better make certain it's Mr. Parsell and Mrs. Gamble you're gettin' dressed up for and not Baron Cain."

Kit's mouth flew open in indignation. "Just what do you mean by that?"

"Leave him to Mrs. Gamble, honey," Sophronia said, walking over to Kit and pushing back a stray lock of dusky hair. Unconsciously she echoed the words Magnus had spoken to her only a few weeks before. "He's a hard man with women. There's something as cold as ice inside him." She paused and then went on hesitantly, trying to convince Kit of what she had sensed about Cain from the very beginning. "Any woman tries to get past that ice will only end up with a bad case of frostbite for her efforts. You got to realize, Kit, that when he looks at a woman, all he sees is a body to bring his own body pleasure. If a woman understands that about him, like I 'spect that Mrs. Gamble does, she can enjoy herself and no hard feelin's afterwards. But any woman who's fool enough to fall in love with him is only goin' end up with a broken heart."

"Really, Sophronia, you've got an overactive imagination. You know better than anyone how much I hate that man. He's standing in the way of everything I want from life. Risen Glory's mine! It's where I belong! I'll die before I let him keep it! I'm going to marry Brandon Parsell, Sophronia. And as soon as I can, I'm going to buy this plantation back!"

Sophronia snatched up the lilac voile from the foot of the bed. "And what makes you think the major will sell it to you?"

"Oh, he'll sell all right," Kit said confidently. "It's just a matter of time."

"You got no way of knowin' that."

"I know what I know," Kit replied mysteriously. She wasn't about to tell Sophronia of her late-night forages through the plantation's calf-bound ledgers, adding and subtracting her way down columns of boldly entered figures. It hadn't taken her long to discover that Baron Cain had overextended himself badly. He was hanging on to Risen Glory and his spinning mill by the most fragile of threads, and the smallest disaster was going to send him right under.

Kit didn't know much about spinning mills, but she did know about cotton. She knew about unexpected hailstorms, about hurricanes and droughts, about insects that fed off the tender bolls until nothing was left. Where cotton was concerned, sooner or later disaster was bound to strike, and when it did, she would be ready. She'd buy the plantation right out from under him, and his mill, too. And she'd buy it at her own price.

With a quick peck at Sophronia's cheek, she left the room and made her way downstairs.

Veronica Gamble's smooth forehead betrayed nothing of her thoughts as Kit swept, somewhat breathlessly, into the sitting room. So the little kitten had decided to fight. Somehow she wasn't surprised. The gown was outrageous, of course, and quite wonderful, its remote ice-maiden perfection a delicious foil for the girl's vivid beauty. She noticed that Mr. Parsell—somewhat subdued after having so blatantly wangled a dinner invitation—seemed rather stunned by her appearance, while Baron looked like a thundercloud. The poor man. He would have done better to have left her in that dirty yellow dress.

Veronica wondered again what had happened between the two of them in the room upstairs. As soon as Kit had come into the sitting room, she had noticed the faint red smudges, like thumbprints, on her upper arms. There had been a struggle, that much was evident, but somehow Veronica did not think they had made love. The girl didn't have the look about her, and Cain was still as tightly coiled as a jungle beast about to spring, a fact that excited her immeasurably. Later that night, she planned to relieve that tension, perhaps even try to make him angry as the girl had done. Forceful lovemaking from a delicious man was a treat she had not enjoyed in much longer than she cared to admit.

Veronica was seated at Cain's right during dinner, with Kit at the foot of the table and Brandon to her right. The meal was delicious—fragrant jambalaya accompanied by oyster patties smothered in a cucumber curry sauce, green peas flavored with mint, beaten biscuits, and, for dessert, rich slabs of pecan pie—but Veronica was fairly certain she was the only one who noticed the food.

She was excessively attentive to Baron throughout the meal, leaning close to him as she told him one amusing story after another, laying her fingers lightly on his sleeve, occasionally squeezing the hard-muscled arm beneath with deliberate intimacy. He gave her his total attention and his obvious admiration. If she had not known better, she would have believed he didn't notice the subdued laughter and conversation taking place at the other end of the table.

After dinner, Cain suggested the men take their brandy and cigars in the sitting room with the women instead of remaining at the dinner table. Brandon agreed to the suggestion with more eagerness than was polite. It was obvious the two men had no desire to be left alone together. Before dinner, Cain had barely been able to conceal his boredom with Brandon's formality, while Brandon could not quite hide his contempt for Cain.

In the sitting room Veronica deliberately took a place on the settee next to Kit and engaged her in conversation, even though she knew very well the girl had taken a dislike to her. Still, Kit was courteous and, to Veronica's surprise, thoroughly entertaining once they began to talk. She was wonderfully well read for a young woman, and before long they had discovered they liked many of the same books. Veronica suggested that Kit borrow her copy of a scandalous new book by Gustave Flaubert that she had just finished reading. The offer drew a thunderous look of disapproval from Cain.

"I get the impression Baron doesn't approve of your reading *Madame Bovary,*" Veronica said when Cain's attention had been drawn back to a question from Brandon. "Perhaps we'd better leave it on my shelf for the time being."

"Baron is my guardian, Mrs. Gamble, not my keeper," Kit replied coolly. "I would love to read the book. Thank you for offering it to me."

Veronica had given the girl a mental salute and an open invitation to call. All in all, it had been a most entertaining evening.

Her pleasure faded, however, when Cain took her home. To her surprise, after planting a light kiss on her lips at her front door, he bid her good night and strode back to his carriage. She told herself she was a fool to be so disappointed, but that evening as she sat at her dressing table clad only in a loose silk wrapper, she found herself regarding the barely perceptible fishtails forming at the corners of her eyes with unaccustomedly intense scrutiny.

Only a dim light burned in the entry hall as Cain let himself back into the quiet house. Despite the fact that he planned an early start the next morning, he didn't immediately mount the stairs to his bedroom, but crossed the hall and let himself into the library instead. The room was warm. Without bothering to light the lamp on his desk, he pulled off his coat and opened the windows.

Why tonight of all nights had the memories come back to nag at him? As he had driven home from Veronica's, the years had seemed to peel away like the layers of an onion. He settled the side of his hip on the high windowsill and gazed out into the darkness with unseeing eyes. The nighttime rasp of crickets and the soft, wheezy cry of a distant barn owl gradually became less real to him than the voices of the past and the yellowed, brittle-frail memory of his father.

Nathaniel Cain was the only son of a wealthy Philadelphia merchant. He lived in the same brownstone mansion in which he had been born and was a competent, if unexceptional, businessman. He was nearly thirty-five when he married sixteen-year-old Rosemary Hewitt. She was much too young, of course, but her parents had been anxious to rid themselves of their troublesome daughter, especially to such a well-heeled bachelor.

From the beginning, it was a marriage made in hell. She hated her pregnancy, had no interest at all in the son who was born to her exactly nine months after her wedding night, and grew to regard her adoring husband with contempt. Over the years she embarrassed him in public and cuckolded him with a succession of other men, but he never stopped loving her or blaming himself for her restlessness. If only he had not forced a child on her so soon, he thought, she would have been content. As time passed, he ceased blaming himself for her misdeeds and blamed only the child. It took her nearly ten years to run through his fortune and destroy his business. She left him for a man who had been one of his employees.

Baron had watched it all, a bewildered, lonely child. In the months after his mother's departure, he stood by helplessly as his father was consumed by his unhealthy, obsessive passion for his faithless wife. Filthy, unshaven, drowning in alcohol, Nathaniel Cain sealed himself inside the lonely, decaying mansion and constructed elaborate daydreams of everything his wife had not been.

Only once had the boy rebelled. In a fit of anger, he had spewed out to his father all his resentment against the mother who had abandoned them both. Nathaniel Cain had nearly gone mad with rage—screaming at his son, calling him an unnatural child, blaming him for his mother's desertion. And then he had begun to beat the boy, slapping him across the face again and again until the child's nose was streaming with blood and his eyes swollen shut. Afterward, he did not even seem to remember what had happened.

The lessons of his parents had been hard ones, and Baron Cain had never forgotten them. He had learned that women are faithless and that love is a weakness that twists and perverts. And so he gave away books when he finished them, traded horses before he could grow too fond of them, and sat in the window of the library at Risen Glory staring out at the hot, still night thinking about his father and his mother . . . and Kit Weston.

He found little comfort in the fact that the emotions she aroused in him were negative ones. What bothered him was that she made him feel anything at all. But since the afternoon she had come into his house, veiled and mysterious and wildly beautiful, he had not been able to get her off his mind.

He stood up and glanced over at his desk, dimly illuminated in the moonlight. His papers seemed not to have been disturbed, so she hadn't been in there tonight. He supposed he should have locked all the ledgers and bankbooks away after he had discovered evidence of her snooping, but he had felt a perverse sense of satisfaction in being able to add dishonesty to all her other unpleasant attributes.

Now he knew it was time he settled with her. Past time, in fact. Her month was almost up and she would be going off soon to marry Parsell. Before that happened, he had to free himself from the mysterious hold she had on his thoughts. There was only one way he knew how to do that, and he had waited long enough. He was going to take for himself what so many other men already had enjoyed.

Chapter Twenty-two

Kit had forgotten how hot it could be in South Carolina so early in the summer. The heat haze shimmered like a living curtain in the air above the cotton fields, covered now with creamy white four-petaled blossoms. Merlin, who had accompanied her on her morning ride, had deserted her this afternoon, preferring to nap in the lengthening purple shadows of the hydrangea that grew near the kitchen door. Kit knew it would have been wiser for her to do the same in her bedroom, which was shuttered now like the rest of the house to keep out the afternoon heat, but she was still too restless from the dinner party the night before.

Brandon had stolen a few moments alone with her just before he had left and asked her to meet him after church tomorrow. From the urgency of his request, she was reasonably certain he would propose to her then, and she told herself it was this that had put her in so fitful a mood today.

Impulsively she turned Temptation off the path they had been following and into the trees. The pond lay like a small glimmering jewel in the center of the woods, safely tucked away from the bustle of the plantation. It had always been one of her favorite places. Even on the hottest August days, its spring-fed water was cold and clear, and the thick barrier of trees and underbrush growing around it acted like a fence, keeping the spot quiet and private, perfect for secret thoughts or napping or reading a book without being disturbed.

She led Temptation close to the water's edge, slipped down out of the saddle, and tied him so he could drink his fill. As she ambled around the pond's perimeter, she tugged at a willow switch, stripping the leaves off in neat stacks in her fingers. The willows that lined the edge had always reminded her of women with their hair tossed forward over their heads, the ends just dipping into the water.

Snatching off her hat, she sprawled down on the ground and tugged at her boots. The workers never came near here, Cain and Magnus had gone into town, and there was no one to disturb her. She was going to take advantage of her privacy and swim in the inviting waters.

Stripping off her breeches and her shirt, she tossed them down on the grass, then followed with her chemise and drawers. When she was naked, she ran toward the pond and made a shallow dive, cutting into the water like a silverfish. She came to the surface gasping at the cold, laughed, and dived under again. After a while, she settled on her back, her hair unfolding like a black silk fan around her head. As she floated, she closed her eyes against the flaming copper ball of sun hanging just over the tops of the trees. She felt suspended in time and space, part of the water and the air and the land around her. The sun touched the hills of her body. The water lapped at the valleys. She felt almost content.

A bullfrog croaked from a stand of rushes, disturbing her revelry. She rolled over onto her stomach and began to swim in lazy circles. When she started to feel chilled, she swam toward the shallower water at the edge and lowered her feet to the sandy bottom.

Just as she was about to step out, she heard Temptation nicker and then, from the far edge of the woods, the ominous answering whistle of a stallion. Her heart racing, she scrambled up the bank and dashed toward her clothes. Ignoring her undergarments, she grabbed the khaki breeches with numbed fingers and tugged them on over her dripping legs. She could hear the stallion coming closer, its hooves muffled by the sandy soil, but still audible. No time for the row of buttons that secured the front. Snatching up her shirt, she shoved her wet arms into the sleeves. She was trying to fasten the button between her breasts when the chestnut stallion broke through the line of trees and Baron Cain invaded the private world of her pond.

He reined in near the spot where her undergarments still lay and, loosely crossing his hands in front of him on the pommel of the saddle, looked down at her from the great height of Vandal's back. His eyes were shaded by the brim of his tan hat, leaving their expression unfathomable. His mouth was unsmiling, a forbidding slash that showed no trace of kindness or softness or compassion of any kind.

She stood frozen in position, as if she were playing a child's game of statues. Her fingers were motionless on the button they had not yet been able to fasten. Her lips were slightly parted and one leg was bent, elevating the heel of her bare foot just above the ground. The wetness of her dripping hair and skin had made her white shirt translucent and changed its color to the pale, creamy peach of the skin it clung to. She might as well have been naked. The wet film of the material exposed every detail of her chilled breasts and then parted to reveal her ribs and the open waistband of her breeches. The late-afternoon sun glistened golden on the skin of her flat stomach and on the beads of water that clung in amber droplets to the circlet of her navel.

Cain slowly swung his leg over the saddle and dropped soundlessly to the ground. He took his time tying his mount, but it was not until he walked toward her that she came to her senses and once again began struggling with the buttons at the front of her shirt. It was all wrong, she thought wildly, for so large a man to move so quietly.

A pair of dusty boots and fawn trousers worn low on narrow hips came into her view. She lifted her eyes, taking in the pale-butternut shirt, the open collar, the determined jaw and hard, unrelenting mouth. As she lifted her gaze still higher, she saw that his eyes remained shadowed under the brim of his hat, and not being able to see their expression frightened her more than anything else.

As if he were reading her mind, he lifted off the hat and dropped it to the ground where it landed next to her undergarments. It would have been better for her if his eyes had remained hidden, for they held not the slightest hint of warmth or emotion. In a quick, self-protective reflex, she began jerking at the buttons of her shirt again.

His voice was as quiet and chilling as the icy spring that fed the pond. "Don't bother fastening it. It's just going to come back off again." He lifted his hands to his own shirt and slowly unbuttoned it.

"What—what do you think you're doing?" Kit stammered.

He tugged his shirt free of the waistband of his trousers and then stripped it off and let it fall to the ground. "You're not stupid, Kit. Figure it out."

She stepped backward. "I—I don't know what you mean."

"No?" He took his time exploring with his eyes the soft curves that the wet clothing outlined with such obliging attention to detail, the curves that his hands and mouth had been aching to discover for far too long. "Somehow I can't believe that."

She could no longer bear his intimate scrutiny, and she turned her back to him, wanting to run, but knowing she must not, knowing he would only drag her back. She heard him coming closer, sensed his presence behind her in the heat that was transferring itself from his sun-warmed body to the chilled skin of her back, even though they were not touching.

"We have something to settle between us before I turn you over to Parsell."

She spun around, pulling the thin cotton material of her shirt away from her skin as she did. "We have nothing to settle between us. Now go away and let me get dressed. Sophronia will send somebody to look for me if I don't come back soon."

"Nobody's coming after you, Kit," he said. "I told them not to expect us back until very late. We have all the time in the world."

"You knew I was here?" The idea that his assault on her privacy was premeditated chilled her. "I thought you were going into town with Magnus."

"I was. Until I saw you heading out on Temptation. I decided to get rid of everybody and come after you. I would have been here earlier, but I wanted to make certain we wouldn't be interrupted. I'm going to have you now, Kit Weston. I've waited long enough. Right here, next to this pond. I'm going to take you again and again until I've had my fill of you."

Kit felt fear clutching at her like a great, clawing beast. Fear, and an awful sense of inevitability.

"You're no innocent, Kit," he went on with chilling calmness. "You know as well as I do that this has been between us from the very beginning. It's time we put an end to it."

Never before had the danger she had always sensed in him been more real than it was at that moment. His arms hung loosely at his sides, the burnished muscles of his bare chest smooth and relaxed. Yet she knew if she made one sudden movement those muscles would quiver with tension and crush her with unyielding strength.

She took her first step, keeping her eyes locked with his. Then she took another, moving slowly toward Temptation. No sudden motions. No loud noises.

He chuckled, a dry, hard sound that bore no trace of amusement. With one stride he was upon her, catching her shoulders in his great hands and pulling her to him. She could not keep herself from struggling, yet even as she fought him, she knew that she could not win against his superior strength. He pinned her head between his hands, and she clawed futilely at his wrists. She waited for the bruising crush of his mouth against hers and pressed her lips tight to cushion them against the hurt he would inflict.

To her surprise, the hurt did not come. When his mouth descended, it found not her own, but her eyelids instead and pressed each one closed with a soft, quieting kiss. The gentleness took the struggle from her and, although she still held fast to his wrists, she stopped fighting him. She felt his breath on her cheek, and then his open mouth, like a warm cave, settled over her closed one. The tip of his tongue gently played with her lips, sliding along them, trying to coax open the seal of fear and uncertainty that held them shut. Her breasts that had been so cold were now crushed against the warm, cushioning fur of his bare chest. With a soft moan, she opened her mouth and let him in.

This time he was a welcome invader, exploring every part of the velvet interior that she made so freely accessible to him. When he was finally satisfied, he touched the tip of his tongue to hers, playing them together one against the other, gradually guiding her into his own mouth. She hesitated for only a moment, and then she slid past the barrier of his teeth and boldly took what he offered her.

The aggressor now, she entwined her arms around his neck as she tasted him, knowing there was something desperately wrong in what she was doing, but unable to stop herself. She felt his hands slip under her shirt to the cold, bare skin of her back. And then one hand moved between their bodies, impatiently pushing aside the open V of her breeches and flattening itself on her stomach. The tip of a finger settled in the moist hollow of her navel.

She dug her fists into the thick, tawny hair at the back of his head. Inside their mouths she relinquished her role as aggressor and gave in to an inflamed, mutual tongue play.

His hand deserted her stomach and climbed beneath her shirt to her breast. He cupped it from the bottom. Then he lifted his thumb and moved it slowly upward. It circled the taut coral crest and then brushed the small, hard bud at the center. She pulled her mouth away from his with a soft, smothered cry. It seemed as if that hard bud he was caressing so thoroughly contained every nerve in her body. Would she go to hell for this? It was a sin what she was letting him do, a man who was not her husband, a man she hated. . . .

She felt herself falling, realized he was taking her to the ground with him. He cushioned their landing with his body and rolled her over onto her back.

The earth was soft and mossy beneath her. There was a tug at the button between her breasts, and his hands pushed aside the wet fabric, exposing her to him. She opened her eyes.

"God, you're beautiful," he said huskily, as he lifted his gaze from her breasts to her face. With their eyes locked, he covered her nipples with his thumbs and began making a series of small circles, gentle at first and then gradually growing more forceful.

She slammed her head to the side, biting her lip to keep from crying out at the frenzied sensations he was arousing in her. He dropped his mouth, letting it travel from the hollow of her throat to one of the nipples he was torturing so expertly. He brushed it with his moustache and then caught it in his mouth.

So far, he had played a gentle, seducer's game with her, but now his own desire became his master. His play at her breasts grew more intense, then he lowered his head, sucking at the soft flesh of her waist. His mouth trailed still lower, to the patch of flat, smooth stomach exposed to him by the open V of her breeches.

It was exciting, inflamed lovemaking, but it was intended for an experienced woman, and Kit was not experienced. He was going too fast for her.

Fear rose up to meet the heat he had aroused in her. "No!" The cry sprang from deep inside. Her fingers sunk like talons into his shoulders, frantic to push him away from her, to give herself time to think, to protect. . . . Cain's head shot up, his eyes still darkly glazed.

"Get up! Get off me! Oh, please! Please get off me!" She balled her hands into fists and hit him.

He snatched her fists before they could do damage and pinned them harmlessly to the ground on each side of her head. "What's wrong, Kit?" he asked, more puzzled than angry.

"I want up!" she sobbed. "I don't want this! I don't understand. . . ."

"Don't want it?" he growled, confusion fleeing as a deep anger took hold of him. "It's a little late for that, isn't it?"

"I don't care! Let me up!" She tried to twist her body out from under his, but he threw his leg over her and pinned her down.

"You cheap little tramp!" His fingers bit into her wrists. "Are these the kinds of games you play with Parsell? Is that why he's so anxious to marry you? I should have known you'd be too smart to let him have free what you were giving away to everybody else."

"No! It's not like that!" She was crying now. "Please, Baron . . ."

"Then what is it?" Fury burned in him, white hot and dangerous, blinding him to her tears. "Was I going too slow for you? Is that it? Were you getting impatient?" He shook her hard, driven by a sense of outrage and an emotion that he refused to identify as pain. "Did you want me to play rough with you? Play rape games so you could pretend you weren't enjoying it? Pretend you didn't have any choice?"

"Do I?" she screamed through her tears. "Do I have a choice?"

He looked at her then, long and hard. "No," he finally said. "Not now." Grabbing both of her wrists in one of his hands, he dropped his other hand to her breeches.

She went wild with fear, twisting beneath him, trying to bite at his neck and shoulders with her teeth.

"Stop it, Kit!" he commanded. "You're only going to get hurt."

"No! I won't let you! I don't want this!"

"You decided that too late." He jerked the breeches down on her hips.

"Oh, God, please, Baron. Don't do this to me. Don't you understand?" She took a great, shuddering breath. "I've never been with a man!"

"No more of your lies!"

"It's true." She sobbed. "Please believe me. You have to believe me!"

"Liar!" He yanked the breeches free of her legs and threw them with all the strength of his anger across the clearing.

She lay beneath him, naked except for the open white shirt. Her cheeks were red-blotched and wet with tears, her nose was running, her hair a wild tangle around her head. Dirt from the sandy soil clung to her stomach and her hips and the long, lean legs he had just exposed. She was crying more quietly now, her head turned to the side so she would not have to look at him when he did to her what it was that men did to women.

Abruptly he released her wrists. Never had she been more beautiful to him than she was at that moment, and he hated her for it and for his sudden, paralyzing uncertainty. Without giving himself time to think, he pushed her knees far apart and, ignoring her sharp, horrified gasp, tested with his touch the truth of what she had told him.

The membrane was there, taut as a drumhead, strong as she was strong, tenacious survivor of her childhood, protecting her now even as it seemed to damn him.

A growl erupted deep in his throat, animallike and curiously defenseless. He sprang to his feet. *"God damn you! Isn't there anything about you that is what it should be?"*

She turned her head and stared up at him without comprehension. He reached over and snatched up his shirt, the moment of his awful vulnerability gone. She realized her legs were still open and slowly, painfully, moved them together.

He walked across the patch of grass to where his horse was tied. Before he mounted, he turned back to her, all feeling washed from his face. "I'm going to settle with you, Kit Weston. It's not over between us."

Chapter Twenty-three

Brandon proposed to her the next day after church. She accepted his offer of marriage, but, pleading a headache, declined his invitation to lunch with his family. He pressed a kiss to her cheek as he helped her into the carriage and told her he would be calling at Risen Glory late that afternoon to secure Cain's permission.

Kit hadn't lied about having a headache. She, who never got sick, had felt ill since her encounter with Cain at the pond. She had barely slept last night, trying to understand Cain's anger and the strange, tortured expression she had glimpsed on his face when he'd discovered she still was a virgin. What right had he to be angry with her when she was the wronged party? She had done nothing to him, while he had done everything to her. Even now she grew hot with shame as she remembered his invasion of the most private part of her body. And then there was the humiliation of her first passionate response to him. How could she have forgotten herself so? Once again she was plagued by the notion that there was something very, very wrong with her.

She rode Temptation hard for nearly an hour and then changed into an old dress and took a long walk with Merlin. When she returned, she met Brandon, who was on his way to the paddock where Lucy had told him he could find Cain. They exchanged a rather formal greeting as they passed each other, and then Kit headed for the kitchen where she pushed Rose aside and began mixing the ingredients for a batch of Miss Dolly's favorite beaten biscuits. Sophronia came in while she was working and watched with a frown as Kit banged the wooden mallet again and again at the dough, her forehead knitted in angry concentration.

They all knew what was happening—Sophronia, Rose, even Lucy, who kept finding excuses to come into the kitchen and dart glances out the back window. Rose picked up her paring knife and began peeling peaches for cobbler. Sophronia took some coffee beans from a burlap bag in the pantry, put them in the big wooden grinder, and slowly turned the wheel.

Lucy saw him first. "Mr. Parsell's comin' dis way. By hisself."

Kit snatched up a muslin dish towel and wiped her doughy hands on it, then ran out the back door. She knew as soon as she saw Brandon's face that something had gone wrong. "What happened?" she asked breathlessly as she reached him.

Brandon did not break his stride. "He refused to give his permission," he said stiffly.

Kit felt as if all the wind had been knocked out of her. "What?" she gasped, rushing to catch up with him. "I don't believe it. But why?"

"He said he didn't think we would suit each other." He turned the corner onto the flagstone path that skirted the side of the house. "It's insufferable! A Parsell bein' dismissed like that by a Yankee ruffian."

Kit grabbed his arm, and he finally stopped walking. "We can't let him get away with this, Brandon. It's too important. I have to get Risen Glory back."

"I don't see what we can do about Risen Glory. You're still a minor, and he's your guardian." Neither of them seemed to notice anything unusual in the fact that they did not speak at all of love, but only of the plantation.

His resigned attitude angered her. "You may be ready to give up, but I'm not!"

"There's nothing more I can do, Kit. You have to be reasonable."

But she did not hear him. She had already turned away and was striding determinedly toward the paddock.

He watched her for a moment, and then, with a sigh, headed for the front of the house and his horse, trying to convince himself that it was all for the best. There was something about Kit Weston that made him feel uneasy. He had tried to dismiss it and concentrate on Risen Glory instead, and, indeed, her captivating beauty had made it easy. But even so, it would never quite go away, the feeling that she wasn't at all the right sort of wife for a Parsell—even an impecunious one.

Cain was standing at the white-washed fence, one foot propped up on the bottom rail, staring idly out at the grazing horses. He didn't bother to turn when Kit came up behind him, although he would have had to be deaf not to have heard her angry footsteps approaching.

"Why did you refuse Brandon's request?" she demanded without preliminaries.

"I don't want you to marry him," Cain replied, not looking at her. "And I don't have to tell you my reasons."

She clenched her teeth tightly together. "Is this your idea of some sort of punishment for what happened yesterday at the pond?"

"This has nothing to do with yesterday." It was a lie, and he knew it. He only hoped she didn't.

Kit was so overcome with rage, she felt as if she were strangling on it. All her life, everything she had ever wanted had been snatched away from her. And now this. "Damn you, Baron Cain!" She choked the words out, each one a killing dart with a sharp, poisonous tip. "I won't have you controlling my life any longer. You send Brandon word that you've changed your mind, or I swear by God Almighty, I'm going to make your life a living hell!"

She was so small and he so large that her threat should have been humorous. But somehow it wasn't. She was deadly serious, and they both knew it.

"Maybe you already have." Cain threw a leg across the fence and dropped to the other side. He headed across the paddock toward Vandal.

Kit had never considered the possibility that Cain would refuse Brandon. The day before at the pond, he had even made a reference to her marriage. Now, as she stumbled off toward the orchard, not seeing where she was going, knowing only that she had to be alone, she could find no consolation in the hope that he would change his mind, for she knew as surely as she drew breath that he would not.

She forced herself to sort through the men who had been showering her with attention since she had returned. All of them would be more than happy to get their hands on Risen Glory, but not one of them would understand how she felt about the plantation. Only Brandon. And Cain was not going to let her marry him.

She was left with Bertrand Mayhew. The memory of his pudgy, woman's-soft body was repulsive to her. She wanted Brandon. How could Cain have done this to her?

The question haunted her for the rest of the evening. She sealed herself in her bedroom, pacing the carpet in her bare feet. She refused dinner. Miss Dolly came to the door, and then Sophronia. She sent them both away. Long after dark there was a sharp knock on the door that led from her bedroom to the adjoining sitting room.

"Kit, come in here," Cain barked out. "I want to talk to you."

"Go away! Unless you've changed your mind about Brandon, I don't have anything more to say to you."

"You know damn well I haven't changed my mind! Now you can come in here, or I'll join you in your bedroom. Which is it going to be?"

She pressed her eyes shut for a moment. Choices. He presented them to her and then took them away. Slowly she walked to the door and turned the knob.

Cain had sprawled down on an old sofa with an upholstered seat and a caned back, part of the hodgepodge of furniture that filled the room. "Were you planning on sulking in there for the next week?" he growled.

"Sulking? Is that what you think I'm doing?" How like him to belittle honest human emotions.

"I think you're like a child who's had a piece of candy snatched from her. You weren't really hungry, but the candy was pretty and now you're crying because you can't have it."

Without a word, she turned on her heel and headed back to her room. He sprang up from the sofa and caught her in the doorway.

"Use your head, Kit!" he exclaimed. "Brandon's weak. He can't make you happy. He lives in the past and whines because things aren't the way they used to be. He was born and bred for only one thing, and that's running a plantation on slave labor. He doesn't know how to do anything else."

"You don't know anything about him," Kit retorted. "Brandon is twice the man you are. He's never insulted me or treated me with disrespect. And he's never mauled me, either."

He looked down at her beautiful, willful face, now drawn taut with emotion. "And does he make your heart pound the way it was pounding yesterday when I held you in my arms?"

His clasp on her arm was a loose one, more to keep her attention than to detain her. When she jerked away and fled into her room, he made no attempt to pull her back to him.

"I'm sending you back to New York," he said quietly, resting the heel of his hand against the door frame. "I've already spoken to Miss Dolly about it. You're leaving on Tuesday."

She made a queer, choking sound and spun around in disbelief. Seeing the expression on her face, he felt as if he had driven a knife into her. Wanting to say more but knowing he must not, he reached down for the knob and closed the door between them.

He stood for some time on the other side, one hand on his hip, his head slightly bowed, a muscle twitching in his cheek. Kit Weston had gotten under his skin, and it scared the hell out of him. All his life he'd watched men make fools of themselves over women, and now it looked like he was in danger of doing the same.

From the beginning he'd wanted to think the worst of her. It was more comfortable for him to believe that she was deceitful and treacherous, the same kind of woman his mother had been. Now, no matter how hard he tried to convince himself, he didn't believe it. She stirred him as no other woman ever had. It was more than her beauty, more than the proof he now had that no man had ever claimed her. There was something sweet and vulnerable about her that unearthed feelings inside him he had not known he possessed, feelings that made him want to keep her by his side, laugh with her instead of snarl, hold and caress a yielding body instead of a struggling one, make love to her until her face lit up with a joy that was meant for him alone.

Idly he traced with his finger one of the panels in the door that separated them, and then as he realized what he was doing, he snatched his hand away, oddly embarrassed by the vulnerability of the gesture, even though he was alone in the room. He couldn't send her back to New York. He knew it now. Tomorrow he would tell her. They would make a new beginning. For once in his life, he was going to set his cynicism aside and reach out to a woman. The thought made him feel young and foolishly happy.

Kit heard Miss Dolly climb the stairs for the night. She heard Cain leave the house and then return later and go to his room. At first the pain was so great she could hardly think. How could he do this to her? In two days she would have to leave Risen Glory. It was a blow so devastating, so unexpected, it was almost incomprehensible.

This time she knew there would be no hope, no foolish schemes to sustain her as there had been during her three years at the academy. There was nothing else she could do. He had won. He had finally beaten her.

As the hours passed, rage rose to the surface, intensifying her pain instead of easing it. She wanted vengeance. If she were to live with herself, she had to strike back at him before she left, strike back at something he cared about and destroy it as he was destroying her. Maybe then she could find some measure of peace.

She stumbled over to the washstand and, with trembling hands, poured water from the china pitcher into the bowl. As she splashed the water on her face, she tried to clear her mind, to force it to work. What did he care about most? She could think of nothing he seemed to attach any real importance to, not even Risen Glory itself. Hadn't he turned the plantation over to Magnus while he completed his cotton mill?

The mill. . . . Her mind raced. It was important to him, perhaps more important than the plantation itself, because it was his alone.

The devils of her rage prodded her on. An idea took shape in her mind, seemingly without any effort on her part. It would be so simple and so perfect. Let him suffer for a change. He was not the only one who knew how to destroy!

Picking up the kid slippers she had kicked off hours earlier, she crept from the room on bare feet and noiselessly followed her childhood escape route down the back hallways and staircases of the great house and out through a small window in the rear of the kitchen.

The night was clear, with just enough moonlight to see where she was going. Thrusting her feet into her slippers, she headed toward the outbuildings beyond the house, keeping herself well hidden in the fringe of trees that surrounded the yard. The storage shed was dark. Ignoring the dusty lantern that hung on the wall, she dipped into the pocket of her blue muslin dress, pulled out a stub of candle, and lit it with one of the matches that she had picked up in the kitchen.

She saw what she wanted right away and tested its weight. The can wasn't as heavy as she had feared it would be, but still, transporting it was going to be difficult, since she couldn't risk saddling a horse and would have to carry it on foot almost two miles. Wrapping a rag around her hand so the narrow handle wouldn't cut into her palm, she picked up the cumbersome can and let herself out of the shed.

She had to stop to rest several times as she walked down the road that led to the cotton mill. The kerosene sloshed inside the half-empty can, the sound amplified by the deep quiet of the Carolina night. Tears ran down her cheeks. As she thought about how much he must hate her to prevent her marriage to Brandon and once again banish her from her home, she began to hate him in return. Ignoring the prick of conscience that warned her what she was about to do was wrong, she clung to her anger and her despair instead. An eye for an eye, a tooth for a tooth, a dream for a dream. . . .

She used her petticoats and the sawdust, pushing it into a pile with her hands around the base of one of the central supporting posts on the second floor of the building. The outer walls were brick, but the fire would climb the post to destroy the roof as well as the interior partitions, which were made of wood. She saturated it all with kerosene and then, cursing the tears that were blurring her vision, stepped back and threw in the lighted match.

It ignited in a quick, deadly explosion. She threw up her arm to shield her eyes and stepped backward toward the stairs, unable to look away. Great tongues of flame lashed at the wooden post, climbing it like twisting orange snakes. This was her destruction. This was the vengeance that was supposed to give her comfort when she left Risen Glory.

But she derived no comfort from the destruction she saw before her. She pressed her fingers to her mouth, sickened by the ugliness of what she had done, realizing, too late, that it was hateful and wrong. It proved nothing except her ability to inflict pain just as well as Cain could. Without giving herself time to think, she dashed over to a sawhorse and picked up the empty burlap sack that had been slung over it. And then she began beating at the flames.

Ignoring her streaming eyes and the burning in her lungs, she desperately tried to control the blaze, but the fire was burning faster than she could have believed possible, and soon she was fighting for breath. A shower of deadly sparks rained on her, stinging her hands and forearms. She was forced back down the stairs, gulping for air. At the bottom, she fell.

For a moment she lay stunned as great billows of smoke began sweeping down toward her. Then the smell of burning cloth dimly penetrated her consciousness, and she saw that the hem of her blue muslin dress was smoldering. Grabbing the fullness of the skirt in her hand, she began to smother out the embers, crawling toward the doorway at the same time. Just as she felt the clean air on her face, she heard the great bell at Risen Glory begin to ring and knew the fire had been spotted. Pushing herself up from the ground, she stumbled off into the trees.

The men had the fire out before it could destroy the mill, but even so, there was damage to the second floor and over half the roof. In the pre-dawn light Cain stood wearily off to the side, his face streaked with soot, his clothing torn and blackened by smoke. At his feet lay what was left of a kerosene can.

Magnus came up beside him and silently surveyed the damage. "We were lucky," he finally said. "That rain we had yesterday kept it from spreading too fast."

Cain stabbed at the can with the toe of his boot. "Another week and we'd have been installing the machinery. The fire would have gotten it, too."

Magnus looked down at the can. "Who do you think did it?"

"I don't know, but I intend to find out," Cain said tonelessly. He looked up at the gaping roof and shook his head. "I guess I shouldn't be surprised that someone decided to get back at me. I'm hardly the most popular man in town. I just can't understand why they waited so long. But I'll tell you the truth, Magnus. They couldn't have found a better way to hurt me than by burning this mill, because I sure as hell don't have any money right now to rebuild it."

"Maybe things'll look brighter after you've had something to eat," Magnus said. "Why don't you go back to the house and get yourself fed and cleaned up."

"In a minute. I want to take another look around first. You go ahead."

"All right. I'll meet you at the house."

It was nearly an hour before Cain saw it. The glint of metal near the bottom of the staircase caught his eye, and he bent down, one knee to the floor, to study it. At first he did not recognize the tarnished metal object, for the heat of the fire had melted several of the prongs together, and the delicate silverwork across the top had folded in upon itself. But then, with a sudden wrenching in his gut, he knew it for what it was, a silver filigree comb, one of a pair that he had so often seen caught up in a wild tangle of black hair.

The twisting inside him grew into an actual physical pain. The last time he had seen her, both combs had been in her hair. He remembered how the shiny metal had glinted in the lamplight when she had turned suddenly the night before. There was only one way her comb could be here now. It was she who had set the fire.

There was a moment when his face was raw with undisguised emotion. He, of all men, should have known better than to begin letting down the barriers he had so carefully erected over the years. Now, as he stared down at the misshapen piece of metal, something inside him shattered like a crystal teardrop, something that had been fragile and tender, and all that was left was the ugliness of betrayal and cynicism and self-loathing. What a fool he'd been. She was just like all the rest.

He stood and pocketed the comb, every trace of pain wiped from his face. His handsome features twisted with a vicious, deadly sense of purpose. She'd had her revenge. Now it was his turn.

Chapter Twenty-four

It was midafternoon before he found her. She was huddled beneath an old broken wagon abandoned during the war in some brush near the swampland at the northern edge of the plantation. He saw the soot streaks on her face and arms, the scorched places on her blue dress. Incredibly, she was asleep. He prodded her hip with the toe of his boot.

Her eyes flew open at once, but he was standing against the sun, and all she could see was a great menacing shape looming above her. Still, she did not need to see his features to know who he was. She tried to scramble to her feet, but he slammed the sole of his boot down on her skirt, pinning her to the ground.

"You're not going anyplace," he said, in a low, chilling tone.

Something dropped in front of her. She looked down to see the melted silver hair comb.

"Next time you decide to burn something down, don't leave a calling card."

Her stomach churned with fear. "Let me up," she whispered hoarsely. "Let me explain." It was a stupid thing to say. How could she explain? He already understood all too well.

He made no response, nor did he move the foot that was

holding her down. His head shifted slightly, blocking the sun for an instant. She winced as she glimpsed the deathly pale gray of his eyes and the cruel line of his mouth before the sun mercifully blinded her again.

"Did Parsell help you?" he finally said.

"Brandon? No! Of course not. Brandon wouldn't do such a . . ." What was she saying? She was only making it worse for herself. Somehow she had to try to make him understand.

"Don't you see? You've taken it all away from me. Risen Glory is my life. It's all I've ever had. I wanted to marry Brandon. When I had control of the money in my trust fund, I was going to buy Risen Glory from you. All it would have taken was one bad year, and you'd have gone under. I would have given you a fair price. I wasn't out to cheat you. You could have kept the mill if you wanted."

"So even a Parsell isn't above marrying for money."

"It wasn't like that. We're genuinely fond of each other. It's just that. . . ." Her voice trailed off. What was the use? He would only see it his way.

He lifted his foot from her skirt and, turning his back on her, walked over to Vandal. She scrambled to her feet, feeling the first faint stirrings of hope. What could he do to her, after all, that was any worse than sending her back to New York City?

But her hopes were short-lived. He came back toward her and, with a push, sent her sprawling to the ground again. She landed hard on her hip. As she twisted around, she saw to her horror that a long, thin cord was dangling from his fingers. Before she could move, he caught up her wrists and whipped the cord around them. Then he tied the ends with cruel efficiency to the axle of the old wagon.

"Are you crazy?" she cried. "What do you think you're doing?"

He turned on his heel and headed back to his horse.

"Baron!" she screamed, twisting against the cords that cut into her flesh. "Don't do this! You can't leave me here!"

It was as if she had not spoken. He vaulted up into the saddle and spun the stallion out. As suddenly as he had appeared, he was gone.

The afternoon passed with agonizing slowness. For the first few hours, she struggled until her wrists were raw and her shoulders felt as if they were being pulled from their sockets. But he had done the job well, and she finally gave up. Hunger and thirst added to her miseries, and by evening it seemed to her as if she would have been better off if she'd died in the fire.

He came back at dusk, dismounting with the slow, easy grace that no longer deceived her. Even in the dim light she could see that he had bathed and changed into a clean white shirt and tight-fitting fawn trousers, all of it at odds with her own filthy condition. He pulled his saddlebags from his horse and came toward her, the brim of his tan hat shadowing his face.

For a moment he looked at her, and then he dropped the saddlebags to the ground and squatted down beside her. With a few deft motions, the cords she had struggled so hard to untie came loose. As he released her wrists, she sagged against him, unable to support her own weight. She felt something hard at her lips, and then tasted water, stale and metallic. He tilted the canteen up and she drank until she could hold no more.

Pulling a small bundle from the saddlebags, he opened it. Inside were several soft rolls, a chunk of cheese, and a slab of cold ham. "Eat," he said roughly.

She was weak from hunger, but her body had another need that was even more pressing than food. "I have to have some privacy," she muttered. He didn't seem to hear her. "I need some privacy," she said more loudly.

He pulled a cheroot from his pocket and lit it. The blaze of the match cast a jagged, bloodred shadow across the stark planes of his face, and then the match went out and there was only the glowing ember at the tip of the cheroot and the ruthless slash of his mouth.

He jerked his head toward a clump of bushes barely six feet from him. "Right there. No farther."

It was much too close for privacy, but once again he had robbed her of choices. As she climbed awkwardly to her feet, she could feel humiliation rising like a great wave inside her. She stumbled toward the bushes, praying that he would move farther away, but he stayed where he was, and the mortification of it was almost more than she could bear.

When she was done, she kept her face averted from him and returned to the wagon and the food he had brought her. She ate slowly, trying to give her body as well as her mind a chance to recover. He made no attempt to hurry her, but leaned against the trunk of a tree as if he had all the time in the world. It was dark when she was done. All she could see of him was the massive outline of his body and the burning tip of the cheroot.

He sauntered over to her, picked up the canteen and the saddlebags, and carried them back to the horse. She stood up, watching him unsurely, waiting to see what he planned to do next. The moon, which had been hiding behind a cloud, came out, washing them in silver light. It glittered on his brass belt buckle as he turned back to her.

"Climb on up. You and I have an appointment."

The flat, deadly tone of his voice chilled her. "What kind of an appointment?" she asked.

He mounted and looked down at her. "With a minister. We're getting married."

"Married!" She couldn't believe she had heard him right. "Have you lost your mind? I'd marry the devil first!"

"We're one and the same," he said finally. "But, then, you'll find that out. You burned down my mill, and now you're going to pay to rebuild it. Parsell isn't the only one who'll marry you for the money in your trust."

"You're insane! I'd die before I'd marry you."

"That's your choice. But it's the only one you've got, and as long as your heart's still beating, you'll do what I say. Now come on and mount up. Cogdell is waiting for us."

At the mention of the minister's name, Kit felt her knees go weak with relief. Cain really had lost his mind! The Reverend Cogdell would never go along with anything like this. He was her friend. Once she told him what Cain had in mind, he'd protect her and keep her safe from him. She walked unprotestingly over to Vandal and began to climb up behind Cain.

"In front," he growled. "I've learned the hard way not to turn my back on you." Reaching down, he swung her up before him and then dug his heels into the stallion's belly. As they shot forward, a low, mirthless chuckle echoed in her ear. "You'll get no help from Cogdell, if that's what you're thinking. I confirmed all his worst fears about both of us, and nothing on earth will keep him from marrying us now."

She could feel her heart skip a beat. "What do you mean? What fears are you talking about?"

"I told him you were pregnant with my child."

"No!" Even as they raced through the night, the world seemed to come to a thundering stop. "How could you do such a thing? You'll never get away with this! I'll deny it!"

"You can deny it all you want. As a matter of fact, I already told him you would. I explained to him that since you found out you were pregnant, you haven't been acting rationally. You even tried to kill yourself last night in the fire, and that's why I couldn't let you have your way any longer."

"You bastard!"

He went on as if she had not spoken. "I told him I'd been begging you for weeks to marry me so that our child wouldn't be a bastard, but you wouldn't agree to it. He said to bring you over tonight, and he'd do the job, no matter how much you protested."

For the first time there was the barest softening in his voice. "He cares for you, Kit. You can spare him and yourself a lot of pain if you go along with this, because, in the end, fighting it isn't going to do you any good."

"You go to hell!"

"Have it your way," he said coldly.

Cogdell and his wife, Mary, were waiting for them at the old slave church. Kit pulled away from Cain and ran to Mary, telling her she wasn't pregnant, trying to make her understand what was happening. But Mary had been well prepared by her husband, and, with tears clouding her kind brown eyes, she patted Kit's arm soothingly and told her she mustn't upset herself for the baby's sake.

She fought them all then, until Cain caught her against him and dragged her in the vise of his arm up the rickety wooden steps into the church. He held her that way through the ceremony, her back pressed to his chest, her right arm pinned at an angle between their two bodies. When it came time for her to respond to a vow, he pressed ever so slightly upward on the trapped arm until, despite herself, the proper answer sprang from her lips. By the time it was over, Cogdell and Mary were badly shaken, and Cain was pale, his lips edged in white.

He spoke to them briefly. She dimly understood that they had taken Miss Dolly into their home for the night. The Cogdells kissed her cheek. Mary urged her to listen to her husband and do what she was told. And then Cain led her back outside to Vandal and pulled her up in front of him in the saddle. They set off for Risen Glory.

Her struggle at the church had exhausted her, and the arm he had held pinioned behind her was aching. She forced herself to lean back against him and remain still. Soon she would need all her strength.

When they reached the front of the house, Cain dismounted and handed Vandal over to Samuel, then he clasped Kit around the waist and pulled her to the ground. For a moment her knees threatened to buckle under her and he steadied her, but she quickly recovered and pulled away.

While he spoke with Samuel, she looked desperately around her. The lights in the front of the house had been lit, but Kit realized she couldn't count on any help there. Miss Dolly was gone. Sophronia was the only servant who slept in the house, and how much help could Sophronia be against Cain? She could feel her throat tightening with desperation.

And then she thought of Magnus. Her eyes darted off to the right, just beyond the orchard where his house lay. Magnus had always been her friend. She was sure he would help her if only she could reach him before Cain stopped her.

She slowly lifted the front of her skirt, pulling it well off the ground so it would not trip her. Judging the distance she had to cover, she knew the best she could hope for was to get near enough to Magnus's house so he could hear her screams before Cain caught her. For catch her he would, she had no doubt about that. Still, she was fast, and she had the advantage of surprise. The way she had slumped against him as they rode home might have convinced him that the fight had gone out of her. Besides, it was her only chance.

He had turned slightly away from her. Bracing herself, she took a deep breath and then she darted forward, her skirts held high, racing into the darkness like a small, woodland creature fleeing a deadly predator.

She heard a curse behind her. The sound forced her legs to move even faster. She began to scream Magnus's name over and over. Desperation pushed her faster still, her legs churning away at the soft ground. She dashed into the orchard, leaping over the jutting roots that were as familiar to her as her own palm, feeling a flash of triumph when she heard him trip in the darkness over one of those same roots. But her triumph was short-lived. From behind, she could hear him gaining on her.

"Magnus!" she screamed. "Magnus! Help me!"

She whipped around the trunk of the tree, abruptly changing direction. Out of the corner of her eye, she saw him hurl himself through the air. She shot forward, but not in time. He tackled her from behind, and they both slammed to the ground.

She fought him then, twisting her body around and slashing at him with fists and wildly flailing legs. He pinioned her with his body, but she had a strength born of desperation, and it was several minutes before he could catch her arms. Even then, she wasn't finished. With a snarl, she lifted her head and sank her teeth into the muscled flesh of his shoulder.

He gave a yelp of pain and, abruptly releasing one of her arms, shot his hand back with the palm open, ready to slash her across the face. He caught himself just in time, and his hand froze in midair. With a growl he jerked her to her feet and shook her until she thought her neck would snap.

"Damn you! If you ever try something like that again, you won't sit down for a year!"

"What's going on here?"

Kit gave a sob of relief and spun from Cain's temporarily slackened grip. "Magnus!" she cried, dashing over to him and clutching at his shirt. "Help me! Please!"

He put his hand gently on her arm and turned to Cain. "What are you doin' to her?" he asked coldly.

"Stay out of this, Magnus. It's none of your business."

"I'm makin' it my business."

"She's my wife," Cain said. "I married her not an hour ago."

Magnus looked down at her questioningly.

"I didn't want to marry him," she cried, pleading with him for understanding. "He forced me into it. Please, Magnus, don't let him take me."

A frown formed across Magnus's wide brow. "I can't keep him from you if he's your husband," he said. "You belong to him now. You'd better make your peace with that."

"No!" she cried, her fingers curling into taut, angry claws. "No, I won't! I hate you both. You're exactly the same. I don't belong to anybody except myself!"

She turned to run, but this time Cain was too quick for her. Before she could move, he had caught her to him and tossed her over his shoulder. As the blood rushed to her head, she began to flail at his back and hips, but her blows were ineffective.

A hand slapped smartly down on her upturned buttocks. "Stop it before I drop you," he growled.

Magnus's feet came into view standing next to them. "Major, that's a fine woman you got there," he said slowly, "and you're handlin' her mighty rough. Maybe you'd better give yourself some time to cool off."

Cain's grip tightened on the back of her thighs. "Like I said. It's none of your business." He began to walk toward the house, his shoulder pushing uncomfortably into her stomach.

"You pigheaded fool!" Magnus exclaimed, walking rapidly to keep up with him. "You don't know a damn thing about women!"

Cain silently turned the corner to the front of the house, his boots crunching on the gravel drive.

Magnus's next words sent Kit's already uneasy stomach pitching. "I'm tellin' you this, Major. If you ruin her tonight, you're goin' regret it the rest of your life. You just remember what happens to a horse gets broken too fast."

There was the clattering sound of feet on the piazza steps. "Kit! Sweet Jesus, what's happened?"

"Sophronia!" Kit screamed, trying to jerk upright. "Help me! Don't let him do this to me!"

Like a mother cat defending a kitten, Sophronia leaped forward and grabbed at Cain, shaking his arm. "Let her go!" she shrieked. "What kinda man are you? Put her down!"

Cain shook her off and spun toward Magnus. "Get her away from me before she gets hurt," he snapped. "And keep her out of the house tonight." With that, he carried Kit up the steps and into the house.

Sophronia struggled inside the circle of Magnus's arm. "Let me go!" she shrieked. "I have to help her. You don't know what a man can do to a woman. Let me go!"

But Magnus held her to him, stroking her head and shoulders. He spoke to her in calm, soothing tones, telling her that Cain was now Kit's husband and that she could not interfere with what took place between man and wife. "He won't hurt her, honey. He won't hurt her." He kept repeating the words, praying she wouldn't hear the doubt in his voice.

As she tried to absorb the news of the marriage and understand what it meant, he led her across the dark orchard. She did not seem to be aware of their destination until she was standing in front of his white clapboard house.

Her head shot up. "Where do you think you're takin' me?"

"I'm takin' you home with me," he said calmly. "We're goin' go inside and have a little bite to eat. Then, if you feel like it, we'll sit in the kitchen and talk for a spell. Or if you're tired, you can go in the bedroom and sleep. I'll get myself a couple of blankets and make a bed right out here on the porch with Merlin where it's nice and cool."

For a moment Sophronia said nothing, she just stood watching him and assessing what he was saying. He waited quietly, letting her take her time. Finally she nodded her head and went into his house.

Chapter Twenty-five

Cain sat slumped in the wing chair that rested near the open window of his bedroom. His shirt was open to the waist to catch the breeze from the window; his ankles were crossed on a footstool in front of him. A glass of brandy dangled from the scarred hand that hung over the arm of the chair.

He liked this room. It was comfortable, with enough furniture to be functional but not enough to crowd him. The bed with its four, pencil-slim posters and summer veiling of mosquito netting was large enough to accommodate his tall frame, and its light design kept him from feeling as if he were being hemmed in. Next to it was a washstand and across the room a chest and a bookcase. In the winter the highly polished wooden floorboards were covered with braided rugs for warmth, but now they were bare, the way he liked them.

He heard the sound of water splashing from the copper tub behind the screen that was unfolded in the corner of the room, and his mouth tightened. He hadn't bothered to inform Sophronia that the bath he'd ordered her to have ready upon his return was for Kit, not himself. Despite the fact that the water could no longer be warm, she had fled to it gratefully, and now she was obviously trying to extend her time in the tub with a foolish hope to postpone the inevitable.

And foolish it was. Raising the brandy to his lips, he took a small sip and then set the glass down on the floor. He wanted to be stone cold sober for what was about to happen. For the accounts he was going to settle with her.

He thought about the trust fund he'd married her for. Marrying for money was something he would have despised another man for doing, yet that part of it didn't bother him. He wondered why. And then he stopped wondering because he suddenly realized he didn't want to know the answer, he didn't want to acknowledge that his marriage to Kit had little to do with money or rebuilding the cotton mill. What it had to do with was one single moment of vulnerability when he'd abandoned the caution of a lifetime and decided to open his heart to a woman. What it had to do with was one moment when his thoughts had been tender and foolish and ultimately more dangerous to him than anything in his life.

In the end it wouldn't be the cotton mill he was going to make her pay for tonight, but his paralyzing fear that he would end up just like his father, the victim of a woman. He was going to hurt her for that. And he was going to hurt her in the most basic way a man could hurt a woman, the way no woman could ever forgive. The antagonism between them would be sealed forever, and he could go on with his life without being tantalized by phantom hopes for the future.

Impatiently he pushed the footstool aside with his heel and stood up. Tonight he was going to break her.

Kit heard the scrape of wooden legs across the bare floor and jumped so quickly from the tub she sent some of the chilly bath water splashing out over the edge. She grabbed for a towel and twisted it around herself, frantically wishing she had something more substantial to cover her nakedness. But her own clothing was gone; Cain had made her pass the smoke-scorched garments to him after she had disrobed so he could get rid of them.

Her head shot up as one end of the folding screen was pushed back and Cain stood before her, legs slightly apart, one hand resting on the top of the screen's wooden frame. She had no idea how beautiful she looked to him, standing in the copper tub like Botticelli's Venus rising from a seashell. Her skin glowed golden in the light of the lamp that stood on a low table nearby. Her hair, sleek and wet, fell down behind the curves of her shoulders, its inky blackness emphasizing the pale cream of her skin.

"I—I'm not finished yet," she stammered.

"You've had enough time."

Her hands convulsively clutched the edge of the towel, and she was nervously aware of the thin gold ring that fit tightly around her finger. It was small and pretty, with two tiny hearts at the top delicately outlined in diamond and ruby chips. She had rebelliously studied it while she was scrubbing the soot from her body, yearning to jerk it off and fling it across the room, but not quite daring to.

"Where did you get this ring?" she asked, not caring about the answer, but desperate to stall for time.

"From Miss Dolly," he said coldly. "Now how about getting out of that tub."

"I don't have anything to put on."

"You don't need anything."

"Yes, I—" She groped for the frailest of straws. "I have to comb out my hair before it dries. Otherwise, it'll be so tangled tomorrow I won't be able to get a brush through it. I can't comb my hair wearing nothing but a towel."

The flicker of scorn in his pale eyes left her little doubt about what he thought of her flimsy excuse. Still, he didn't argue with her. Slowly, without taking his gaze from hers, he unbuttoned his own shirt and passed it over.

"I don't want to take your shirt." She spoke courteously, almost as if she were a guest at a garden party politely refusing the last piece of cake. Only the white, stretched skin over her knuckles betrayed her. "If you'll just let me go to my room, I can get my robe."

"Don't push me, Kit."

She hesitated for only a moment before she stepped out of the tub and, holding the towel to her body with one hand, reached for his shirt with the other. As he seemed to have no intention of moving away to allow her privacy, she clumsily slipped the shirt on over the towel and then, turning her back to him, pulled the towel out from beneath and rapidly fastened the row of buttons, a job made more difficult by the fact that the long sleeves trailed down over her hands.

When the buttons were fastened, she turned the cuffs up and, without looking at him, slipped past him out into the room. The shirttails brushed her still-damp thighs, and she was agonizingly conscious of the thinness of the material and the fact that she was damply naked beneath it.

To her surprise he did not approach her, but walked over to the door that led to the adjoining sitting room and disappeared through it. Her hopes for some sort of deliverance from the awful nightmare she was caught in were abruptly dashed when he quickly reappeared holding her comb and brush.

She took them from him with shaking fingers and walked toward the mirror that hung over the bureau. In its reflection she saw that he had slouched down into the wing chair. She watched as he lifted one leg and idly crossed the ankle over his knee. His eyes caught hers in the mirror. She jerked her gaze away and began pulling the comb through the long strands of wet hair, stripping out the water and sending droplets spattering over her shirt and across her bare feet.

Just as it had when she was taking her bath, her mind began frantically searching for some escape from what lay ahead, but she was possessed by a paralyzing sense of inevitability. She had so little strength left. If she tried to run, he would only catch her. If she fought him, he would quickly overpower her. Logic told her that her best course lay in submission, just as Mrs. Templeton had advised little more than a month ago in that other life that she had lived. But submission had never been an easy course for her.

She heard a sound of movement, and her eyes darted back to the mirror. Cain had picked up a glass from the floor and was lifting it to her reflection.

"To wedded bliss, Mrs. Cain."

"Don't call me that."

"It's your name. Or have you forgotten already?"

"I've forgotten nothing."

"Good. Then why don't you put down that comb and turn around so I can look at you."

Slowly she did as he said, her mind working all the time,

trying to find a way to distract him. Her eyes settled on the scars that marred his half-naked body. "Where did you get that scar on your shoulder?" she asked quickly.

"Missionary Ridge."

"What about the one on your hand?"

"Petersburg. And I got the one on my gut fighting over a crooked poker game in a Laredo whorehouse. Now unbutton that shirt and come over here so I can take a better look at my newest piece of property."

"I'm not your property, Baron Cain!"

"That isn't what the law says, Mrs. Cain."

"I told you not to call me that."

"I guess I can call you anything I want. Just like I can do anything I want with you. Women belong to the men who marry them."

"I don't belong to anybody but myself!"

He set down his glass and stood up, walking toward her with the slow, deliberate steps she had come to dread. "Let's get something straight between us right from the start," he said quietly as he stopped in front of her. "I own you. And from now on, you'll do exactly what I say, when I say it. If I tell you to polish my boots, you'll polish them. If I tell you to muck out my stable, you'll do that, too. And when I want you in my bed, you'd better be flat on your back with your legs spread by the time I have my belt unbuckled."

His words were deliberately crude, and they found their mark. She winced as if he had slapped her, and for a fragment of an instant, he felt something like shame. Then the instant passed as he reminded himself that tonight was to be his exorcism.

His hand whipped out and caught her chin. He raked his thumb down over the delicate line of her jaw. "When you married me, you lost your last bit of freedom. Now I can do anything I want with you, short of killing you. And if I'm not too obvious about it, I think I can probably do that, too."

It was too much! She lifted her arm and slashed at the hand that imprisoned her chin. His grip had loosened, and he released her. "I won't let you talk to me like that!" she exclaimed. "I did a terrible thing to you. It was wrong of me. But you've more than paid me back, so let's call an end to all this. You have my money. It's triple what it should cost you to rebuild that mill."

"Some things don't have a price."

She was too distraught to wonder what he meant. She went on, desperate to convince him to leave her alone. "The fire had already reached the roof when I realized that what I was doing was just as ugly as what you were planning to do to me. I tried to put it out, but it was too late. I'm sorry. I—" She stopped herself. What was wrong with her? Had she lost every shred of her pride? She was practically begging him.

"I'd already made up my mind not to send you back to New York," he said coldly. "I was going to tell you in the morning."

"No," she whispered. "It's not true."

"Oh, it's true all right. So you'll have to forgive me if I'm not in a very charitable mood at the moment. Now I think we've talked enough." He reached out his hand and began unfastening the buttons of her shirt.

She stood perfectly still, the color fleeing from her face, no strength left to fight him, the awful feeling of inevitability once again taking her prisoner. "Don't do this to me."

"It's too late." He parted the shirt and gazed down at her breasts.

"I'm afraid." The humiliating, cowardly admission sprang unwillingly from her lips.

"I know."

"Will it hurt?"

"Yes."

She pressed her eyes closed. Tonight would be the worst, she told herself, and then it would be over. He would have lost all power to ever hurt her so badly again. The thought brought her a strange kind of comfort.

Something twisted inside Cain at the sight of her closed eyes and the resignation in the beautiful heart-shaped face. What had it cost her proud spirit to admit her fear to him? Damn it! He didn't want her like this. He wanted her spitting and fighting, cursing him, sparking his anger as only she knew how so that it would be easier for him to do what he had to do.

With a smothered exclamation, he stripped the shirt from her and threw it to the floor. Catching her up under the knees, he carried her to his bed and tossed her down. She turned her head away from him, her eyes still closed.

He stripped off his clothing, looking down at the slim, pretty shape of her—the small, firm breasts, the tapered waist and flat belly. Despite the turmoil raging inside him, he was hard and ready by the time he was naked.

The bed sagged beneath his weight as he lowered himself to the side and reached out to cup her knees. She flinched at his touch, but still she didn't fight him. He pushed her legs apart and shifted his weight to kneel between them. Then he looked down at the secret part of her, bathed in lamplight.

Leaning forward, he separated the dark, silken threads with his fingers. His wild rose of the deep wood. Petals within petals. Protectively folded around the heart of her. His stomach knotted at the sight. He knew from the afternoon at the pond how small she was, how tight.

From the corner of his eye, he saw one delicate hand curled in a fist on the counterpane. He waited for her to swing at him, to fight him for what he was about to do to her. Wished for it to happen. But she did not move, and her very defenselessness filled him with a rage darker than anything he had ever known.

Reaching out, he slapped her hard across the cheek. "Damn you! Fight me!"

Her eyes snapped open, huge and terrified. Sickened, he watched as they filled with tears.

With a groan, he twisted his weight to the side of her and pulled her trembling body into his arms. "Oh, God, Kit. I'm sorry." His hand cupped the softness of the cheek he had just abused. Never in his life had he hit a woman. It was a coward's act. All part of this madness that had overcome him. "I couldn't stand the way you lay there so resigned," he muttered. But she had begun to cry—deep, shaking sobs—and he did not even know if she had heard him.

He held her against his bare chest, cupping her injured cheek and then stroking the damp tendrils of hair around her ears and then returning to her cheek. When she began to quiet, he moved the counterpane out from beneath their bodies so they were resting on the sheet and pulled a thin blanket up to their waists.

Kit must have dozed, for when she awakened, the room was bathed in moonlight and she felt refreshed, even though she could not have slept for very long. She shifted slightly. The hair on Cain's chest tickled her nose. His arm around her was solid and ironically comforting.

She tilted her head back and saw that he was awake watching her. There was something about the quiet room silvered in moonlight, something about the hell they had both been through and the hell that no doubt lay ahead for them, that made questions possible.

"Why do you hate me so much?" she asked. "Even before the cotton mill. From the first day I came back to Risen Glory."

He was quiet for a moment before he answered her. "Hatred's a funny emotion. It's got a lot of different faces to it."

She thought about that. "I guess you're right. It was inevitable that I would feel the way I do about you from the moment you inherited Risen Glory."

"It always comes back to Risen Glory, doesn't it? Do you love this plantation so much?"

"More than anything in the world," she said fervently. "Risen Glory is much more than a home to me. It's all I have. All I've ever had. Without Risen Glory, I'm not anything."

"You're a beautiful woman, and you have courage."

His response surprised her. "You can say that about me after what I did?"

"I guess we all do what we have to do."

"Like forcing this marriage on me?"

"Like that."

"I thought you were going to—" she faltered over the word, "rape me tonight."

"So did I."

"But you didn't."

"No. But I'm going to make love to you, Kit. Before the night is over."

She pulled away from him, turning on her side so her back was to him, suddenly aware of her own nudity and of his. "I don't want you to."

He elevated himself on his forearm, gazing down at her without attempting to touch her. "You've got a passionate nature. I've tasted it in your kisses. Don't be afraid of it."

"I don't want a passionate nature," she lashed out. "It's wrong for a woman."

"Who told you that?" he asked quietly.

"Everybody knows it. And Mrs. Templeton, when she talked to us about Eve's Shame, said that—"

"Eve's what?"

"Eve's Shame. You know."

"Good God." He sat up in bed. As he looked down at her, he was suddenly struck by an awful suspicion. "Kit, do you know exactly what happens between a man and a woman?"

"Well, I—I mean, I've seen horses and—Yes, I think I do."

"I don't think you do," he said harshly. And then he put his hands on her shoulders and turned her toward him. "Look at me. Whether you like it or not, we're married now, and there's no way I'm going to even try to keep my hands off you. But I want you to know what's happening between us. I don't want to scare you again the way I did earlier."

Patiently, in language that was simple and direct, he told her about her own body and about his. And then he told her what happened when they were joined. She listened, curiosity and embarrassment battling inside her until curiosity won and she asked a few shy, hesitant questions.

He answered each one carefully, and then he slipped out of bed and walked naked over to the table where he had put down his brandy glass. Picking it up, he turned and stood quietly, letting her satisfy the curiosity she would not give voice to.

Kit's eyes swept over the body that was so clearly illuminated in the moon-drenched room and saw beauty of a kind she had never before witnessed, a beauty that was lean and rugged and muscular, that spoke of strength and hardness and things she still did not understand. Her eyes went to the center of him, drawn by a force greater than her will. He quickened under her gaze.

The sight brought back all her fear. He seemed to sense what she was feeling, for he returned to her at once. Sitting on the edge of the bed, he tilted the glass of brandy to her lips. She did not like the taste of it, but she swallowed it nonetheless, glad there was so little of it to drink. It slid down her throat like fire.

He set the glass on the table beside the bed and gazed deeply into her eyes. She wanted to look away, but found she could not. Their gray depths held a challenge, and even though she was afraid, she had never been one to refuse a challenge.

The corner of his mouth twisted in what might have been a smile and then was gone as he lowered his head and brushed his lips against hers. His touch was feather-light and soft, his mouth firmly closed. Whether it was the brandy or the fact that there was no hard, probing tongue to remind her of the other, less friendly invasion that would soon take place, she could feel some of her tension dissolve. His moustache brushed her cheek as his lips trailed a path to her ear. He kissed the valley below it and then took the lobe with its tiny, silver ear stud gently between his teeth and teased it with his lips.

She could feel her eyes drifting shut at the sensations he was arousing in her, but then they snapped open again as his hands clasped her wrists and stretched them up above her head.

"Don't be afraid," he whispered, trailing his fingers down the soft underskin of her arms. "It'll be good. I promise you." He paused at the crook of her elbow, brushing his thumb back and forth across the sensitive inner surface.

Everything that had passed between them should have made her wary, but as he played with her skin and then went on to trace delicate circles in the quivering hollows under her arms, she found the past slipping from her and the exquisite sensations of the present taking her prisoner.

He slid the sheet down to her waist and gazed at what was revealed. "Your breasts are beautiful," he muttered huskily.

A more gently reared woman would almost certainly have lowered her arms, but Kit had not been gently reared, and modesty did not occur to her. She saw his head slowly begin to drop, watched his lips part, felt his warm breath on her tender flesh, felt his tongue dart out. . . .

She gave a moan as he circled the small nipple, transforming its softness as if by magic into a tight, pulsing peak. She arched her body ever so slightly, and he opened his mouth to encompass what she offered. Tenderly he suckled her.

Without willing it to happen, she reached up and caught the back of his head in her palms, pulling him closer. As his mouth encompassed one breast, he attended to the other with the tough, callused pad of his index finger, teasing the tip and then catching it with his thumb and squeezing it ever so gently.

Not knowing men, she could not understand what a tight rein he was keeping on his own raging passion as he pleasured her. All she knew was that her body suddenly seemed to possess hidden wires, running from her nipples to the other part of her, and that the pull of his mouth at one breast and then the other was like a hot, moist sucking deep inside her.

The bed moved as he slid down next to her, pushing the sheet away so she felt the great length of his body against her. Once again his mouth found hers, but this time he did not have to coax it open, for her lips were already parted for his pleasure. Still he took his time, letting her become accustomed to the feel of him.

As he played at her lips, Kit's own hands began to grow restless. They moved down to his sides. She clasped him there, one of her thumbs settling over his hard, flat nipple.

With a groan he plowed his hands into her damp, tangled hair and drew her head up off the pillow. Forgetting all caution, he plunged his tongue into her mouth and took possession of the slippery-hot interior. The wildness that had always been part of her nature met his passion with her own. She arched beneath him, splaying her fingers over his chest. He could feel the last vestige of his self-control slipping away. His hands were no longer content with her neck and shoulders and breasts. They slid down her body to her belly and then into the dark, silky triangle.

"Open for me, sweet," he whispered huskily into her mouth. "Let me in."

She did open. It would have been unthinkable not to. But the access she offered was still not enough for him. He stroked the inner surface of her thighs until she thought she would go mad with a desperate longing she did not even understand, until her legs were finally splayed wide enough to satisfy his desire.

"Please," she gasped, the sound coming from deep within her.

He touched her then, his wild rose, the center of her, gently opening so it would not be so hard for her, taking his time even though he was nearly crazed with the drive of his own passion, full and bursting and needing her as he'd never before needed a woman.

He moved on top of her, kissing her breasts, kissing her sweet young mouth as it sucked at his lips. And then, unable to hold back any longer, he poised himself at the very center of her and slowly entered her.

She cried out at the invasion. He caught the cry in his mouth and held it there as, with one sharp thrust, he split her maiden's veil and put innocence behind her.

She plummeted back to reality at the sudden, tearing pain. It was a betrayal. His caresses had lied to her, promised her something magical and extraordinary when in the end it had been a devil's promise.

His hand cupped her chin and turned her face. It was a moment before she could meet his eyes, for she was too conscious of the searing hot rod of him buried deep inside her, massive and swollen.

"It's all right, sweet," he murmured. "The hurt is over."

But this time she didn't believe him.

And then he smiled a smile that was deep and smoky. His hands returned to her breasts and she could feel the melting begin at the very core of her body.

He began to move inside her. Thoughts of betrayal disappeared. She dug her fingers into the hard muscle of his shoulders, buried her mouth in his neck so she could taste him with her tongue. His skin was sea salt and clean, and the stroking inside her was growing deeper, piercing womb and stomach and lungs and heart, melting her bones and her flesh and even her soul.

She arched and strained and let him ride her through day and night and space itself, clinging to him, to the sweet male of him, the hard shaft of him, driving deeper and deeper into her, carrying her higher, flinging her up and up and up into the blinding brightness of the sun and moon where she hung for eternity and then shattered into a million slivers of light and darkness, answering his own great cry with her own.

Part Four

KATHARINE LOUISE

"Nothing can bring you peace but yourself."
Ralph Waldo Emerson, *Self-Reliance*

Chapter Twenty-six

She was alone in the great rumpled bed when she opened her eyes the next morning. She blinked against the sunlight that flooded the room. It was very late. Why had no one awakened her? And then she saw where she was and bolted upright in the bed.

The sudden movement made her wince. Gingerly she pushed the covers away from her naked body and looked down. There was a pale stain on the inner flesh of her thighs. She shifted her weight and saw that the sheet beneath her bore a matching stain.

She kept her mind carefully blank as she went to her room, washed herself, and dressed in a candy-cane–striped dimity. She was working at the snarls in her hair when there was a knock at the door. The brush in her hand froze in midair.

"Yes?" she called out somewhat unsteadily.

The door opened immediately.

"Sophronia!" Kit jumped up and ran to her. The two women held each other tightly for several moments. Kit was the first to recover. She disengaged herself and turned away, unwilling to meet Sophronia's eyes.

"Magnus wouldn't let me leave his house or I would of been here earlier," Sophronia said.

Kit sat down at her dressing table and resumed brushing her hair. "You stayed with Magnus last night?"

"The major didn't give me much choice, did he?" Sophronia replied sharply. "Magnus slept on the porch. I slept in the bedroom."

"I see."

Sophronia began wandering aimlessly around the room. They frequently visited on mornings when Kit wasn't going riding. While Kit dressed, Sophronia would tidy the room and make the bed. But this morning, there were no discarded nightclothes to pick up, and the bed had not been slept in.

She finally broke the silence that had fallen between them. "Are you all right?"

"I'm fine." Kit picked up her comb and began working at a stubborn tangle.

Sophronia noticed the sharp, nervous gestures. "Did he hurt you, honey?"

There was no response.

Sophronia sat down on the straight chair next to the dressing table, her hands clasped in her lap. She suddenly knew what she had to do, but knowing and doing were two separate things, and the words were sticking in her throat from having been buried so long.

She looked over at Kit, who was staring determinedly into the mirror. "I—I never told you about this, but I think I better. I know what it's like to be hurt by a man." She finally had Kit's attention, but now she was the one who had to look away. "I was fourteen the first time. He—he was a white man. I wanted to die afterward, I felt so dirty. All that summer he would find me no matter how hard I tried to stay away from him. 'Gal,' he'd call out. 'You. Nigger gal. Come over here.' "

"Oh, Sophronia." Kit's voice was ragged with her friend's pain. She reached out and covered Sophronia's hand with her own. "I didn't know."

"I didn't want you to."

"Couldn't you have gone to my father and told him what was happening?"

Sophronia's nostrils flared. "He knew what was happenin'. White men always know what happens to the nigger women they own."

Kit didn't know what to say. Still, as horrible as Sophronia's confidence was, she somehow wasn't completely surprised by it. It explained a lot.

"What happened to me is all in the past," Sophronia went on. "It's you I'm worried about now."

Kit opened the center drawer of her dressing table and began clumsily searching through it for a new set of hair combs to replace the silver ones she would never wear again. "You don't have to worry."

"Don't lie to me, Kit. I've never seen anything like the expression on his face when he carried you in this house. It doesn't take much imagination to know you had a hard time of it. But listen to me, Kit. I know better than anyone that you can't keep ugliness like that stopped up inside you. You have to let it out before it changes you."

Kit slammed the drawer closed and stood up. "I don't want to talk about it." She walked to the bureau and began sorting through the contents of a wooden jewelry box on top.

"You have to talk about it," Sophronia pressed. "No matter how ugly or how awful it was. I understand, honey. You can tell me."

"No, you don't understand."

"I do. I know what it's like. I know how—"

"You don't know!" Kit spun around. "It wasn't ugly, Sophronia. It wasn't ugly or awful or anything like that."

Sophronia shook her head slowly. "You mean that he didn't. . . ."

"He did."

There was a moment of silence, and then the chair bumped hard against the wall and Sophronia shot to her feet, her face ashen. Without a word, she ran from the room.

Kit stared after her, feeling sick and guilty, and then she sank down on the edge of her bed. It was some time before she could force herself to get back up again and finish dressing. After slipping on her shoes, she began to search through her bureau drawers for another set of hair combs. When her search proved futile, she tied her curls back with a pumpkin-colored ribbon that clashed with her dress and went downstairs.

Just as she was getting ready to step into the dining room, the front door opened and Cain walked in with Miss Dolly. The old lady spotted her at once. "Oh, my sweet, sweet precious!" She scampered down the hallway, cap and curls fluttering. "This is the happiest day of my life, 'deed it is. To think that you and the major have cherished deep and tender feelin's for each other all this time, and I didn't suspect a thing."

Kit looked at her sharply. Never had she heard Miss Dolly voluntarily refer to Baron as the "major." But before she could judge the older woman's state of mind, she was swept into a peppermint-scented embrace.

"I've already chastised the major for keepin' me in the dark, and I shall give you the sharp edge of my tongue, too, don't think I won't, but right now I'm too consumed by happiness." She stepped back and clasped her hands to her flat bosom. "Just look at her, Major, in her pretty frock with a ribbon in her hair. She doesn't look old enough to be a bride. Not a day over sweet sixteen. Now I must go see Rose about a cake. I know just the recipe." With a quick peck at Kit's cheek, she headed for the kitchen, the clatter of her tiny heels on the wooden floor gradually receding until Kit was finally forced to look at her husband.

She might have been staring at a stranger. His face was carefully void of any expression, his eyes cool. It was as if the passion of the night were only something she had imagined. Not until that moment did she realize that she had expected to see something far different on his face, some acknowledgment of what had passed between them, a trace of tenderness or softness.

She felt something tighten deep inside her. How could she have been so foolish to expect anything else? She should have known this was the way it would be with him.

"Miss Dolly's right," he said curtly, tossing the hat he held onto the hallway table. "You do look like a child with your hair like that. Wear it up from now on, unless you're getting ready for bed. Then I want it loose."

Kit could feel her hands begin to tremble at his autocratic manner. She clasped them tightly together and, with more willpower than she knew she possessed, bit back all the words she couldn't afford to fling in his face when she felt so betrayed. "Why is Miss Dolly calling you Major?" she asked instead, the question sharp and snappish. "What did you say to her?"

"I told her we were married"—he shrugged—"and then I pointed out that if she went on believing I was General Lee, she'd have to reconcile herself to the fact that you were living with a bigamist, since everyone knows General Lee has been married for years."

"What did she say to that?"

"She accepted it, especially after I reminded her that my own military record was nothing to be ashamed of."

"Your military record!" Kit exclaimed, perversely glad that she finally had a target on which to pin at least one small portion of her pain. "How could you frighten her like that? If you bullied her—"

"She wasn't frightened at all. As a matter of fact, she was

quite pleased to hear how well I was serving under General Beauregard."

"General Beauregard? But he fought for the Confederacy."

"Compromise, Kit. Maybe someday you'll learn the value of it." He turned to head for the stairs and then stopped. "I'm leaving for Charleston in an hour. Magnus will be here if you need anything."

"Charleston? You're leaving today?"

His eyes narrowed mockingly. "Were you expecting a honeymoon?"

"No, of course not," she replied. "But don't you think it's going to look a little strange if you leave so soon after our—our wedding?"

"Since when have you cared what people think?"

"I don't! I was just thinking about Miss Dolly and her cake. Go to Charleston! Even better, go to hell!" She pushed past him and dashed out the front door, half expecting that he'd come after her. But the door remained shut and the only sound that came from the house was the distant murmur of women's voices drifting from the open windows of the kitchen.

She went to the live oak behind the house and leaned against one of the great, drooping branches, close to the trunk where no one could see her. What was she going to do? How was she to survive being the wife of a man she hated?

For the next few days she stayed away from the house, donning her breeches at first light and spending the daytime hours on Temptation riding from one corner of the plantation to the next, every place but near the spinning mill. She talked to the women about their gardens, the men about the cotton crop, and walked between the long rows of plants until the blazing afternoon sun drove her into the refuge of the woods or to the banks of the pond.

But the pond was no longer the sanctuary it had once been. He had spoiled that, too. As she sat beneath the willows and gazed out on the light-speckled water, she saw how clearly he had managed to take it all—her home, her money, and finally her body. And then she would remember how freely she had given herself to him, making his victory all that much sweeter. Sometimes she felt almost sick from the force of her hatred for him and what he had done. But there were other times when she was tired or it was late in the afternoon. Then she would think about what had happened and she would feel a restlessness inside her body that had nothing to do with hatred. When that happened, she would jump on Temptation's back and ride him hard until the restlessness was subdued.

Sophronia kept her distance, treating her with a servant's formality, even addressing her as "ma'am." Miss Dolly was nearly frantic because Kit wouldn't receive any of the callers who were appearing at the door to offer their best wishes. Never in her life had Kit been a coward, but now she couldn't find the courage to face them. Although she was certain the Cogdells would never reveal the awful details of her wedding, the rest was bad enough. She had married the enemy in a hurry-up affair that would leave them all counting on their fingers and darting covert glances at her waistline for months to come. Nearly as humiliating was the fact that her husband had abandoned her the morning after their marriage without even having the courtesy to tell her when he would return.

Only once did she agree to receive company, and that was early Saturday afternoon when Lucy announced that Mr. Parsell had come to call. Kit felt an irrational rush of hope and dashed to the mirror to check her appearance. Brandon knew how she felt about Baron Cain, so he must realize that she had been forced into the marriage. Surely he would have thought of some way to help her. She hurriedly made her way to the sitting room, where he rose from the settee to greet her.

"Mrs. Cain." He bowed formally. "I came to extend my felicitations as well as the best wishes of my mother and my sisters on your marriage. I'm certain that you and Major Cain will be very happy."

Kit could feel a hysterical bubble of laughter rising up inside her. How like him to be so proper and polite. He behaved as if there had never been anything between them but the most distant of friendships.

"Thank you, Mr. Parsell," she replied, matching his tone with the greatest of efforts.

Propelled by her pride, she flawlessly played the role for which the Templeton Academy had trained her. For the next twenty minutes, she skillfully moved the conversation from one impersonal topic to another—the condition of the roses that grew near the front of the house, the health of the president of the Planters' and Citizens' Bank, the possibility of purchasing new carpeting for the church. He responded to each topic she put forth and never once attempted to refer to any of the events that had transpired between them less than a week before. As he took his leave of her, precisely twenty minutes after his arrival, she could see his relief at the civilized manner in which she had conducted what could have been an awkward interview for him, and she wondered why it had taken her so long to admit to herself what a weakling he was.

She spent the evening after Brandon's visit curled in a chair in the back of the sitting room, her old, battered copy of Emerson's *Essays* on her lap. She finally abandoned any pretense of reading and gazed at the mahogany desk Sophronia had taken over as her own when she had assumed the duties of housekeeper. Behind the upraised lid, she knew that the pigeonholes of the desk were filled with neat stacks of inventories and recipes, with lists of supplies that needed to be ordered as well as the household bills Sophronia turned over to Cain at the end of each week.

He would probably expect her to take charge of all that now, and Sophronia wasn't going to like it any more than she was. She had no interest in counting linens or in clipping out formulas for furniture polish from the newspaper. She didn't want to be mistress of the house; she wanted to be mistress of the land, to know that Risen Glory was securely hers. With a more amenable husband, it would have been possible for her to have that security, but with Baron, never. He could do anything he wanted to her plantation, and he probably would, too.

Kit's mind, like a tongue probing a sore tooth, considered all the horrible possibilities. He was already neglecting the plantation in favor of the mill. Maybe he would decide to slice up the fields to make way for a road; she had heard him talking to Magnus about how difficult access to the mill was from the north and east. He was a gambler. What if he squandered the money from her trust at cards and then decided to sell off part of the land for ready cash? It would be like watching a part of her own body being cut off.

The clock in the hallway chimed midnight and her thoughts grew darker. She knew from Magnus that Cain had been something of a wanderer. He'd already been there for three years. Maybe he was getting restless. What if he decided to sell Risen Glory and set off for someplace new?

The burning of the cotton mill had taught her a hard lesson about her own impulsiveness. This time she knew she had to consider carefully before she did anything, for she couldn't afford to make any more mistakes.

Tossing down her book, she began to pace the first-floor rooms of the house. Despite her bleak thoughts, it should be obvious that, for the moment anyway, Risen Glory was safe. Cain was going to be preoccupied with rebuilding the spinning mill and putting it into operation, so he wasn't likely to do anything drastic for a while. As difficult as it would be for her, she didn't seem to have any choice but to bide her time. The decision made her deeply unhappy, but she could find no alternative. Her first concern had to be Risen Glory.

And what of herself? The thought intruded like an unwelcome visitor. What of the hot, primitive pounding of her blood when he touched her? What of that instant of heightened awareness that shot through her like a thunderbolt every time she saw him? These were the questions she had not let herself ask because they were the most dangerous questions of all.

She forced herself to admit what she had secretly known for a long time. There was something about Baron Cain that excited her, piercing through her hatred for him to make her feel more vital and alive than anyone had ever made her feel in her life. Perhaps it had always been there, even in those days long ago when she had been his stable boy. Perhaps the strong attraction that underscored her hatred for him was something she couldn't even help—history repeating itself—Weston blood calling out to Cain blood as it had done before in the union between Garrett and Rosemary that had nearly destroyed Risen Glory.

And was that what this union would accomplish? Was that what the surgings of her body would lead to? Risen Glory destroyed? She couldn't let that happen. Somehow she had to hold her body apart from him.

Eventually her late-night wanderings woke Miss Dolly, who forced several teaspoons of laudanum down her throat and sent her to her room. When she finally fell asleep, it was only to have her rest disturbed by vague, opium-induced shadow-images that seemed to hover just on the other side of her consciousness. Toward dawn, the images faded, and it was then that she began to dream.

A great, tawny lion was coming toward her. She could smell his male, jungle scent, but she felt no fear at his presence. Instead, she wanted to snake her fingers through his lion's mane and pull him closer, but her arms were leadened and would not respond.

And then the lion changed into her husband, his expression full of a tenderness she had never seen. He whispered love words in her ear and began caressing her, lightly at first and then more demandingly. She could feel his flesh through the fabric of her dream. It was warm and as moist as her own.

"I'll fill you now," her dream-husband whispered.

"Yes," she murmured. "Oh, yes."

He entered her then, and her body caught fire. She moved with him and climbed with him, and just before the flames exploded around her, she called out his name.

Chapter Twenty-seven

The dream was still with her the next morning. She stretched and, through half-closed eyelids, gazed up at the pink and green silk hangings above her bed. How real it had seemed—the lion who had changed beneath her hands into. . . .

She was suddenly conscious of a soft, scraping sound. Her eyes flew open to see Cain standing at her washstand and shaving in the mirror that hung above it. He was naked except for a white towel wrapped around his hips.

"What are you doing in here?" she sputtered.

"Shouldn't I be asking you that question?" Chin jutted forward, he slid the straight blade of the razor along the line of his jaw with well-practiced efficiency. "When I got back from Charleston last night, I expected to find you in my bed, not hiding in here like a child."

"I wasn't hiding! This is my room."

He didn't even bother to look at her, merely went on with what he was doing. "Not any longer."

She refused to let him get away with such high-handedness. "Go into your own room to shave," she demanded.

He turned and stared pointedly at her chest. "The scenery is better in here."

Her gaze fell to where he was looking, and she saw to her dismay that the sheet lay around her waist and she was naked beneath it. She yanked it to her chin and jerked upright, ready to do battle with him. It was then that she noticed the nightgown she had worn to bed lying in a crumpled heap on the floor. Her sudden intake of breath was like a thunderclap in the room.

He chuckled and turned back to the mirror.

Her eyes took in the rumpled bedcovers and the dented pillow next to her own. But it was not until she reached over to snatch up her nightgown that she became aware of the wetness between her thighs. Even then she did not completely understand what had happened. She reached under the sheet, touching herself apprehensively to see what was wrong with her.

"It's all right, Kit." Cain, a dab of white lather still clinging to his chin, walked toward her holding out a damp cloth. For the first time since their wedding night, there was a softening in his features.

She understood then. It had not been a dream. While she was asleep and vulnerable, unable to protest, he had come into her bed and made love to her.

"How could you?" Batting the cloth from his hand, she sent it flying across the room, furious at the thought of having been robbed of her will.

The shuttered look slammed down over his face. "How could I what?"

"You know very well what I mean," she replied angrily. "Last night, when I was asleep, you—you—"

"I took what was mine," he growled, his lips barely moving. "You keep forgetting that you belong to me. I meant what I said, Kit. Your freedom is a thing of the past. You're my wife, and you'll do what I say. Now get out of bed and get dressed. You've been hiding out long enough."

"What do you mean?"

He went back to the washstand and, picking up a towel, wiped the remaining lather from his face. "I ran into one of our neighbors in Charleston yesterday. She took a great deal of pleasure in telling me you were refusing to receive visitors."

"Well, what did you expect? Am I supposed to invite them into my house so they can cluck their tongues over the fact that I married a Yankee who abandoned me the morning after our wedding?"

"That really rankles, doesn't it? Unfortunately I didn't have much choice. There's a little matter of a spinning mill that has to be rebuilt in time for this year's crop. I had to arrange to get the new lumber and building supplies shipped here as quickly as possible."

Setting down the towel, he walked to the door of the connecting sitting room. "I want you dressed and downstairs in half an hour. The carriage will be waiting."

She eyed him suspiciously. "What for?"

"It's Sunday morning, and we're going to church."

"Church!"

"That's right, Kit. This morning you're going to face them all. I won't have you skulking around any longer like a yellow-bellied coward with jelly where her backbone used to be."

Kit jumped from the bed, taking the sheet with her. "Damn you, Baron Cain! I've never been a coward in my life!"

"That's what I'm counting on." He turned and disappeared through the doorway leaving her alone in her bedroom.

She realized she had played right into his hands, but she didn't care. She was done with hiding. She'd face them all this morning, and teach Baron Cain a thing or two in the process.

She donned the blue-and-white muslin dress with forget-me-nots printed on the skirt that she had worn on her first night back at Risen Glory and pulled up her hair into a loose chignon with soft, inky wisps of curl feathering around her face and behind her ears. She was wearing it up, she told herself, not because Cain had ordered her to, but because she didn't want to look the least bit childish this morning. She perched her hat, a tiny confection of chip straw and blue satin ribbon, high on her head. The only jewelry she wore was her wedding ring and small silver ear drops set with moonstones.

It was a warm morning, and a crowd of worshipers had gathered on the pavement outside the church where they were waiting until the last moment to go inside. Through the open window of the carriage, Kit watched heads turn beneath shabby bonnets and faded parasols and worn silk hats as first one group and then another became aware of their arrival. Only the young children darting about in a final burst of energy seemed indifferent to the arrival of Baron Cain and his bride.

Cain helped Miss Dolly out and then reached inside the carriage to assist Kit. She stepped gracefully down onto the pavement, but as he began to release her arm, she moved closer to him. With an intimate smile that made more than one gentleman who was watching clear his throat and tug on his shirt collar, she slid first one gloved hand and then the other up the length of his sleeve and clung to it in a pose of helpless and adoring femininity.

There was a narrowing at the corners of Cain's eyes, but whether it was an expression of amusement or cynicism, she wasn't certain, and the well-wishers who descended upon them gave her little time for speculation. Cain briefly acknowledged the men's congratulations, while the women clustered around Kit, who continued to cling to his arm.

"Why, Katharine Louise," Mrs. Rebecca Whitmarsh Brown called out as she swept over to them, her daughter Celia firmly in tow. "We didn't expect to see you this morning. It goes without sayin' that your very sudden marriage to Major Cain has surprised us all, hasn't it, Celia?"

"It certainly has," Celia answered tightly. Yankee or not, she had had her own eyes fixed on Major Cain for some time, and she didn't appreciate being passed over for a hoyden like Kit Weston.

Kit gave her husband's arm an intimate squeeze and even went so far as to press her cheek to his sleeve. "Why, Mrs. Brown, Celia, I believe you're teasin' me, 'deed I do. Surely everyone in the entire county who possesses a pair of eyes guessed from the very beginnin' how Major Cain and I felt about each other. Although he, bein' a man, of course, was much better able to hide his true feelin's than I was."

Miss Dolly blinked twice, wondering if it were only her imagination or if Katharine Louise's accent had deepened considerably since they had chatted together only moments before in the carriage.

Kit sighed and clicked her tongue. "I fought and fought our

fatal attraction, of course—the major bein' a Yankee and one of the enemy. But as Shakespeare wrote, 'Love conquers all things.' " She gazed innocently up into Cain's face. "Isn't that so, darlin'?"

"Virgil wrote that," he replied dryly. "Not Shakespeare."

Kit beamed at the women. "Isn't he just the smartest thing? You wouldn't think a Yankee would know so much, would you?"

His hand was suddenly covering hers and squeezing it in a manner that seemed affectionate to the onlookers but was, in actuality, a pointed warning.

She decided not to push him any farther. "Goodness, it certainly is warm this mornin'. Baron, darlin', maybe you'd better take me inside where it's cooler. I seem to be feelin' the heat."

The words were barely out of her mouth before she wished she could take them back. A dozen set of eyes traveled to her waistline.

This time there was no mistaking Cain's amusement. "Of course, my dear," he said solicitously. "Let's get you inside right away." Disengaging his arm from her hand, he wrapped it around her shoulders and led her slowly up the steps as if she were, indeed, a delicate, fruit-bearing flower in need of his protection.

Kit was helpless to protest, and he knew it. She could almost feel their eyes piercing into her back and hear their tongues clacking as they counted off the months. She lifted her chin higher. Let them count, she thought defiantly. They'll soon see for themselves that they are wrong.

And then a horrible thought struck her.

She sat through the service, not hearing or seeing anything, thinking only that in a few months she might very well find herself with a swollen belly. She couldn't have a baby, she thought desperately, not while there still was a chance for her, some kind of miracle that would make everything right again. If she had a baby, she would be bound to Baron Cain for the rest of her life. All the way home in the carriage, she searched for an answer.

Cain disappeared soon after they returned home, but it was not until late in the afternoon that Miss Dolly left Kit alone, announcing that she was retiring to her bedroom to read the

Bible. As soon as Kit heard her door close, she sent word to Samuel in the stables that he was to put a sidesaddle on Lady. Then she rushed to her room to change into her riding habit.

The Conjure Woman lived in an old, ramshackle cabin on what had once been Parsell land. She had been at Holly Grove for as long as anyone could remember. Some said old Godfrey Parsell, Brandon's grandfather, had bought her at a slave market in New Orleans. Others said she had been born at Holly Grove and was part Cherokee. No one knew for certain how old she was. Estimates varied from seventy to a hundred. No one remembered her ever having any other name but Conjure Woman.

White and black alike, most of the women of the county came to see her sooner or later. She could predict the future, cure warts and monthly female pain, make love potions, and determine the sex of unborn babies. She was the only one Kit could think of who might be able to help her.

"Afternoon, Conjure Woman. It's Kit Weston—Katharine Louise Cain now—Garrett Weston's daughter. You remember me?"

The door creaked open far enough for an old, grizzled head to protrude. "You Massa Weston's young 'un?" Kit nodded her head. The old woman let out a dry, rasping cackle. "Yo' daddy, he be burnin' in hellfire fo' sho."

It wasn't an auspicious beginning. "May I come in?"

Without answering one way or the other, the old woman disappeared into the cabin. Kit hesitated for a moment and then pushed the door open and stepped inside.

The cabin's single room was tiny and immaculately clean, despite the fact that every space was filled. Bunches of onions and garlic and herbs hung from the open rafters, odd pieces of furniture filled the corners, an old spinning wheel with an overturned chopping bowl supporting one leg sat near the cabin's only window. One wall of the room was lined with crude wooden shelves that had bowed in the center from the accumulated weight of assorted crocks and jars.

The Conjure Woman stirred the fragrant contents of a kettle that was hanging by an iron hook over the fire and then sat down in a rocker next to the hearth. As she rocked, she began to hum, "There is a balm in Gilead" in a voice as dry as fallen leaves.

Kit sat in the chair closest to her, a ladder-back with a sagging rush seat, and listened to her for a while, not saying anything. It was the Conjure Woman who finally spoke.

"Chile, you lay yo' troubles on Jesus, you goin' feel whole lot better."

Kit said, "I don't think Jesus can do much about my troubles."

The old lady looked up at the ceiling and released another cackle. "Lawd," she called out, laughter rattling in her bony chest, "Lawd, you be listenin' to dis here chile? She think you cain't help her. She think ole Conjure Woman can help her, but she think yo' son Jesus Chris' cain't." Her eyes were beginning to water from her amusement, and she lifted the corner of her apron and dabbed at them. "Oh, Lawd," she cackled, "dis chile so young."

Kit leaned forward to touch the old woman's knee. "It's just that I need to be certain, Conjure Woman. You see, it's very important that I don't have a baby. That's why I've come to you. I'll pay you well if you'll help me."

The old woman stopped her rocking and looked Kit full in the face for the first time since she'd entered the cabin. "Chillun be de Lawd's blessin'."

"They're a blessing I don't want!" The heat in the small cabin was suffocating her, and she jumped restlessly to her feet. "A long time ago, I overheard some of our slave women talking. Then I didn't understand what they meant, but now I realize they were talking about you. They said you sometimes helped them so they wouldn't have any more children, even though you could have been put to death for keeping them from breeding."

The Conjure Woman's yellowed eyes narrowed with something like contempt. "Slave womens goin' hab dey chillun sold away. You a white woman. You neber hab to worry none 'bout habin' yo' babies ripped out yo' arms so you neber goin' see dem again. You a white woman."

"I can't have a baby," Kit repeated stubbornly. "Not now."

The old woman began to sing tunelessly as she rocked back

and forth, "Dey is a balm in Gilead to make de wounded whole. Dey is a balm in Gilead. . . ."

Kit walked over to the window and stared out unseeingly. It was no use. There wasn't any help for her here.

"Dat Yankee man. He got de debbil in him, but he got goodness, too."

Kit shouldn't have been surprised that she knew about Cain. "A lot of devil and very little goodness, I think," she replied sharply.

The old lady chuckled. "Man like dat, he gots strong seed. Ole Conjure Woman need strong med'cine to fight dat seed." She struggled out of her chair and shuffled over to the wooden shelves, peering into first one container and then another before she finally poured a generous supply of grayish-white powder into an empty jelly jar and then covered the top with a piece of calico she tied on with a string. "You stir a little dab dis powder into a glass water and drink all of it in de mawnin' after he hab his way wid you, missy."

Kit took the jar from her and gave her a swift, grateful hug. Then she took several greenbacks she had tucked into the pocket of her riding habit and pressed them into the old woman's hand. "Thank you, Conjure Woman. Thank you so much."

"You jes' do what ole Conjure Woman tell you, missy. Ole Conjure Woman, she know what's bes'." And then she let out another wheezy cackle and turned back to the fire, chuckling at a joke known only to herself.

Chapter Twenty-eight

Kit was standing on a low stepladder in the library about to pull a book from the top shelf when she heard the front door slam. She jumped at the sound, her hand freezing in midair. Now that it was too late, she wished that she had sealed herself away in her bedroom before he'd returned. But something inside her had rebelled at the idea of hiding away from him like a coward, and so she had forced herself to act as if this were an ordinary evening. Still, she'd been nervous as a cat since it had grown dark.

He'd gone to the mill as soon as they had returned from church, nearly twelve hours earlier. Kit had caught a glimpse of him in the distance on her way back from the Conjure Woman's, and she had reined in Lady so she could watch him for a moment. Since it was Sunday, he was working alone. Stripped to the waist, he'd been unloading a wagon of lumber he'd brought back from Charleston.

"Kit!" A deep, angry bellow came from the hallway.

"I'm in the library."

"Get out here!"

She tensed, knowing at once that she was in for a difficult time of it. Don't let him make you lose your temper, she admonished herself as she descended the steps of the ladder. Keep your mouth shut no matter what he says, and then get out of his way as soon as you can.

"When I call you, I want you right away." His muscular form filled the doorway. As she stepped off the ladder, she noted his sweat-stained shirt and dirty nankeen trousers tucked into boots that had undoubtedly left muddy tracks down the hallway. Sophronia was going to be furious.

"What do you want?" she asked calmly.

"I want my wife waiting for me when I come home, for one thing. I don't appreciate having to look all over the house for you."

He was being so outrageous that she could barely restrain herself from delivering a scathing retort. With admirable self-control, she asked, "Would you like something?"

"You're damn right, I would. A bath, for one thing, and clean clothes. Then I want dinner."

"I'll get Sophronia." She started to slip past him, but he reached out and caught her arm, leaving a dusty stain on the sleeve of her pale green and yellow plaid dress.

"Sophronia isn't my wife," he glowered. "You'll tend to me." He dropped her arm and leaned back against the doorframe, blatantly daring her to defy him.

"Very well," she said tightly. "I'll see about your bath."

"You do that."

She pushed past him without a word and made her way to the kitchen. As soon as the door had closed behind her, she balled her fists and slammed them down on the wooden table in front of her. Damn him! She knew what his game was. On their wedding night he had told her he regarded her as his property and expected her to follow his orders. Now he had decided to put her through her paces. Damn his soul to hell!

Lucy and her sister, who helped out in the kitchen, were getting ready to leave for the night, and Sophronia was nowhere in sight. She sent the girls scurrying upstairs to get a bath ready and then looked around for something to feed Cain. To her relief she saw that Rose had left a covered plate for him on the back of the stove. In the dining room she found a place had been set for him.

Lucy appeared somewhat breathlessly at the door. "De major, he say he want you upstairs right now, Miz Cain."

"Thank you, Lucy," she said stiffly. She stood motionlessly for a moment after the girl had disappeared, knowing she had to see this thing through but not certain she would be able to do it. He wasn't going to make it easy for her. He would push her just as far as he could.

She was still looking for a way out as she climbed the stairs to his room. She had no doubts about what would happen if she openly defied him. He had never been averse to using physical force on her in the past, so she could hardly expect that he would hesitate now, and in any physical battle between them, she was predestined to be the loser. The only other option was for her to run away, and she rejected that idea as soon as it occurred to her. It was going to take more than an evil-tempered husband to make her leave Risen Glory!

By this time she was at the door of his room. Drawing a deep breath, she pushed it open.

He was sprawled in a chair, still fully dressed, his bath waiting for him in the corner. "Where the hell have you been?"

"Seeing to your dinner," she replied evenly.

She saw surprise flicker on his face and felt a stab of satisfaction. It quickly fled, however, at his next words.

"Get these boots off me."

He stretched out his leg imperiously and lifted his boot. There was mud on the sole as well as bits of straw from the stable, and even from several feet away, she could catch the unmistakable odor of fresh manure. Clamping her teeth together, she walked over to him and reached down for the heel. The muck squished into her palm.

"That's not the way to take off a pair of boots," he said with a silky condescension in his voice that made her want to slap him.

She swallowed hard and, turning her back to him, lifted her skirts and straddled his leg. She had just grabbed the heel when, without warning, he jammed the muddy sole of his other boot hard against her backside. She did not need a mirror to know that her pretty yellow and green plaid dress was ruined.

With a savage jerk she pulled off the boot and tossed it aside. Then she removed the other one, smearing the front of her skirt in the process. She turned back to him, the boot still dangling from her grimy hand, her expression mutinous.

"Now clean them," he drawled.

He watched her, waiting to see if she would defy him. There was speculation in his gaze and something more. For a moment she couldn't define it, and then she saw what it was. Anticipation. He wanted her to defy him!

"My pleasure," she said sweetly. Reaching over, she scooped up the hem of her skirt and calmly began wiping the filthy boot with it.

There was a queer, choking sound, but she didn't dare look at him to find out what it meant. Behind her, she heard clothing being dropped to the floor and then a splash as he lowered himself into the tub. She applied herself more diligently to the boots, first one and then the other. Her chignon was coming loose, and a lock of hair fell down. She pushed it back from her face with the heel of her hand, leaving a smudge on her cheek. The grandfather's clock in the sitting room downstairs struck ten.

"Come over here and scrub my back."

The boot slid from her fingers and fell to the floor with a thud. Swallowing hard, she looked over at him.

He was slouched low in the tub, his arm propped on the side. A cigar was clamped between his teeth, and one wet calf dangled over the edge. "Get that dress off first. And throw it outside in the hallway so I don't have to look at it."

He wasn't going to win that easily! She hesitated for only a moment before she reached around to unfasten the ruined garment. Beneath it she wore a modestly cut chemise and several petticoats, more than adequate protection from his lechery. Disposing of the dress, she approached him cautiously.

He looked up at her, his eyes glittering through a cloud of blue-gray smoke. "Scrub my back."

She spotted the sponge near the foot of the tub. Averting her eyes from the dangers that lay beneath the crystal-clear water, she plucked it up and sudsed it with a cake of soap. Then she gingerly put it to Cain's back.

"Scrub, damn it!"

Setting her teeth firmly together, she did as he ordered, running the sponge firmly across his shoulder and along the ridge of his spine. He leaned forward. "Lower."

She dipped the sponge beneath the water, sliding it down over the small of his back and across the top of his hips. "There," she said with what she hoped was cool detachment. "You're all done."

"Not quite." He leaned back lazily. "My chest."

Taking a deep breath, she lathered the sponge for the second time and reached gingerly around him from behind. He caught her wrist and pulled her to the side of the tub, soaking the front of her chemise in the process. "Over here where I can see you."

Refusing to meet his eyes, she put the sponge to his chest and began soaping the mat of hair that stretched across it. A piece of dead ash from his cigar drifted down and fell into the water. She worked with brisk efficiency, making white, lathery circles over his skin. Unable to force herself to push the sponge lower, she chose to move it higher instead and wash his arms. As she leaned across his body to get to his far arm, her hair finally pulled free of its pins and tumbled down over one shoulder, its ends dipping into the water.

Cain caught a handful of it and reached up to tuck it behind her ear. She quickly sat back on her heels, pulling away from his touch. His eyes drifted down from her face to her breasts, and she knew without looking that the water had made her chemise transparent.

She rose unsteadily to her feet. "I'll go put your dinner on the table. You can join me in the dining room when you're done."

His smile did not quite reach his eyes. "I'm too tired to go back downstairs. Bring my dinner up here." She nodded stiffly and headed for the door. "And, Kit. Don't bother to get dressed."

She walked out of the room without even acknowledging that she'd heard him. In the kitchen she took as much time as she could fixing a tray. Before she carried it back upstairs, she plucked Sophronia's blue wool shawl from a peg near the back door and draped it over her shoulders.

She entered the bedroom to see that he was dressed only in a pair of trousers. His hair was damp and combed free of curl. Setting the tray down on a small table near the window, she pulled the shawl closer with one hand and pushed a chair up to the table with the other.

"There. I think that's everything." Turning, she made her way briskly to the door.

"Sit down, Kit. I don't like to eat alone."

She walked resignedly back to the table and took a chair across from him. Somehow she had known it wouldn't be that easy to get away from him.

He picked up his fork and started to eat, his movements sharp and economical. Occasionally he looked over at her, but he did not speak at all. She could feel herself growing more and more tense. Out of the corner of her eye, she caught sight of the four-poster bed, and once she had spotted it, she could not seem to think of anything else.

She tried to distract herself by studying the sparkling prisms hanging from the lamp globe on the table, and then by running her eyes over the bindings of the books on the shelf. Thackeray's *Vanity Fair*—how much she had enjoyed that book. Richard Henry Dana's *Two Years Before the Mast*—around the Horn to California. Perhaps she would visit California some day. *The Speeches of Abraham Lincoln*—better left unread. . . .

The bed loomed larger and larger, filling the room, filling her mind. She was warm beneath the shawl, much too conscious of the heat of her skin.

Her gaze settled on Cain's hands as they set down the knife and switched the fork over from left to right, manipulating the cutlery as efficiently as he did everything else. Broad-palmed hands with lean, blunt-tipped fingers. Hands that had stroked her body and cupped every curve. Fingers that had explored her. . . .

"Coffee?"

She jumped to her feet, the single word an explosion in the quiet room. He was holding out the cup she had poured for him earlier and offering it to her.

"No. No, thank you," she stammered foolishly, her earlier composure finally deserting her.

He set down the cup and then leaned lazily back in the chair to scrutinize her. His right hand, the scarred one, reached up and tugged absentmindedly on the corner of his moustache. "Maybe you'd better go get ready for bed," he said quietly. There was a soft, creaking sound as he shifted his weight slightly in the chair.

For a moment she stood without moving, and then she turned and left the room without a word.

He watched her disappear into the connecting sitting room and then shoved his plate away from the edge of the table, knocking off the knife in the process. She was so damned beautiful, he hurt inside just looking at her. Was this the way his father had felt about his mother?

It was some time before he realized she wasn't returning. The thin line of his mouth was grim as he got up and walked through the sitting room to her door. It was locked against him.

At the sound of his hand rattling the knob, Kit backed away toward the far corner of the room. She still wore her chemise and petticoats, although the blue shawl had slipped from her shoulders and lay in a heap on the floor. "Go away! I'm not feeling well."

For a moment everything was quiet, and then there was the sound of splintering wood as the door crashed back on its hinges, kicked open by Cain's foot. He was across the room before she could move, catching her shoulders and dragging her up until her weight was balanced on her toes and his breath was falling hot on her cheek.

"Don't you ever lock a door against me again!"

"I won't go to bed with you!" she cried. "I'll clean your boots, damn you, but I won't go to bed with you!"

"You'll do whatever I tell you!"

"I won't do that!" she exclaimed. "Not voluntarily anyway.

You're stronger than I am. You can force me if you want to. But when you take me, you'll know it'll be against my will."

His mouth thinned into an ugly sneer. "We'll see about that." He crushed his lips to hers, the pressure relentless and demanding.

But there had been enough humiliation for her that night, and she would have none of it. She kept her mouth determinedly closed against him, her spine stiff and unyielding to the force of his hands.

Cain knew women, and he knew their bodies. Although he had only made love to Kit twice, he knew her passion as well as he knew his own. It would not take much to break through her resistance. He could give her the soft kisses his mouth yearned to bestow and then he could follow with the secret touches that produced those strangled whimpers deep in her throat, exciting him almost beyond bearing. With a little patience on his part, he could melt her resistance. But he did not feel patient.

He jerked her petticoats down. She tried to kick at him, but he picked her up and roughly tossed her onto the bed. Then he stripped off the rest of her thin, cotton undergarments as effortlessly as if they were made of tissue paper.

As he reached down to unfasten his belt buckle, he saw the hatred burning in her eyes, and lurking just behind the hatred, he saw fear and the unwilling edge of desire. Her fear checked his anger, but not his sense of purpose. Within seconds, he was rid of his own clothing and lowering himself to the bed.

He took her quickly and efficiently, being scrupulously careful not to hurt her and equally careful to give her no pleasure. When he was done, he lifted himself from her small, damp body and stalked from the room, his thoughts turned bitterly inward. Let her discover for herself that what had passed between them before was something rare and special, something that she should not have rejected so lightly.

He would not admit to himself as he left her how much of the fault was his own. He had meant to push her tonight by forcing her to perform the menial tasks that he knew she would hate—tending to his boots and his bath, responding to his deliberately unreasonable commands. He had wanted to inflict the small humiliations that would tell her only too clearly how little he cared for her. Then, he had thought, when she had understood how unimportant she was to him, it would be safe for him to take her into his arms and love her the way he wanted to.

Only it hadn't worked out that way, and he determinedly fixed the blame on her.

Chapter Twenty-nine

During the long summer of 1868, South Carolina slowly climbed from her back to her knees. In June the state was readmitted to the Union, but the action made little difference to its inhabitants. The Negroes, impoverished and uneducated, were still waiting for the fulfillment of the shining promise of freedom. In a protest against the Fifteenth Amendment and Negro suffrage, the white citizens boycotted the election of 1868. Despite the disenfranchisement that had followed the war, almost forty-seven thousand of them were eligible to vote. Forty-two thousand refrained. As a consequence the state's new lawmakers were a corrupt group of men, both black and white, whose primary interest was in lining their own pockets even if it meant bleeding the state dry.

It was not only in the legislature that the state was in turmoil. Two years earlier in Pulaski, Tennessee, an organization had been formed whose purpose was to maintain white supremacy. South Carolina embraced the Ku Klux Klan as its own. Its members, many of whom were former Confederate soldiers, covered their horses with white sheets and dressed in long robes. They rode at night with their horses' hooves muffled and preyed upon the superstitions of the illiterate Negroes by claiming they were the ghosts of Confederate soldiers. Sometimes their actions were little more than children's pranks—waking a Negro family at night with eerie sounds and then offering for a handshake a skeleton's arm that had been concealed under the sleeve of a robe. Sometimes their actions were not pranks at all. There were whippings and, eventually, lynchings.

Cain was enraged by the strength the Ku Klux Klan was gaining in South Carolina. He and Kit had several arguments over the Klan. While she did not approve of the organization, she insisted it was an inevitable result of the unjust policies of

Reconstruction. Cain refused to acknowledge that the policies were unjust and, to her fury, steadfastly maintained that South Carolina had gotten what she deserved. Despite the corruption of the state legislature, he believed in organized government, and he made trips to both Charleston and Columbia trying to force federal officials to take action against the vigilantes.

The rest of the time, he was at the mill. He hired extra men and paid them to work a fourteen-hour day. The damage from the fire was repaired in little more than a month. Then it was time to install the machinery.

Surprisingly enough, since the night Cain had taken her with such businesslike efficiency, their only arguments had been political ones. Otherwise, the two had fallen into a pattern of polite coexistence, rather like two neighbors who nod formally to each other over their mutual fence but seldom stop to chat.

At first she had been filled with anger at the impersonal way he had used her body the night she had locked her door against him, but as the days of the summer ticked away, her anger gave way to confusion, especially at bedtime when he would bid her a polite good night as she climbed the stairs to her room. The first time it happened, she had waited apprehensively for him to come and claim her. But he did not, neither that night nor any of the nights that followed.

Her confusion was not as much about why he wasn't coming to her room as it was about the nature of the physical act of lovemaking between men and women. Pleasure, she now understood, was not something that happened by chance. It could be given or withheld.

To Kit's relief Cain did not expect her to take over for Sophronia. When she finally spoke with him about assuming Sophronia's housekeeping duties, he looked at her quizzically and asked her why on earth she would want to do something like that. He did remain adamant, however, about her responsibilities toward him and insisted she see to his personal needs, although he no longer humiliated her with degrading tasks. As long as she served him his meals when he came back from the mill, saw that his bath was ready, and superficially, at least, played the role of a dutiful wife, he treated her courteously.

Although he wanted her waiting for him when he arrived home, he did not seem to care what she did with the rest of her time and even let her take one of his rifles when she told him she wanted to hunt for rabbits for a stew Rose planned to make that evening. As she was tramping through the woods in muddy boots and breeches, the wooden stock of his Spencer carbine tucked under one arm, a burlap bag holding the carcasses of four rabbits under the other, it occurred to her that, with the exception of Cain's view of her responsibilities toward him as a wife, he seemed to place no importance at all on having her conform to proper female behavior. She could not imagine herself having such freedom if she were Brandon's wife.

The realization disturbed her. She thought about it the next day when Cain told her a fox had gotten into the chickens sometime during the night and asked her, quite casually, if she'd spend the next few days trying to track it down.

She got the fox the first morning.

Cain didn't seem particularly surprised.

One afternoon Miss Dolly took to her bed, announcing that the *Merrimac,* the great Confederate ironclad, had been sunk. Since it wasn't like her to acknowledge the South's defeats, Kit suspected something was wrong. She was certain of it when she went to Miss Dolly's room and found her talking about rag babies, as she had her first day at Risen Glory. It did not take her long to discover the problem. It had finally occurred to Miss Dolly that now that Kit was married, she had no need of a chaperone, and she was terrified she would be sent away. Kit assured her that no such thing would happen and that she would always have a home at Risen Glory.

She waited for Cain to finish dinner before broaching the subject with him. To her relief he made no protest, but merely shrugged and said, "I guess there's not much we can do about it. Looks like Miss Dolly's ours now." And then his mouth curved into a shadow of his old grin. "Probably for the best anyway, since neither of us gives a damn about convention. Miss Dolly will keep us respectable."

The day after Miss Dolly's future had been settled, a letter arrived from Elspeth:

My dearest, dearest Kit,

When I received your letter telling me of your marriage to Major Cain, I let out such a whoop, I quite terrified poor mama, who feared I had injured myself. You minx! To think how you used to complain about him! It is positively the most romantic *histoire d'amour* I have ever heard. And so perfect a solution to all of your troubles. Now you have both Risen Glory and a loving husband!

You must tell me if his proposal was as romantic as I have imagined it. In my mind I see you in your beautiful gown (the one you wore to our graduation ball) with Major Cain on his knee in front of you, his hands clasped imploringly to his breast just as we used to practice it. Oh, my dear Kit (my dear Mrs. Cain!), do tell me if my imagination has done justice to the event.

You will be amused, I know, to hear what a wicked thing I did after I received your letter. I went to call on Lilith Samuels, using as my excuse an inquiry after the name of her new milliner. We talked about nothings for some time. I made no effort to introduce your name, for I suspected she would ask about you as she always does. (I still do not understand why she took it into her head to dislike you so.) My guess proved correct. Over our second cup of tea, she said, with a sigh that was excessively patronizing, "And how is poor Kit Weston?" I replied, with as much innocence as I could muster, "Quite fine, I should think. Of course, being a new bride has its responsibilities." If anything, her smile became more condescending. "Come now, Elspeth, what responsibilities could be attached to marrying someone like Bertrand Mayhew?" I lifted my eyebrows in what I hoped was an expression of surprise. "Bertrand Mayhew?" I said. "Why, what on earth gives you the idea that Kit married him?" "Really, Elspeth," she replied, "everybody knew she had set her eyes on him. Although nobody understood why, of course. Still, I suppose Bertrand was the best she could do." At this I began to laugh. (I know it was unkind, but I really could not help myself.) "Lilith, you silly goose," I said, "Kit Weston didn't marry Bertrand Mayhew. She married Baron Cain."

How can I describe what happened next? Lilith jumped to her feet, dropping her teacup as she did, and for a moment I feared she would faint. "You're lying,

Elspeth Woodward," she cried out, sounding more like a street vendor than a Templeton girl. "I assure you, I am not," I replied with surprising calm. "Kit Weston is now Mrs. Baron Cain." And then, I blush to admit, I embellished ever so slightly on the facts in your letter. (Really, Kit, how could you have left me so in the dark?) "You must remember, Lilith," I said sweetly, "he had not seen her for three years. And she's so beautiful, of course. He fell deeply in love with her the instant he set eyes on her. Kit writes that they are blissfully happy and he is the most doting of husbands."

Then, I must admit, I was truly ashamed of myself, for she began to cry most pitifully, and her mother had to lead her from the room. I am certain that what upset her was not the fact that Major Cain had married someone other than herself but that he had married you. Still, I was ashamed of the satisfaction her misery gave me, but really, Kit, she was most unkind to you and she deserved some retribution.

I have saved my own wonderful news for last, although I suspect it will not come as a complete surprise. You are not to be the only bride, for in October I shall be joining you in the state of wedded bliss! You will remember that in my letters I have told you I have been spending much time with my cousin (twice removed) Edward Matthews. Although we have known each other all our lives, he is eight years older than I and has, until quite recently, thought of me as a child. I assure you, he no longer does!

Dearest Kit, I detest the distance between us. How I wish we could talk together as we used to and exchange confidences about the two men we love, your Baron and my darling Edward. Now that you are a married woman, I could ask you some of the questions I can not bring myself to ask my own dear mama. Can Eve's Shame really be as horrible as Mrs. Templeton suggested? I am beginning to suspect that she must be wrong, for I can not imagine anything (even E.S.) that could take place between my darling Edward and myself that would be repulsive. Oh, dear, this is all quite improper, and I should not be writing any of it, even to you, but it has been so much on my mind lately. I will close now before I am any more indiscreet. How I miss you!

Ta chère, chère amie,
Elspeth

For nearly a month, Elspeth's letter stared accusingly at Kit from the top of her bureau. She sat down to answer it a dozen times, but did not pick up her pen once. Finally she knew she could put it off no longer. It took her most of an afternoon, and the result was glaringly unsatisfactory, but it was the best she could do.

Dear Elspeth,

I am sorry it has taken me so long to respond to your letter, but it seems I never have a moment to spare.

You must realize how happy I am for you. Your Edward sounds perfect, just the husband for you. I know you will be the most beautiful bride in New York. How I wish I could see you. Lilith will be green with envy.

I am amazed at how close your imagination hit upon the truth of Baron's marriage proposal. It was just as you imagined it, down to the graduation gown.

Forgive me for such a short note, but I have a hundred things still to do this afternoon. Do not worry about Eve's Shame. Mrs. Templeton lied to us.

All my love,
Kit

It was the end of August before Kit could bring herself to visit the spinning mill, and then it was only because she knew Cain wouldn't be there. It was harvest time, and he was in the fields with Magnus from well before dawn until long after dark, leaving Jacob Childs in charge at the mill.

Even though Kit hadn't seen the mill since the awful night she had tried to burn it down, it had never been far from her thoughts. She finally admitted to herself what had been nagging at her from the very beginning—the mill fascinated her even while she hated it.

The reason for her hatred was obvious. The mill was a threat to Risen Glory. She did not believe Cain would be content to keep it small, and each time he expanded it, it would be at the expense of the plantation. The reason for her fascination was less obvious. It had to do with the fact that she was a Southerner and born to cotton. Looking back, she wondered why the full implication of the spinning mill hadn't struck her at once, why it had taken her so long to understand that maybe, just maybe, it was the miracle of the gin all over again.

She knew the story as well as she knew the lines in her own palm. All the children of the South did. They had heard it told again and again, even before they could understand it. The story knew no boundaries of creed or color. It was told by rich and poor alike, by free men and slaves. How the South was saved in ten short days.

It was the end of the eighteenth century, and the devil seeds were killing them. Oh, you could talk all you wanted about Sea Island cotton with its long, silky fibers and smooth seeds that slipped out as easily as the pit of a ripe cherry. But if you didn't own sandy soil along the coast, you might as well forget about Sea Island cotton, for as sure as God made heaven and earth, that cotton wasn't going to grow anyplace else in the South.

There was tobacco, of course. But tobacco sucked the life out of the soil within a few years, and then what did they have left? Land that wouldn't grow anything, that's what.

Rice? Indigo? Corn? Good crops, but they wouldn't make a man rich. They wouldn't make a country rich. And that's what the South needed. A money crop. A crop that would make the whole world come banging on her door.

It was the devil seeds. The South could grow green seed cotton anywhere. It wasn't temperamental. It didn't need sandy soil or sea air. Green seed cotton grew like a weed. And it was worth about as much.

The fibers were short and tough. And those devil seeds. They clung to those short, tough fibers like burrs, they clung like glue, they clung like they'd been nailed in, they clung like the devil had put them there just so he could laugh at any man foolish enough to try to get them out. A man had to work ten hours to separate one pound of cotton lint from three pounds of those devil seeds. Three pounds of seeds for one small pound of cotton lint. Ten hours' work. The devil was having a fine time in hell laughing at them all.

Where was the money crop going to come from? Where was the money crop that was going to save the South? They stopped buying slaves and promised manumission to those they owned. Too many mouths to feed. No money crop. The devil seeds.

And then the schoolteacher came to Savannah. A Massachusetts boy with a mind that was different from other men's. He dreamed machines. They told him about the devil seeds and those short, tough fibers. He went to the cleaning shed and watched how they had to fight to pull out the seeds. Three pounds of seed for one pound of cotton lint. Ten hours.

The schoolteacher set to work. It took him ten days. Ten days to save the South. When he was done, he had made a wooden box with some rollers and wire hooks. There was a metal plate with slots and a crank on the side that turned like magic. The teeth hooked the cotton and pulled it through the rollers. The devil seeds fell into the box. One man. One day. Ten pounds of cotton lint.

The miracle was made. The South had her money crop. She had the whole world banging on her door. The South was Queen and King Cotton was on the throne.

They bought more slaves. They were greedy for them now. Hundreds of thousands of acres of land had to be planted with green seed cotton, and they needed strong black backs for that. Promises of manumission were forgotten. Eli Whitney, the schoolteacher from Massachusetts, had given them the cotton gin. The miracle was made.

Now, as Kit tied Temptation to the rail and walked toward the brick building, she thought about the gin and the spinning mill. The gin had saved the South, but had it destroyed it, too? Without the gin slavery would have disappeared by itself because it wouldn't have been economical to maintain slaves. Then there would have been no war. Was it going to be the same with the spinning mill?

Cain wasn't the only man who had seen what it would mean for the South to have its own mills instead of shipping the raw cotton to the northeast or to England. She had learned that there were a few others building spinning mills in the South—a small handful, it was true, for an ocean of cotton, but it was only a matter of time before there were more. Then the South could control its cotton from beginning to end—grow it, gin it, spin it, and eventually weave it. The mills could bring back the prosperity the war had stripped away. But like the gin, might they bring unforeseen changes, too? Changes to plantations like Risen Glory? Changes to Risen Glory itself?

Jacob Childs showed her through the mill, and if he was curious about why the wife of his employer should suddenly reappear after a two-month absence, he gave no sign of it. As far as Kit knew, Cain had told no one that she was the person who had tried to burn down the mill, and Childs seemed to suspect nothing. It appeared that only Magnus and Sophronia had guessed the truth.

Although the machines were not yet in operation, Childs explained to her how they would work and even told her something of the development of the various spinning frames from the famous spinning jenny of the eighteenth century to the highly efficient ring-spinning frame, invented only eighteen years before, that the mill at Risen Glory would use. Despite herself, she found she was looking forward to seeing the huge machines at work when the mill opened in October.

On her way home, she caught sight of Cain standing beside a wagon filled with cotton. He was stripped to the waist, and his chest glistened with sweat. As she watched, he took a burlap sack filled with cotton from the shoulders of one of the workers and emptied it into the wagon. The worker moved off, his gleaming black skin in marked contrast to Cain's paler bronze color.

Cain took off his hat and lifted his forearm to wipe the sweat from his brow. At the movement, the taut, sinewy tendons rippled across the sheath of his skin like wind over water. Kit could feel a sudden, piercing weakening inside her. He had always been lean and hard-muscled, but the back-breaking work of the last few months had brought subtle changes to his body. Every tendon, every muscle, seemed to have tightened and further defined itself. She had a sudden, unexpected vision of that naked, sinewy strength pressed upon her, and she shook her head to clear the image from her mind.

When she returned to Risen Glory, she indulged in a frenzy of cooking, despite the fact that the weather was oppressive and the kitchen heavy with heat. By the end of the day, she had produced a terrapin stew, corn rolls, and a jelly cake, but she still hadn't managed to shake her restlessness, and she decided to ride to the pond for a swim before dinner. As she left the stable on Temptation, she remembered Cain was working in a field she would have to cross and would almost certainly guess where she was going, but instead of upsetting her, the thought excited her.

He did see her, as it turned out. He even lifted his hand in a small, mocking salute. But he didn't come near the pond. She swam in the cool waters, naked and alone.

She awakened the next morning to find that her monthly time had come upon her. By afternoon, her initial relief at discovering that she was not pregnant had been displaced by racking pain. She was seldom sick with her monthly courses, and never this badly.

At first she tried to ease the pain by walking, but before long, she gave it up and, stripping off her dress and petticoats, went to bed. Sophronia dosed her with medicine, Miss Dolly read to her from *The Christian's Secret of a Happy Life,* but the pain did not ease. She finally ordered them both out of the room so she could suffer in peace.

She was not to be left alone for long, however. Near dinner time her door banged open unceremoniously and Cain strode in, still dressed from the fields. "What's the matter with you?" he demanded belligerently. "Miss Dolly told me you were sick, but when I asked her what was wrong, she began twitching like a rabbit and ran to her room." Only the creases across his forehead marked his true concern.

Kit was lying on her side, her knees clutched to her chest. "Go away," she moaned.

"Not until you tell me what's wrong."

"It's nothing," she groaned. "I'll be all right tomorrow. Just go away."

"Like hell I will. I come home to find the house as quiet as a funeral parlor and everybody in it acting like somebody just died. My wife is locked away in her bedroom, and nobody will tell me anything!"

"It's my monthly time," Kit muttered, too sick to feel more

than a momentary pang of embarrassment. And then, almost apologetically: "I never get this bad."

For a moment Cain said nothing, and then he turned and left the room. As much as Kit had wanted him gone, she couldn't help but feel resentful at his abrupt and unsympathetic departure.

To her surprise, however, he was back in less than half an hour. He sat down next to her on the bed and, lifting her shoulders, held a cup to her lips. "Drink this. It'll make you feel better."

She was too dazed by pain to argue. She took a swallow, and then gasped for breath. "What is it?" she sputtered weakly.

He put the cup back to her lips, forcing more down her throat. "Lukewarm tea with a heavy dose of rum. It'll take the edge off."

It tasted foul, but it was easier to drink it than put up a fuss, and she swallowed it all. As he gently laid her back on the bed, her head beginning to swim pleasantly, she was dimly conscious of the smell of soap about him and realized he had bathed before he had come back to her. The gesture touched her. And then she felt a tug at the sheet that covered her. Beneath it she wore only a plain schoolgirl's cotton chemise from her days at the academy and, mismatched with it, a pair of expensive, delicately ruffled pantalettes threaded with emerald-green ribbon.

She tried to grab at the cover, but her reflexes were dulled, and she did little more than bat weakly at the air. The sheet slipped from her body. "No," she muttered. "I don't want. . . ."

"Shhh. Just close your eyes and let the rum do its work."

Indeed her eyelids suddenly seemed much too heavy to hold open. As they drifted shut, his fingers touched the small of her back and began to massage her through the thin cotton. It felt so good.

His hands climbed gently along the line of her spine, and she could feel the tight cords inside her begin to loosen. Then he moved down again, kneading at the small of her back and across her hips, applying a gentle yet insistent pressure. She was not even aware when he pushed the camisole up out of his way and touched her skin directly. As she drifted off to sleep, she knew only that the power of his touch seemed to have drawn the knife edge of pain from her body.

The next morning she found a great bunch of yellow foxgloves thrust into a drinking glass at her bedside.

Chapter Thirty

Spring slipped into fall. The harvest was in and the cotton being ginned. It would not be long before the mill sprang alive. An air of tense expectancy hung over the house and its inhabitants. It was as if they were all waiting for some cataclysmic event to either sort out their lives or leave everything so hopelessly jumbled that they would be forced to put the past behind them and start over again. But life isn't made up of cataclysmic events. Instead, it is a series of everyday occurrences, much like beads strung on a necklace, with each one little different from the other.

Sophronia moved belligerently through the days, increasingly snappish and difficult to please. Only the fact that Kit was not sharing Cain's bed brought her any comfort at all. It was not that she wanted Cain for herself—she had finally relinquished her hold on that particular piece of her past—instead, it was a feeling that as long as Kit stayed away from Cain, Sophronia would never have to face the awful possibility that a decent woman like Kit, a decent woman like herself, could find pleasure lying with a man. For if that was possible, all her carefully arranged ideas about what was important and what was not might be meaningless.

The truth was, Sophronia had nearly run out of time. James Spence was pressing her to make up her mind whether or not she would be his mistress, safe and well protected in the small, doll'shouse he had found in Charleston. He had made it clear that if she did not agree, he had someone else in mind to take her place. Never one to be idle, Sophronia now found herself staring out the window for long stretches of time, looking in the direction of the overseer's house.

Magnus waited, too. He could sense Sophronia coming to some sort of crisis, and he steeled himself to face it. How much longer, he wondered, could he be patient, and how was he going to live with himself if she left him for James Spence with his fancy red buggy and his phosphate mine and his skin as white as the underbelly of a fish?

Cain's problems were different, and yet the same. Despite himself, he began to resent Magnus and Jacob Childs. They were both honest and so remarkably efficient that there was no longer any need for him to spend fourteen hours a day in the fields or at the mill, driving himself to exhaustion. He was discovering too late that he needed that exhaustion so his body would be too tired to realize the great joke that was being played on it.

The very idea of celibacy was as foreign to Cain as jumping off a bridge or throwing himself in front of a train. The word itself conjured up images in his mind of robed monks and cool, cloistered monasteries set into the sides of inaccessible mountain ranges. Yet now he found himself without the will to take another woman to his bed. He, who had never been faithful to a woman, was now being faithful to a woman who wouldn't make love to him.

And then there was Kit. It seemed as if her body, once awakened, would not go back to sleep. Strange, erotic fantasies began to bite into her thoughts when she least expected them. She tried to read Emerson again, but his philosophy of individuality and self-reliance did not bring her the comfort it once had. Out of curiosity, she picked up a collection of poems by Walt Whitman called *Leaves of Grass,* remembering as she opened the green cover with its curious design of leaves and flowers and sprouting roots that Cain had once recommended she read this unknown poet.

By the time she had finished, she felt as if she had been stripped bare. Never had she read poetry like this, sprawling free verse stuffed with images that were so blatantly sexual they left her body burning:

> Love-thoughts, love-juice, love-odor, love-yielding,
> love climbers, and the climbing sap,
> Arms and hands of love, lips of love, phallic thumb of
> love, bellies press'd and glued together with love. . . .

The poem left her weak and finally ready to admit that she was aching with a need to be touched and to touch in return. She found herself rushing back to her bedroom in the afternoons for long, soaking baths before dinner and then, fragrant with jasmine scent, dressing in her most attractive gowns. She no longer wore her hair down unless she was riding, in which case she still twisted it into a single thick braid down her back. Otherwise, she arranged it either in a loose chignon high on her head with wispy curls framing her face like soft, inky feathers, or in the severely sophisticated Spanish style so few women could wear successfully, parted in the center and pulled into a heavy knot at the nape of her neck. Both styles suited her well, depending upon her mood. The chignon, as impish and mischievously impulsive as she, formed a delicious contrast to her heavy, dark brows and startling eyes, while the Spanish style emphasized the pure classic beauty of a bone structure that age would only enhance.

She suddenly found her clothes too tame for her and cut off a dozen tiny silver buttons from the bodice of a cinnamon silk gown so that the modest neckline fell open from her throat to the middle of her breasts and then filled in the space with a string of purple glass beads the color of juniper berries. She replaced the belt on a pale-yellow morning dress with a long swath of vermilion and indigo striped tafetta that Miss Dolly hemmed for her. She wore bright pink slippers with a tangerine gown and then was unable to resist threading lime-colored ribbons through the eyelet that capped the sleeves. She was outrageous and enchanting, rather like a peacock spreading its tail to attract a mate.

Cain, however, didn't seem to notice, even though he was now home more frequently for dinner. She mentioned to him that she had read *Leaves of Grass,* and they had a lively and satisfying discussion about the merits of the maverick work, but afterward, Cain bid her an indifferent good night and went to Magnus's house for a companionable cigar. She began to read at night in the sitting room that connected their two bedrooms, telling herself it was more comfortable than remaining downstairs. Cain, however, did not seem to be aware that she was there.

Veronica Gamble came to call on her one rainy Monday afternoon, and once again Kit found herself looking less than her best, having volunteered to sift through the dusty clutter in the attic for a pretty set of floral china that no one seemed to be able to find. Other than exchanging a few courteous words when they saw each other at church or in town, they had not spoken for any length of time since the night Veronica had visited Risen Glory, althought Kit had sent her a polite thank you note for the handsome, calf-bound copy of *Madame Bovary* that had been Veronica's wedding present—a most inappropriate gift, Kit had discovered when she read it.

Since her marriage, Kit had deliberately distanced herself from Veronica, despite the fact that she appreciated the older woman's worldliness and intelligence. Still, she couldn't bring herself to like her. There was something subtly threatening about such cool beauty and total self-assurance.

While Lucy served them frosty glasses of lemonade and a small plate of cucumber sandwiches with the crusts neatly trimmed from the bread, Kit dismally compared Veronica's well-cut biscuit-colored suit with her own soiled and rumpled cotton frock. Was it any wonder that her husband showed such obvious pleasure in Veronica's company whenever they met? Not for the first time, it occurred to Kit that all those meetings might not be taking place in public.

"And how do you find married life?" Veronica asked after they had exchanged pleasantries and Kit had consumed four cucumber sandwiches to her one.

"Compared to what?" Kit replied bluntly.

Veronica's laughter tinkled through the room like a string of glass bells. "Dear Kit, you are without doubt the most refreshing female in this decidedly tedious town."

"If it's so tedious, why do you stay here?"

Veronica fingered the cameo brooch at her throat. "I came here to heal my spirit," she said thoughtfully. "I'm certain that sounds melodramatic to someone as young as you, but my husband was very dear to me, and it has not been easy for me to accept his death. In the end, though, I'm finding boredom almost as great an enemy as grief. Once one has become accustomed to the company of a fascinating man, it is no longer easy to be alone."

Kit did not know what to say to this, especially since she sensed a subtle calculation behind the words, an impression that Veronica quickly reinforced.

"Enough! You cannot want to spend your afternoons listening to the maudlin reflections of a lonely widow when life is so new and young for you. Besides, you have not yet told me how you are enjoying your new married life."

"I'm adjusting to it much like any other new bride," Kit answered after a small pause.

"What a perfectly conventional and proper response." Veronica sniffed. "I'm quite disappointed. Somehow I had expected you to tell me with your customary bluntness to mind my own business, although I'm certain you shall do just that before I leave, since I came here with the express purpose of prying into the intimacies of this most interesting marriage of yours."

"Really, Mrs. Gamble!" Kit exclaimed, feeling an unreasonable flicker of panic. "You go too far."

"Of course I do. I always have. That's why my life is so amusing. And now I find I am caught up in a fascinating mystery that presents itself beneath my very nose." Veronica tapped her cheek thoughtfully with one oval fingernail. "Why, I ask myself, does what is unquestionably the most attractive couple in South Carolina seem to be at loggerheads? Why do their eyes seldom meet in public? Why do they never touch each other in the casual way lovers do? That, of course, is the most interesting question of all because it makes me wonder if they truly are lovers."

Kit sucked in her breath indignantly, but Veronica waved her silent with a lazy flick of her hand. "Spare me any dramatics until you have heard me out. You may discover I am doing you a favor."

A small, silent war took place inside Kit, with caution on one side and curiosity on the other. In the end there was little doubt about which side would win. "Go on," she said frostily.

"As I was saying," Veronica continued, "there is something not quite right about this couple. The husband has a hungriness about him that is foreign to a well-satisfied man. While the wife. . . . Ah, the wife! She is even more interesting than the husband. She watches him when he is not looking, drinking in his body in the most immodest fashion, letting her eyes actually caress him. It is most puzzling. The man is virile, the wife unquestionably sensuous, and yet I am convinced the two are not lovers." Having had her say, Veronica was now content to wait.

Kit had gripped her hands tightly together in her lap to keep them from trembling. She felt stripped and humiliated; yet, in a strange way, she was not ready for the conversation to end. If she ended it now, in some subtle way Veronica Gamble would have beaten her. The woman had come here with a purpose, and now she had to know what it was. "I will refrain from commenting on your ridiculous suppositions, Mrs. Gamble," she said with dignity, "and merely ask what possible concern all this could be of yours."

Veronica looked somewhat surprised. "But isn't it obvious? You can't be so naive that you don't realize how attracted I am to your husband. I am here simply to give you fair warning that, if you don't intend to make use of him, I certainly do."

It was all so absurd that Kit found herself almost calm. "Am I to understand, Mrs. Gamble, that you have come here today to warn me that you intend to have a liaison with my husband?"

"Only if you don't want him, my dear." Veronica picked up her lemonade, took a slow sip, and then set the glass back down. "Despite what you may think, I formed an exceptional fondness for you the first time I met you. You remind me so much of myself at nineteen, although I was not quite so undisciplined. Still, friendship can only extend so far, and in the end, it will be better for your marriage if I share your husband's bed, and not some scheming hussy who will try to come between the two of you permanently."

Up until that moment, she had been speaking lightly, but now her green eyes bore uncompromisingly into Kit's like small, polished emeralds. "Believe me when I tell you this, my dear. For some reason that I can not possibly fathom, you have left your husband ripe for the picking, and it is only a matter of time until someone does just that. I intend that someone to be me."

Kit knew she should sweep indignantly from the room, but there was something about Veronica Gamble's utter frankness that reached deep inside and caught at the part of her that had so little patience with dissemblance. Still, she kept her face expressionless, her spine as rigid as an iron bar. "For the sake of conversation, Mrs. Gamble," she said stiffly, "suppose some of what you say is true. Suppose, for example, that I have no interest in my husband. Or suppose—again for the sake of conversation—that my husband has no interest in me." She could feel the hot color flooding her rigidly set features, but she plunged determinedly on. "How might you suggest I go about . . . getting him interested?"

"Seduce him, of course."

There was a long, painful silence in the room. "And how," Kit asked stonily, "might one do that?"

Veronica considered her answer for a moment before she spoke. "A woman seduces a man by following her instincts without giving the slightest thought to what she has heard is proper or improper. Seductive dress, a seductive manner, a willingness to tantalize, to give a glimpse of promises to come. You're an intelligent woman, Kit. I'm certain if you truly put your mind to it, you will find a way. Just remember this. Pride has no place in the boudoir. It is a room devoted to giving, not holding back. Do I make myself clear?"

Kit nodded stiffly.

Veronica gathered up her gloves and reticule, having accomplished the purpose of her visit. As she stood, she turned to Kit who had also risen. "I warn you, my dear," she said softly, "you had best learn your lessons quickly, for I shan't give you much time. You've had quite enough already." With that, she swept from the room.

As Veronica mounted the steps to her carriage, she smiled slightly to herself. What a delightful young woman. How Francis would have enjoyed this afternoon. It was not often that she got the chance to play the role of fairy godmother, but she had to admit that she had performed splendidly. As she settled back in the tufted leather seat, her brow knitted ever so slightly. If only she could make up her mind whether or not she would actually carry out her threat.

For nearly a half hour after Veronica had left, Kit sat on the settee. She felt like an utter fool. How could she have let the conversation get so entirely out of hand? Slowly she worked up a full lather of righteous indignation. Veronica Gamble was a sinful, hateful woman! Before long, Kit was stalking about the room, her mind racing at a furious pace. She wouldn't let it happen! She would never let that woman have the satisfaction of being able to smirk at Kit Weston!

With an angry exclamation, she rushed up the stairs to her own bedroom and began pulling open the drawers of her bureau, searching through them until she found what she was looking for. She finally had the excuse to do what she'd been wanting to do for so very long.

Dinner was torture for her, made worse by the fact that Cain seemed to be in the mood to prolong it. He talked to her about the mill and then asked her what she thought the market for cotton would be like within the year, listening intently as she gave him her opinion. While the main course was being cleared away, he flirted with Miss Dolly and, through dessert, teased the older woman unmercifully about breaking the hearts of all the gentlemen in Rutherford. He was charming and so achingly handsome that Kit found it hard to look away from him.

She escaped to her room as soon as she could after dinner. Slipping out of her clothes, she donned a faded cotton wrapper and sat down in front of her mirror to take the pins from her hair and brush it into a soft, midnight cloud around her face. It was not long before she heard Cain climbing the stairs and then moving about in his bedroom. Still, she took her time—replacing her moonstone ear drops with a small pair of pearl studs, dabbing a touch of jasmine scent to her wrists and the hollow of her throat, pinching her cheeks to bring out a touch of color in a face that was unnaturally pale.

When she was finally satisfied, she slipped off her wrapper and picked up the scandalous black silk gown and peignoir set that she had pulled from the bottom of her bureau that afternoon. It had been a wedding present from Elspeth, along with a silver tray.

Lifting her arms, Kit slipped the garment on. It slid like oil down over her naked flesh. The garment was starkly simple, with small capped sleeves and a rounded bodice that dipped so low it barely covered the peaks of her breasts. The skirt clung to her body in long, soft folds that outlined the shape of her hips and legs when she moved.

Over the gown she slipped on the peignoir, made entirely of

sheer black lace and, with shaking fingers, fastened the single small button at the throat. Through the black lace, the pale white of her skin gleamed like winter moonlight. As she stepped forward, the peignoir fell open in a great, inverted V and, had she turned her head at that moment to catch a glimpse of her reflection in the mirror, she would have seen that the silk had shaped itself like a second skin to the front of her body, not only outlining every detail of her breasts, but even clinging to the delicate indentation of her navel and, more seductively, to the small gentle lamb's wool mound that lay at the base of the flat slope of her stomach.

She walked through the sitting room, her bare feet padding noiselessly on the carpet. When she reached the door to his bedroom, she nearly lost her nerve. Quickly, before she could think further about what she was going to do, she lifted her fist and rapped on the door.

"Come in."

He was dressed in shirt-sleeves and sitting in the wing chair next to the window, a sheaf of papers on the table by his side. At first he looked up at her quizzically, but when he saw how she was dressed, his eyes darkened to a deep smoky gray. She walked toward him slowly, head high, shoulders proud.

"What do you want?" His question was laced with hostility, the charming man at the dinner table a distant memory.

Kit had thought it over carefully. She could have invented an excuse to visit him in his room—a cut finger that needed his attention, a request to borrow a book—but in the end she had known that he would see through her excuse and she would end up looking like a fool, so she lifted her chin and met his gaze directly. "I want to go to bed with you."

Something flickered in his expression for a fraction of a second and then was gone. She watched uneasily as his mouth curved in a small, mocking twist. "My beautiful wife," he sneered. "Always so forthright." His eyes dropped to the pale mounds of her breasts riding above the edge of the gown and the small nipples so clearly defined against the thin fabric. "Let me be just as straightforward, then. Why?"

This was not the way she had played the scene in her imagination. Somehow she had expected him to put out his arms and take over. "We're—we're married," she faltered. "It's not right for us to be sleeping apart."

"I see." He tugged thoughtfully on the corner of his moustache and then jerked his head in the direction of the bed. "It's a matter of observing the amenities, is that it?"

"Well, no. Not exactly that."

"Then what?"

She could feel a slight sheen of perspiration gathering between her shoulder blades. "I just want to," she finally said in a small voice and then, overcome with humiliation, turned toward the door. "Forget it! Forget I ever said anything! It was a stupid idea!" She reached out for the knob only to find, as his hand settled over hers, that he was not going to let her get away so easily.

"No gentleman would ever let a lady so obviously in need go unsatisfied," he drawled, turning her around by the shoulders. "Even if the lady in question hasn't shown the smallest sign over the past few months of giving a damn about any of the gentleman's needs."

Kit's eyes dropped. She wished she had never started this. It had been a stupid idea. If she were to be honest with herself, she knew she could not even blame it on Veronica Gamble. She had wanted him. It was that simple. Veronica had merely given her the excuse.

Cain released her shoulders and moved away. When she looked up, it was to see him leaning against the mantel of the fireplace, gazing down at her sardonically.

"What's wrong?" she asked uneasily.

"Nothing's wrong. I'm just waiting for you to start."

"Start what?" She was becoming more nervous by the second.

"Really, Kit." He sighed with mild exasperation. "Haven't you learned enough about men yet to understand that it's more than a matter of simply saying you want to make love? A man can't perform on command. I'm afraid you'll have to arouse my interest."

Had she thought to drop her eyes, she would have seen that his interest was already well aroused, but she was too busy trying to fight down the queer jumble of feelings twisting about inside her. "I—I don't know how to do that," she confessed miserably.

He leaned his shoulders back against the mantelpiece and crossed his ankles indolently. "Experiment," he said. "I'm all yours."

She turned her back on him, unable to bear his mockery any longer. Throat clogged with tears, she stumbled toward the door.

"Coward," he challenged softly.

She spun around in time to see that the mockery had faded from his expression and something far warmer had taken its place. A light that was in part mischievous but underlaid by something far more serious danced in his eyes. "I dare you, Kit Weston," he said.

She could feel a wild pounding beginning deep inside her. Follow your instincts, Veronica had advised. But was that possible? Would she know what to do?

He lifted a brow in silent acknowledgment of her turmoil, the light of challenge shining brighter than ever in his eyes. Suddenly a rush of courage that defied all logic surged through her, a courage that was based, perhaps, on her own desperate need. Slowly she raised her fingers to the single button that held the peignoir together, fumbling with it a moment before it would release. The garment slid to the floor in a cascade of black lace.

His eyes drank in the slim, silk-clad body so clearly revealed before him. "You've never been one to refuse a dare, have you?" he observed huskily.

Her mouth curved into a smile as she walked toward him slowly, feeling a sudden, unreasonable surge of self-confidence. As she moved, she let her hips sway ever so slightly from side to side so that the slim skirt of the gown clung even more revealingly. Stopping in front of him, she stared directly into the smoky depths of his eyes, and then, without dropping her gaze, reached up and rested the palms of her hands lightly on his shoulders. She could sense the tension of him beneath her outspread fingers, and she was suddenly possessed by a feeling of power such as she had never known before in his presence. Lifting herself on her toes, she leaned forward and placed her lips directly on the dancing pulse at the base of his throat.

He groaned softly and buried his face in the raven cloud of

her hair, but otherwise he did not move, and his arms still hung passively at his sides. Excitement quivered through every nerve of her body. She parted her lips and flicked at the dancing pulse with the tip of her tongue until its rhythm beat faster and faster, and then she moved her mouth up along the line of his neck as far as she could reach.

Greedy for more of him, her fingers tugged at the buttons on his shirt. When it was open, she shoved the fabric out of her way and slipped her hands beneath. She pushed her splayed fingers through the mat of hair on his chest and then dropped her head to press her lips over the hard, flat nipple that she had exposed.

He could bear it no longer. With a strangled excitement, he caught her in his arms and pulled her body against him. But it was her game now, and she was determined he would play by her rules. With the soft, wicked laugh of a vixen, she slipped from his grasp and backed across the room.

When she was satisfied that she was far enough away from him, she lifted her eyes to his and wet her lips with the tip of her tongue. Then she slid the palms of her hands down over her silk-clad sides, cupping her ribs and waist and the curve of her hips in deliberate provocation. She saw his nostrils flare and heard his quickening breath. Slowly she slid her hands back up again, this time over the front of her. Thighs . . . stomach . . . ribs . . . *A woman seduces a man by following her own instincts without giving the slightest thought to what she has heard is proper or improper. . . .* She cupped her own breasts in her palms, thumbs resting over the bare mounds that rose above the edge of the gown.

A muffled exclamation escaped his lips. The word was unintelligible, but it was uttered with a sense of wonder, as some sort of tribute.

She moved so that the bed was between them, confident now of her power. Lifting the gown at the front, she climbed up onto the mattress. Then she bent her knees and spread them apart, leaning back to rest her weight on her heels. With a shake of her head, her hair tumbled forward over her shoulder. She smiled a smile that had been passed down from Eve and tugged on one sleeve, pulling it far down on her arm. Beneath the veil of her hair lay one exposed breast.

It took all of Cain's self-control not to close the agonizingly wide distance between them and devour her as she was meant to be devoured. Never had a woman been more maddeningly enticing. His own passion raged inside him, hot and thickly liquid, aching for release.

But she was not done with him yet. Still resting back on her heels, the skirt of her gown lying loose across her open knees, she began to play with her tousled hair, using her fingers to toy with it so that the raven locks fell open and closed in an erotic game of peek-a-boo.

Cain could hold back no longer. He came to the edge of the bed and, reaching out with his scarred hand, pushed the dark curtain of her hair back behind her shoulder. He gazed down at the perfectly formed breast with its taut, rosy crest. "You learn fast," he said, his voice thick as he reached for her breast.

But once again she eluded him, sliding back against the pillows so that she was resting on one elbow, the black silk skirt of her gown loosely gathered across her thighs. "You wear too many clothes," she told him softly.

His bottom lip curved beneath his thick moustache. With a few deft motions, he unfastened the cuffs of his sleeves and pulled the garment off. She watched as he undressed, her heart pounding with a wild, savage rhythm.

Finally he stood before her fiercely naked. "Now who's wearing too many clothes?" he murmured, placing his hand on her knee, just under the hem of her gown. But the gown excited him, and he did not remove it. Instead, he slowly slid his hand upward beneath it, moving along the inner flesh of her thigh until he found what he was seeking. He touched her lightly once, then again, then once again more demandingly, more deeply.

This time it was she who moaned, tossing her head to the side and arching her back. The black silk fell free from her other breast and presented an invitation he could not resist. As he continued to caress her beneath the gown, he dipped his head to claim first one and then the other of her ripe, moist nipples. He played at them deeply and lovingly, his own passion surging to molten heat as they swelled within his mouth.

The double caress at her breasts and beneath her gown was

more than she could bear. With a moan that came from her very soul, she shattered beneath his touch.

It could have been seconds or hours later before she came back to herself. He was stretched beside her, staring intently into her face. As she opened her eyes, he dipped his mouth to hers and kissed her lips. "You've learned your lessons well," he whispered. "I think you're ready for more."

She looked at him questioningly, but he only smiled, and then he kissed her again, a deep, passionate kiss that she returned with abandon. His kisses moved to her breasts and then, pushing her gown high above her waist, on to her stomach.

She sensed what was to happen even before she felt the brush of his moustache against the soft inner surface of her thigh. At first she thought she must be mistaken. The idea was too shocking, too impossible. Surely she must be wrong. It could not be . . . He could not . . .

But he did. And she thought she would die from the pleasure he gave her. After it was over, she felt as if she would never be the same again.

He held her close to him and stroked her hair, idly curling the long, dark tendrils around his finger, giving her the time she needed to recover, although he could barely repress his own desire. Finally, when he could be patient no longer, he rolled his body over hers, only to feel the heels of her hands on his chest pushing him away. Now the question was in his eyes as he lay back against the pillows and she rose to her knees beside him. Puzzled, he watched her cross her arms modestly in front of her kneeling body, and then his puzzlement vanished as she picked up the hem of her gown and pulled it off over her head, revealing the feast of her nakedness to him.

She pressed her body over his and, covering them both with the curtain of her hair, clasped his head between her small, strong hands. She took his mouth aggressively, boldly female, using her tongue to plunder and ravish, to take pleasure for herself and return it in abundance. And then she caressed the rest of his body, pressing her mouth to scars and muscles and hard, male flesh until there was only sensation between them.

They held each other through the night, making love when they awakened, dozing with bodies still joined and lips pressed together. Sometimes when they were awake, they talked. They spoke of the pleasure in their coming together, but never once did they speak of the things that held them apart. Even in their most intimate moments, they established subtle limits that could not be crossed. You may touch me here . . . You may touch me there . . . Oh, yes . . . oh, yes . . . and there . . . But do not expect more. Do not expect daylight to bring a change in me. There will be no changes. You would only hurt me . . . Take from me . . . Destroy me . . . I will give you my body, but do not, *dare not,* expect more.

Chapter Thirty-one

It was just before Christmas, and Sophronia had finally made up her mind—or rather her mind had been made up for her two days before when James Spence had met her beside the road that led into Rutherford and shown her a deed with her name on it to a house in Charleston. He described it as a pretty pink stucco with a fig tree in the front and a trellis covered with wisteria in the back. She had taken the deed from him, studied it carefully, and then said she would go with him.

As she gazed out the kitchen window at the wet, dreary December day that lay heavy over the fields of Risen Glory, she reminded herself that she was twenty-two years old and her life had been standing still long enough. James Spence was a well-to-do man who could give her all the things she'd wanted for so long. He treated her with courtesy, and he was pleasant enough in appearance not to make her skin crawl every time he touched her arm. He'd take good care of her, and in return, she would take care of him. It really wouldn't be all that much different from what she was doing now, she told herself, except that she would have to sleep with him.

She shivered and then reprimanded herself for being foolish. What difference did it make anyway? It wasn't as if she were a virgin. The house would be hers—that's what was important—and she would finally be safe.

Besides, she had to go. Between Magnus and Kit and the major, she would go crazy if she had to stay at Risen Glory much longer.

Every time she stepped out of the house, it seemed as if Magnus were watching her with those soft brown eyes of his, and she hated the pity she saw in them. Sometimes she found herself reliving that Sunday afternoon when he had kissed her in the orchard. She hadn't been able to forget that kiss, even though he'd never attempted to touch her again, not even the night Kit and the major had been married and she'd slept at his house. Now she wished he would just go away and leave her in peace.

She wished they'd all go away, especially Kit. Ever since she had gone back to the major's bed, there had been something almost frantic about her behavior. She was demanding and unreasonable with everybody, even poor Miss Dolly. She rushed from one thing to another, never giving herself time to think. It was as if she were afraid if she stopped running, she'd have to face something she'd rather avoid.

In the morning when Sophronia went to the hen house to gather eggs, she sometimes saw Kit in the distance, riding Temptation as if there were no tomorrow, taking him over jumps that were too high, pushing them both to the limit. Even on the wettest days, she rode from one end of the plantation to the other. It was almost as if she were afraid the land had disappeared during the night while she and the major were carrying on in that great bed upstairs. Sophronia's lips compressed into a tight line. Kit had taken leave of her senses, that was the only explanation.

When the major was around, things were even worse. There was so much bad feeling between the two of them, you could cut it with a butter knife. Sophronia hadn't heard Kit speak a civil word to him in weeks, and when the major talked to her it sounded as if his voice had been frozen inside a big block of ice. Still, Sophronia had to give the major credit for at least trying to be polite. Kit made no effort at all. Time and again she'd seen him ignore one of her sullen remarks. He'd even given in on the matter of putting a road to the mill through those acres of scrub to the east, when anybody with half a brain could see Kit was being unreasonable about the whole thing since the land was useless, and the road would save everybody miles of traveling time.

Yesterday Sophronia had been afraid they would actually

come to blows. The major, after warning Kit for weeks to stop riding Temptation so recklessly, had finally put his foot down and told her she could no longer ride the gelding at all. Kit had gone half crazy, calling him all kinds of names and threatening horrible things that no woman should even know about, much less mention. He had stood there like a granite statue not saying a word, just watching her with that stone-cold expression of his that sent shivers down Sophronia's spine.

Still, it seemed that no matter how bad things were between them during the day, when nightfall came, the door of that big front bedroom upstairs would slam shut on the two of them and not open again until morning. Last night had been no different.

Through the window, Sophronia saw Kit, dressed in those shameful breeches of hers, walking back from the paddock to the house. She couldn't put it off any longer. Her satchel was packed, and Mr. Spence—she couldn't think of him yet by his first name—would be waiting for her at the end of the drive in less than an hour. So far, no one knew she was going, although she wondered if Magnus suspected something; he had looked at her so strangely when he'd come to the kitchen for breakfast. Sometimes she had the feeling he could read her mind. She told herself she was just as glad he'd gone into Rutherford for the day and wouldn't be here when she left, but she knew it was a lie. More than anything, she wanted one last glimpse of that kind, handsome face.

She jerked on the strings of her apron and pulled it off, hanging it for the last time on the peg next to the sink where she'd been hanging aprons since she was a child. She met Kit by the front door.

"It's cold out there, Sophronia." Kit shivered, bringing a chilly gust with her as she strode in. "That wind has a real bite to it. Tell Rose to make chowder for dinner tonight."

Sophronia sighed with exasperation, temporarily forgetting that such things were no longer her responsibility. "What's wrong with you?" she scolded. "It's nearly five o'clock. If you wanted chowder, you should of told me this mornin'. Rose has been workin' all day on a nice okra pilau. You can't go changin' menus so soon before dinner."

Kit jerked off her woolen jacket and shoved it irritably onto the newel post. "I think it's about time you remember who's the mistress of this house, Sophronia," she said scathingly. "I'm not ten years old any longer, and I don't appreciate being treated as if I am." With that, she began climbing the stairs to her room.

"People get treated accordin' to the way they behave."

Kit paused and looked down at Sophronia. "And what's that supposed to mean?"

"It means that you've been actin' like a spoiled child for months now, and you're makin' everybody in this house miserable."

It wasn't the first time Sophronia had reprimanded Kit for her behavior, but today Kit didn't seem to have the energy to come to her own defense. She had been feeling edgy and listless lately, not sick exactly, but not entirely well either. "If Rose can't manage chowder tonight, I'll expect it tomorrow." She sighed wearily.

"You'll have to tell her yourself," Sophronia said. "I won't be here."

"Oh? Where are you going?"

Kit asked the question so innocently that Sophronia's irritation dissolved, and she was abruptly recalled to her purpose. "Why don't we go into the back sittin' room for a few minutes so we can talk."

Kit looked at her curiously, but then followed her down the hallway. Once inside, she sat on the rose damask settee, sensing, for the first time, Sophronia's agitation.

Sophronia remained standing, clasping her hands in front of her butternut wool skirt, nervously making a church steeple with her index fingers. "I—I'm goin' away to Charleston."

"Are you going on a shopping trip?" Kit inquired tentatively. "I really think you might have discussed it with me before you decided. Maybe I should go, too."

"No! It's not a shopping trip." Sophronia reached over to straighten a magazine on the table, lining it up precisely with the edge. "I—I'm goin' for good. James Spence bought me a house there. I won't be comin' back to Risen Glory."

"Not coming back!" Kit exclaimed in dismay. "How can you even say such a thing?" And then her forehead knit in puzzlement. "But why would Mr. Spence buy you a house? Are you going to be his housekeeper? Is he paying you more money than we are? How could you even think of leaving? Whatever he's paying you, I'll match it."

Sophronia shook her head, her eyes still firmly fixed on the cover of the magazine. "I'm not goin' to be his housekeeper. I'm goin' to be his mistress."

Kit's hand gripped convulsively around the arm of the settee. "No! I don't believe it! You'd never do anything so horrible."

Sophronia's chin shot up proudly. "Don't you dare judge me!"

"Judge you!" Kit exclaimed harshly. "This doesn't have anything to do with judgment. What you're talking about is wicked, plain and simple." Her voice softened, becoming faintly pleading. "How could you even consider such a thing, Sophronia?"

"I'm doin' what I have to do," Sophronia said stubbornly. "Did you ever think I might want some of the same things you want—a house, pretty clothes, bein' able to wake up in the mornin' knowin' nobody can hurt me."

"But nobody can hurt you here. It's been three years since the war's been over. Nobody has bothered you."

"That's just 'cause everybody assumed I was sharin' your husband's bed." At Kit's sharp look, she added, "Which I wasn't." And then, maliciously because she felt so awful: "He was takin' his amusement, though. Don't you think any different. But it wasn't with me. Still, nobody 'cept Magnus knew that." The sleek, sculptured lines of her face set into bitter planes. "Now that you're married, everything's different. It's just a matter of time before somebody decides I'm free for the pickin'. That's the way it is for any black woman doesn't have a white man lookin' out for her. I can't go through the rest of my life like that."

"But what about Magnus?" Kit argued desperately. "Magnus is a good, strong man. Anybody can see that he loves you. And no matter how much you pretend otherwise, I know you have tender feelings for him. How can you do this to him?"

Sophronia's mouth formed a straight, stubborn line. "I have to look out for myself."

Kit jumped up from the settee, finally understanding how deadly serious Sophronia was. "I don't see what's so magic about having a white man watching out for you!" she exclaimed fiercely. "When you were a slave, my father was supposed to be watching out for you, and look what happened? Maybe Mr. Spence won't be able to protect you any more than my father could! Maybe he won't care either. Maybe he'll look the other way the same as my father! Did you ever think about that, Sophronia? Did you?"

"Your father didn't try to protect me!" Sophronia cried. "He didn't try, do you understand what I'm tellin' you? It wasn't just a matter of not seein' what was happenin'. He was the one who was givin' me away for the night to his friends."

Kit felt a sick stab deep in the walls of her stomach.

Sophronia went on, unable to stop herself.

"Sometimes he'd let them throw the dice for me. Sometimes they'd race their horses. I was the prize in the games they played."

Kit ran to Sophronia and took her in her arms. "I'm sorry. I'm so very, very sorry. He was a horrible, wicked man." She stroked Sophronia awkwardly. "Listen to me. As awful as it must have been for you, it was all a long time ago. You can't let it ruin your whole life. You're young. Lots of slave women—"

"Don't you tell me about slave women!" Sophronia cried out savagely as she jerked away from Kit. "Don't you dare tell me about slave women! You don't know nothin' about it!" She took a deep gulp of air, as if she were strangling. "He was *my* father, too!"

Kit froze. "No!" she cried hoarsely. "No! It's not true! You're lying to me. Even he wouldn't give away his own daughter. Damn you! God damn your soul, you're lying to me!"

Sophronia did not flinch. "I'm his daughter, no different from you. He took my mama when she was only thirteen and kept her right in this house with him, right under your mama's nose. Kept her there until he found out she was carryin' a baby, then he tossed her back to the slave cabins like a piece of week-old trash. He never touched her again after that. At first, when his friends came sniffin' after me, I thought maybe he might of forgot I was his. But he hadn't forgot. He just didn't attach any significance to it, do you understand what I'm sayin'? Blood had no meanin' because I wasn't human. I was property. Just another nigger gal."

Kit's face was chalk-white. "I don't believe you," she said in a ragged whisper.

Sophronia was finally calm, almost at peace now that her heartbreaking secret was no longer locked inside her. "I'm just glad my mama died before it all started. She was a strong woman, but seein' what was happenin' to me would of broke her." Sophronia reached out and touched Kit's immobile cheek. "We're sisters, Kit," she said softly. "Didn't you ever feel it? Didn't you ever feel that tie between us, bindin' us so tight together nothin' could ever pull us apart? Right from the start, it was the two of us. Your mama died not long after you was born, and my mama was supposed to take care of you, but she didn't like to touch you unless she had to. She couldn't help herself. You was too much a reminder of what had happened to her. So I took care of you, right from the beginnin'. A child raisin' a child. I can remember holdin' you in my lap when I couldn't of been more than four or five myself. I used to set you next to me in the kitchen when I was workin' and play doll babies with you in the evenin'. And then Mama died, and you was all I had. Except when Miz Weston came, she wouldn't let me take care of you anymore. But I used to try to watch out for you all the same. That's why I never left Risen Glory, not even when you went away to New York City. I had to make sure you was goin' to be all right. But when you came back, it was like you was a different person, part of a world I could never belong to. I was jealous, and I was scared, too." She put her arm around Kit's stiff shoulders and hugged her. "You got to forgive me for what I'm goin' to do, Kit, but you got a place in the world. Now it's time for me to find my place and start livin' my own life." Without waiting for a response, she turned and left the room.

Not long after, Cain found Kit there. "What's going on?" he barked. "I just saw Sophronia running from the house, and none of the servants knew where you were. I—" He broke off as he noticed the rigid set of her features and the stiff way she was standing. In an instant he was beside her, touching her arm. "Kit? What's wrong?"

It was as if his touch had pulled her from a trance. She sagged ever so slightly against him, choking on a sob. He quickly led her to the settee and took her into the circle of his arms as he lowered her onto the seat. "Tell me what happened, Kit."

Her tears were flowing freely now, dampening the front of his shirt. His arm felt so good around her. She could not remember him ever holding her like this—protectively, with no trace of passion. "Sophronia's leaving me." She barely managed the words. "She's going away to Charleston to be James Spence's mistress."

Cain swore softly. "Does Magnus know about this?"

"I—I don't think so." She caught her breath on a sob. "Oh, Baron, it's so awful. Sophronia is—she's my sister."

"Your sister?" he said slowly.

Kit nodded. "Garrett Weston's daughter, just like me."

He gently tilted her chin up so he was looking her full in the face. "You really shouldn't be so surprised. You've lived in the South all your life. Sophronia's skin is light."

"You don't understand!" Kit's face was streaked with tears. "My father used to give her away to his friends for the night. He knew she was his daughter, his own flesh and blood, but he gave her away anyway."

Kit's disclosure sickened Cain but there were no words he could offer to comfort her, so he simply held her, resting his cheek against the top of her head as she cried. Gradually she filled in the details of the story for him, and then she suddenly pulled away. "I have to stop her, Baron! I can't let her go through with this!"

"Sophronia isn't a slave any longer," he reminded her gently. "If she wants to go off with Spence, there's nothing you can do about it."

Kit leapt up from the settee. "She's my sister!" she exclaimed fiercely. "I love her! I won't let her do it!" Before Cain could stop her, she had run from the room.

He sighed wearily as he slowly uncoiled himself from the settee. Willful, headstrong, impulsive as always. She was hurting badly, and, as he knew only too well, that would probably mean trouble.

Outside, Kit hid in the trees near the piazza, waiting for Cain to come after her. When he appeared, as she had known he would, she huddled further back in the damp, wintry shadows, grateful for the presence of mind that had made her grab her jacket as she fled the house. She watched as Cain rapidly descended the steps of the piazza and looked toward the drive. When he didn't see her, he turned abruptly on his heel and, uttering a particularly offensive obscenity, headed for the stable.

As soon as he was out of sight, she ran back into the house, making her way directly to the gunrack in the library. It had suddenly occurred to her that carrying the carbine might be a sensible precaution. She didn't really expect trouble from James Spence, but you could never tell, and as she had no intention of letting Sophronia go off with him, the gun would add weight to her arguments.

Chapter Thirty-two

Several miles away on that same road, James Spence's crimson-and-black buggy had just swept around the buggy Magnus was driving. Spence was in an all-fired hurry to get wherever he was going, Magnus thought to himself as he watched the back of the vehicle disappear. With so many of the plantations still deserted, there wasn't much along this road except Risen Glory and the cotton mill. He decided that Spence must have business at the mill. It was a logical conclusion, but somehow it didn't satisfy him. Suddenly anxious to get home, he gave the horses a sharp slap with the reins.

Spence's buggy had already stopped at the bottom of the drive when Magnus caught up with him. Its occupant, fashionably dressed in a long black frock coat and bowler with a walking stick in his gloved hand, was just stepping out onto the road. Magnus, however, barely spared Spence a glance. All his attention was fixed on Sophronia standing at the side of the road with her blue woolen shawl wrapped around her and a satchel resting at her feet.

He pulled up the buggy and jumped out in what was nearly a single motion. "Sophronia!"

Her head shot up, and for an instant he imagined he saw a flicker of hope in her golden eyes, but then they clouded over. "You leave me alone, Magnus Owen," she declared, clutching the shawl more tightly. "This doesn't have nothin' to do with you."

Spence stepped around from the side of the carriage, looking at Magnus with surprise. "Something the matter here, boy?"

Magnus tucked one thumb into his belt and glared belligerently at Spence. "The lady's changed her mind."

Spence's eyes narrowed beneath the brim of his bowler. "If you're talkin' to me, boy, you'd better call me 'sir.' "

Magnus ignored him, concentrating all his attention on Sophronia. Gone was the gentle, soft-spoken man with the warm brown eyes. In his place stood a tight-lipped, hard-eyed stranger. "Get back to the house, Sophronia."

"Now see here," Spence declared, stepping forward. "I don't know who you think you are, but—"

"Go away, Magnus." Sophronia's voice was tremulous. "I've made up my mind, and you can't stop me."

"I can stop you all right," Magnus said stonily. "And that's exactly what I'm goin' to do."

James Spence was a man accustomed to having his own way. He had started working in an Illinois gravel quarry when he was ten, and he'd been working hard ever since. Although he was not an exceptionally intelligent man, he'd been blessed with a natural shrewdness and an almost limitless capacity for hard work, qualities that had served him well. During the war, he had bought himself out of the draft for three hundred dollars, and while others fought, he had set about the business of making money. After the war, he headed South with a carpetbag stuffed with greenbacks, and he now found himself with a prosperous phosphate mine and a comfortable position in life.

Because his manners were not polished and his money was so new as to be embarrassing, the upper-class women to whom he was attracted would have nothing to do with him, and he couldn't bring himself to settle for the women who'd have him. As soon as he'd seen Sophronia, he had decided she was exactly what he wanted. He'd keep her safely tucked away in Charleston so he wouldn't offend the people who were important to his business, and he'd visit her on weekends. She was beautiful and smart and so light-skinned he could almost make himself forget what she was. His only surprise had been how difficult it was to persuade her to accept his more than generous offer. The experience had left a slightly bitter taste in his mouth.

He sauntered over to Magnus, his walking stick with its gold-headed knob firmly in hand. "I think it might be better for everybody if you went back to wherever you came from, boy," he said dismissively. "Come along, Sophronia."

But as he reached out for her, she was abruptly snatched away, just beyond his grasp. "Don't touch her," Magnus snarled, shoving her firmly behind him. His hands clenched into fists as he took a step toward Spence.

Black man against white. For Sophronia it was as if all her nightmares had come true. "No!" she cried out, flinging herself at Magnus and clutching the front of his shirt. "Don't hit him! You hit a white man, you be hangin' from a rope before mornin'."

"Get out of my way, Sophronia."

But Sophronia wasn't so easily dissuaded. "White man got all the power, Magnus. You leave this be!"

He set her aside roughly, but the gesture of protecting her cost him. Behind his back, Spence lifted his walking stick and, as Magnus turned back around, slammed it against Magnus's chest. "You stay out of things that don't concern you, boy," Spence growled.

In one swift movement, Magnus snatched the cane from him and broke it in half across his knee. He tossed it aside and, as Sophronia screamed, landed a hard blow to Spence's jaw.

It had never occurred to Spence that Magnus would be foolish enough to actually attack him, and so the blow caught him by surprise and sent him sprawling into the dust.

Kit had just reached the line of trees directly behind them, and through the branches she saw what was happening. Raising her rifle, she rushed out to the road and leveled the barrel at Spence. "You'd better get out of here, Mr. Spence," she ordered. "Doesn't seem you're wanted."

A grateful cry escaped Sophronia's lips at Kit's appearance, but Magnus's face grew rigid. Spence slowly rose, glaring at Kit the whole time.

"Looks like things are getting a little out of hand here," a deep voice drawled. Four sets of eyes turned as Cain climbed down off Vandal. He walked toward Kit with the loose, easy swagger that was so much a part of him and extended his hand. "Give me the rifle, Kit," he said, speaking so calmly he might have been asking her to pass the bread across the dinner table.

She started to refuse, and then she realized that giving him the rifle was exactly what she wanted to do. She didn't mind hunting, but as she had discovered once before, she had no stomach for holding a gun on a man. So she handed it over to him without an argument, confident that he would see to it that Magnus came to no harm.

To her surprise he took her by the arm and pulled her, none too gently, toward Vandal. "Accept my apologies, Mr. Spence," he said, as he shoved the rifle with one hand into the scabbard that hung from his saddle. "My wife has an excitable temperament."

As far as Spence was concerned, Cain's apology was the first sensible thing that had happened since he had arrived. And Baron Cain was an important man. It would be to his advantage to have him for a friend. "Don't mention it, Major," he replied magnanimously, reaching over to dust off his trousers. "I'm sure none of us can ever predict the ways of our little womenfolk."

"Those are true words, Mr. Spence," Cain replied, oblivious to the baleful glare Kit was focusing on him.

Spence leaned over and picked up the black bowler hat that had been knocked off when he fell, his mind working rapidly as he set it back on his head. "Let me ask you something, Major. You value this nigger of yours?"

"Why do you ask?"

Spence smiled a companionable man-to-man smile. "Seems to me niggers are about as much trouble as the ladies sometimes. Now if you was to tell me you valued him, I'd assume you wouldn't be too happy to see him dangling from the end of a rope." His smile grew broader. As much as he wanted to settle with Magnus Owen, business was business. "Seeing as how we're both gentlemen, if you was to tell me you valued this nigger, I'd be more than willing to forget what happened here."

Cain barely seemed to have heard Spence. Instead, he was looking at Magnus. Their eyes locked for several long, hard seconds, with Cain the first to look away.

"What Magnus does is his own business." He shrugged indifferently. "It doesn't have anything to do with me, one way or the other." And then, to Kit's astonished outrage, he scooped her up and, settling her in front of him on Vandal, spurred the horse back up the drive.

Sophronia stared after them in stunned disbelief. It wasn't possible. The major was supposed to be Magnus's friend. A great wave of cynicism rose up inside her and engulfed her. She had forgotten the most basic rule of survival, passed down in African blood from one generation to another. White stood together against black. Now and forevermore. That's the way it always had been; the way it always would be.

She looked over at Magnus, surprised to see that Cain's betrayal did not seem to have bothered him at all. He stood with his legs slightly apart, one hand lightly balanced on his hip, and a strange light shining in his eyes. At that moment the love that she had felt toward him for so long but had refused to admit to herself burst into shining glory inside her, breaking invisible shackles of the past and sweeping away the rubble in a great, cleansing rush.

How could she have denied it for so long, this feeling she had for Magnus Owen? He was everything a man should be—strong and good and kind, a man of compassion, a man of pride. And now, because of her own selfishness, that pride was going to destroy him. She had put him in a perilous position. She, who had been ready to sell herself like a painted whore, had placed the best man in the world in danger.

They were standing in a triangle, with Sophronia at the apex and Spence and Magnus facing each other like opponents in a duel. Sophronia saw at once what she had to do. Turning her back firmly on Magnus, she walked toward James Spence and reached out to touch his arm. "Mr. Spence, it's my fault what's happened here today. I been flirtin' with Magnus. Makin' him believe he meant somethin' to me. You got to forget all this. I'll go with you, but you got to promise me you won't let any harm come to Magnus. He's a good man, and all this is my fault."

Magnus's voice came from behind her, as soft and mellow as an old hymn. "It's no good, Sophronia. I won't let you go with him." She heard him move closer, felt him come up beside her. "Mr. Spence," he said quietly, "Sophronia is goin' to be my wife. You try to take her with you, and I'll stop you. Today, tomorrow, a year from now. Doesn't make any difference. I'll stop you."

Spence licked his lips nervously, beginning to wish Cain had stayed instead of ridden off. Magnus Owen was a bigger man than he, taller and more muscular. In a physical match Spence would clearly be the loser, and he hadn't gotten where he was today by losing. It seemed he was going to have to stage a retreat for the moment. Inconvenient, but necessary, he decided. Sophronia might not be in his bed tonight, but she'd be there by tomorrow night. No nigger could get away with hitting a white man and then threatening him. Not in South Carolina, anyway. If the sheriff wouldn't do something about it, Spence knew a group of men who would.

He walked over to the buggy and climbed up on the seat, but before he picked up the reins, he turned back to Magnus. "You've made yourself a big mistake, boy." And then, to Sophronia: "I'll be back for you tomorrow."

"Just a minute, Mr. Spence." Magnus bent over to pick up the broken halves of the walking stick and then made his way toward the buggy. "I consider myself a fair man, so I think it's only right I tell you what kind of risk you'd be takin' if you got any ideas about comin' after me or about sendin' any of your acquaintances wearin' bedsheets after me. I don't think that'd be a good idea, Mr. Spence. Matter of fact, I think that'd be a real bad idea."

"What's that supposed to mean?" Spence sneered.

"It means I got a talent, Mr. Spence, that you should know about. And I got three or four friends with the same talent. Now they're only niggers like me, you understand, so you might not think their talent is worth your notice. But you'd be wrong, Mr. Spence. You'd be dead wrong."

"What're you talkin' about?"

"I'm talkin' 'bout dynamite, Mr. Spence. Nasty stuff, but real useful. Learned to use it myself when we had to blast some rock to build the mill. Now most people don't know too much about dynamite, since it's so new, but you strike me as a man who keeps up with new inventions, so I'll bet you know a lot about it. For example, I'll bet you know just how much damage dynamite could cause if it were set off in the wrong place in a phosphate bed."

Spence could hardly believe what he was hearing. "Are you actually threatening me?"

"I guess you might say I'm just tryin' to make a point, Mr. Spence. I got good friends. Real good friends. And if anything was to happen to me, they'd be mighty unhappy about it. They'd be so unhappy they might set off a load of dynamite in the wrong place. Now we wouldn't want that to happen, would we, Mr. Spence?"

"Damn you, Owen!"

Magnus put his foot up on the step of the buggy and rested the broken pieces of the stick on his knee. "Every man deserves his happiness, Mr. Spence, and Sophronia's mine. I intend to live a good long time so I can enjoy her, and I'm willin' to do anything necessary so as to make sure I have that time. Whenever I see you in town, I'm goin' take off my hat and say, 'Howdy, Mr. Spence,' real polite. And as long as you hear that 'Howdy, Mr. Spence,' you'll know I'm a happy man wishin' you and your phosphate mine all the best." Drilling his eyes directly into Spence's, he extended the broken halves of the walking stick.

Taut with anger, Spence looked down at them and then, with a growl, snatched the pieces from Magnus and grabbed the reins. As he turned the horses and took off down the road, he tried to console himself by remembering that a cautious man knew when to cut his losses.

At first Sophronia couldn't move. She felt breathless and giddy with happiness. What she had just seen ran contrary to her entire way of thinking, and yet it had happened. She had seen it with her own eyes. She had just seen Magnus Owen stand up against a white man and win. He had fought for her. He had kept her safe, even from herself. Safe.

"Oh, Magnus!" She threw herself across the border of dry, wintry grass that separated them and tumbled into his arms. "Magnus, Magnus, Magnus . . ." She repeated his name over and over and over again until its rhythm became one with the beating of her heart.

"You're a trial to me, woman," he said softly, cupping her slim, straight shoulders in his powerful hands. Slowly she lifted her gaze until her eyes found his. They were steadfast and true, promising all the strength and goodness that was so much a part of him. He lifted one hand from her shoulder and moved his index finger over the line of her lips, almost as if he were a blind man, staking out the boundaries of the territory he was about to claim. And then he lowered his head and pressed his mouth to hers in a kiss that was firm and possessive.

Sophronia accepted his lips shyly, as if she were a young girl again. She felt pure and innocent, untouched by any man, newly awakened to love. He pulled her closer to him, his kiss growing more demanding, thrilling her with its power until she molded her body to his, no longer afraid. This man, this one good man, was hers for ever and ever, more important than houses and dresses, more important than anything.

It was a long time before they drew apart, and when they did, Sophronia saw that Magnus's eyes were glistening. The strong, hard man who a few moments before had been coolly threatening to blow up a phosphate mine was now as soft and gentle as a lamb.

"You've been givin' me a lot of trouble, woman," he said gruffly, the words catching slightly in his throat. "Once we're married, I won't stand for any more nonsense."

"We gettin' married, Magnus?" she inquired saucily. And then she splayed her long, elegant fingers along the side of his head and pulled his mouth back for another deep, lingering kiss.

"We gettin' married, Sophronia," Magnus affirmed when he was finally able to catch his breath.

Chapter Thirty-three

Sophronia and Magnus were married a week later in the old slave church. Kit stood at Sophronia's side, trying not to remember a far different ceremony that had taken place in the same church barely six months before. Through the corner of her eye, she saw her husband standing next to Magnus and wondered if his thoughts were the same as hers.

She frowned and looked down at the floorboards, worn smooth and gray by hundreds of feet. She and Cain had barely spoken to each other in the past week. She had been horrified when he had pulled her up on Vandal and abandoned Magnus and Sophronia to James Spence. All the way back to the house, she had ranted at him, and as she stormed out of the stable at his heels, her anger still had not run its course.

"I figured you for a lot of things, Baron Cain, but I never figured you for a coward!" she called out. "How could you walk out on Magnus like that? He's going to be a dead man, and it'll be on your conscience. All you had to do was nod your head, and Spence would have made himself forget that Magnus hit him. What you did was contemptible, and you're only making it worse by not giving me that rifle back. If you're not man enough to defend your friend, I'll do it myself."

Cain spun around, the carbine held across his chest by fingers that were white at the knuckle. "You even look like you're going back there," he growled venomously, "and I'll lock you up and throw away the key!"

Despite herself, Kit drew back from his rage. "You're contemptible, do you know that?"

"So you tell me," he jeered. "You know something, lady? I'm getting tired of the sound of your voice. It's shrill and nasty and it sets my teeth on edge. Did it ever occur to you to ask me about what happened before you started throwing your accusations around?"

"What happened was obvious."

"Was it?"

Suddenly Kit felt unsure of herself. Regardless of what she had said in the heat of anger, she knew that Cain was no coward. He also never did anything without a reason. "All right," she snapped begrudgingly, "suppose you tell me just what you had in mind when you left Magnus there with a man who isn't going to be happy until he sees him lynched." She thrust her hand on her hip and glared at him belligerently.

For a moment he looked at her, saying nothing, and then he shrugged. "I think I'm going to let you figure that one out for yourself."

He began walking toward the house, but Kit stopped him, thrusting her small body in front of his larger one and taking a few backward steps with him until he finally came to a stop.

This time he was the belligerent one. "Well? What do you want?"

"I have to know," she said, making some effort to be conciliatory. "Tell me. Please."

At first she thought he would refuse, but then he gave a short nod. "All right." He shifted the carbine so that its barrel rested on his shoulder pointing upward. "Magnus is a man, Kit. There are some things a man has to do alone. He didn't welcome your interference, and he wouldn't have welcomed mine."

"But you might as well have signed his death warrant."

"Let's just say I have more faith in Magnus than you seem to have."

"But he's a Negro, Baron. This is South Carolina, not New York City."

"Don't tell me you're finally admitting your native state has some flaws," he said mockingly. "He's a man, Kit. He doesn't need anybody to fight his battles for him. What you were doing back there was castrating him! If you knew anything about men, you'd have known that."

She understood now that, from Magnus's viewpoint anyway, Cain had been right, but from her viewpoint, so much male pride was foolhardy. To her surprise, that evening when she had finally found Sophronia alone, her half sister had sided with Magnus and Cain.

"It was something Magnus had to do, Kit," Sophronia explained. "I didn't understand it at the time, but I do now. It was all my fault. I made him feel like he was less than a man. I just thank Jesus it turned out right, because if anything had happened to him, I'd never been able to live with myself."

There was a soft rustle beside her, and Kit realized with a start that the ceremony was over. Sophronia, wearing a starkly beautiful silk gown that had been Kit's present to her, seemed almost ethereal in her happiness, while Magnus was visibly bursting with pride at his exquisite bride as he gently claimed her lips in their first kiss as man and wife. And then Kit was hugging Sophronia and Cain was shaking Magnus's hand, while Miss Dolly fluttered around urging them all back to the house where her special wedding cake was awaiting them.

It was after dark when Magnus and Sophronia left for the overseer's house. Kit was relieved to see that, although Sophronia seemed somewhat nervous about the night ahead of her, she did not seem frightened. Cain excused himself and went into the library to work on some papers. Kit grabbed a shawl and made her way out the back door to the darkened stable. As soon as she was inside, she lit the kerosene lamp that hung near the door. She heard a soft whinny and made her way down the center aisle to the end stall where Temptation waited for her.

"Hello there, boy," she cooed, holding out the apple she had brought with her. "Do you miss me as much as I miss you?" As she stroked the gelding's silky muzzle, she still could not believe that Cain had actually given the order that she was not to ride him. He knew how much this horse meant to her. She leaned back against the wooden half-door, nursing her resentment and repressing the small voice that told her she had only her own recklessness to blame.

After he had issued his order, she had considered breaking the unwritten rule between them and carrying the raging argument that had followed into their bedroom. But in the end, she had not been able to do it, not even for Temptation, for she had known as surely as she drew breath that she would ruin it all, and at that moment, the big front bedroom was the only place where she ever felt happy.

Lately even that happiness was slipping from her. It seemed the more passionate their nights were, the worse the next day would be. Sometimes she could feel Cain's scorn as tangibly as if it were her own flesh. And the more she sensed his contempt, the worse she behaved toward him. With each passing day, she became more shrewish, more unreasonable, more unlikable. Worst of all were those moments when he seemed to soften toward her with a look or a word or a kind gesture. Then she would turn the full force of her sharp tongue on him and kill the softness with a swift, clean blow.

And then with his capitulation to her wishes on the matter of the road to the mill, their daytime and their nighttime relationships no longer seemed so different. Recently their loving had become tinged with violence. Occasionally a kiss would bring a speck of blood or a caress would leave a bruise. In some unfathomable way, they seemed to be losing control of their own humanness and coming together in a primitive, atavistic mating that frightened her and perhaps even frightened him.

She wanted it to stop. The soft, treacherous, most female part of her begged that she give up the struggle and open her heart before it burst with the feelings she dared not put a name to, but the devils of her past were driving her with a force that she didn't seem to be able to fight. Risen Glory was all she had ever had, the only thing in her life that was secure. People appeared and disappeared, but Risen Glory was everlasting, and she would let nothing threaten it, certainly not her tumultuous unnamed feelings for Baron Cain—Baron Cain with his mill and his ambitions for expansion that, gone unchecked, would eat up her fields and spit them out like so many discarded cotton seeds until nothing was left of it but a worthless husk.

Chapter Thirty-four

Veronica Gamble left Rutherford shortly before Thanksgiving and went to Charleston where she purchased a three-story mansion and immediately turned it into a center of fashion and culture by filling it with an everchanging procession of artists. Some were struggling, others famous, but all of them were drawn to her strength and gaiety. A celebrated actor from New York and an unknown sculptor from Ohio were her earliest guests. By the end of the first month, she had entertained painters and poets, a harpist, several writers, and even a world-famous horticulturist.

To celebrate her new home as well as her new contentment with an assortment of lovers, she decided to hold a ball during the dull days immediately following the New Year. In addition to the artists and with a total disregard for politics, she invited everyone in Charleston who interested her as well as several of her old acquaintances from Rutherford, including Baron and Kit and Brandon Parsell. Brandon was to be accompanied by his fiancée, Alice Ann Dunforth, and her father, a former Bostonian who had taken over the presidency of the Planters' and Citizens' Bank after the war.

When Kit received the invitation, she told Cain that she did not want to attend. Sophronia's newfound happiness had made her more conscious than ever of her own misery, and she was in no mood for a party, especially one hosted by Veronica Gamble. But Cain turned a deaf ear to her protests. They were going, he informed her. He wanted to get away from Risen Glory and the cotton mill for a while. Besides, he liked Veronica, and he missed seeing her.

His openness about his affection for Veronica infuriated her, and that night when they went to bed, she turned her back to him. To her dismay, he made no effort to touch her, and they had not made love since.

Kit was pale and exhausted by the time they reached Charleston, despite the fact that the ride had been an easy one. After a cordial greeting from Veronica, which Kit returned with cool politeness, Cain left to attend to some business and Kit was shown the spacious room that the two of them would share for the next few nights. It was light and airy, with a narrow balcony that looked down upon a brick courtyard, appealing even in winter with its green border of sea island grass, the white bloom of camellias, and the scent of sweet olives.

Kit, however, barely noticed the room and the balcony. As soon as the maid that Veronica had sent up to her had finished unpacking and left her alone, she threw herself down on the bed and closed her eyes, too drained of emotion even to cry.

To her surprise, she fell into a deep sleep, awakening several hours later, refreshed in body if not in spirit. Sliding her legs over the edge of the bed, she reached for the thin cotton wrapper that lay across the foot. After she had knotted the sash, she walked over to the windows and pushed back the drapery. It was already dark outside. She was going to have to get dressed soon, even though she could not imagine how she would get through the evening after what she had discovered such a short time ago.

Immediately after breakfast that morning, while Cain had gone off to give some last-minute instructions to the mill's manager, Kit had set out for Rutherford on an errand she had been putting off for several weeks. Lady had proved to be tractable for once, and it was not long before she was dismounting in front of a modest white clapboard house with a green shingle nailed next to the front door. Patients who paid cash were hard to find, and the doctor had seen her immediately. She had been in and out in less than half an hour.

She lay her cheek against the cool window glass, trying to absorb what the doctor had told her. It didn't seem possible that she was actually going to have a baby, and yet she knew it was. Why had it never occurred to her to attribute the recent changes in her body to the most probable cause?

She pressed her open palms to her flat stomach, trying to make herself accept the fact that there was a small speck of life growing inside her. Baron Cain's baby. A child that would bind her to him for the rest of her life. A tight sob rose inside her, but she bit it back at the sound of a knock at the door and the maid's voice telling her she had water for a bath.

The bath took away the last of her grogginess from the nap but none of her panic. After she had dried herself and slipped into her wrapper, she sat down in front of the dressing table and fumbled for her brush. It was then she noticed the blue ceramic jar that had once held candied ginger resting next to her other toiletries. Lucy had obviously packed it along with the rest, never suspecting how ironic her efficiency was.

The jar contained the grayish-white powder Kit had gotten from the Conjure Woman to keep her from conceiving. As soon as she had returned from the Conjure Woman's cabin, she had taken it just as she had been instructed, and then again that same evening after Cain had left her bed. She had never taken it again.

At first there had been the long weeks when she and Cain had slept apart, and then, after their nighttime reconciliation, she had found herself strangely reluctant to take the powders. It had been foolish, she now realized, but after a night spent in Cain's arms, she had not wanted to take them. They had seemed almost malevolent, like old, dry bones ground fine—life-destructive, when, on those mornings, she had felt as if she were bursting with life. And then she had heard several women talking about how difficult it had been for them to conceive, and she had justified her carelessness by deciding that the risk of pregnancy was not as great as she had feared.

Eventually Sophronia had discovered the jar. She had been horrified to learn that Kit had even considered doing something so shameful. According to Sophronia, only fallen women tried to interfere with conception. It was a sin against God's law. And then, in one of her customary twists of attitude, she calmly informed Kit that the powders were worthless anyway since the

Conjure Woman didn't like white women and had been selling them useless prevention powders for years.

Kit was fingering the domed lid of the ginger jar when the door behind her flew open and she jumped, knocking over the jar with her hand and spilling its contents over the top of the dressing table. "Damn it!" she swore, springing up from her stool. "Can't you ever enter a room without tearing the door from its hinges?"

"Just eager to see my devoted wife," Cain said sarcastically, as he tossed a pair of leather gloves down on a chair. And then he caught sight of the mess on the dressing table. "What's that?"

"Nothing!" Kit exclaimed, much too quickly. She grabbed at the towel that she had used to dry herself and began wiping vigorously at the powder.

Cain came up behind her and pushed his hand down hard on top of hers, stopping the motion of the towel. With his other hand, he picked up the overturned jar, looking at the powder that still remained inside before he set it back down. "What is this, Kit?"

"It's nothing," she answered, again too quickly. She tried to pull her hand from beneath his, but he held it down with an unrelenting pressure, and she realized he had no intention of letting her go until she told him what he wanted to know. "They're headache powders."

"I don't believe you."

"It's true. I—"

His hand pressed down harder on hers. "Don't lie to me," he growled. "I've taken a lot from you lately, but I won't take lies."

"It's something I got from the Conjure Woman," she admitted reluctantly. "Lucy packed it by mistake." And then, because it didn't seem to make much difference now: "I—I didn't want to have a baby, Baron."

Something dark and bitter flashed across his face. Slowly he released her hand and, turning his back to her, walked across the room. "I see," he said, and then, casually: "Maybe this was something we should have talked about."

"We don't seem to have that kind of marriage, do we?" Kit snapped, perversely hurt by his indifferent attitude.

He shrugged. "No, I guess we don't." With his back still to her, he took off his pearl-gray coat and tugged at his cravat. When he turned back to her, his eyes were as cold as a Northern winter. "Actually, I should be glad you were so sensible. It was careless of me not to have thought of it myself. Two people who detest each other don't exactly make the best parents. I can't imagine anything worse than bringing some unwanted little brat into this sordid mess we call a marriage, can you?"

Kit looked at him stonily. "No. No, I can't."

Cain turned away from her and finished dressing for the evening in silence. He was ready before she was and left her without a word. As soon as he had gone, Kit dropped the hairpin she had been trying to push into her curls and stared at the woman before her in the mirror. Her face was pale, her features rigid. And then she dropped her eyes, unable to bear the sight of her own misery. What was she going to do? How was she going to bear the child of a man who hated her?

"Understand you own that new spinning mill out past Rutherford, Mr. Cain."

"That's right." Cain stood at one end of the foyer next to John Hughes, a beefy young Northerner with pleasant features and a receding hairline who had claimed his attention just as he had been about to go upstairs to escort Kit to dinner. A half dozen or so of Veronica's guests mingled nearby in the doorway leading into the sitting room and by a tufted settee resting against the far wall.

"Hear you're doing a good business, there. More power to you, I say. Risky, though, don't you think, with the price of cotton dropping every day? Why, just yesterday I heard—" He suddenly broke off, gazing over the top of Cain's shoulder to the staircase. "Whoa now! Would you look at that!" He whistled softly under his breath. "Now there's a woman I'd like to take home with me. And not to meet my mama, either!"

Cain didn't need to turn around to know. He could sense her through the pores of his skin even before he caught the whiff of her perfume. But still he turned, unconsciously steeling himself as he did.

She wore her silver-and-white gown with the crystal bugle beads, but the dress had been altered since Cain had last seen it.

The white satin bodice had been sliced away to just below her breasts and replaced with a single, fine layer of silver organdy that rose up over the curves of her breasts to her throat, where it was gathered by a glimmering ribbon into a high, delicate ruffle. She wore nothing beneath the bodice, and the organdy was completely transparent, revealing the warm flesh tones of her bare skin. Crystal bugle beads taken from the skirt had been restitched in strategic clusters over the transparent fabric, producing a breathless combination of icy spangles and warm, rounded flesh.

The gown was both beautiful and shocking, a product of those long weeks when all her clothing had seemed so tame. She had ordered it packed on impulse—remembering how immature Veronica Gamble always made her feel—even though she fully intended to wear the more modest jade-green velvet that she had also brought with her. But this night of all nights had not seemed to be the time for modesty. With her old defiance she had determined that no one would see her beaten. Fortified by the two glasses of champagne she had asked the maid to bring her when the girl appeared to help her dress, she had cast the velvet aside for the gown of an ice maiden set afire.

It was outrageously lovely, and Cain had never seen anything he hated more. One by one, the men around him turned to her, their eyes greedily devouring flesh that should have been his alone to see. Jealousy bit at him like a poisonous reptile, and then, his heart pounding, he forgot even that as he lost himself in the sight of her. She was savagely beautiful, his wild rose of the deep wood, as untamed as the day he had met her, still ready to stab a man's flesh with her thorns and draw his blood.

And then he felt the first prickle of uneasiness as his eyes took in the high color smudging her delicate cheekbones and the queer, voltaic lights that glittered in the deep purple depths of her eyes. There was something almost frantic lurking inside her tonight. He could feel it pulsing from her body like a drum beat, straining to break loose and run free and wild. He took one quick step toward her, and then another. Her eyes locked with his and then deliberately drew away. Without a word she pushed past him and swept across the foyer to Brandon Parsell.

"Brandon! My, don't you look handsome tonight. And this must be your sweet fiancée, Alice Ann Dunforth. Alice Ann, I hope you'll forgive me if I steal Brandon from you every once in a while. We've been friends for so long—like brother and sister, you understand—that I couldn't possibly give him up entirely, even for such a pretty young lady."

Alice Ann tried to smile, but her lips could not quite manage it. She was, in fact, not pretty at all, as she very well knew, and next to such an exotic beauty as Katharine Cain, she felt even more shy and awkward than usual. It did not help to see her dearest Brandon so obviously captivated by the glittering creature who clung so possessively to his arm.

She had heard rumors about the two of them, of course, but Brandon had led her to believe all that was over. He had even told her once that he could not entirely approve of Katharine Cain, saying that her behavior was far too forward for a lady, a statement with which Alice Ann, born and bred in Boston, was in hearty agreement. And yet here he was, gazing at her in that shocking dress as if she were the only woman in the world. Alice Ann felt her lip begin to tremble. She had always cried easily, and now the ever-ready tears were pressing against the back of her eyes.

She was saved from disgrace by the sudden appearance of Cain at Kit's elbow. "Parsell." He nodded coldly. "Miss Dunforth. If you'll excuse us, I'd like to have a word with my wife."

His fingers sunk into Kit's organdy-draped arm like the talons of a hawk, and before she could protest, he was pulling her across the foyer toward the steps.

"What do you think you're doing?" she whispered fiercely.

He hissed at her through taut, thin lips. "I'm taking you upstairs where you're going to get out of that whore's dress and put on something respectable."

She could feel curious gazes on them and realized that even though the other guests could not hear the words of the argument, they could certainly guess what was happening. She reached out for the bottom of the banister and held tight. "I'm not going anywhere," she declared.

Just at that moment, Veronica appeared, gliding toward them in a jet-black evening gown and instantly taking in the small drama being played out before her. There was a slight lift to her forehead, and then she smiled gaily. "Baron, Katharine, just the two I was looking for. I'm late as usual, and for my own party. Cook has been ready to serve dinner for a quarter of an hour. Baron, be a darling and escort me into the dining room. And, Katharine, I want you to meet Sergio. A fascinating man and the best baritone New York City has heard in a decade. I have given him to you as a dinner partner."

Cain ground his teeth in frustration. There was no way he could remove Kit now without causing a scene. For the two of them, he didn't care, but Veronica had extended her hospitality to them, and he would not embarrass her.

He watched as a much too handsome Italian stepped forward and kissed Kit's hand. She smiled at him and said something Cain could not quite hear. The Italian cocked his head to the side in a gesture Cain thought too pretty for a man and then turned over the small hand he had not yet released and pressed his lips intimately to Kit's palm.

Cain moved quickly, but Veronica was even quicker. With surprising agility, she placed herself between him and the Italian. "My dearest Baron," she cooed softly, "you are behaving like the most boring sort of husband. Escort me into the dining room before you do something that will only make you look foolish."

Veronica was right, and he knew it. Still, it took all his will to turn his back on his wife and the Italian.

Dinner lasted for nearly three hours, and at least a dozen times during the meal, Kit's laughter rang out as she divided her attention between Sergio and Brandon and an assortment of other men who sat near her. The men flattered her outrageously, showering upon her one compliment after another. Sergio taught her the Italian words for "You are beautiful" and then looped his arm around her shoulder and pulled her closer to whisper a more intimate compliment into her ear. When she spilled a drop of wine on the tablecloth, he dipped his index finger into the spot and then pressed it to his lips.

The attentive servants kept her wine glass full, and she drank more freely than usual while eating very little. Each time she heard the sound of Cain's laughter echo from the other end of the room, she picked up her glass and, with a gay smile at the most convenient male, took a deep sip.

Brandon claimed her for the first dance, abandoning Alice

Ann to her father. Kit tilted her head and looked directly into his handsome, weak face. For the first time she seemed to see him clearly. Brandon, who talked of honor, was willing to sell himself to the highest bidder. First it had been for a plantation; now it was for a bank. Somehow she could not imagine Cain selling himself for anything at all.

Out of the corner of her eye, she saw Alice Ann rush from the ballroom, and she felt a sudden stab of remorse that her flirtatiousness had caused Brandon's fiancée such unhappiness. Poor girl. Still, Brandon had made himself a ridiculously easy target.

In a flash of champagne-induced insight, Kit saw quite clearly what she had to do. Women should stick together against men like Brandon Parsell. Besides, she had a small score of her own to settle with him.

"Brandon," she whispered in his ear as the music began, "I've missed you so."

"I've missed you, too, Kit," he murmured. "Oh, Lord, you're so beautiful, and you smell so good. It's nearly killed me these past few months to think of you with Cain."

"Dear Brandon." She pushed closer to him and whispered mischievously, "Run away with me tonight. Let's run away from both of them, from Baron and from Alice Ann. Let's leave it all, Risen Glory and the bank. It will only be the two of us." She could feel him stiffen beneath the cloth of his coat, and she became more dramatic. "We won't have any money or any home, but we'll have our love. Our love will shelter us, dear Brandon."

"Really, Kit, I—I don't think that would be—would be very wise," he sputtered with great consternation.

"But why not?" She stopped moving so abruptly that he nearly stumbled, and then she pulled him determinedly to the edge of the floor. "Come, Brandon, let's go tell Alice Ann right now. Or maybe we should tell her father and let him break the news to her. That might be kinder. Oh, Brandon, what should we do? Perhaps we should just sneak away and not tell any of them. Of course my husband will come after us, but I'm certain you can take care of him."

Brandon clutched at her arm before she could move any further toward what he saw as certain disaster. "Let's not—That is to say, I think, perhaps—Too much haste—"

She had not meant to let him off the hook so easily, but she could no longer contain herself, and although she ducked her head, the sound of her laughter drifted up to him like the bubbles in a glass of champagne.

"You're making fun of me," he said stiffly.

Kit lifted her head to see that he was deeply offended. His reaction produced an odd mixture of satisfaction and remorse inside her. "You deserve it, Brandon. You're an engaged man."

"I don't understand you at all," he muttered, with some attempt to regain his dignity.

"Of course you don't. You never have. But everything would be a lot easier for you if you were honest enough to admit that you don't like me very much. And you certainly don't approve of me. Admit it, Brandon. All you feel for me is a most ungentlemanly lust!"

Such unvarnished honesty was more than Parsell could accept. "I beg your pardon if I have offended you," he said stiffly. For a moment his eyes caught on the crystal-spangled bodice of Kit's gown. With great effort, he tore his gaze away and, smarting with humiliation, went in search of his fiancée.

With Brandon's departure, Kit was quickly claimed by Sergio. As she took the Italian's proffered hand, she glanced toward the far end of the room where her husband and Veronica had been standing only a moment before. They were both gone, and a half hour later when Veronica reappeared, Cain was not with her.

Her husband's indifferent desertion prodded Kit to the limits of what even she considered acceptable behavior. She whirled from one partner to the next, dancing with Rebel and Yankee alike, complimenting each one extravagantly and letting several hold her much too closely. She didn't care what any of them thought. Let them talk! She danced every dance, laughed her intoxicating laugh, and only Veronica Gamble sensed the quiet edge of desperation behind it.

Many were shocked by Kit's bold behavior, although a few of the younger women were secretly envious. They looked around anxiously for the dangerous Major Cain, but he was nowhere in sight. Someone whispered that he was playing poker in the library and losing badly.

There was open speculation about the state of the Cain marriage. After all, the couple had not once danced together. There had been rumors, of course, that it had been a marriage of necessity, but time had proven those rumors false, for five months after the wedding, Katharine Cain's waistline was as slim as ever.

The poker game folded shortly before two. Cain had lost several hundred dollars, but his black mood had little to do with money. He stood in the doorway of the ballroom, watching his wife sail across the floor in the arms of the Italian. Some of her hair had come loose from its pins and tumbled in disarray around her shoulders. Her cheekbones still held their high color, and her lips were rosy smudges, as if someone had just kissed her. The baritone could not seem to tear his eyes away from her face except for those moments when his appreciative gaze dropped to her breasts.

A muscle twitched in the corner of Cain's jaw, and the last vestige of self-control deserted him. He pushed past several people in front of him and was about to stride into the swirling couples on the ballroom floor when John Hughes came up and caught at his arm.

"Mr. Cain, Will Bonnett over there claims there wasn't a bluecoat in the whole Union army could outshoot a Reb. What d'ya think about that? You ever meet a Reb you couldn't pick off if you set your mind to it?"

This was dangerous talk, and Cain knew it. He slowly tore his eyes away from his wife and turned his attention to Hughes. Even though nearly four years had passed since Appomattox, social interaction between Northerners and Southerners was still tenuous, with talk of the war pointedly avoided by both parties on those few occasions when they were pushed together. He looked over at the group of seven or eight men made up of former Union soldiers as well as Confederate veterans. They were standing off to the side of the orchestra, and it was obvious that, like his wife, they had all had more than enough to drink. Even from where he was standing, he could hear that their discussion had progressed from polite disagreement to open antagonism.

With a last glance toward Kit and the Italian, he walked with Hughes over to the men. "War's over, fellows. What do you say we all go sample some of Mrs. Gamble's ten-year-old whiskey?"

But the discussion had gone too far. Will Bonnett, a former rice planter who had served in the same regiment as Brandon Parsell, punched his index finger in the direction of one of the men who worked for the Freedmen's Bureau. "No soldier in the world ever fought like the Confederate soldier, and you know it!"

The angry voices were beginning to catch the attention of the other guests, and as the argument grew louder, people stopped dancing to see what the commotion was about.

Will Bonnett spotted Brandon Parsell, who was standing off to the side with his fiancée and her parents. "Brandon, you tell 'em. You ever see anybody could shoot like our boys in gray? Come on over here. Tell these bluebellies how it was."

Parsell moved forward reluctantly. Cain frowned as he saw that Kit had moved up, too, instead of remaining discreetly in the back with the other women.

By this time Will Bonnett's voice had reached the musicians, who gradually put down their instruments so they could enjoy the argument. "We were outnumbered," Bonnett declared, "but you Yankees never outfought us, not for one minute of the war."

One of the Northerners moved forward. "Seems like you got a short memory, Bonnett. You sure as hell got outfought at Gettysburg!"

"We didn't get outfought!" an older man standing next to Will Bonnett exclaimed. "You got lucky! Why, we had boys twelve years old could shoot better than all your officers put together."

"Hell, our *women* could shoot better than their officers!"

There was a great roar of laughter at this sally, and the speaker was slapped heartily on the back for his wit. Of all the Southerners present, only Brandon, still stung by his earlier humiliating encounter with Kit, didn't feel like laughing.

His eyes fell first on her and then on Cain. There was a horrible injustice about their marriage that seemed to nag at him more each day. At first he had been foolishly relieved not to be married to a woman who didn't behave as a lady should, even though it meant the loss of Risen Glory. But as the weeks and months had passed, he had watched Risen Glory's fields bursting white with bolls and seen the wagons laden with ginned cotton head for Cain's spinning mill. And even though he'd become engaged to a woman who, although a Northerner, was a well-bred lady and would bring him the Planters' and Citizens' Bank, he could not quite erase the memory of a pair of wicked violet eyes. His relief at not having married Kit had turned into bitterness. It seemed as if everything in his life had soured. A great injustice had somehow taken place. He was a Parsell, and yet he seemed to have nothing, while they had everything—a disreputable Yankee and a woman who didn't know her place.

Impulsively he stepped forward, his proud bearing immediately commanding the attention of the gathering. "I believe you do have a point about our Southern women," he observed quietly. "Why, I once saw our own Mrs. Cain shoot a pinecone out of a tree from seventy-five yards, even though she couldn't have been more than ten or eleven at the time. There's talk to this day that she's still the best shot in the county."

Several exclamations met this piece of information, and once again Kit found herself the object of admiring masculine eyes. But Parsell was not quite finished. It wasn't easy for a gentleman to settle a score with a lady and still remain a gentleman, but that's exactly what he intended to do. And he would settle with her husband at the same time. There was no way Cain could go along with what he was about to propose, but he would still look like a coward when he refused.

"I've heard that Major Cain is a good shot," Brandon continued. "I guess we've all heard more than enough about the Hero of Missionary Ridge. But if I were a bettin' man, I'd put my money on Kit. I guess I'd give about anything to send Will home for that matchin' set of pistols of his, set up a row of bottles on Mrs. Gamble's garden wall, and see just how good a Yankee officer can shoot against a Southern woman, even if she does happen to be his wife. Of course, I'm sure Major Cain would never permit his wife to take part in a shootin' contest, especially when he knows he has a pretty good chance of comin' out the loser."

There were hoots of laughter from the Southern men. Parsell

had certainly put that Yankee in his place! None of them seriously believed a woman, even a Southern one, could outshoot a man, but they'd enjoy seeing the match all the same. It would be a story to tell long after it was over. And because she was only a woman, there'd be no honor lost to the South when the Yankee beat her.

The women were deeply shocked by Brandon's proposal. What on earth could he be thinking of? No lady could make such a public spectacle of herself as he was suggesting and still be considered a lady. If Mrs. Cain went along with this, she would be a social pariah. They glared at their husbands, who were encouraging the match, and silently vowed to curtail the supply of spirits for the rest of the evening.

Kit could feel Cain's eyes on her and wondered if she was the only one present who could see the contempt in his gaze as it slid down over her gown. As clearly as if he had said the words aloud, she understood his unspoken message. None of this would have happened if she had not set out, from the very beginning, to make a public spectacle of herself. She thrust her chin higher and returned his glare defiantly.

The Northerners urged Cain to accept the challenge. "Come on, Major. Don't let us down."

"You can't back out on us now!"

Cain finally lifted his eyes from her, although the force of his contempt lingered, burning against her skin like acid. "I will not permit my wife to engage in a public shooting contest," he said.

His words were uttered so coldly, so without feeling, that Kit felt as if she had been slapped. It was as if he were talking about a mare he owned instead of his wife, as if she were merely another piece of property. But then, why should she let that hurt her? He had made it clear from the very beginning that was exactly how he regarded her. Was that how he would regard their child, too? With contempt? As just another piece of property?

She stepped forward, the candlelight setting sparkling golden fires to the beads of her gown. "I've been challenged, Baron. This is South Carolina, not New York. Even as my husband, you have no right to interfere in a matter of honor. Fetch your pistols, Mr. Bonnett. Gentlemen, I will face my husband, or, if he should decline, any other Yankee who would like to shoot against me."

The shocked gasps of the women went unheard beneath the triumphant whoops of the men. Only Brandon did not join in the male joviality. He could not believe she had actually accepted. He had meant to embarrass them both, but he had never meant to ruin her. After all, he was still a Parsell and a gentleman.

"Kit—Major Cain—I—I believe I was somewhat hasty. Surely you cannot—"

"Save it, Parsell," Cain growled, his own mood now as reckless as his wife's. He was tired of being the conciliator, tired of losing the battles she seemed determined to thrust them into. He was tired of her scorn and her hatred. Most of all, he was tired of himself for caring so damned much about her.

"Set up your bottles, John," he exclaimed roughly. "And bring as many lamps as you can find into the garden so we can see."

With a great deal of laughter, the men moved off, Northerner and Southerner suddenly drawn together as they figured the odds on the match. The women were not anxious to remain too close to Kit, although all were nearly bursting with the excitement of being firsthand witnesses to such a scandal, and so they moved off, too, leaving husband and wife standing alone.

"You've got your match," he said bitterly, "just like you've gotten everything else you've ever wanted."

She was angered by his words. When had she ever gotten anything she wanted? "What's the matter, Baron? Are you afraid you'll get beat?"

He shrugged. "I figure there's a pretty fair chance of it. I'm a good shot, but you're better. I've known that since the night you tried to kill me when you were only sixteen."

Kit was suspicious of his honesty. "If you feel that way, why are you doing this?"

"Maybe I'm not afraid of losing," Cain replied. "Or maybe I just figure all the champagne you've been drinking has tilted the odds in my favor."

"I wouldn't count too much on that champagne," she warned. But it was false bravado, and they both knew it. Although she would never admit it to him, she realized she was far from sober.

At that moment Veronica descended on them, genuinely distressed by what had taken place while she was in the dining room conferring with the butler about the buffet that was being set up. If this were Vienna, she argued, it would be different, but in South Carolina, such a thing was impossible. Kit knew that better than any of them. And then she reprimanded Cain for not having had more sense than to be swept along by his wife's impulsiveness.

But her words fell on deaf ears. Within minutes, Will Bonnett had reappeared with a large wooden pistol case, and Kit and Cain were swept out through the back doors onto the piazza.

Fresh torches had been shoved into the iron brackets that were placed at strategic intervals along the brick wall of the garden. Their flames were supplemented with a number of kerosene lamps that had been brought outside from the house, and despite the moonless night, the garden shone as brightly as if it were daytime.

Along the far wall, a dozen champagne bottles had been set up, and Veronica noticed, with alarm, that only half of them were empty. She gave hurried orders to the butler to replace them quickly. Reputations might be won or lost, civilizations rise and fall, but Veronica Gamble would not stand by and see good champagne wasted.

The wooden case was opened, and Kit and Cain each picked up the weapon nearest them. They were both familiar with the gun. It was the Confederate version of a Colt revolver, made in Baton Rouge during the war. It was plain and serviceable, with walnut grips and a brass frame instead of the more expensive steel frame of the Colt. The Southerners groaned and let out loud protests when they saw the guns Will had produced. The revolver was heavy, designed for hard, wartime use by a man. It was no gun for a woman.

Kit, however, was accustomed to the weight and barely noticed it. She'd fired revolvers like this a hundred times before. She slipped six of the paper cartridges Will had provided into the empty chambers of the cylinder, pulling the loading lever down each time to press them into place. Then she fitted a copper percussion cap on each of the six small metal nipples at the other end of the cylinder. Her fingers were smaller than Cain's, and she was done first.

The distance was marked off and then checked. They would stand twenty-five paces away from their target. Each would fire six shots. Ladies first.

Kit stepped up to the line that had been scratched in the gravel. Under normal circumstances, the empty champagne bottles would have held little challenge for her, but the slight swimming in her head made her all too conscious of the truth of Cain's words. If only she hadn't drunk so much.

She turned sideways to the target and lifted her arm. As she sighted through the notch in the hammer of the gun and the bead at the end of the barrel, she made herself forget everything except what she had to do. Slowly she pulled the trigger, and the bottle exploded. There was a surprised exclamation from the men. She moved on to the next bottle, but her success had made her careless. She fired too quickly, forgetting to take her intoxication into account, and just missed the second target.

Cain watched from the side as she picked off the next four bottles and found that his anger was giving way to admiration. Five out of six, and she wasn't even sober. Damn, but she was one hell of a woman. There was something primitive and wonderful about her, standing silhouetted against the torch flames, arm extended, the deadly revolver in her hand in such marked contrast to the loveliness of her. If only she were softer, somehow. If only. . . .

She lowered the revolver and turned to him, lifting a black slash of brow in triumph. She looked so pleased with herself that he couldn't quite suppress a smile.

"Very nice, Mrs. Cain, although I believe you left one."

"That's true, Mr. Cain," she replied with the barest shadow of a smile. "You just make sure you don't leave more than one."

He inclined his head and, with mock gallantry, turned to the target.

A hush had fallen over the crowd as the men became uneasily aware of what Cain had known from the start—they had a serious match on their hands. Cain lifted the revolver. It felt familiar and comfortable in his hand, exactly like the Colt that had seen him through the war. He picked off the first bottle and then the second. One shot followed another. When he finally lowered his arm, all six bottles were gone.

Kit couldn't help herself. She grinned. He was a wonderful shot, with a good eye and a steady arm. Something tight and proud caught in her throat as she watched him in his formal black and white evening dress, copper lights from the torches glinting in his crisp, tawny hair. She forgot about her pregnancy, she forgot her anger, she forgot everything in an all-encompassing rush of feeling for this difficult and splendid man. He turned to her, his head tilted slightly to the side as if in inquiry.

"Good shooting, my darling," she said softly.

She saw the surprise on his face and wished at that instant that the earth would open up and swallow her. The endearment had slipped out, humiliating her, making her feel naked and vulnerable at a time when she already seemed to have lost so many of her carefully erected defenses against him. It was a bedroom expression, part of a small dictionary of love words that were the private vocabulary of their passion, words that were never, ever to be used in any other place, at any other time.

She wanted to run and hide, and those cowardly feelings hardened her. Tossing her chin high, she turned to the onlookers. "Since my husband is a gentleman, I'm certain he'll give me a second chance. Would someone fetch a deck of cards and pull out the ace of spades?"

"Kit!" Cain's voice was a brusque, warning bark.

She spun around to face him. "Will you shoot against me?" she demanded. "Yes or no?"

The two of them might have been standing alone instead of in the midst of dozens of people. All of their former pleasure in the other's skill had vanished. Although the onlookers did not realize it, the purpose of the contest had just undergone a subtle shift. The war that had raged for so long between them had found a battleground.

"I'll shoot against you."

There was a deadly quiet as the ace of spades was fastened to the wall. "Three shots each?" Kit inquired as she reloaded her gun.

He nodded grimly.

She lifted her arm and sighted the small black spade at the exact center of the playing card. She could feel a tremble beginning in her hand, and she lowered the revolver until she felt steadier. Then she lifted her arm again, sighted the small target, and fired.

She had hit the top right corner of the card. It was an excellent shot, and there were amazed murmurs from the men as well as the women, several of whom could not help but feel a burst of pride at seeing one of their own sex excel at such a decidedly masculine sport.

Kit cocked the hammer and adjusted her aim. This time she was too low, hitting the brick just below the bottom of the card, but it was still a respectable shot and the crowd acknowledged it. She could feel her head beginning to reel, but she forced herself to ignore it and concentrate everything on the small black dot at the center of the card. She had made this shot dozens of times before. All she needed to do was concentrate. Slowly she squeezed the trigger.

It was nearly a perfect shot, taking the pointed top off the spade. There was a trace of disquiet in the subdued congratulations of the Southern men. None of them had ever seen a woman shoot like that. Somehow it didn't seem quite right. After all, the Southern code of chivalry decreed that women were to be cosseted and protected, and how could a man go about protecting a woman like her?

Cain lifted his own weapon without looking at her. The crowd had once again fallen silent, so that only the nighttime rustle of the sea breeze in the sweet olives disturbed the quiet of the garden. The gun exploded, hitting the brick wall just to the left of the card. Cain corrected his aim and fired again, and this time hit the top edge of the card.

Kit held her breath, praying that his third shot would miss, praying that it wouldn't, wishing too late that she had not forced this contest upon them.

Cain fired. There was a puff of smoke, and the single spade in the center of the playing card disappeared. His final shot had drilled it out.

The onlookers went wild. Even the Southerners temporarily forgot their animosity in their relief that the natural law of male physical superiority had not been upset after all. They surrounded Cain to congratulate him.

"Fine shootin', Mr. Cain."

"A privilege to watch you."

"Of course, you were only firin' against a woman."

The men's words of congratulations grated on his ears. As they pounded him on the back, he looked over their heads at Kit, standing off by herself, the revolver nested at her side in the soft folds of her skirt.

One of the Northerners shoved a cigar into his hand. "That woman of yours is pretty good, but when all is said and done, I guess shootin' is still pretty much a man's game."

"You're right there," another said. "Never much doubt about who was going to win."

Cain felt contempt for their casual dismissal of Kit's skill. He thrust the cigar back and glared at them all. "You fools! Can't any of you see that she's half drunk. If she'd been sober, I wouldn't have had a chance against her. And neither, by God, would any of you!" Turning on his heel, he stalked out of the garden leaving the men gaping after him in astonishment.

For a moment Kit stood unmoving, stunned by his incredible defense of her. She suddenly thrust the revolver at Veronica and, picking up her skirts, ran into the house after him.

He was already in the bedroom when she reached it, and her brief happiness faded as she saw that he was throwing his clothing into a satchel that lay open on the bed.

"What are you doing?" she asked breathlessly.

He didn't bother to look up at her. "I'm going to Risen Glory. I'll send the carriage back for you the day after tomorrow. I'll be gone by then."

"Gone?" she cried. "What do you mean? Where are you going?"

He tossed a shirt into the satchel. "I'm leaving you," he said tonelessly. "I'm getting out now while I can still look myself in the eye. Don't worry, though. It won't really affect you. I'll see a lawyer first and put your name on the deed to Risen Glory. You won't ever have to worry about having your precious plantation taken away from you again."

Kit's heart was pounding in her chest like the wings of a trapped bird. "I don't believe you! You wouldn't walk away just like that. You can't just pack up and leave. What about the cotton mill?"

"Childs can manage it, or maybe I'll sell it. I've already had an offer." He grabbed a set of brushes from the top of the bureau and shoved them inside with the rest. "I'm done fighting you, Kit. You've got a clear field now."

"But I don't want you to go!" The words sprang spontaneously from her lips. Even as she said them, she didn't understand them, but she knew they were true.

He finally looked up at her, his mouth twisted in its old mockery. "Now that surprises me, especially since you've been trying your best to get rid of me one way or another since you were sixteen."

"That was different. Risen Glory—"

He slammed the open palm of his hand against the bedpost, making the heavy wooden spindle vibrate. "I don't want to hear about Risen Glory! I don't ever want to hear that name again! God damn it, Kit, it's just a cotton plantation! It isn't a shrine!"

"You don't understand!" Kit cried. "You've never understood. Risen Glory is all I've ever had."

"So you've told me," he said contemptuously. "Maybe you'd better start thinking about why that is."

"What do you mean by that?" she demanded, grabbing the bedpost for support as she took a step closer to him.

"I mean that you don't *give* anything! You're like my mother. You take from a man until you've bled him dry. Well, I'll be damned if I end up like my father. And that's why I'm leaving."

"I'm not anything like Rosemary, and you know it!" she exclaimed furiously. "You just can't accept the fact that I won't let you dominate me."

"I never wanted to dominate you, Kit," he said quietly. "I never wanted to own you either, no matter what I said. If I'd wanted a wife I could grind under my boot heel, I could have gotten married years ago to any of a dozen different women. I never wanted you to walk in my dust. But, by damn, I won't walk in yours either!"

He slammed the satchel closed and began fastening the leather straps. "Do you know that when we got married, I actually had this idea that maybe it could be all right between us—especially after that first night. And then it went bad right away, and I decided I'd been a fool. But when you came to me in that black nightgown, and you were so scared and so determined, I forgot all about being a fool and let you creep right back under my skin again."

He released the satchel and straightened up. For a moment he looked at her, and then he slowly closed the small distance left between them. When he reached her, she saw to her amazement that his eyes were full of pain. It pierced through her as if it were her own.

Slowly he lifted his hand and touched her cheek. "When we made love," he said huskily, "it was as if we stopped being two separate people. You never once held back from me. You gave me everything—all your wildness and your softness and your sweetness. But there wasn't any real foundation beneath that lovemaking—there wasn't any understanding, and that's why it all turned sour. I could feel myself trying to hurt you." He rubbed his thumb gently over her dry lips, his voice barely a whisper. "Sometimes when I was inside you, I would use my body to punish you. I hated myself for that, and I hated you, too." He dropped his hand. "Lately I've been waking up at night in a cold sweat, afraid that someday I'd really hurt you, and tonight when I saw you in that dress and watched you with those other men, I finally realized that I had to go. It's just no good between us. We started out all wrong. We never had a chance."

As he began to turn away, Kit clutched at his arm, her eyes filled with desperate tears that she barely understood. "Don't go, Baron! It's not too late. If we both tried harder—"

He shook his head. "I don't have anything left in me. I'm hurting, Kit. I'm hurting bad." Bending down, he pressed his lips to her forehead, and then he picked up the satchel and walked out of the room.

Chapter Thirty-five

True to his word, Cain was gone when Kit returned to Risen Glory. At first she would not let herself believe it. He'd come back to her. He had to come back! And then a young lawyer appeared at the door with a thick stack of documents and a pleasant, unassuming manner, and all her illusions crumbled.

She was shown papers that gave her clear title to Risen Glory as well as control over her trust fund. She listened as the attorney explained that Cain had deeded over a wedge of prime land surrounding the overseer's house to Magnus and Sophronia and that the loans that had been taken from her trust fund to rebuild the cotton mill had all been repaid. The lawyer told her that the mill was in the process of being sold, and that the money from the sale was the only thing Cain was taking with him from their marriage. She listened to his lengthy explanation, but she didn't care about any of it.

For the next month, she moved like a sleepwalker, losing track of time, forgetting to eat, spending entire days locked away in the big front bedroom. Magnus came to her for orders concerning the plantation, and she sent him away. She shut out thoughts of the new life growing inside her and turned a deaf ear to Sophronia's increasingly anxious scoldings and Miss Dolly's tearful frettings.

One dreary afternoon in late February as she sat in the bedroom pretending to read, Lucy appeared to announce that Veronica Gamble was waiting for her in the sitting room.

"Tell her I'm not feeling well," Kit said listlessly.

Veronica, however, was not so easily put off. Brushing past the maid, she made her way to the bedroom and entered without knocking. She took in Kit's uncombed hair and sallow complexion and said scathingly, "How Lord Byron would have loved this. The maiden withers like a dying rose, growing more frail each day. She refuses to eat and hides herself away. You silly child, what on earth do you think you're doing?"

"Get out of here!" Kit glared at her, furious at having her privacy interrupted. "I've never liked you very much, Mrs. Gamble, but I thought better of you than to imagine you would come here to gloat over my husband's desertion."

"Oh, I'm not gloating, my dear," Veronica said, shrugging off an elegant topaz velvet cloak and tossing it down on a chair. "Far from it. The greatest disappointment of my return to South Carolina has been that I didn't get to sleep with your husband. And now, thanks to you, it looks like I'll never have the chance."

"How dare you!" Kit exclaimed, springing to her feet.

"And how dare you," Veronica replied coldly. "If you care nothing for yourself, you could at least consider the child you're carrying."

Kit caught her breath. "How did you know about that?"

"I met Sophronia in town last week. She told me everything that has been happening since Baron left, and she told me about the baby, too."

"You're lying. Sophronia doesn't know. No one knows."

"Really, Kit, you didn't imagine something that important could get past Sophronia," she scoffed. "You didn't tell Baron about the child, did you?" Kit's closed face told her what she wanted to know. She sighed and said, somewhat more gently, "Of course not. You're much too proud for that."

"It wasn't pride," Kit said softly, and then she sagged down into the chair, all the fight gone out of her. "I didn't think of it. Isn't that silly? I was so stunned by what he was telling me that I didn't think of it."

Veronica wandered over to the front window, pushed back the curtain, and stared outside. "Womanhood has been hard coming to you, I think. But then, I suppose it's hard coming to all of us. For men, growing up seems easier. They have rites of passage that are clear and well defined. They perform acts of bravery on the battlefield or show that they are men through physical labor or by making money. For women, it's so much more confusing. We have no rites of passage. Do we become women when a man first makes love to us? If so, why do we refer to it as a *loss* of virginity? Doesn't the word 'loss' imply that we were better off before? I will tell you in all honesty, Kit, that I abhor the idea that we become women only through the physical act of a man. We become women when we learn what is important in our lives, when we learn to give and to take with a loving heart." She turned around and was somewhat surprised to see that Kit was actually listening to her.

"My dear," she said softly as she walked over to the bed and picked up her cloak, "it really is time for you to put childhood behind you. There are certain things in life that are temporal and others that are everlasting. You'll be much happier when you decide which are which."

She was gone as quickly as she had arrived, leaving only her words to linger in the room. As soon as Kit heard the carriage moving off down the drive, she grabbed the jacket that went with her riding habit and threw it over her rumpled woolen dress. Then she slipped out of the house.

She made her way to the old slave church without anyone seeing her, and, letting herself in through the sagging back door, she sat down on a rough, wooden bench. The interior was dark and chilly, with only the scratching of a mouse to disturb the quiet. She thought about what Veronica had said and recognized the truth of it.

It was the pain she had seen on Cain's face before he had left her that had finally unlocked the door she had kept so tightly shut and let her see inside her own heart. No matter how hard she had tried to deny it, no matter how hard she had fought him and fought herself, she had fallen in love with Baron Cain.

It had been written in the stars long before that July night when he pulled her down off the wall by her breeches. All of her life since birth had shaped her for him and for him alone. He was the other half of herself. She had fallen in love with him during the mornings and the afternoons and the evenings of their days together, through his anger and his indifference, through his mockery and his sudden, surprising gentleness. And she had fallen in love with him during the deep, secret hours of the night when he had stretched her and filled her and spilled his seed into her with all his force.

How she wished she could do it all over again. Over the past weeks she had relived their times together like scenes in a play. If only she had said this or done that. If only on those times when he had softened toward her, she had opened her arms and met his softness with her own instead of killing it with a cutting phrase or sharp gesture. He was gone, and she had never uttered the words of her love. But then, neither had he, and that was what had tortured her ever since he'd left.

If only she knew that he really loved her, she could go after him and make him listen to her. Surely the lawyer who had come to see her knew where he was. They could start over again, and this time she would hold nothing back from him.

But at this point Kit's thoughts had come around in a full circle. She couldn't go after him. The pain she had seen in his eyes was undoubtedly the result of all the misery her shrewish, selfish behavior had caused him. Not only had she been a poor excuse for a wife, she had been a poor excuse for a woman, and Baron Cain was undoubtedly glad to be rid of her.

She stood up and let herself out of the church. Perhaps it was Veronica's visit, or maybe it was just her own common sense coming to her rescue, but she knew she had to stop feeling sorry for herself and get on with her life. She could cry in the privacy of her bedroom at night, but during the day there was work to be done. People depended on her and cared about her.

For the first time in weeks, her lips curved in a smile. It was a small, infinitely sad gesture that bore little resemblance to her high-spirited, intoxicating laughter, but still it was a smile. It was time she started taking care of herself. After all, she was going to have a baby.

The child was born in July, four years, almost to the day, since the hot afternoon Kit had arrived in New York City to kill Baron Cain. The baby was a girl, with fair hair like her father's and startling violet eyes fringed with tiny, black lashes. Kit named her Elizabeth and called her Beth.

Her labor had been long, but the birth had gone without complications. Sophronia had stayed by her side the entire time, while Miss Dolly fluttered about the house getting in everyone's way and shredding two of her best lace handkerchiefs. Afterward, her very first visitors had been Rawlins and Mary Cogdell, pathetically relieved to see that a baby had finally been produced from the Cain marriage, even though it had taken twelve months from the time of the shameful forced marriage in the slave church for the event to happen.

Kit spent the rest of the summer regaining her strength. She sat by the hour in a wicker rocker on the shady piazza and held her daughter, slipping inside only to nurse her in private. Beth was a sweet, good-natured baby, happiest when she was in her mother's arms. At night, when she would awaken to be fed, Kit would pick her up and tuck her in bed beside her where the two of them would doze until dawn, Beth content with the milky-sweet breast of her mother and Kit full of love for this tiny, precious infant who had been God's gift to her when she had most needed it.

Veronica came to visit her frequently, as she had done during the final months of Kit's confinement, and a deep affection grew between the two women. Veronica still said outrageous things about wanting to make love to Cain, but Kit now recognized them as none too subtle attempts to prod her own jealousy and keep her feelings for her husband alive. Sometimes she smiled to herself at Veronica's outrageousness. As if she needed someone to remind her of her love for her husband. Not an hour of the day went by that she did not think of him and wish she could do it all over again.

With the secrets of the past swept away, Kit's relationship with Sophronia deepened. Although the two still bickered occasionally, it was more out of habit than animosity. Sophronia talked to her freely now, and Kit took comfort from her presence. Sometimes, however, Kit would watch as Sophronia caught sight of Magnus unexpectedly, and she would feel a stab of bittersweet pain as her half sister's face softened with deep, abiding love for her husband. Magnus's goodness had laid to final rest the ghosts of Sophronia's past.

Of them all, Magnus was the least changed by the past year's events. For a very long time he had known exactly what he wanted, and now that he had it, he was a contented man. He alone understood Kit's need to talk about Cain, and in the evening as she sat on the piazza, he told her all that he knew about her husband's past: his childhood, the years of drifting from place to place and job to job, his bravery during the war. She listened intently to everything he told her.

The beginning of September found her with renewed energy and a deeper understanding of herself. Veronica had once said that she should decide which things in life were temporal and which were everlasting. As she once again rode the fields of Risen Glory, she finally understood what Veronica had meant.

Part Five

KIT

"Hitch your wagon to a star."
Ralph Waldo Emerson, *Civilization*

Chapter Thirty-six

Kit reached Texas the first of November. It had been a long, arduous journey, made all the more complicated by the fact that she had not traveled alone. The trip to New Orleans was difficult enough, but that had been only the beginning. From New Orleans, they had traveled by steamer to Galveston and then overland by rail and stagecoach to the small cow town of San Carlos.

It had not been easy to locate Cain, for the lawyer who was handling his affairs no longer knew where he was. To her dismay Kit learned that profits from the sale of the cotton mill were lying untouched in a bank in Charleston. She knew that all Cain's money had been tied up either in Risen Glory, which he had deeded over to her, or in the cotton mill. For some reason he had left himself virtually penniless.

She ordered inquiries made in Natchez, the last address the lawyer had for Cain, but although many people remembered him, no one seemed to know where he had gone. She finally mentioned her difficulties to Veronica, who quietly informed her that Cain had kept in touch with her through occasional letters ever since he had left and that he was in San Carlos, Texas.

Kit had been furious with her. How could she have held back such important information?

Veronica had remained unaffected by Kit's anger. "Really, my dear, you're being quite unreasonable. After all, you never asked me if I knew where he was. Why don't you admit that the real reason you're upset is because he wrote me instead of you? Dear Kit, don't you see this was his way of keeping in touch with you? He knew that, if anything was really wrong, I would inform him."

Kit wanted to believe what Veronica was telling her, but she couldn't quite suppress her jealousy or her pain. "So he knew about Beth, but even then he didn't come back to me?"

Veronica sighed. "No, Kit, he doesn't know about Beth, and I'm still not certain I did the right thing by not writing him about her. But I wasn't sure it was best for you, and I couldn't bear to see either of you hurt any more than you have been."

Kit had been touched by Veronica's genuine concern, and her anger had evaporated. She learned that Cain had traveled on the riverboats for several months after he had left Risen Glory, apparently living on what he won at the poker tables. Then he'd moved on to Texas where he'd ridden shotgun for one of the stagecoach lines. For a while he had herded cattle, and now he was running a gambling palace in San Carlos. Kit felt a wrenching inside her as she realized that the old patterns of Cain's life were repeating themselves. He was drifting again.

Texas had been a surprise to Kit. Never had she imagined there could be so much uninhabited space. It was all so different from South Carolina—the vast, flat East Texas prairie that stretched unbroken for mile on unending mile, and then the rougher country farther inland where twisting trees grew from jagged rocks like gnarled fingers and where tumbleweed chased itself across the harsh, hilly terrain. They said that when it rained, the canyons flooded, sometimes washing away entire herds of cattle, and that in the summer, the sun baked the earth until it hardened and cracked. Yet there was something about the land that appealed to her, despite its harshness. Perhaps it was the challenge it posed.

Still, the closer she came to San Carlos, the more uncertain she grew about what she had done. She was no longer an impulsive sixteen-year-old taking off on a quest to New York City. She had responsibilities now, yet she had left the familiar behind her to go off in search of a man who had never even said he loved her.

As she climbed the wooden steps that led to the Yellow Rose Gambling Palace, she could feel her stomach twisting into tight, painful knots. For several days now she had hardly been able to eat, and this morning not even the mouthwatering smells that had drifted up from the dining room of the Ranchers' Hotel had been able to tempt her. She had dallied while she dressed, fixing her hair one way and then another, changing outfits several times, and even remembering to check for any buttons or hooks that might have escaped her notice. Now that she had reached her destination, she was strangely reluctant to see her journey at its end.

She had finally decided to wear her dove-gray dress with the soft rose piping. It was the same outfit she had worn on her return to Risen Glory, including the matching hat with its spiderweb-thin veil draping her features. It comforted her somehow to wear the rose and gray outfit, as if she could turn the clock back and start all over again. Still, the dress fit differently now, clinging more closely to her breasts as a reminder that nothing ever remained the same.

Her gloved hand trembled slightly as she reached out for the swinging door that led into the saloon. For a moment she hesitated, and then she pushed hard against it and stepped inside.

The Yellow Rose was the best and most expensive saloon in San Carlos. Its red-and-gold wallpaper and oversized crystal chandelier had been imported from St. Louis. An ornately carved mahogany bar ran the length of the room. Behind the bar hung a portrait of a reclining nude woman with Titian curls draping her plump shoulders and a yellow rose caught between her teeth. She had been painted against a map of Texas so that the top of her head rested near Texarcana and her feet curled along the Rio Grande. Despite her nervousness, Kit smiled at the portrait. The woman reminded her of Veronica.

There were only a few patrons inside, for it was not quite noon. One by one they stopped talking and turned to study the slim, veiled figure who stood by the door. Even though they could not see her features clearly, her dress and her bearing told them she was no ordinary woman, certainly not one who belonged inside a saloon, even the elegant Yellow Rose.

The bartender cleared his throat nervously. This could only mean trouble. "Can I help you, miss?"

"I'd like to see Baron Cain."

He glanced uncertainly toward a flight of curving stairs at the back and then down at the glass he was polishing. "There's no one here by that name," he muttered.

Kit knew that he was lying. Walking past the men at the bar, she began to make her way singlemindedly toward the stairs.

The bartender dashed around the edge of the bar. "Hey! You can't go up there!"

"I certainly can," Kit replied without slackening her pace. "And if you don't want me to invade the wrong room, I suggest you tell me exactly where I can find Mr. Cain."

The bartender was a giant of a man, with a barrel chest and arms like ham hocks. Long accustomed to dealing with drunken cowboys and gunslingers out to make a reputation for themselves, he was suddenly helpless in the face of a woman who was so obviously a lady. "Last room on the left," he mumbled. There'd be hell to pay, but he didn't know what else he could do.

"Thank you," Kit said graciously, and then she began to climb the stairs like a queen, shoulders back and head held high. None of the men watching could have guessed just how frightened she was.

Her name was Ernestine Agnes Jones, but nobody knew that. To the men at the Yellow Rose, she was simply Red River Ruby. Like most people who had come west, Ruby had buried her past along with her name and never once looked back.

Despite powders and creams and carefully rouged lips, Ruby looked older than her twenty-eight years. She had lived hard, and it showed. Still, she was an attractive woman with rich, chestnut hair and breasts like pillows. Until recently, little had come easy for her, but all that had changed with the convenient death of her last lover. Now she found herself the owner of the Yellow Rose and the most sought-after woman in San Carlos—sought after, that was, by every man except the one she wanted for herself.

She pouted as she looked across the bedroom at him. He was tucking a linen shirt into a pair of black broadcloth trousers that fit his lean hips just tightly enough to renew her determination. "But you promised you'd take me for a ride in my new buggy. Why not today?"

"I have things to do, Ruby," he said curtly.

She leaned slightly forward so that the neck of her red ruffled dressing gown fell open even further than it had been when she had entered his room, but he didn't seem to notice. "Anybody would think you was the boss around here instead of me," she said sharply. "What do you have to do that's so important it can't wait?"

When he didn't answer her, she decided not to press him. She had done that once before, and she wouldn't make the mistake of doing it again. Instead, as she walked around the bed toward him, she wished for the hundredth time that she could break the unwritten rule of the West and ask him about his past. She suspected he had a price on his head. That would account for the unmistakable air of danger that was as much a part of him as the set of his jaw. And there was a hard, empty look to his eyes that made you feel cold just staring into them. She had discovered right away that he was as good with his fists as he was with his guns. Still, he could read, and that didn't fit with being a man on the run.

One thing was for sure. He wasn't a womanizer. He didn't even seem to notice that there wasn't a woman in San Carlos who wouldn't lift her petticoats for him if she got the chance. Ruby had been trying to get into his bed ever since she'd hired him to help her run the Yellow Rose. So far she'd not been successful, but he was about the handsomest man she'd ever seen, and she wasn't going to give up yet.

She stopped in front of him and put one hand over the buckle of the belt he had just fastened and another against his chest, slipping her fingers inside his shirt where he'd not yet secured the buttons. There was a knock at the door, but she was too intent on her seduction to notice. Gazing up at him from beneath painted eyelids, she murmured, "I could be real nice to you if you'd give me the chance."

She wasn't aware that the door had opened until he lifted his head and looked past her. Impatiently she turned to see who had interrupted them.

At first Kit felt an absurd desire to apologize for barging in on what was so obviously a private moment, but that lasted for only an instant before the pain hit her. She saw the scene in front of her in separate pieces—a gaudy, red-ruffled dressing gown, a pair of doughy white breasts, a brightly painted mouth open in indignation. And then she could see nothing else but her husband.

He looked years older than she remembered him. His features were thinner and harder, with deep creases at the corners of his eyes and near his mouth. She noticed that his hair was longer, lying well over the back of his collar, and his moustache shaggier. He looked like an outlaw. She wondered if this was the way he had been during the war, watchful and wary, like a piece of fine wire drawn so taut it was ready to snap.

Something raw and violent passed over his features as he saw her, and then his face closed like a locked door.

The woman rounded on her furiously. "Just who the hell do you think you are, bargin' in like this?" she raved. "If you come here lookin' for a job, you can just drag your tail downstairs and wait until I get to you."

Kit welcomed the anger that rushed through her. Pushing the veil of her hat up on the brim with one hand, she shoved the door all the way back on its hinges with the other. "You're the one who'd better drag her tail downstairs. I've got some private business with Mr. Cain."

Ruby's eyelids narrowed as she took in Kit's elegant outfit. "I know your type," she sneered. "High-class Eastern girl who comes west and thinks the world owes her a livin'. Well, this is my place, and there ain't no la-de-da lady gonna tell me what to do. You can put on airs back in Virginny or Kentucky or wherever you come from, but not in the Yellow Rose."

"Get out of here," Kit said in a low voice.

Ruby tightened the sash of her dressing gown and moved forward menacingly. "I'm gonna do you a favor, sister, and teach you right off that things are different here in Texas."

Cain spoke quietly from across the room. "My best piece of advice to you, Ruby, would be not to tangle with her."

Ruby gave a contemptuous snort. As if she could be afraid of a woman like this! And then, before she knew what had happened, she found herself looking down the barrel of a snub-nosed pistol.

Kit's hand never wavered. "Get out of here. And close the door behind you."

Ruby gaped at the pistol and then back at Cain.

"I tried to warn you." He shrugged. "Go on, Ruby."

She didn't need any more persuasion. With a last assessing glance toward the lady with the pistol, she hurried from the room, closing the door behind her with a decisive bang.

Now that they were finally alone, Kit's carefully rehearsed speech deserted her, and she couldn't think what to say. She suddenly realized she was still holding the pistol and that it was pointed at Cain. Swiftly she shoved it back in her reticule. "It wasn't loaded," she muttered.

He made no reply. She looked up at him. She had imagined their reunion a hundred times, but nothing she had ever imagined had been like this. How could she have ever been foolish enough to hope that this cold-eyed stranger, fresh from another woman's arms, might care for her?

"What are you doing here?" he finally asked.

"I came looking for you."

There was another lengthy silence. "You've found me. What do you want?"

If only he'd move, maybe she could find the words to say what she'd come to say, but he was standing stiffly in place, as if her very presence were contaminating him. Suddenly it was all too much—the grueling journey, the horrible uncertainty, and then finding him with that awful woman.

Fumbling inside her reticule, she drew out a thick envelope and put it on the table next to the door. "I wanted to bring you this," she said, and then she turned and fled.

The hallway seemed to go on forever, and so did the stairs. She tripped halfway down, barely catching herself before she fell. She could feel the men who were leaning against the bar watching her, and she glimpsed Ruby standing at the bottom of the stairs, still wearing her red dressing gown. Brushing past her, she made her way toward the swinging doors of the saloon.

She had nearly reached them when she heard the sound of movement behind her, movement that was swift and decisive. Before she could react, a pair of hands clasped her shoulders and spun her around. She felt herself being swung through the air as Cain caught her beneath her knees and swept her up into his arms. Holding her tightly against his chest, he carried her back through the saloon.

He took the stairs two at a time. When he reached his room, he kicked the door open with his foot and then closed it the same way. She let out a startled gasp as he dumped her roughly down on the bed, knocking off her hat. For a moment he looked at her, his expression still closed and inscrutable. And then he crossed the room and picked up the envelope she had dropped on the table.

She lay quietly as he read it. He glanced through the pages once, very quickly, and then went back to the beginning and read them through more carefully. "I don't believe this," he finally said. "I don't believe you did this. Why, Kit?"

"I had to."

He looked at her sharply. "Were you forced to?"

"No. Of course not. Nobody could force me to do something like that."

"Then why?"

She sat up on the edge of the bed. "It—it seemed like the only way."

"What do you mean by that?" he demanded. "The only way to do what?"

When she didn't immediately answer him, he threw the paper down on the table and stalked toward her. "Kit! Why did you sell Risen Glory?"

She stared down at her hands, too numb to explain.

He thrust his fingers back through his hair, talking as much to himself as he was to her. "I can't believe you sold that plantation! Risen Glory meant everything to you. And for ten dollars an acre! Did you need money that badly? That's only a fraction of what it's worth. Did you know that?"

She nodded her head miserably. "I knew it. I wanted to get rid of it quickly. I had the money deposited in your account in Charleston."

Cain was stunned. "My account?"

"It was your plantation, Baron," she said. "Your money put Risen Glory back on its feet again." He said nothing. The silence stretched between them until she thought she would scream if it weren't filled. "You'd like the people who bought it," she said in a rush. "They're a nice family from up near Columbia. They have six children and another on the way. Things have been hard for them since the war."

"So you sold them Risen Glory?"

"I didn't sell it for their sake. I sold it for my own."

"Maybe you'd better explain that."

Was she imagining it or could she detect a slight thawing in his voice? She thought of Ruby pressed up against him. How many other women had there been since he'd left her? So much for all her dreams. She was going to look like a fool when she explained it to him, but suddenly she didn't care. She needed to speak the truth whether he deserved it or not. There would be no more lies from her, spoken or unspoken.

She plucked at a fold of her skirt and then lifted her head, fighting the lump she could feel forming in her throat. He was standing in the shadows of the room, and she was glad she did not have to see his face while she talked. "When you left me," she said slowly, "I thought my life was over. I felt so much anger, first with you and then with myself. It wasn't until you were gone that I realized how much I loved you. I'd loved you for a long time, but I wouldn't admit it to myself. I'd hid it away under so many other feelings. I wanted to come to you right away, but that wasn't—it wasn't practical. Besides, I needed to make sure of what I was doing. I've acted on impulse too many times. And I wanted to make certain that when I did find you, when I did tell you I loved you, you would believe me."

"And so you decided to sell Risen Glory." She could not see his expression clearly, but his voice was thick, almost slurred.

Kit could feel her eyes filling with tears. "It was going to be the proof of my love. I was going to wave it under your nose like a banner. Look what I did for you! But when I finally sold it, I discovered that Risen Glory didn't really mean anything to me anymore. It was just a piece of land. It wasn't a man who could hold you and love you and make a life with you." Her voice broke, and she rose to her feet to try to cover her weakness. "Then I did something very foolish. I wish now I hadn't, but when you plan things in your head, they work out a lot better than they do in real life. I gave away my trust fund to Sophronia."

There was a soft, startled exclamation from the shadows of the room, but she barely heard it. The words were coming in short, choppy bursts now. "I wanted to get rid of everything so you would feel responsible for me. It was sort of an insurance policy in case you told me you didn't want me. I could look at you and say that whether you wanted me or not, you were going to have to take care of me because I didn't have any money or anywhere to go. But now I realize that wasn't a very good idea. I'm not really a helpless person. I couldn't stay with you just because you felt responsible for me. That would be even worse than being apart from you."

"And was it so horrible being apart from me?"

She jerked her head up at the unmistakable tenderness in his voice and watched as he stepped out of the shadows. The years seemed to have fallen away from his face, and the gray eyes that she had always thought were cold were full of feeling. "Yes," she whispered.

And then he was beside her, catching her up and pulling her to him. "My sweet, sweet Kit," he groaned, burying his face in her hair. "Dear God, how I've missed you! How I've wanted you. All I've dreamed about since I left was being with you again!"

She was in his arms again. She tried to take a deep breath, but it turned into a sob as she sucked in the familiar clean male scent of him. The feel of his body against hers after so many months was almost more than she could bear. He was the other part of herself, the part that had been missing for so long.

"I want to kiss you now and make love to you more than I've ever wanted anything in my life," he said.

"Then why don't you?"

There was a sense of wonder in his expression as he looked down into her upturned face. "You'd let me make love to you after you just found me with another woman?"

The pain was a sharp, keen stab, but she lifted her chin and fought it down. "I guess I don't have a whole lot of pride left right now."

The smile that he gave her was soft and tender. "You love just like you do everything else, don't you? Without condition. It took you a lot less time than it took me to figure out how to do it right."

He drew back ever so slightly from her. "I'm going to let you go now. It won't be easy, but there are some things I have to say to you, and I can't think straight when I'm holding you like this."

He released her with agonizing slowness and stepped just far enough away so he was not touching her. "I knew long before I left you that I loved you, but I wasn't as smart as you. I tied strings to it. I made conditions. I didn't have the guts to go to you and tell you how I felt, to put everything on the line the way you just did. Instead, I ran. Just like I've done all my life when I felt somebody or something getting too close to me. Well, I'm tired of running, Kit, and I want you to listen to what I'm going to tell you. I don't have any way to prove it to you. I don't have a banner to wave under your nose. But I love you, and I was coming back to fight for you. I'd already made up my mind. As a matter of fact, I was just getting ready to tell Ruby I was leaving when you barged in that door."

Despite the unmistakable message of love she was hearing, Kit couldn't help but wince at the mention of the saloonkeeper's name.

"Get that fire out of your eye, Kit. I have to tell you about Ruby."

But Kit didn't want to hear it, and she shook her head, trying to fight down the thought that what he had done while they were apart was a betrayal.

"I want you to listen," he insisted. "No more secrets. This part isn't easy for me, but you have to know." He drew a deep breath. "I—I haven't exactly been the world's greatest lover since I left you. As a matter of fact, I haven't been any kind of lover at all. For a long time I stayed away from women, so I didn't think much about it. Then I came to work at the Yellow Rose and Ruby was pretty determined, but what you saw today was all one-sided on her part. I never touched her."

He shoved one hand deep in his pocket and turned slightly away from her, some of his former tension coming back to him. "I guess to another woman, Ruby doesn't look like much, but it's a little different for a man. She's ripe and experienced, and it had been a long time for me. She was making it easy, too, coming to my room all the time dressed like she was dressed today and letting me know that she wanted in my bed. But I didn't *feel* anything for her!"

He stopped talking and looked at her as if he were waiting for something. Kit was confused. He sounded so unhappy, more like a man confessing infidelity than one confessing fidelity. Was there more?

Her confusion must have shown on her face because now Cain spoke more sharply. "Don't you understand, Kit? She offered herself to me in every way she could, and I didn't want her!"

This time Kit did understand, and the happiness that burst inside her was like the whole world had been made anew just for her. "You're worried about your virility! Oh, my darling!" With a great whoop of laughter, she threw herself across the room and into his arms. Pulling his head down, she pressed her mouth to his, talking and laughing and kissing him all at the same time. "Oh, my dear, dear darling! My great, foolish darling! How I love you!"

There was a hoarse, tight sound deep in his throat, and then she was trapped in his embrace, and his mouth was alive with need for her. Their kiss was deep and bittersweet, full of love that had finally been spoken and of pain that had finally been shared.

But they had been apart for too long, and their bodies could not be content with a kiss, however passionate. Cain, who only moments before had doubted his manliness, now found himself aching with desire. Kit felt it and wanted it and, in the last instant before she had lost her reason, remembered that she had not told him everything.

With her last ounce of will, she pulled herself back and gasped out, "I didn't come alone."

His eyes were glazed with passion, and it was a moment before he understood her. "No?"

"No. I—I brought Miss Dolly with me."

"Miss Dolly!" Cain laughed, a deep, joyous rumble that started in his boots and grew louder as it rose upward. "You brought Miss Dolly to Texas?"

"I had to. She wouldn't let me go without her. And you said yourself that we were stuck with her. She's our family, Baron. Besides, I needed her."

"Oh, you sweet! God, I love you." He reached for her again, but she stepped back quickly. "I want you to come to the hotel with me."

"Now?"

"Yes. I have something to show you."

Cain pointed out some of the sights of San Carlos to her as they walked along the uneven wooden sidewalk, his hand tightly clasped over hers where it rested in the crook of his elbow, but it was soon evident by her absentminded responses that her mind was elsewhere, and he fell silent, content to have her beside him.

Miss Dolly was waiting in the room Kit had taken. She giggled like a schoolgirl when Cain picked her up and hugged her, and then, with a quick, worried look at Kit, excused herself, saying that she had to visit the general store across the street and make some purchases for the dear boys in gray.

When the door closed behind her, Kit turned to Cain. She looked pale and nervous.

"What's wrong, Kit?"

"I have a—a sort of present for you."

"A present? But I don't have anything for you."

"That's not," she said hesitantly, "exactly true."

Cain watched, his forehead creased in puzzlement, as she slipped through a second door leading to an adjoining room. When she came back, she was holding a small white bundle in her arms. She approached him slowly, her expression so full of entreaty it nearly broke his heart. And then the bundle moved.

"You have a daughter," she said softly. "Her name is Elizabeth, but I call her Beth. Beth Cain."

He looked down into a tiny valentine of a face. Everything about her was delicate and perfectly formed. She had a fluff of light-blond hair, dark slivers of eyebrows, and a dab of a nose. He felt a tight prickling inside him. Could he have helped create something this perfect? And then the valentine yawned and fluttered open pink shell lids, and he lost his heart to a second pair of bright, violet eyes.

Kit watched him and saw how it was and felt that nothing in her life could ever be as sweet as this one moment. She pushed away the blanket so he could see the rest of her, and then she held their child out to him.

Cain looked at her uncertainly.

"Go on." She smiled tenderly. "Take her."

He gathered the baby to his chest, his great hands nearly encompassing the small body. Beth wriggled once and then turned her head to look up at the strange new person who was holding her.

"Hello, Valentine," he said softly.

Chapter Thirty-seven

Cain and Kit spent the rest of the afternoon playing with Beth. Kit undressed her so her father could count her fingers and her toes. Beth performed her gamut of tricks like a champion: smiling at the funny noises that were directed toward her, grabbing at small and large fingers put within her reach, and making happy baby sounds when her father's shaggy moustache tickled her tummy.

Miss Dolly looked in on them, and when she saw that all was well, slipped into the room where Beth had been sleeping earlier and lay down to take her own nap. Life was peculiar, she thought, as she drifted to the edge of sleep, but it was interesting, too. Now she had sweet little Elizabeth to think about. It was certainly a responsibility. After all, she could hardly count on Katharine Louise to make certain the child learned everything she needed to know to be a great lady. So much for her to do, it made her head spin like a top. It was a tragedy, of course, what was happening at Appomattox Court House, but it was probably all for the best. She was certainly going to be far too busy from now on to devote herself to the war effort. . . .

In the other room Beth finally began to fret. Puckering up her mouth, she directed a determined yowl of protest toward her mother.

Cain looked alarmed. "What's wrong with her?"

"She's hungry. I forgot to feed her." She picked Beth up from the bed where they had been playing with her and carried her over to a soft chair near the window. As she sat down, Beth turned her head and began to root instinctively at the dove-gray fabric that covered her mother's breast. Nothing happened, and she grew more frantic. Kit looked down at her, understanding her need, but suddenly feeling shy about performing this most intimate of acts in front of her husband.

Cain lay sprawled across the bed, watching them both. He saw his daughter's distress and Kit's obvious reluctance. Slowly he uncoiled himself and walked over to them. Reaching down, he touched Kit's cheek, and then he lowered his hand to the cascade of gray lace at her throat. Gently he loosened it with his fingers, exposing a row of rose-pearl buttons beneath. Unfastening them, he pushed apart the gown.

There was a blue ribbon on her chemise. It fell open with a single tug. He saw the small trickle of tears on Kit's cheek, and he leaned down to kiss them away. Then he opened the chemise so his daughter could be nourished.

With the last barrier gone, Beth jerked her head to the side and made a ferocious grab with her tiny mouth. Cain laughed at her determination and kissed her on the chubby folds of her neck. Then he turned his head and pressed his lips to the sweet, full breast that fed her. He felt Kit's fingers coil in his hair and knew he had finally come home.

That evening, with Beth fed and safely tucked in bed where Miss Dolly was watching over her, they rode out to a canyon north of town that Cain said he wanted Kit to see. It was only an excuse to get away, and they both knew it, but there were promises that had to be sealed between them in private.

As they rode, they talked about the lost months between them, at first only the events, and then their feelings. They spoke quietly, sometimes in half sentences, frequently finishing each other's thoughts. Cain spoke of his guilt at deserting her, especially now that he knew she had been pregnant at the time, and Kit of her guilt at using Risen Glory as a wedge to drive them apart. Each of them felt better for the sharing.

Tentatively at first, and then with more enthusiasm, Cain told her about a piece of land he had seen to the east, near Dallas, and asked her how she would feel about building another cotton mill. Cotton was going to be a big crop in Texas, he told her; bigger than any state in the South. And Dallas seemed like a good place to raise a family. Or maybe she would like to go back to South Carolina and build another mill there. That would be all right with him, too.

But Kit didn't want to go back to South Carolina. This was a new land for them and a new life. Besides, she liked Texas. Somehow it seemed the right place for her, and the right place for them together.

The deep, cool shadows of evening were falling over them as they rode into the small, deserted canyon. Cain tied their horses to a black willow and then took Kit's hand and led her to the edge of a lazy creek that meandered through the floor of the canyon. Although it was not quite dark, the moon was already out, a full, shining globe that would soon bathe them in silver light.

He looked down at her. She was wearing a flat-brimmed hat and a warm, flannel shirt that was one of his own over a pair of tight fawn breeches. "You don't look much different than you did when I pulled you down off my wall," he said. "Except now, nobody could mistake you for a boy."

His eyes traveled to her breasts, visible even under his oversized shirt, and she delighted him by blushing. Reaching out, he took off first her hat and then his own, tossing them both down onto the mossy creek bank. He touched the small silver studs in her ear lobes and then her hair, coiled in a thick knot at the nape of her neck.

"I want to take your hair down."

Her lips curved in gentle permission, and she moved closer to him, cupping his sides with her hands. He took the pins out, one at a time, and set them carefully inside his own hat. When the great cloud of hair finally fell free, he caught it in his fists and brought it gently to his lips.

"Dear God, how I've missed you."

She moved her hands around to his back and gazed up at him. "It's not going to be a fairy-tale marriage, is it, my darling?"

He smiled softly. "I don't see how. We're both hot-tempered and stubborn. We're going to have our problems."

"Do you mind very much?"

"Fairy tales are for little girls. You're the one who needs to answer that question."

She hugged him tightly, pressing her cheek to his chest. "I'm not a little girl any longer. Besides, I never cared much for princes. They always seemed awfully dull to me."

"My wild rose of the deep wood," he muttered into her hair. "I don't think things will ever be dull."

"What did you call me?"

"Nothing," he whispered, stilling her question with his lips. "Nothing at all."

The kiss that began gently grew in intensity until it set fire to them both. Cain plowed his fingers through her hair and cupped her head between his hands. "Undress for me, will you, sweet?" he groaned softly. "I've dreamed of it for so long."

Happy that he had asked something of her she could give so easily, she nodded her head. He fetched a bed roll from the back of his saddle and spread it on the ground. By the time he sat down upon it, she had discarded her boots and her stockings and was waiting for him.

She had already decided how it was going to be, the way she could give him the most pleasure. Tossing him a teasing grin, she unfastened her breeches and peeled them down over her legs. He groaned as the long, flannel shirttail fell modestly below her hips. Reaching beneath it, she pulled off her white pantalets and dropped them next to her.

"I don't have anything on under this shirt," she said mischievously. "I forgot my chemise. On purpose."

He could barely keep himself from leaping off the ground and taking her. "You're a wicked woman, Mrs. Cain."

Her hand traveled to the button at the top of her shirt, and she opened it. "You're going to find out just how wicked I am, Mr. Cain."

Never had a shirt been unbuttoned so slowly. It was as if each unfastening were a delicate operation that could only be accomplished successfully if it were performed with the most leisurely of movements. And even when it was finally unbuttoned, the fullness of the material held the front together.

"I'm going to count to ten, Kit . . ." he said huskily.

"You can go ahead and count all you want, Yankee," she replied, with a devilish crinkling at the corners of her eyes. "It's not going to do you a bit of good."

With one hand she held the shirt together at the waist; with the other, she pushed it open at the throat and shrugged her shoulders. The sleeves fell down far on her arms, and Cain forgot all about counting. Then she let it go and stood naked before him.

"I didn't remember it right," he muttered thickly, "how beautiful you are. Come to me, love."

Suddenly serious, she walked across the chilled ground toward him. Only then did she wonder if she could still please him. What if having a baby had changed her in some way?

He reached up his hand for her, and she took it. Then she knelt down beside him. Gently he cupped her fuller breasts. "Your body is different."

She nodded her head and then lowered it. "I'm a little scared."

"Are you, love?" He tilted up her chin and grazed her mouth with his own. "I'd die before I'd hurt you."

His moustache was soft beneath her lips. "It's not that. I'm afraid it will be different. That I won't please you anymore."

"Shhh," he breathed softly. "I'm a little scared, too. Maybe I won't be able to please you."

She wrapped her arms tightly around him. "Silly," she murmured.

"Silly," he whispered back.

They smiled and kissed each other, and then the barrier of his clothing was suddenly too much for them. They worked at it together until nothing was left between them. As their kisses deepened, they fell back on the bed roll.

A wisp of cloud skidded over the moon, casting moving shadows on the ancient walls of the canyon, but the lovers did not notice. Clouds and moons and canyons, a baby with a valentine face, and an old lady who smelled of peppermint—all had ceased to exist. For now, their world was small, made up of only a man and a woman, joined together at last.